FIRE

HEART

Fire
Heart

**A Coming of Age Novel that tackles
Fear at its Heart and
Embraces the
Fire of Love**

Broken Bottles Series: Book 2
Pamela Taeuffer

OPEN
HEART
PRESS

Published 2014

Printed in the United States of America

ISBN: 978-0-9899529-2-7

Library of Congress Control Number: 2014912867

For information, address: pamelataeuffer@gmail.com

Fire Heart is dedicated to all the women in my family who, in their hearts, were mustangs trying to run free. May women and men everywhere shake their hair and stomp down their fences, unafraid and with an open heart.

Table of Contents

WARNING

Nicky here.

This book is part of an ongoing series with steep cliffs.

Hang in there!

There is a very good reason for them. When coming home to face my family's battle with alcoholism, I never knew what waited behind the front door—just turning the doorknob was an exercise in fear.

I know from living with my family's addiction that:
- Good things will end.
- My opinions don't matter.
- Peace never lasts.
- Those who love me will abandon me.

This is my family's saga and what we endured to break the chains of dysfunction and my love story: love of friends, parents, siblings, those relationships that give us life lessons and of lovers. This is about intimacy in all levels. Despite the lack of trust I have for others I'm desperate to have it. I'm only eighteen, but my entire life I've longed for the sweet touch of someone who wasn't afraid, raging, or drunk. I want joy.

Be patient, please. I formed years of bad habits, fears, and irrational behavior while trying to survive my dysfunctional family. This is my story.

When you finish, can you please leave a review for me?
I'd really, really appreciate it if you would:

Amazon: bit.ly/FireHeart
Goodreads: bit.ly/GoodreadsFireHeart

The Story So Far

In Shadow Heart, the first novel of the Broken Bottles series, we meet a woman who has come of age. Nicky Young tells the story of her family's battle with alcoholism. Hers is a love story about the challenges of trust and belief in others and intimacy in relationships. Those people she's loved the most have been the biggest disappointments.

Left to fend for her own emotional survival, one way she's kept her sanity has been the pursuit of higher education—especially when it comes to getting into Stanford, the college of her choice. Hoping to pad her college application with accolades, she proposed a plan to feature a high school cheer team at the San Francisco Goliaths baseball games. When it was accepted, she knew Stanford was in reach and in her control—or so it seemed.

Enter Ryan Tilton, one of the Goliaths' star pitchers, who has set his sights on her. At 6'2" with blue eyes, golden brown hair, and biceps that turn women's heads, Ryan appears to have it all. Few people know the private side of him or the losses he's suffered. To protect and hide his hurt, he plays hard to avoid his demons. He's begun to reveal himself to Nicky in ways he never has with anyone. Ryan has a reputation with women, and the very innocent Nicky Young won't be an easy mark.

That nagging feeling of being played, in combination with the steeled armor surrounding her heart keeps Nicky shut down. Fight as she may, desire seems to have awakened. A virgin, she's never felt these strong urges until now. She writes about Ryan in her journal: *That* smile. *That* chest. *Those* arms.

Also in her line of sight is Jerry Stowe, her childhood friend. His innocence appeals to Nicky. She feels they are on a level playing field and can experience the newness of sex together—

until their classmate tells Nicky he has been making advances on other girls.

Is either boy sincere?

Does it matter?

Will she dip her toes into the hot, sensual heat of passion and experience one or both of them?

A ticking time bomb has been planted inside her from the dysfunction of her childhood, repeating: No one will last. Abandonment will rear its ugly head sooner or later and the promises made to her will all fall away.

Will she step backward into the shadows where she's made it a habit of seeking refuge and cover herself in the secrets of her twisted family?

She knows in order to move forward a healthy woman she must allow herself to be vulnerable. She's made a baby step and opened up to her sister again; has new relationships with two women—one a fiancé and the other wife to two of the Goliaths' players. All she's ever done is play it safe. Hold back, and analyze when it's safe to step forward.

Can she leap from the edge of her cliff, the one she clung to all her life, when rising and dramatic emotions challenge her to her very core?

Can she lose the fears from her childhood that hang on fiercely and dare to be loved?

Will she let her heart—a heart on fire—take her to new places?

Prologue

I'd been standing by myself. Reflected back to the year I was eighteen and had experienced first love. A tug on my hand caught my attention.

"Great auntie Nicky!" Five-year-old Olivia whined. I'd been a friend with Olivia's grandmother, Lorraine, since the sixth grade and took comfort in having a friend with me from those innocent years.

Friends and family were gathered together for my thirty-fifth wedding anniversary. Children were shouting. Grandparents smiling. Perhaps they were reminiscing about the old days, just as I was.

Thirty-five years ago, I'd been getting closer with Jerry Stowe. We'd always been friends, but felt something else when we turned eighteen. At the same time, Ryan Tilton, a professional baseball player, had been making a full on press to make me his girlfriend.

Had I not fallen in love with a boy who encouraged me to explore intimacy on every level, I'd have kept my heart shrouded in mistrust and in the fear of abandonment because of my dysfunctional family and alcoholic father.

Because of that man, everything opened.

"Oh, sweetie. Why are you upset?" I asked Olivia.

"He hit me!" she sobbed.

"Who hit you?"

"Bobby!" She pressed her head into my hip as she continued whimpering. "He's a mean boy!"

I took her into my arms and listened to her story. As she dramatically embellished the tale of her woes, I remembered back to the day I was getting ready to check on Ryan Tilton's contacts. They were people who, with his say so, could help my family.

When I was finished speaking with them, I not only understood his wide circle of influence, but the generous spirit of his heart.

I was falling in love.

A Child's Cry

Shadows and darkness are my cover
My hiding places are many
I have them even in my own home
I've witnessed his rage and red face
My father's become a stranger

Tonight my mother didn't notice
When I reached for her love
Every day I crave the moment
When I'm alive in my parents' eyes
I'm tired of keeping family secrets
They seem to have gone deaf
And don't hear me anymore

It seems I am a part of a permanent sunset
Never enough light at our house
I have a television and a bag of cookies
I need to fill up with *something*
My father has changed
My mother is damaged and hurt
I know it's up to me if I'm going to make it
Will anybody love me
With my fences so very high
The boards are steel
Reach inside if you can
I'm calling out, but you can't hear me
I'm looking for you, but you can't see me
I'm here, waiting to get out
Waiting to get
Waiting to
Waiting

Chapter 1

Hollow Eyes

"*F*ollow me," the man at Municipality's reception area motioned. He'd reappeared after checking with Dad's supervisor.

We made our way to his office. In only minutes I'd find out how much trouble my father was in and if Stanford was still a realistic goal for me. He knocked on the door.

It was only an interview. Still, dread filled me.

When it came to my father, there was no safety net.

I knew the answers could be everything I didn't want to hear.

Then again, I'd heard those kinds of answers all my life.

"Come in," the man behind the smoky glass shouted.

* * * * *

Before my appointment at Municipality, I'd stopped at a nearby diner. I not only craved a cup of strong, black java, I needed to review the questions I'd prepared for my day of interviews with Ryan's contacts a second time.

Sniffing in the rich aroma wafting up in the steam from my coffee mug, I took a nice slow sip of the delicious dark French roast and practiced my first interview out loud.

When the alarm rang at seven ninety minutes earlier, it took me longer than usual to shake out the cobwebs. I'd had another late night—which seemed to be a habit of late—after a beach party with my friends. The gathering would be one of our last. In only two months we'd take off like seeds blowing in the wind and begin our adult lives and celebrated having a party at the beach.

Jerry Stowe, a boy I'd grown up with, had tried to make moves on me when we were in his sleeping bag. We were considering a deeper relationship, but his attempt at intimacy backfired when the park rangers broke up our party.

With strobe lights and megaphones they threatened to throw us in jail if we didn't clean and vacate the beach immediately. I laughed aloud as I recalled the ranger's spotlight ready to find Jerry's naked bottom as he rushed to put on his jeans.

We were two of a few people who were sober, proved after the rangers made us take a Breathalyzer Test. After that, we were charged with cleaning up the beach and making sure everyone got home safely. Since Colleen, my best friend, lived next door to me and I'd gotten a ride in her boyfriend's car, I volunteered to take them home as well as a few of our friends.

When I finally walked into my house, I saw I'd missed a few calls from Ryan. Only twenty-four hours earlier, we'd spoken about honesty and trusting each other. I felt uneasy about calling him back. I went upstairs to my room. Climbed into bed. Lay with my thoughts.

Why was I hiding from Ryan the way I had with Jerry? Was it because ultimately I knew I'd chose friendship?

Wouldn't I surrender completely and my own goals weaken the moment I admitted my feelings for one of them?

In those early morning hours, I realized a desire had definitely ignited inside me.

I was far from certain about who stirred me the most. One thing that was clear—Ryan Tilton and my friend Jerry Stowe had everything to do with my awakening.

It was as if a spark from the bonfire had come home with me and settled in my belly.

Tired as I was, I sat in the diner before my first interview, sipping my coffee and rehearsing my questions so I'd appear prepared and ready to meet with some of Ryan's contacts—people who could help my friends and family. Through a candid conversation with him, I found out my father's job was in danger. Translation? An education at Stanford was in jeopardy.

What was Ryan's goal from these interviews? I would agree that his heart was in the right place and try a relationship with him.

My goal? I needed to find out what these people could do for my family.

One final sip of coffee and I pushed up from the table.

I went into the bathroom and took a moment to check myself in the mirror. I made sure my hair was in place and I hadn't stained the black slacks and white blouse I chose to wear.

I wasn't sure I was ready to confront my father's mess—could I ever be ready for the uncertainty of his path of debris?

Tugging on my waist-length, flared-at-the-waist purple jacket, I adjusted the amethyst pin I'd fastened to its collar.

The pin was my grandmother's.

She'd come to stay at our house seven years earlier because no one else would take her. Before that, she had been admitted to St. Agnes Hospital and Sanitarium.

I remembered it as a place of terror.

The generational chains of dysfunction rattled somewhere in my mind. I shivered.

* * * * *

"Girl!" The old woman moaned in a low, wretched voice, the word shaking as it came from her body.

Her bony fingers reached for me as if crawling from a casket to rise and walk among the living in a hallway on the fifth floor of St. Agnes Hospital and Sanitarium.

The box-shaped building was painted in a faded cream color. A rusted iron cross was hung above its doors. It was as if the rust from it had become blood and stained the stuccoed fascia underneath it an ugly reddish-brown.

Bars covered many of the windows—especially on the upper floors. If not for the bright Red Cross on the lit sign near the road, passersby could have easily confused St. Agnes with a prison—especially on floors five and six.

Inside, the faded, pastel-pink linoleum floors were polished to a glossy finish. They led visitors down cream-colored halls to cream-colored doors leading into cream-colored rooms. Iron beds were painted white, covered with white blankets that covered white sheets.

As soon as we walked in the front door, a smell hit me I never forgot—a combination of something unsanitary, mixed with heavy amounts of bleach and Pine-Sol. I wondered if the patients crept from their rooms at night and smeared the floors with their feces to rebel and show their wardens they had lie yet to live. Mopping the floors failed to hide what went on when visitors left.

Screams, moans, and the constant chant of otherworldly sounds—those well and unwell—filled the air of the unholy sanitarium. The upper floors should have been off-limits to the public. I'd gotten lost and found myself in the halls with hollow, frightened eyes.

Some stared, unfocused, at nothing. Others accompanied open mouths, mumbling and begging for anyone to listen—gray-haired people were everywhere.

Pale, wrinkled skin adorned the skeletons on wheels.

All of them pushed toward me.

Surrounded me.

Tried to touch me.

The day I'd gotten lost at St. Agnes, my family was visiting my grandmother. I knew from hearing my parents talk that with each ascending floor, the patients were more violent, disturbed, unreachable, and nowhere for a child to be without an adult.

Always wanting something to eat for comfort, I'd asked Mom for money to get a candy bar and something to drink. The vending machines were on the first floor. I took the elevator down, got my goodies and then stopped in the gift shop for a small note pad. I wanted to jot down some ideas I had for a story—this one was about flying.

Sent to me in a dream during the night, magic dust had filled my sleep, perhaps sprinkled into my thoughts by an angel. In it, I first skipped and then ran in our back yard, opened my arms, and flew high above my neighborhood, watching my house fade away as I ascended into clouds and rainbows.

I was so busy writing I didn't notice I'd passed the fourth floor. When the elevator doors opened, I walked down several hallways and suddenly realized I wasn't where I should be.

Bang! It was like a hammer hit my chest.

Panic.

Confusion.

My heart beat hard and my throat tightened when I saw the pink heads of thinning gray hair wheeling down the hallways, bumping into walls, furniture, and people.

Some of them seemed to purposefully slam into each other as if trying to get attention from someone—anyone. Was this a way they screamed for help?

Wide, frightened eyes asked silent questions. Screams and yelling crowded the end of a hallway filled with locked doors.

I wondered if they were ever acknowledged or touched.

What would bring them back to life?

How could *anyone* stand this?

I ran through the halls trying to find a familiar face.

They all looked the same—the rooms, the doors, and the nurses' station . . . something . . . something wasn't right. I stopped. A fleeting thought crossed through my mind during my confusion—I realized it was the patients that made the place come alive. They *were* alive. I was frightened beyond words, but my mind spun with curiosity as I realized *they were in there*.

Eyes revealed more than pink scalp and grey hair.

In some ways, they were just like the patients who were two floors down—lonely, confused, some sad and all of them counting down the days until they could go home—if they could.

But two floors down, the patients didn't try to touch me.

Two floors down, they stared at the ground, looked away, or smiled gently; their eyes were focused, their words understandable.

"Who are you looking for?" A male nurse grabbed and spun me around.

I gasped.

He was the biggest man I'd ever seen.

I thought he must be a giant.

He wore green pants and a matching shirt and looked like a doctor. Bunched on a clip, keys jingled from his belt. His expression was stern. When he grabbed me, the moving skeletons backed off. I wondered if they feared this giant, too.

"Grandma Young." My lips quivered. The words came out broken and laced with hidden tears ready to flow.

He held my hand. Brought me behind the desk at the nurses' station, so I would be out of the hallway and the nightmare.

Was this scary-looking man actually a *gentle* giant?

As he stared at the computer, the hollow eyes in the hallway continued to stare.

"Maureen Young?" He lifted his head to look at me.

"Yes." I was shaken. "That's my grandma."

"How did you get up here?" His voice was stern.

"That elevator," I pointed.

"Daniel!" He shouted to a man who'd come from a door behind the desk. "The elevator isn't stopping at four. Call it in, will you?"

The other man grumbled and then picked up the phone.

"Come on. I'll take you back down to see your grandma." The enormous man took my hand. I followed him into the elevator. We rode down silently. The ding announced we had arrived and the doors opened again. "Here we are." He held them so I could step out, but remained inside; ready to return to his duties. "Flora, this girl is lost. She's looking for Maureen Young's room and she's had quite a scare up on five. Can you escort her?"

"Sure can." She lifted her index finger. "Give me a minute."

"I know where to go now, sir." I put on my best smile. Inside, I was anything but calm.

"What's your name?" He knelt down and spoke to me at eye level.

"Nicky Young. What's yours?"

"Edward King. I'm a nurse here." With his smile it seemed my body warmed in golden colors. "Nicky, the patients you saw upstairs didn't run into you on purpose or grab at you to hurt you. Try and remember them as people. Like you and me, only they need a different kind of help. Can you?"

"I'll try," I folded my hands. "That was scary."

"I know." His voice softened. "They don't understand how you see them. They only saw a sweet little girl and they wished she could be their granddaughter."

"Thank you." I waved goodbye as he disappeared in the elevator ascending into the madness of St. Agnes.

Chapter 2

On the Case

𝓔xiting the coffee shop, I walked in a rhythmic pace. Breathed deeply. Kept my eyes focused on Municipality's corporate offices. Built in the early 1900s, the hub of my father's work was in one of the oldest brick buildings in San Francisco. Almost condemned twelve years earlier, a decision was made to save its one-hundred-year-plus history.

Its three-stories was graced with several dramatic archways. Inside, large planks of hardwood creaked as I walked across the floor. It reminded me of a great old hardware store—the kind that sells old copper colanders for cooking and an assortment of nails in big, silver buckets.

Antique clocks hung on the walls. The chimes were slightly off in timing the hour and their symphony of bells rang in nine o' clock in the large reception area for several minutes. Massive oak desks with roll-up tops and heavy wooden chairs were placed intermittently throughout the office.

Surrounding the entire room and lining the upper walls were historic photos of old streetcars and early Market Street when horses were used to pull the trollies.

I could feel the many layers of its masculine history. It was as if I was surrounded by the whispers and stories from the era of my great grandparents. Those photos and antiques had voices.

The man at reception had just called for me to follow him.

I was completely entranced as I walked down a hallway decorated with dark wood walls and doors that had smoky glass windows. Stenciled on them were the names of each occupant.

Mr. Freeman's office was one of the farthest from the reception area. The receptionist knocked on his door and then opened it.

"Come in," the man behind the smoky glass shouted. The door opened. "Thank you, Max. I'll take it from here."

I entered the room of the person who apparently held my father's job, and possibly my future, in his hands.

The door closed behind me.

"Ms. Young?" He stood up. "Sid Freeman. What can I do for you?" His face was youthful. I guessed he was somewhere in his early thirties. Possessing average height and a gorgeous head of black hair, his striking brown eyes warmed as I shook his hand.

"Thank you for seeing me. I know you're busy and I'm sorry about the short notice. I understand you're Robert Young's supervisor?"

"Please, sit down." He nodded and then gestured to the two chairs in front of his desk. "Technically, I'm in charge of his superior. Indirectly, yes. I oversee the administrative personnel as well."

"*And* you're a friend of Ryan Tilton's?" I blurted.

"Yes."

"Well, I'm checking on something that might seem a little bizarre to you." I pulled out my journal of notes.

"You want to know if Ryan can help your father," he offered confidently.

"Yes. I was told he's on *Probation Level 3*. Could he lose his job if he gets another write-up? What exactly does that kind of probation mean?"

"Because of privacy issues, I can't reveal all that you probably want to know, but since you're Robert's daughter and a friend of Ryan's, I'll tell you as much as I can."

I should hope so. After all, Ryan must have told you about it and vice versa.

"First, let me assure you no one, including me, wants to terminate your father or hurt your family. Quite the contrary, I'd like nothing better than to help him. However I can't sit by while he endangers others."

"How is he a danger to others?"

"Do you know anything about what he's done?" Mr. Freeman reached for his coffee cup. "Would you like some?"

"No thank you. No, to answer your other question." *Here we go. What have you done now, Dad?*

"He's come to work drunk, been caught drinking and sleeping on the job, wrote incorrect orders because of it and found non-responsive in his office."

"Non-responsive?" I momentarily held my breath.

"Passed out." His eyes were focused. "Incapacitated because he's drunk—really drunk—and can't move because he's in an alcoholic's blackout."

My father let himself sink to this level? He's given up?

"Ms. Young, part of his job involves working with electricity, which is dangerous all by itself. He's also responsible for making split-second decisions with the men and women who work with that danger. More than twenty mechanics, over one hundred streetcars and buses and some responsibility for the drivers who check into his barn—that's his responsibility.

"If there's an incident such as a fight, accident, or mechanical emergency, even the occasional court appearance, he has to be able to speak with police and fire personnel, the press, attorneys, and the public. You can see the difficulty facing us. What do I do when his coworkers come to me and lodge a complaint against him? How many times do I refrain from reprimanding him when I send the sub-foreman to the scene because your father is passed out? Worse, how do I explain we were aware of his problem?"

I knew my father's back was against the wall.

He'd put himself there and had no one to blame but himself.

How many times had I heard, *I'm not hurting anyone but myself when I drink?* Not one of us was untouched by his alcoholism. His addiction affected our entire family.

"We're incredibly liable if we do nothing," he admitted.

"You can't ignore it, sir, I know that. But what about his record of service before, you know . . ." I cleared my throat. "I'm sure it's in his file, but did you know he was threatened with a gun a few years ago? You must understand how that could shake anyone."

I'm using the same excuses my mother did. But this is different, isn't it? Am I using them now because I'm directly involved?

Haven't you always been affected, Nicky?

"Yes, I know about his close call." Mr. Freeman leaned back in his chair. "I've offered him counseling and rehabilitation. His medical plan would cover it. Your father won't accept the help. I'm running out of options."

"Okay then, can you tell me if Dad's situation has anything to do with Ryan?"

"*Ryan?* How so?"

"What I mean is, no one can help or hurt my father except you and your superiors, right? And himself, of course; I didn't mean to suggest he's not in control of his own destiny."

"Ryan already called me to better understand how he can help protect your dad."

"I didn't know that." *He already called? But he said I needed to date him exclusively before he'd call you.*

"You understand what we're talking about here?" He leaned forward on his desk.

"Being terminated."

"It's much more than that." He took in a deep breath and let it out in a rush. "Robert's eligible for retirement now. In fact, I wish he'd just give up and file for it. What another write-up means? He'd lose everything. Thirty years of service and he'd have no retirement or medical benefits."

"I see." I hung my head.

"There is good news, Ms. Young. Ryan knows the head of your father's union, Mr. Tremmel. It's how we were introduced, in fact. Tremmel has agreed to get involved and once the process starts, your dad will be protected. Robert will go out on sick leave so he doesn't get into any more trouble."

"How soon can that happen?" I noted his comment on my yellow tablet. *Please tell me tomorrow.*

"Eight to twelve weeks."

Crap.

"And then what?" I pressed.

"Typically what's next is mandatory rehabilitation. That will qualify him for long-term disability while everything is sorted out. What I'm saying, and doing a damn poor job of it," he laughed confidently, "Is that if Ryan hadn't made a call to me, I'd go through the usual procedures. Now, I'm making it a priority."

"I really appreciate that, Mr. Freeman. May I ask who's above you in the chain of command?"

"My dad, Jack Freeman." He smiled. "Would you like to speak with him about me?"

"No, that's not what I meant." I looked away, embarrassed. "I just need to be clear about everything. Well, thank you." I stood up to leave. "I'm supposed to go to Stanford next year and if anything happened to my father's income, it affects me, too." I stared at the floor a moment and then back to Dad's supervisor. "I sure appreciate your time today."

"My pleasure, Ms. Young. Stanford, huh? You're lucky. In fact, you're both lucky."

"How so? With my father's situation, I don't feel that way."

"You're well-spoken, intelligent, driven, and so is your boyfriend. I suspect you're a good woman or he wouldn't be with you. Ryan's funny with people. Once he becomes a good friend, he's very dedicated."

He told you I was his girlfriend?

Chapter 3

My Family's Legacy

$\mathcal{N}$ext on my list was interviewing Niles Woodson, the head of the Architecture Department at San Francisco State. He introduced himself and couldn't have been more different than Sid Freeman. This professor and department head was tall and thin, with salt-and-pepper hair and wore wire-rimmed glasses. In contrast to my father's supervisor, Niles seemed at ease, spoke freely about opportunities for Jenise and how Ryan's recommendation could make a big difference.

"I don't understand why that's true. Isn't the award something my sister can achieve through her own efforts? Why does she need a personal reference, especially a baseball player, of all people? I mean, no disrespect, but why does his input have to do with any student here?"

"If your sister were going to another college, Mr. Tilton's input probably wouldn't mean anything. Water?" He held a paper cup under the water cooler by his office window. I shook my head. He drank it down quickly, crumpled the cup, and tossed it in the trashcan.

"Mr. Tilton started several networking groups here. One of them is for helping veterans reenter college. It has received national recognition. In part because of what he's set up, we are one of *the* go-to schools in the entire country for helping veterans. In fact, Ryan helped us design some of the orientation classes and put together mentor groups that have been invaluable to our men and women of the military."

"Oh, I . . . I didn't know that. Wow, I, um . . ." *Can his generosity really be so big?*

"He continually fundraises to help support them. Beyond giving his money, he gives his time. I've been in some of his workshops." He showed me a brochure for one of the seminars. "When he shares his stories with the students, the room falls silent. He's—"

"Magical." When I interrupted, I never thought about sounding ridiculous. I spoke with honest spontaneity bursting from my heart. I was certain Ryan had magical gold dust inside him. Somehow I knew Mr. Woodson had witnessed it.

"Yes," he smiled. "I believe he *is* magical, Ms. Young. I think he's someone who comes around once in a lifetime. So, now you know why a recommendation from him means so much."

"I'm beginning to understand the importance of networking in a whole new way," I admitted.

"Makes a difference who your contacts are sometimes," he replied. "Jenise hopes to work for City Architecture. They have an amazing intern program that opens up every four years. The current offering coincides with your sister's graduation. If her project were chosen, she'd have a five-figure starting salary. Have you heard of them?"

"I know *of* them. In fact, my next appointment is with their president, Mr. Blockley."

"Careful," his said with a playful grin.

"What do you mean?"

"He'll have fun teasing you when you see him," he warned.

"Great. That's just what I need."

"You should know they're one of the biggest architectural firms in the country and the largest by far in the Bay Area. If they hired your sister and she did well, she could relocate just about anywhere *and* on her own terms."

"I understand everything much better now, Mr. Woodson. You're very kind to have met with me." I grabbed my backpack, ready to leave.

"My pleasure. And where are you going to college? Will we have the chance to see you follow in your sister's footsteps?"

"I'm going to Stanford in the spring to study business marketing."

"Good luck with that." He shook my hand. "And don't worry too much about your sister. She's a smart woman and she'll do well whether or not she receives the internship."

"Thank you," I shook his hand. "I completely agree." I left the campus and drove to City Architecture.

Thoughts about Ryan and his charity work seemed to swirl around me. *Are we as good of a match as it seems we are? Doesn't he need someone older and more experienced?*

Early for my appointment with Mr. Blockley, I went into a deli for a fruit smoothie. It gave me a chance to make notes about the conversations I'd just had. I didn't want to forget the details. As I wrote, my right hand wandered again to my grandmother's amethyst pin. I didn't often wear jewelry. When I did, I couldn't help fiddling with it.

Before Grandma Young came to stay with us and after her nightmare at St. Agnes, she lived with her sister, Ruthanne. She had called my father to come over and discuss taking his mother to live with us. As I listened to my father's aunt, even as young as I was, I considered, how do children learn about love?

Can anyone have real intimacy when living in a home that had lost those feelings?

One example of my family's relationship was watching how addiction numbed our emotions. My parents gradually withdrew from activities with friends and relatives—and later from my sister and me—unless they were forced to interact with us in some way. Rather than gain control over the substance and familiarity of their roles, Jenise and I became Mom and Dad's sacrifice.

We sunk deeply into our family dysfunction.

It had been passed from generation to generation.

Without fully understanding why, I needed to manage even the smallest details all my life. I wondered if I'd ever be able to calm the anxiety I felt; it was so extreme.

In many ways, I mimicked my mother's behavior choices.

Staying calm—at least on the outside—prevented me from being vulnerable. I made sure to detach from my relationships so the hurt—or love—wouldn't get too close. Over the years I'd seen my mother's angry face—and also the sadness—as it washed over her, countless times.

I knew from the way my grandmother was discarded and tucked away in St. Agnes, my parents had shut down. In spite of my grandmother's plight, she made the best of it. I suppose because she was at the mercy of others, she didn't complain, but there was something humbling about her.

The pin she gave me was one of three gifts.

The second was a silver cross that I hung above my door.

The third? It was intangible and priceless—time with her.

* * * * *

A big house stood on Dolores Street in San Francisco. It belonged to my great aunt, Ruthanne Dunne.

It was a spooky old place and had plenty of dark corners and creaks, which traveled like a snake down the dimly lit halls. Moans seemed to hide behind walls framing its wooden floors.

Jenise and I were two little girls filled with a desire for exploration and mischief. As our parents discussed adult matters upstairs, we snooped into the dark, moldy basement. There were dozens of shelves lined with old dusty novels and bibles.

We opened her beautiful old books and ran our fingers over the musty pages. Even as we read through the pages about murder and mystery, history and fiction, I wondered if many were first editions. Old bibles were edged with gold, and written in the old language of thee, thy and thou.

After reading an especially delicious tale of intrigue, we pretended a killer lived in the cellar's shadows, carefully picking the right time to take his next victim into the darkness. When we found a small statue of Mother Mary with her head severed and another of Jesus tipped over and broken in half? In our mind, that moment confirmed we were in the devil's lair. Running into her large garden, filled with rhododendrons and roses, we screamed and then laughed in the relief of making it out of there alive.

The first time I remembered my great aunt speak with my parents about the "burden" my grandmother had become to her, she mentioned how she'd already been charged with the care of another sister named Ethel. That sister was kept—no, more like *stowed away*, in the parlor room. It was a room built to receive guests in older homes. Although physically in her sixties, Ethel's mind hadn't progressed beyond the age of six—at least that's what I was told.

Jenise and I were warned not to go in the parlor. My sister even told me some crazy story she'd heard about a stabbing that involved Ethel and a pair of scissors. Of course, that danger made her all the more intriguing.

Never one to heed my parents' warning, and another way to rebel silently, I dared myself to meet Ethel on a day Jenise hadn't come with us.

I took a deep breath.

Opened the door.

The furniture looked turn of the century. The sofa and chairs had carved wooden backs. A round table with claw feet provided a resting place for a beautiful antique lamp. The carpet was pale green with a pale rose pattern dotted throughout.

Ethel sat on the floor playing with paper dolls.

Her legs tucked under her.

"Hello!" she said sweetly. "Play!"

I knelt beside her.

"What's your name?" I threw a small test her way—at least in my mind.

"Ethel."

"Mine's Nicky."

"Before."

"What?"

"I saw you," she revealed. "I wanted to play. You want to play?" She responded like a child. Her body was that of an older woman but her eyes were still innocent. It was certain I could see joy behind them.

"Where did you get these nice clothes for your paper dolls, Ethel?" The details were brilliant, imaginative, and all cut from construction paper, the tabs that fastened to the dolls precisely, and the design seemingly crafted by hand.

"I make!" Enthusiasm and pride shone on her face.

With that visit, I understood creativity had no age or mental limitations. With the right encouragement, things might have been different for her. Instead, her family gave up and tucked away the beautiful and talented silver-haired lady.

Each time we visited, I carefully opened the parlor door, hoping she would be there with her dolls. I no longer cared if

Jenise came with us when we visited Grandma Maureen because that would mean I couldn't play with my new friend. Plus, I didn't trust that she wouldn't tell our parents and we'd be forced to stay with them during the visit.

Ethel loved showing me the new paper outfits she created: jackets, shoes, purses, and dresses. She even made a second set for a doll she'd made for me. With her cardboard, crayons and pencils around her, she was ready to make or change an outfit at any time.

We walked them under the sofa and chairs, making little rooms and houses for them, took them shopping to pretend stores, and even made them fly through the air. The imaginary adventures we dreamed up were like little fairy tales.

I wished I would have kept a journal back then so I could remember more of them. Time with her was like nothing I'd ever again experience.

The day inevitably came when I slid open the parlor door and Ethel was gone. No longer were her boxes of colored papers and markers strewn about the room.

I knew I'd never see her again.

I knelt in prayer, asking that she hadn't been abandoned.

I never asked where she'd gone.

I was afraid I'd hear, "She's on the fifth floor at St. Agnes."

Children know intuitively—before they grow older and become jaded—when they find sweetness and honesty. I knew it was inside my great aunt Ethel.

Not too long after she died, Ruth admitted to my father that she could no longer care for her other sister, his mother, Maureen Young. She said she'd been drained and saddened with the grief of losing her sister. If Dad didn't take her, St. Agnes would once again claim my grandmother. As much as he'd numbed himself, even he realized readmitting her to that hellish place was wrong.

When Grandma came to stay with us, Jenise was fourteen and I was eleven. It wasn't too many months earlier my sister had been raped, which apparently made her room off limits to me. It was as if my parents thought I might catch a disease if I got close.

I had a choice between sleeping downstairs by myself, or in my parents' room. I chose my parents' room. I was afraid to be on a whole floor by myself, but not because of ghosts and skeletons of St. Agnes. It was the haunting from my father and his drunken talks at my bedside, which might last all night if there was no one around. I had to deal with enough of those living nightmares and I didn't need to be surrounded with more as I tried to fall asleep.

After grandma moved in, I was given new household chores. I resigned myself to them although I didn't understand why I had to shoulder any of the responsibility. Why weren't those given to my sister, or for that matter, why not my parents?

I made her breakfast: a simple bowl of cereal, usually cornflakes, or toast, a cup of juice, and coffee. When I got home from school I checked on her and took her lunch dishes away. I brought her dinner and also cleared those plates later on.

One night as I set her tray down, she seemed more pensive than usual. Dad had stumbled down the hall and into his room. On the way, he'd unintentionally knocked her door open.

"Is your dad polluted?" she looked at me bashfully, folding her book closed and placing it on her lap. I realized from her question, she hadn't known how far into his addiction my father had gone.

"Yes, Grandma." I held her tray. "He's been drinking."

She lowered her head and sighed. Her hair was gray, short, thin, and curly. In many spots, the pink of her scalp was exposed. She couldn't have weighed more than eighty pounds.

"Can you get me that book on the dresser?" She pointed with a shaky finger. I put the tray down and retrieved it. Still resentful of her being in my room and sleeping in my bed, a fresh dusting of anger settled on me.

Now, in addition to these extra duties that cut into my time, I have to listen to her stories.

I wanted her gone.

I needed out of my parents' room and wanted to be back into my comfort zone. I hated the stale stink of my father's breath, saturated from alcohol, and the drunken snore that rattled from his throat.

My fear of being tender with anyone kept me from embracing my grandmother. I was especially frightened to get close with someone her age. I knew it was only a matter of time that she'd leave me—she was one of the gray people.

"What's in the book, Grandma?" *I might as well take an interest. She doesn't seem to be going anywhere and no one else talks with her.*

"I want to read you something in the pages of our family bible." She began reading her family's history, going all the way back to Ireland. "Your dad wanted to name you after me."

"Maureen Young." I said out loud. "That would have been nice. I wonder what my middle name would have been? Maureen Marie is kinda weird."

She smiled and then told me about her own parents and grandparents. I found out my father was no angel when a boy. He was expelled from high school for defying authority and rather than pursue continuation school or get his GED he went to work at a local market. As I listened, I finally appreciated the opportunity in front of me.

Why had it taken me so long to accept her? It was because of the things I saw every day: in our house, family wasn't cherished or held. None of us were touted as special. It was up to us to create love for ourselves.

That day, my grandmother became interesting.

That day, I shared my first cup of coffee with her and loved it.

That day became a tradition, a memory of talking with Grandma over breakfast and savoring a cup of coffee together.

That day, one link in the chain that bound our addicted generations together, weakened just a little and was replaced with a golden thread.

I listened to a different story every night and looked forward to bringing dinner to her and sitting by her side while she ate.

Patience and understanding made their introduction.

Although she'd given me her amethyst pin and silver cross, my grandma's *real* gifts taught me to appreciate my family's history and how loving each other shouldn't be a sacrifice.

It was what family did.

The difference I felt in her being at our house, in my room, getting to know her, even at eleven-years-old, was life changing.

Instead of resenting her, now I helped Grandma on her portable potty.

Instead of rushing out of the room after I brought her breakfast, I got up a little earlier to make sure we had our coffee together and had a chance to chat.

I made sure she had her doctor-approved treats when I went grocery shopping with Mom—especially the butter mints she loved—putting them in the cart along with my bags of cookies.

I brought her extra napkins and a box of tissue so she didn't have to keep used paper towels on her nightstand. While she was on her potty I stripped her bed and changed her sheets.

A privilege—that's what I understood it was to be with her. Some days, I skipped playing with my friends and instead listened to her stories.

She began leaving a dollar for me underneath her empty plate in the evening. When I told her it wasn't necessary she put her finger to her lips. I never said anything about it to anyone. Sometimes I used the money to go on bike rides with Jerry and we stopped at the corner store to get candy. Most of the time, I tucked it away, saving for my future.

They abandoned her and brought her to live here and yet did as little as possible, leaving her in bed night after night. They could have set up the family room near the kitchen so she could sit in her wheel chair with us.

I knew the bottom line—they really didn't want her close.

Like the months immediately following Jenise's rape, they kept their distance.

After all, getting too close was our fear.

Dad brought her home so she wouldn't stay at St. Agnes, but left the rest of her care to his wife and daughters.

In the end, because of Grandma Maureen, I was able to appreciate older people quite differently. I loved being around them and no longer feared the ghosts on wheels.

Because we visited her, I met Ethel.

Because my great aunt Ruthanne didn't want her sister, I came to love my Grandma Maureen.

I came to associate the smell of powder and butter mints with love—she kept them both on her nightstand. Sometimes, I'd sit with her and we'd eat all of the mints.

The day she gave me the amethyst pin, she said it was because I gave up my room for her and I was brave for doing it.

"It's so pretty!" I rubbed it between my fingers. "What is it?"

"An amethyst. Your grandfather gave this to me as an anniversary gift. I want you to have it. My bible and this pin is the only thing I have left to remind me of him."

A few weeks later, my parents took her to the hospital. I didn't know she was in her final days of life.

I wasn't told they were taking her there.

I wasn't told I could have my room back.

During the week she was away, she broke her hip.

She died a week later.

I never got to say goodbye.

It heightened my fear of good things ending.

I was afraid of people leaving—I might not see them again.

Is it any wonder why?

* * * * *

Tucking my journal safely in my backpack, I checked my wallet and make sure I had my ID handy for security at City Architecture. I popped a butter mint in my mouth.

"Thank you, Grandma and Grandpa." I patted the pin. "Thank you for your gift of compassion."

Just as I was about to leave the café, I got a text from Ryan: *Thinking of you and your deliciousness. I am being a Boy Scout.*

I texted him: *Through with SF State and Municipality, glad you are Boy Scout. Love you for my dad.*

He returned: ☺ *Love you.*

I sent: *Remind me to tell you about my amethyst pin.*

He replied: *Call you later.*

Chapter 4

A Future for Jenise

City Architecture was located in one of the tallest buildings on Stockton Street. I stood in front of it and looked up to the rooftop, considering what it would mean to work at such a company. A few seconds later, I walked through the revolving glass doors.

The large lobby had marble floors that echoed with the hard footsteps of men and the high heels of women's shoes. Two men sat behind a large security desk. I thought the atmosphere was seductive and easily imagined myself in that kind of world.

One of the guards took my name, checked it off the "approved" list, and directed me to the top floor where the company president, Mr. Blockley, was located.

I took the long ride to the top, finally stepping off the elevator into the beautiful reception area. Photos of their many projects hung on the walls. A definite modern design echoed throughout, with chrome, glass, shining blacks, pale grays and swishes of red, boldly proclaiming the themes of the company.

A striking man and woman, each in their mid-twenties and dressed as if they were models, sat at the large, black, marble-topped desk. I introduced myself and the man called back to someone to announce my arrival.

I hadn't been sitting for more than a few minutes when a pretty young assistant with long blonde hair wearing a black sheath dress and a Tahitian pearl necklace came through a second set of glass doors. She asked me to follow her.

Like Municipality, we walked down a long hallway. This one was modern and sleek. At the very end, a third set of glass doors guarded its occupant. The glass was opaque with chrome handles and the company's logo—a silver cloud with a red lightning bolt—on each door. The young woman rounded her desk, which was in a large alcove, carved out of the ornate hallway. It was obvious her purpose was to take direction from Mr. Blockley.

"Mr. Blockley, Ms. Young is here. Would you like me to let her in or will you . . . Yes, right away." She hung up the phone and looked up. "Please go right in. May I get you a beverage?"

"No, thank you. I'm too nervous to drink."

She smiled and watched as I opened one of the two heavy glass doors. My hand made prints on the freshly polished chrome handle.

His office had a sweeping view of the bay and it gave me a clear vision of how my office might look someday. I could see myself sitting behind a big glass desk in a big chair. Perhaps I'd reupholster it in white leather and throw some pink, lacy pillows around the room for accents.

The man taking long strides toward me was tall and athletic looking, had dark brown hair, wore a three-piece suit, and was young. I guessed he was somewhere in his late twenties. His eyes were dark and focused. I imagined anyone who was caught in them knew they were in for quite a reward—or a lot of trouble.

Whoa!

"Ms. Young. Caden Blockley." He extended his hand and we shook. "You're a friend of Ryan's."

"Yes. How do you know him?"

"I met Ryan at a charity ball a few years back and was quite taken with the woman he escorted. In trying to determine if they were together, I admit our mutual friend put me in a trance of sorts." He chuckled wickedly. "After that we ran into each other quite often. These society events . . . part of developing contacts, you know. I must say the woman he was with couldn't hold a candle to you, Ms. Young."

Oh, you're smooth. I guess that kind of comment generally gets you what you want.

"I don't take compliments well, but thank you."

"How long have you known him?" He circled the room as if analyzing me.

"A little over a year."

"Did my assistant offer you a beverage?"

"Yes. I passed, but thank you for checking. This is a beautiful view, Mr. Blockley. I'm studying business marketing at Stanford next year and plan to have an office just like it." My eyes swept his office from left to right.

"Thank you, Nicky. May I call you Nicky? I'd hate to continue being so formal. If you're Ryan's girlfriend, I'm certain we'll run into each other at some gathering or another in the near future."

"Nicky's fine," I agreed.

"Good. And call me Caden. The view is spectacular, isn't it? I've worked hard to get this view." The smile on his face was a sensual smirk and full of mischief. "You don't like to talk about Ryan?"

"I like to talk about him fine. I'd like to keep our appointment simple and direct. Only business, please." I gave in a little. "If you must know and I'm being honest, Caden, he overwhelms me. I think he's brilliant."

"I agree." His hand flexed. "He thinks the same about you, by the way."

Really?

"I have a gift for analyzing people and I do it quickly. It's how I've gotten the edge in business. You are an intelligent and dynamic force waiting to light a brilliant fire in my opinion. In fact, I'm sure you'll give me a run for my money someday."

"I hope I'll find a firm that will appreciate my marketing ideas." My voice trembled. "You seem . . . I don't mean to be condescending when I say this, but you appear to be very young. If that's true, it gives me hope I can move up the chain quickly."

"Thank you." With an open hand, he gestured to one of two black leather chairs in front of his desk. Rather than sit behind his desk he took the chair next to me. He was relaxed. His body language conveyed power and being very comfortable in his own skin. He even swiveled in his seat a bit while talking with me.

"Moving up quickly is very possible if you're willing to give it your all. Stanford should help with that. I've been told how hard you've worked to gain admission there—a plan that had never been done in professional baseball?"

"Yes."

"I'm sure that meant long months of preparation. You've given up more than one weekend to achieve your goals. Get used to that. Success means sacrifice. How much . . . up to you, of course."

"I have no problem with hard work. It's what I live for, actually."

"Good . . . *very* good. Now then, what questions can I answer?"

"I understand City Architecture has an internship program, which is offered to students of SF State once every four years. My sister is studying architecture and she's going to try for it."

As he explained the details about the internship, he confirmed what Mr. Woodson had revealed to me an hour earlier.

"Have any of the students submitted their project yet?" I had to ask. "Jenise Young, maybe? Have you seen her presentation?"

"We won't look at any of their plans until early next year. If even one of the students submit the kind of work deserving of the award it will be given at the graduation ceremony."

"May I ask what you look for in a project?"

"The depth of the research, the feasibility of it and the way it fits in the current culture of society to name a few. Changing regulations are some of the biggest challenges that make the project so difficult."

"Can you explain, please?" I pulled out my journal. "Do you mind if I take notes?"

"Be my guest." He laughed and shook his head.

"I'm sorry. Did I offend you?" I closed my journal; suddenly afraid I'd done something wrong.

"No. I should have known Ryan would fall for someone like you. He always did like a challenge and you are definitely that. Please. Open your notebook. I didn't mean to make you uncomfortable."

"Thank you." I reopened my journal. "Caden?"

I've had enough of this flirtation.

"Nicky?"

"I admit I'm naive, but I'm not stupid."

His head jerked back.

"Meaning?"

"I *will* challenge you in a few years." My eyes narrowed as I focused on him. "And it won't be because of Ryan. I'll do it all on my own. Can we continue now?"

"Please." His smile changed from playful to all business.

"You were explaining how you look for a project that fits into a changing society."

"Yes. Right." He pushed up from the chair and walked to the window. Stood a few second. Turned to me. It was as if I'd unnerved him. I hoped that was true and he wouldn't try to intimate women like he had with me in the future. "Regulations and events change. They're fluid, beyond the student's control.

For example, zoning changes, natural disasters, possible permit issues, and current political opinion . . . all of them could change just as the student finishes two years of work. Suddenly, the project is obsolete. Even in an award year, few are given because of the complexities involved."

"That's tough criteria."

"You're studying business?"

"Entertainment Marketing."

"A woman who's ahead of her time," he announced.

"You *know* what that is?" I asked, surprised. "You're the first."

"I practice it." He stood and walked to his desk, lifted a framed certificate and handed it to me. "We hired Lance to help in the cafeteria. When employees started complaining about a boring selection, I circulated a memo for ideas. He emailed me a plan to personally cater our staff and executive meetings as well as a healthy alternative for the cafeteria. I took him up on it. Now I'm a partner in his restaurant. Crouton. It's on Church Street. Ever been?"

He's smart—and also conceited. But smart nonetheless. I know I could learn from him if I could stand to be near him.

"I'll have to check it out. That's exactly the kind of pay-it-forward thinking I plan to study." I shared my ideas. When I was done, he offered a few of his own. Our meeting lasted more than an hour.

"I'd love to continue talking with you. Unfortunately I have a meeting to get to." He handed me his business card. "Call me when you graduate . . . if you dare. You're a fascinating woman."

"Thank you. And I *will* dare." I lifted my chin in defiance and shook his hand.

"Oh. Tell Ryan yes."

"Yes?"

"He'll understand." He took my hand and kissed it. "Charmed."

Although I'd never admit it to anyone, I left his office a little weak in the knees.

A passion started to burn in me for my sister and her career. I wanted her to have a great future.

I'd also found out more concerning Ryan's passions—his drive to succeed was strong. His empathy and love for people seemed on a deeper level than anyone I'd ever met. After meeting his contacts, I saw how he was building layers of protection. Just as I had with volunteering, he was setting up layers of protection and a second career in case his baseball life was cut short.

Suddenly, it struck me how vulnerable he felt.

Suddenly I understood how vulnerable I was.

Suddenly I understood he was afraid his career wouldn't last.

Suddenly I understood he was afraid he'd slip away without being significant in a life he so desperately wanted to make meaningful.

Perhaps, just like his father, he was tortured because of a fear that the memory of his contribution would fade and only his mother or family would remember him.

I wondered, how deep, hot, and furious, the desire burned inside Ryan Tilton for a unique and different life. Was losing his father the root of his fear, leaving him with the feeling that with one misstep, one injury, or one bad decision, anything, everything, could be over?

Chapter 5

Walter Dixon

Walter Dixon was the last appointment of the day. He was Stanford's athletic director and the manager of the men's baseball team. I knew he could be a very important man for Jerry's career.

On the way to his office, I watched and admired the students buzzing around me. With their book bags in tow, they walked and socialized in every direction. I desperately wanted to be there and now regretted my decision to go to junior college for my general education classes.

Why didn't I ask for what I wanted and take the opportunity my parents had initially offered before my father's job was in danger?

Because you took the passive route once again, Nicky. Stop being the peacemaker. It's time to take care of your own needs.

Even after all the upheaval at home, I never thought that my professional life—a life I'd planned so methodically—could be altered in such a significant way. I had been hopeful that through my own hard work, my future was a given.

I should have known better.

As I got closer to the football and track fields, there were more males than females. I began getting the looks and comments that came being in *jock country*. I thought about Ryan *and* Jerry and their raging testosterone.

What am I doing? A relationship with an athlete? There's no way I want to battle other women for my boyfriend, always wondering if someone else has caught his eye. I've got to squash my feelings before this goes any further.

After I was admitted through a large and glamorous checkpoint displaying Stanford's many trophies and awards for athletics, I was directed to Mr. Dixon's office.

There were no thick glass doors guarded by hired personnel, nor a receptionist appointed to him. The intimate waiting area was small, with a few chairs and a sofa, a worn brown rug and a few old pictures of former college stars hanging on the wall. When Walter Dixon finally walked in, he looked haggard. It was obvious he was preoccupied.

"I'm sorry." He shook my hand. "There was a problem with one of our athletes. She takes precedence, of course."

You're the head of the athletics department—the man *who manages* men's *baseball—and you spent time with a* female *athlete? I like you already.*

I watched as he quickly straightened the reception area. He was a man of average height, had a good physique and I guessed was somewhere in his early to middle forties. His rusty hair was beginning to bald and the fine wrinkles of life had settled around his eyes. A goatee adorned his chin. He wore gray sweats and a Stanford T-shirt.

"No apology needed, Mr. Dixon. I appreciate your time on such short notice. In fact, if this isn't the best time for you I'm happy to reschedule our meeting."

"First off, call me Walter." He unlocked the door to his office. It was much larger than his modest reception room. The deep red carpet accommodated a solid looking, dark wooden desk, rows of bookcases and a dozen metal file cabinets. The walls were peppered with photos and plaques. Trophies were lined side by side on a massive oak cadenza.

One of the photos seemed to hang purposefully in the center of the wall. It was a young baseball team and he was standing on the left of them, obviously their coach. Inscribed were the words: Burberry High School, North East Champions. The year and the name of the players were listed. Ryan was one of the boys.

"Second, I promised Ryan I would talk with you today. I'll never hear the end of it if I don't," he chuckled. "Do you find him as relentless as I do?"

"Oh yes," I laughed along with him. "Hell, yes."

"Please have a seat and fire away with your questions. I was warned once you begin I should prepare to keep up."

"Thank you, Walter. Yeah, I um . . . I get nervous, so just put your hand up and I'll stop if I run on too long." I felt my face flush. Ryan had prepared the man in front of me in case I took off on a rant. I pulled out my journal and turned to the page I'd marked. I cleared my throat. "May I ask how you know Ryan Tilton and how he might have influence over your program?"

"Well, that's right to the point." He offered me a contagious smile. "I like that. Before we go much further, you should know Ryan encouraged me to be completely honest in our discussion today. I'll answer all of your questions except any privacy issues regarding Mr. Stowe, who I understand is the primary concern here. Jerry hasn't given me permission to reveal any details about his scholarship. Ryan says you and Jerry have been friends a long time. I assume you probably know most of what I omit."

"We grew up together."

"I'm surprised—actually *beyond* surprised—that Ryan gave me the freedom to speak with you so openly. He's very private. That tells me he cares about you a great deal."

"I care about him, too." I noticed a cobweb in the corner of the room. A daddy longlegs walked delicately on the spun thread. "The more I find out about him, the more certain I am of how different he is than anyone else I know."

"You're right about that." By the thoughtful look on his face, it was obvious they had shared something priceless.

"So about Jerry . . . why would Ryan have any say so for his position on Stanford's baseball team?"

"Let me throw a question back to you. Can you imagine how much a recommendation from a professional baseball player could mean for Mr. Stowe's future at Stanford?"

"I can see the baseball connection, but why should that have anything to do with Jerry making the team?"

"With Ryan's input, your friend might have a spot on the varsity team. For an incoming freshman, that's highly unusual. Professional scouts would notice."

"But Jerry's doing really well on his own. Did you know he has a chance for a golden glove *and* the batting title in his summer league?" Just then the full impact of what Walter said hit me. "Wait—so Ryan *already* recommended him?"

"Yes, but only that we take a closer look, not a full endorsement." He gathered several phone messages together and put them aside. "And yes, we're keeping an eye on Mr. Stowe. I'm aware of his summer baseball league and his entrance to City College in the fall."

"What's the difference in a look and a full endorsement?"

He explained all the advantages Jerry would have with Ryan's input and after exhausting the topic, switched directions. "I'd like to tell you a little bit about my relationship with Ryan. Do you have time?"

"Take all the time you need." I closed my journal. "I'm the one intruding on *you*."

"Do you know about Ryan's father?"

"Yes." I flattened my hands on my thighs.

"He died a few months before I started coaching at the high school. Ryan sat out the first season I was there. Poor kid was in such turmoil. He didn't know I was watching and analyzing him in more ways than playing baseball. I wanted him on the team, but he was a dark, brooding boy. He'd lost his direction, challenged authority and rebelled against everyone in his path."

"You sound like a shrink," I teased. Immediately I was afraid I sounded flippant. "I'm sorry. No disrespect intended."

Shut up with your sarcasm, Nick.

"Minored in psychology," he laughed. "Well, I watched Ryan for a few months before I approached him." He ran one hand through his hair and then shook his head. "He was really something."

"I can see that," I smiled. "As cool as he seems to be, he's got a little devil in him."

"Thank God, right? We should all have a little of that."

What a mentor for Ryan you must have been.

"Losing a parent during his adolescence was devastating." Walter folded his hands on his desk. "Did you know that Ryan never said goodbye to his father?"

"Oh God." I lowered my head. I could hardly stand to keep listening. My stomach turned over at the thought of the hole that might still be inside of him.

"When his dad was deployed to the Middle East—the fourth time in only six years—instead of a hug goodbye, Ryan yelled profanities at him and then rode away on his bike until his father's screams faded. He never turned back. When he came home that night? His dad had already left. I'm afraid the last sounds of his father's voice remain as fresh now as when he was fourteen." He looked out his window. "You remember being that age?"

"Everything is traumatic, let alone losing a parent."

"And we're immortal," he went on. "We just *know* we are at the center of the universe. The thing was, Ryan didn't have the time to mature like most of us before the lesson came down that the world didn't revolve around him."

A knock on the door interrupted us.

"I'm sorry to interrupt, Mr. Dixon." A young man in sweats and a Stanford Track Team sweatshirt stood at the door.

"Do you mind? I'll only be a minute," Walter asked politely.

"Take your time." I walked into the waiting room. Absentmindedly, I leafed through a magazine. *Oh crap, that's right! I still have to pick up the stuff from Ryan's place and take it to Yountville tomorrow. Another short night . . . I'm so tired.*

"Anytime Owen." Walter and the young man stepped out of the office shaking hands twenty minutes later. "Sorry, Nicky? You ready to resume?"

"Thanks," the young man winked. "Going here in the fall?"

"Spring."

"Owen Posley." He shook my hand. "See you in six months, I hope. What's your major?"

"Business marketing."

"Cool. Maybe I'll see you in a class." He reached for the door, which let him into the main hallway and then pointed to himself. "Economics major. Look me up, will you? What a lovely spring it'll be, don't you think?"

"Turn off the charm, Owen," Walter kidded.

"I look forward to it," I laughed.

We sat down once again, ready to continue our discussion.

"Are all the students that polite?"

"When they see a pretty girl? Most definitely. Where were we?" He opened a container of hard candies. "Care for one?"

"Sure." I reached for one that looked like butterscotch. "You were telling me how the death of Ryan's father made him rebellious."

"Right. I knew the first thing I needed to do was gain his trust. Ultimately, however, he had to love and trust himself. It took me a full year to get that boy turned around."

That's easier said than done. I still can't trust anyone.

"I hoped I could reach him before he self-destructed. He burned as if an evil fire roared inside of him." Walter looked at his desk as if those times were still fresh.

"I understand trauma." I reached for his hand. "I've lived with it all my life." The look in his eyes made me feel as if I'd known him longer than only a few minutes.

"I do love that boy." He wiped his eyes and then stopped to use a tissue. "I visited his home, talked with his mother, and invited him to the high school field. I made sure we were alone so he wasn't distracted. You know how boys try to be tough for other boys and at the same time show off for girls. We're all weak for girls at that age, Ms. Young."

"Just call me Nicky. Girls are just as weak for boys." *I'm weak for one right now!*

"True," he smiled. "Thankfully, I had the privilege of witnessing a young man who had raw, natural talent. When his smile broke through, I knew I couldn't let him down."

Walter loves Ryan!

"Judging by that plaque on the wall, I'd say you see him as your friend and star pupil." I nodded to the picture of the high school team he'd coached and proudly displayed.

"The courage it took for him to reach out . . ." He fiddled with his pen. "So many young people close up and bury their youth die in anger. Too late they realize the opportunity for something special has already passed by them. I knew I wanted to—no, correct that—I *needed* to help. I still wonder if I pushed him too hard too soon."

"I'd say you were on the money, Walter. The results seem to speak for themselves, right?"

"So far. I became the father figure in his life. All these years later, we've kept in touch, and miraculously ended up on the same coast. So that's our story."

"That's pretty terrific." I clasped my hands.

"I'm lucky to have seen him achieve his dreams—at least professionally. Another part of his life seems to be opening. Are you the reason he wanted me to reveal our story?"

"Before I came here, I thought it was to help me understand all the things he could do for my friends and family."

"And now?"

"Now, I'm confused." I rubbed my amethyst pin.

As Walter finished talking, I was lost in my thoughts about the friendship of a boy who'd put the pain of his childhood in front of his mentor and me. The fondness I felt for Ryan turned to love as I sat with Walter. It was like a kaleidoscope was turning colors all through my body.

Just as Ryan didn't know how to deal with his emotions when he lost his father, I didn't know how to deal with the same loss from my dysfunctional parents. I didn't understand—yet—that inside I'd been silently grieving for the touch and embrace of my family for many years.

My fears of intimacy and abandonment would soon demand recognition. No longer would I be able to ignore what it meant to let someone see inside me.

"Are you all right?" Walter asked.

"Yes." I took a Kleenex from his desk and dabbed my eyes. "I don't know why I'm so emotional about him. He reaches me in ways I don't understand."

"You love him," his eyes softened. "That's plain enough. Whether that love is friendship or something more . . . the man I've always known? When he cares about you, he cares deeply."

"Thank you, Walter. I've heard that same thing from almost every person I met with today." I got up to leave. "I could sit here for hours and listen to you talk, but I know you're busy."

"Nicky?"

"Yes?"

"I understand your confusion," he moved a puzzle of stacked magnets to the corner of his desk and then looked up at me.

"I think I've got it now. Thanks again for your time." I offered my hand to shake his.

"Ms. Young?" He took my hand to make sure he'd caught my attention. "Be thoughtful about this."

"What do you mean?"

"I'm saying that whatever you do, make sure you don't regret your decision. Let the chips fall where they may, but it's *your* life; not Jerry's, not Ryan's, but yours."

"Would I overstep if I gave you a hug, Walter?"

"I'd be honored." Walter pushed up from his desk to meet me. "You know, when I spoke with Ryan yesterday, the excitement in his voice wasn't about Mr. Stowe."

I forced a smile. I was embarrassed and swimming with emotions that I didn't know how to process. I thanked him again and left his office.

I thought about Ryan's story the rest of the day.

I wonder what his mother and siblings are like? Does he have any brothers or sisters? Does he have any friends from school he still sees? All these social events he attends . . . how big is his circle? What was it like growing up on the east coast?

The ache I felt for him simmered. As I reviewed the conversations I'd had that day, I heard a rumble inside me.

Something was building.

Even I didn't know how strong and furious the oncoming storm would hit me.

Chapter 6

A Buffet of Choices

*A*fter my talk with Walter Dixon, I needed to be alone to sort through feelings. He'd shared a sweet vulnerability that lay within Ryan and while it was fresh in my mind I needed to write down my observations and also process my day.

I knew the perfect place.

The magnificent Cliff House was located on the Great Highway at Ocean Beach in San Francisco. It was where my father had taken me after we went to the Goliaths games, just he and I, when Dad was Dad.

Now, it was where I went when I wanted to be by myself.

Like the biggest diamond in a jeweler's display case, the building sat on the bluffs as if guarding the waves, which crashed on the rocks below. The architectural gem had survived earthquakes, fire, and powerful winter storms that broke her 10 x 20 foot beveled glass windows.

Years earlier, gale force winds and sheets of rain had mercilessly battered the interior. It damaged priceless works of art and caused the eighty-year-old ceiling murals to run like tears; the plaster had turned into mush.

Being there made me feel strong—like I survived with her.

I needed to wrap myself in those kinds of feelings and the memories of having a family that was present and attentive.

The walls were a sky blue. Gods of the sea like Triton, Amphitrite and her husband, Poseidon, were a part of the murals now painted on the ceiling.

Shown to my table for one in the corner of the big room, I stood facing the thick, floor to ceiling windows. Soaking in the sweet beauty of the view outside, I wished the thick walls of glass weren't there to separate me from the ocean. Like so many times before, I ran my hands over them, longing to feel the vibrations and power of the waves beyond my reach. Still, as protected as we were inside, the pull of the wind, sky, and water resonated through the open doors at the entry. It was magical.

The pulsating life of the ocean always drew me to it in a deep way—the barnacle-covered rocks below, the sea lions lying in the sun, barking as they jockeyed for position, the foggy skies above—I bathed myself in the glorious richness around me.

A seafood buffet with my favorite shellfish and a big selection of side dishes, salads, and desserts, waited for me on the well-stocked tables set in the middle of the room. If I kept my plate full, I knew I'd be left alone and could stay as long as I needed at my table for one.

I'd just started to eat one of several salads I'd put on my plate when my cell phone rang.

It was almost seven p.m.

"Hey, sweetness." Ryan's voice was welcoming.

"Hi, my Ryan." My voice trembled. Emotions surfaced unexpectedly.

"Are you all right? You sound—you're not upset with me, are you?" Worry plagued his voice.

"No, I'm not upset."

"Your voice sounds shaky."

"You're trying to help my father."

"Yes."

"Last week you were pretty specific that you wanted an exclusive commitment from me before you'd do that. I haven't given you one. And yet . . ." My bottom lip quivered. "You've—"

"I decided your dad wasn't the only one who might be hurt if I didn't try to do something. My precious woman would be on the end of an unfair situation. When you said we were more than casual friends, you got to me."

I knew you were moved on the beach when we went to Sammy's.

"I considered, here I am asking you to trust me. I wouldn't be much of a boyfriend if I didn't do anything."

I could hear him breathing.

Afraid to ripple the silence, I waited until he began speaking.

"Something else? It's never good when you're quiet."

"You helped Jerry, too." I was still in mild shock from when Walter revealed Ryan had already called him.

"That was for selfish reasons," he admitted.

"How could such a generous act be selfish?"

"I don't want you to see Jerry as a victim because of something I could have done and instead withheld. I want you to see him as an equal and make a decision about two strong men."

"I'm falling for one of those strong men."

"And?"

"It's you, Ryan Tilton. And I'm afraid."

"Of?"

"We'll both get hurt."

"How would you hurt me?" he exhaled softly.

That's just what Jerry said and now I have to tell my friend I'm in love with another man.

"I don't know how to be the woman you're looking for. I've never been with a boy and I have a feeling; actually, I just *know* I'll be a lousy girlfriend. I'm leaving for college in January no matter what. I'm completely focused on it. That's only six months from now. What if we get along great? Then I'll leave."

"You don't think we can figure it out?"

"You'll be disappointed." I stabbed at a forkful of crab.

"We're meant to be." His voice lowered. "I have no doubt about that. By January, I'm hoping you'll look at your home life differently. Maybe you'll decide to live there instead of the dorms. Maybe, you'll live with me."

"You don't mean that." *How could he?*

"Oh, I mean it, Nicky. I'm going to tempt you in every way to consider doing it."

He's murder.

"A lot can happen in six months. You have your life on the road and I'll meet new people at college. I have dozens of fears . . . I have to spit it out, so please listen when I tell you this. Are you listening?"

"Yes."

"Even if I fall head over heels in love with you, the focus on my goals won't change," I insisted. "I won't let myself be distracted by anyone. That means I won't go on the road with you if I have to study or prepare for a test. What will happen then?"

"I'll understand. Of course I want you to go to Stanford and be successful. I'd never get in the way of your dream. You and I are not about killing dreams; we're about soaring. When I asked you to look at us, I meant everything about us. For you that includes Stanford."

"My father says you'll want me to come on the road with you all the time." I almost gasped as I released the words. "He thinks you won't support me or honor that I need to have the college experience. I wonder about it, too, because I'll make new friends and have a separate life. Will you be able to handle that? Dad thinks you want to keep me sheltered and away from the life I see for myself."

"I *will* support you," he almost pleaded. "Sure, I'll want you on the road with me, but I'm not naïve. I know you won't always be able to go. The way I want to shelter you has nothing to do with isolation."

"I really like Walter Dixon." Trying to get my fragile emotions under control, I changed the subject. He seemed ready to explore a level of intimacy I wasn't prepared to hear.

"He's quite a man," Ryan's voice softened.

"He loves you."

"I love him, too."

"Talking with him about your childhood helped me realize how strong my feelings are for you. In fact, everyone I spoke with today made me feel how good it is to know you."

"Thank you for saying that. How could you know Walter and I love each other in so little time?"

"Oh, Ryan," I sighed. "It was so easy. When he told me the story of the reckless boy he'd found he had tears in his eyes. The way Walter mentored you—what a blessing to have in your life."

"I was lost back then."

"He's a special man . . . like you. You know what?"

"What?"

"I think a guardian angel created a miracle and brought the two of you together. Maybe it's your dad watching over you."

"I've thought about that," Ryan's voice was like a soft caress.

"And you know what else?"

"What else, Nicky?"

"I'm fond of the little boy that Walter loves, too."

Ryan suddenly quieted and I wondered if I had shocked him. He probably expected me to talk only about the things he could do for my family. Instead, I'd focused on my feelings for him.

The sense of him as a little boy and the vulnerability hidden beneath his macho man exterior piqued my curiosity in a way that made me want so much more.

You can be that vulnerable, Nick.

"Ryan? Are you there?"

"Who's left on the list?" His voice shook.

Now you're deflecting—I know that tactic very well.

"No one's left."

"What about your sister?"

"I saw Mr. Woodson and Mr. Blockley. By the way, how well do you know Caden Blockley?"

"Why?"

"He seems like he could be a lot of trouble for a woman."

"He told me you called him out," Ryan laughed appreciatively.

"I'm sorry, I guess I did. I was tired of the flirting and game playing. I wasn't in there for any of that."

"You did the right thing," he supported. "He can be overbearing."

"I'll say. I get a feeling you two have hit the town together more than once trolling for women."

"Hit the town?" he laughed.

"Mmm. And he said to tell you yes. What does that mean?"

"Ah, well . . . that's man code. The translation means he's in agreement with my intuition that you're great."

"That's caveman stuff," I laughed.

"No it isn't," he argued. "You women do the same thing."

"True. Anyway, I canceled the other appointments."

"Why would you do that?"

"I'm fairly confident the results will be the same. Each of my friends will have a unique opportunity because of someone you know. Did you win today?"

"Yes."

What's the matter, Mr. Cool? Cat got that golden tongue of yours?

"God, Ryan." I started laughing.

"What?"

"You and the night at my house after I sang the anthem and we were on my front steps. What a faker you were with all your veiled threats."

"You found me out." For the first time since I'd known him, he sounded bashful.

"It wasn't too difficult."

"I needed leverage; something to get your attention. You didn't look at one guy at the stadium all last year or this year—at least so far. I knew I had to be bold."

"You're wrong about that. I did look at one boy last year."

"Who was it?" he asked innocently.

"Did you pitch?"

Are you as quick as I think you are?

"I get it." I could hear the smile in his voice. "That's a sweet thing to say."

"How many saves now? Nineteen?"

"You still track me?" He laughed.

"Of course, I do. I told you I follow the Goliaths," I reminded him. "I was a baseball fan years before the cheer team—or boys. You know what? I'm counting down."

"To what?"

"Nine more days, Ryan."

"Until?"

"Until I get those sweet kisses of yours. Ooh I can't wait." I raised my voice in excitement.

"You're taking me apart piece by piece," he said bravely. "I didn't expect to hear you say these things. You uh, you understand . . . you're seeing us just like I hoped you would. In fact, what you just said is so much more than I dared to let myself dream of this soon. Did you realize you'd open up to me like this?"

I stared out the windows at the raging ocean.

"You know what, Ryan?"

"What, sweetheart?"

"I think we're putting each other *together,* piece by piece. I've been taken apart since I was little. And from what Walter told me today, it seems like you've been through the same."

I can hear you breathing. Ooh, how I'd love to be near that mouth and get your kiss.

"It's almost as if I was fighting a war," he sighed.

"How did you end up with such a big heart?"

"Same way you did." His response was kind.

"I'm so attracted to your generosity—the way you've set up networking groups at my sister's college . . . I knew you'd be amazing. I saw it last year when we went to Yountville. You knew what you were doing taking me there."

A sexy laugh greeted me on the other end of the line.

"And, of course, when I ran my hands over your amazing chest, that did it. Oh, it's so, so, boo-tee-ful," I giggled.

"God, Nicky."

"Don't pretend to be bashful," I kidded. "Well, I should get back to my writing. Let's talk tomorrow. Don't forget, I'm going to Yountville in the morning. If you miss me, then leave me a good time to get back to you. I still have to go over to your place. Does Ross work this late?"

"Until ten."

"Good," I exhaled in relief. "I still have time to finish up here. Whelp, I'll let you know if I have any problems getting your packages. Don't worry if you get in too late. If you're out partying, you can just text me."

"Partying?"

"Yeah, you know. Come on, Ryan. I know about you guys and the way you are on the road. Tara and Alex tell me about you guys and all your women. I'm not stupid. Naive maybe, but not stupid."

"I don't party anymore," he said firmly. "Have you seen me with anyone since I confessed I want to be with you?"

"No, but your physical needs . . . we're not exclusive, so why wouldn't you . . . you know."

After all, it only took me one day to consider things with Jerry.

I couldn't allow myself to trust him even though I hoped he was all mine. Giving him permission to carry on the way he did before his promise kept love and the seriousness of his commitment somewhere in the distance. No way would I set myself up for disappointment.

I had no idea of how I was kidding myself.

Control was so fleeting, unmanageable or attainable.

I still thought I could handle everything.

"I'm not partying. You rely on a gossip chain that has given you false information a few times now."

"Well . . ." I hesitated.

"What does that tell you?" he asked again.

"You don't have to convince me." Secretly, I hoped he'd continue.

"Yeah, I think I do. I wouldn't ask you to see me exclusively or have you talk with the people you did today if I was seeing other women. That would be a waste of everyone's time and I'd be a pretty big asshole."

It's not possible for you to abstain from sex while you wait for me. You'll never be able to love me enough. There isn't any way to really comfort me or make me believe you.

"I know you don't believe me. I'm asking you to give me your attention so I can prove it to you."

"You have my attention," I answered honestly.

"Speaking of, um, promises and trust, what were *you* doing last night? I tried to phone you a few times."

"I was . . ." I tried to disguise my nervousness. "At the beach with friends."

"Uh-huh." He didn't question me, but without saying another word, he let me know—he knew. "So, I'll call you tomorrow to see how your visit went with our vets. What are you doing now?"

"I'm having dinner at the *Cliff House*."

"With your family?"

"By myself."

"Oh, Nicky . . ."

"I'm okay."

"Picturing you sitting by yourself in that big restaurant is . . . sad. I wish I could be there to take you in my arms. I can visualize you sitting alone, the same way you do at the ballpark when your teammates leave you. You're at those big windows; the ocean is pulsing with life, crashing and calling to you as you write your thoughts." His voice was soft. "Your beautiful long hair has fallen around your shoulders. I'll bet your green eyes are sparkling. I can see them beckoning to me."

"After today, I'm certain they're sparkling just for you." *Whoa! Hold back, Nick. Don't reveal so much.*

"I hope that's true. If I were there, do you know what I'd do?"

"Hmm?" *I'm afraid to ask.*

"I'd look into those beautiful eyes, caress your head and kiss your cheeks. We'd sip our coffee and share a decadent dessert. I wouldn't care who was listening or watching as I kissed you. Will you go with me when I get back from my road trip?"

"I'll sit anywhere with you." A large wave crashed on shore. *What am I saying?*

From the time Ryan had come into the outfield to introduce himself, my dam had been cracking open. Now, even the road under my feet started to crumble.

"Don't stay there too long. I hate that you're sitting by yourself."

"It's really not like that. After all of my meetings today, I just wanted to gather my thoughts. I'm writing in my journal."

"Have you written a lot?" Ryan asked.

"Oh, yeah! I've been writing, eating, writing, and eating some more. You should see my plate—crab, prawns, and salad, all piled high so I can sit here a few hours."

"I'm sitting next to you."

"Mmm."

"My hand just covered yours."

"I feel you." I played along.

"My thumb rubs your arm."

"Nice."

"I'm sitting quietly at your side while you write, as long as you need me to stay with you. I'm over my head appreciating the beautiful, giving woman next to me."

"I wish you really were here, Ryan."

"Me, too."

"Truthfully," I stabbed a prawn and dipped in cocktail sauce. "I do enjoy the quiet. I don't get as much time alone as I'd like. That's why I was behind the centerfield fence last year when I accidently heard you and Kevin talking. I needed to be by myself like I am now."

"I want to help with the noises in your head."

"It's not easy letting those go," I cautioned.

"We'll work on it together. Good night, sweet lady."

"Ryan?"

"Uh-huh?"

"When you get home, I want us to know each other better before we have sex."

"Where did *that* come from?"

"I know you're probably dying to have it. Can you wait for me, please?" I was nervous and afraid of his answer, certain by the next call or the one after that, I'd listen to his apology for leading me on. I just knew he'd admit to me he'd met someone else he could be himself with.

"Of course, I'll wait—"

"I feel you're expecting us to go there when you get back, especially when you say you're not partying or seeing other women," I interrupted. "Sex is way too complicated for me right now. I need some time before I add it to my life."

"Do you mean sex in general or . . ." He let me finish his sentence.

"I'm not sure," I thought about it a few seconds. "Penetration, I guess."

"The full Monty?" he laughed gently.

"God, Ryan." I returned the giggle.

"Don't worry, sweetness. Trust me when I say there are volumes written about enjoying each other's body in a gradual way until we're both comfortable. Do you feel more at ease about me now?"

"Yes, I do. I know I'm a pain in the ass. I'm sorry."

"I can't wait to hear your voice again. Goodnight for now."

"Goodnight, my Ryan. You're a very special man."

"*Your* special man." His strong response made me feel as if I belonged with him.

"Yes, *my special man.* Thanks for saying that."

"Until tomorrow, then. Can't wait to hear about Yountville."

I stayed at the Cliff House until the fog rolled in and gulped the sea into its throat. The water vanished from my view.

The day turned gray.

Mist covered the big windows.

My exploration of Ryan Tilton's sphere of influence and the beauty of that Friday, ended.

As I left the restaurant, I felt as if it was our beginning.

Chapter 7

What is the Definition of Home?

Strange didn't begin to describe how I felt when I pulled up to Ryan's apartment building.

The doorman rushed over to the car, ready to motion me away as if he didn't think I belonged there. He wore black slacks and a navy blue jacket with the emblem, "Bayside Residences" sewn onto the breast pocket. I focused on his big brown eyes, thick eyelashes, beautiful brown skin and full lips.

"Excuse me—" His tone was firm and I was certain he was ready to ask that I move along.

"Hi, my name is Nicky Young." I rolled down the passenger window. "I'm a friend of one of your residents, Ryan Tilton."

"I happen to know he's not—"

"Yes, I know he's not home, but he left a package for me. I'm supposed to pick up and take it with me when I go to Yountville tomorrow. Ross has it."

"One moment." He put up one finger as if pausing time. "Could you pull up just a bit?" He pointed to the next parking space and then hurried inside.

I parked after rolling forward fifteen feet. Got out of the car and waited, noting some the details of the neighborhood where Ryan lived. The building was one of the newer developments in San Francisco—modern, sleek, a few dozen floors, and covered in glass that shimmered from top to bottom. Across from one of the small harbors along the embarcadero, it was built on a corner of Chestnut Street, one of the glamorous areas of the Marina district.

Contrasting to the shine of the outside of the building, soft beiges, lavenders and other earthy colors decorated the lobby. Inscribed on a bronze plaque and bolted to the olive green stuccoed front wall, were the same words as on the curb attendant's blazer, "Bayside Residences."

A large B and an R was fixed stylishly above the doors, obviously drawn up by a professional logo designer. I could see a welcoming interior through the glass doors. A desk with a concierge plaque sitting on its top was on the right side of the entry while an attendant of some sort was at a desk on the left. Chairs and sofas covered in chocolate brown upholstery with olive green and lavender accessory pillows dotted the lobby and sat on pastel pink rugs. Several men and women sat about the room socializing.

A red-haired, middle-aged man of average height stepped out to greet me. He wore the same blazer as the doorman and had two large boxes loaded on a dolly.

"I'm Ross." He extended one hand while holding the dolly's handle with the other. "Nice to meet you, Ms. Young. You made it with a half-hour to spare," he pointed to his watch.

"Nice to meet you as well, Ross. I'm sorry, I lost track of time having dinner. Did I inconvenience you?"

"Not at all. Shall we load these in the back?"

"*Those* are what Ryan wants me to take to Yountville?"

He nodded. "Naveed, help me with these, please?" He shouted to the young man who had first hurried to the car.

"My God, that's a lot of something!" I opened the back hatch.

"They're autographed jerseys from the entire Goliaths team." The young doorman said, while lifting each box and sliding them into the back of the car. I immediately understood the order of authority. Ross was in charge.

"Oh, he's so . . ." I closed the door. "They'll be so happy!" *Did I just shout? Calm down, Nicky.*

"He does this all the time," Naveed reported in a charming Pakistani accent. Instead of my original judgment assuming he'd reacted quickly because I didn't belong, I could see he was protective of the residents. I wondered if he'd had any personal encounters he could share about the man I was falling in love with.

"Thanks for your help, Naveed." I offered my hand.

"Nice to meet you." After shutting the hatch, I also shook hands with Ross.

"The feeling's mutual." Ross set the dolly on the sidewalk. "Take it inside and put it in the closet, please."

Naveed hurried inside with it.

"I'm so pleased to meet a friend of Mr. Tilton's." Ross buttoned his jacket and Naveed stood by the door. "Will we see you again?"

"I hope so." I got in the car. "Your resident is making it difficult for me to stay away." Both men laughed. I waved to them and drove home.

When I walked in my front door, my parents were in the living room, watching TV.

What a difference in the way I felt.

For the first time in years, instead of feeling dread when I opened the door, I felt excitement, joy, the anticipation of seeing my family, and being present rather than looking to the future.

Having new choices and the knowledge my father had alternatives with Misters Freeman and Tremmel was like a fifty-pound weight had been lifted from my shoulders.

My house had been empty on so many evenings like this one—realistically and metaphorically. For years I came home from school, took the key from the chain I wore around my neck, or from a rock hidden in the yard.

I'd turn the doorknob and flip on all the lights to make it seem like everyone was home. Sometimes I even turned on the TV downstairs. I made several snacks and carried them with my backpack upstairs to my room, and tackled my homework alone.

Food became the friends I relied on day after day—and year after year. I'd polish off a bag of salty chips in no time at all. Add a sleeve of chocolate chip cookies. Top it all off with a couple of peanut butter sandwiches and a bowl of ice cream or a few candy bars . . . they were company.

Sometimes I downed them all in one afternoon.

Tonight was different; a very sober father and an attentive mother seemed to be waiting—for me.

Uh-oh!

"Hey," I nodded to my parents. "How's it going?"

"Where have you been all day?" Dad put down his newspaper.

If only I could tell you. What would I say? I've been at Municipality talking with Sid Freeman about your level-three probation? Or maybe I should ask if I'm be going to Stanford? Should I lead with, do you want to explain your problem at work?

"Just out and about." I didn't want to reveal anything that might disrupt the fragile balance of the evening. "Tomorrow morning I'm going to Yountville. Is it okay if I take the car again? I have some boxes to drop off and they're huge!"

My parents stared at each other.

"You guys want to come with?"

Silence.

I was uncomfortable.

Kept talking.

"Remember Ryan talked with you about speaking with the vets, Dad? Tomorrow is Saturday and we could have lunch afterward."

"We'll see."

Sure, we will. Just tell me you aren't interested.

"I'll pay for the gas." I hung the keys on the hook by the door. "How can you refuse that?" I smiled, trying to ease their concern, but my parents gave each other *the look.*

Uh-oh.

"There's some dinner that's left over if you want it. It's in the oven," Mom offered.

"I've already eaten."

"Where?" She marked her book.

"At the Cliff House. Why?" I challenged.

"It's expensive." She looked at me head on. "Did Ryan give you the money?"

"No." I could feel my shoulders straighten. "Why?"

"Is he buying you things?" She continued her questions.

"Things? *That's* your concern? Let's stop this dance." I took off my jacket. "What's your real question?"

"We're concerned you're getting serious with Ryan." Dad finally joined in our series of questions that were challenges about my relationship with Ryan in disguise.

"And there's his age difference," Mom added.

"Let's not forget he stayed over," Dad pressed.

"In your bed," Mom finished.

They stopped.

Waited for my response.

"Would you rather I spent the night at his place? I didn't try and hide anything about our plans. You knew that's what I was going to do, Mom. We sat on the couch and I told you about it."

"It's not that, it's . . ." She looked away.

"What? No friend is ever good enough, are they? Neither of you were happy who I played with, where I volunteer, who my cheer team friends are, and now Ryan. Why can't you give me credit for my choices? I've always done the right thing. Have I given either of you a reason to be concerned—*ever*?"

"Not until now." Dad looked worried.

I was going crazy.

I wanted to scream at the two of them.

I'd only been a straight arrow from the day I set foot in grade school. I'd never been in trouble, didn't drink or use substance of any kind. I took care of my own needs . . . now this. I was livid.

"*Not until now*? That's . . . if you must know, Ryan was a perfect gentleman—all night," I reported defiantly. "In fact, *he* was the one who asked if he should stay or go. He didn't want to disrespect you guys."

"That's admirable, but—"

"Neither of you know him." I interrupted my father. "You think nothing of throwing around criticisms and accusations of us not being good together. Why? You should know me by now. I wouldn't have sex in my bedroom with *any boy*."

"No?" Dad stepped right back into the arena.

"What if I'd gone to his apartment? Would you rather I had sex out of sight? Would that make you feel better?" Something about Ryan made me want to protect him. I surprised myself when I defended him so boldly. "Or is it that I shouldn't have sex at all? You guys want me to stay away from boys forever?"

"Don't get upset." My father raised his hand. "We believe he's a good person or you wouldn't be with him. Our concern is the eight year difference between you."

"Well, we already talked about this a few nights ago. Admit it . . . you don't really care about his age. It's only his sexual experience. Yet, Jenise can have sex all day long. You never say boo to her about it. I don't care that she's twenty-one; sex is sex at any age, especially living under your roof."

I got huffy.

My chin went up.

"Neither of you has to worry. If it bothers you so much that he comes here, I'll just go to his place like Jenise does with her boyfriend. You haven't been involved in my social life so far, so why start now?"

I tromped upstairs as if I were a two-year-old and knocked on my sister's bedroom door.

Then the words I'd just said to my parents hit me.

Nervous and shaky—that's how my body reacted talking to them so harshly. I knew I might've hurt them. I didn't want that. Down deep, I understood they were concerned.

I wished they'd shown their love more openly when I was younger and really needed them.

Even so, they were showing it now.

I had to try and let them in.

"Come in," Jenise said.

"Hang on. I'll be right back." I popped my head through her door and left it ajar. I went back downstairs. The guilt I felt was too much for me to handle and I apologized. They looked relieved and I felt better about everything.

That day, I began to bring my family back around me.

That day, I found out about Jenise's college studies and how Ryan's contacts could help her.

That day, I fell in love with my sister again.

And that day, Jenise gave me quite an education.

Chapter 8

Orgasms and Aching

When I knocked on my sister's door a second time, I sat down on her bed and proceeded to spill the details of the two boys who had my attention.

I began with Jerry. He was simple—at least when comparing my thoughts of him to those of Ryan. I told her how nice prom was, that Jerry had asked me to spend the night and had tried to make moves on me at the beach bonfire.

Then I gave her a summary of the things that happened with Ryan, including his visit in the tunnel at the ballpark, the daisy and silver charm he gave me on my birthday, and the lavender roses he'd sent on the day of my prom. I finished by summarizing his call at the Cliff House.

"I have big stirrings, Sis."

"What do you mean *stirrings*?" Jenise smiled. "Sexual?"

"I think so."

"You *think* so? Tell." She lay on her stomach and cupped her chin in her hands.

PAMELA TAEUFFER

"Ryan, God, he's . . . his kisses, the way he touches me . . . speaks to me . . . it's like I start to rev up in my belly. Jerry's are nice too, but . . ." I was losing myself in a daydream.

"Oh, Sis, I know that look." She sat up and tucked her legs underneath her. "Forget about Jerry. He won't have a chance if your face is saying what I think it is."

"I don't know about my face, but I do want to explore Jerry more. I mean, logically he should be the one I go with, right? Ryan is a man and—"

"Yeah, he's a big, fucking, beautiful, man!" She threw her arms in the air. "Hell yes, he's a man. Go and grab him! Let him teach you a thing or two. Forget Jerry. Just strike that boy from your list and go with your sexy Ryan beast."

"I don't think I'm ready for that. God Jenise." I burst in nervous laugher. "I'm really attracted to him and I told him so. He's coming on so strong. I think—"

"You'd better damn well prepare, Sis. What are you using for birth control?"

"Nothing."

"Are you stupid?"

"No, I—"

"Why the hell are you taking a chance like that?" Her expression was mixed with shock and anger. She'd assumed I was having sex and being careless.

"I, um . . . you know, I mean, I haven't . . ."

"Oh no!" Her mouth was open as she slapped her cheek lightly to mock me. "You've never had sex?"

"No and it seems like both of them want to have it with me right now," I confided. "I don't know how much longer I can put them off."

"Why the hell would you want to do *that*?" She tilted her head, obviously questioning my abstinence.

"I'm afraid," I confessed. I knew by her reaction I was missing out on something wonderful.

"Afraid of what?"

"Well, how uh, you know, I don't understand . . . what I mean is, how does it feel when their thing is inside you?" *The real issue is . . . how do you let someone get that close?*

She cracked up, launching into hysterics.

"Shut up."

"I'm sorry." She continued laughing.

"Okay, okay, I'm a dork. I know women deliver babies after all, but they also dilate and their bodies prepare for something big to come through. I just don't get it. How does it wedge in? You obviously enjoy it and lots of women do, too, but how?"

"Yeah, women enjoy it," she laughed. "Billions and billions. How big *are* your two fellas?"

"I've only felt them against me, but oh my God, Ryan's . . ."

"When did you feel his cock?" My sister's eyes widened and her entire face lit with curiosity.

"That night after I sung the anthem, when we walked out to the front porch. He hugged me and we were pressed together when he kissed me. Also when he spent the night. I put my leg right on it! I was afraid I hurt him but he said—"

"He said fuck no, keep moving on it and make me come!" She burst with enthusiasm.

"Jenise! Wow!"

"What about Jerry?"

"When I slept over his house the other night, his you know, was against me, too, and . . ."

"What are you doing, measuring them by having them press their bodies against you?" She was in hysterics once again.

"No." I hit her with a pillow.

"Their penises fit great." She calmed to a giggle. "As long as they give you a chance to get into it and your vagina is lubricated. When you're wet, you expand down there. I assume Jerry doesn't know what the fuck he's doing, but when Ryan starts to tickle your furry bush, does he take his time with foreplay?"

"Kissing?"

"Sensual kissing, playing with your breasts, sucking your nipples and nuzzling into your neck, licking or fingering your vagina . . . Have you done any of that with him?"

"We've kissed a lot and I feel all juicy when his tongue goes in my mouth. I . . . ." I could see his chest in front of me as I began to tell her about it. "Whenever I see his chest, my belly aches. And his arms . . . he's got these tattoos . . . oh, this one on his arm is of a big Phoenix."

She grabbed the pillow I'd thrown at her and hugged it, thoroughly entertained as I shared my thoughts and story.

"He's built, no denying that. I don't know how you can resist him, but since you obviously have some reservations, don't rush it," she sliced the air with her hand. "If something feels *off*, pay attention to what your gut tells you, it's just . . ."

"What? Tell me what you're thinking!" I wanted to reach inside her and pull out the words.

"If you do want to be with Ryan, how long do you think he'll wait for you? I mean, being an athlete and all . . ."

"That's exactly what I'm afraid of. He has so many options. You should see the women trying to get his attention. Still, I do fantasize about having his fingers crawl on my body while his hands and mouth are all over me—actually I think about Jerry that way, too. Then I have them close to me and I chicken out."

"Crawl on your body, huh? That's a damn fine idea."

"I have my sexy thoughts, too," I grinned. "Even if I don't know what to do with them."

"It doesn't take much to get your body going in the beginning." Jenise's *Sex Ed* class had begun. "You're wet all the time. Just hearing their voice, a look they give you, thinking about them on your body . . . pretty much anything."

"Jenise, I get like . . . these waves of awareness. It's as if they're charged with light or something. They take off from my chest and slide down my body."

"Oh, I know how those are. Even a quick, sexy glance from them turns you on in the beginning. A random thought during the day and it's like feathers are in your stomach, teasing the ache inside . . . doesn't your tummy get yummy just thinking about it?" She tickled my belly. "Or should I say, about *him*? You get a little pang that flows down between your legs, your clitoris aches so deliciously, doesn't it?"

"Ooh yeah!" I covered my stomach with both of my hands. "It's like a liquid rush and I want to relieve myself right on the spot. You know what I mean?"

"Hell yeah, I know what you mean!" She pushed her index finger through a hole she'd made with her thumb and middle finger, mocking the movement of intercourse.

"My chest gets tight and my legs . . . they get so weak; I feel like tumbling to the ground. You know, when Ryan and I were going into Sammy's and he kissed me with this long, lingering kiss? I had to ask him to wait a minute so I could lean on him. My legs started shaking. How embarrassing, huh?"

"You wish he'd make your legs shake with an orgasm like there was no tomorrow, don't you?" She was so into our discussion, I couldn't help but smile. "He knows he's got you."

"No he doesn't," I challenged. " I haven't committed to him. We even talked about it. He's waiting for an answer."

"You're only kidding yourself. He knows."

"That's—"

"That's the end of this discussion, because I'm telling you . . . he knows. Anyway, you'll find out by experimenting what feels good for each of you," she interrupted. "Now listen to me and listen to me good. Whichever boy you choose, don't be bashful about guiding either of them when it comes to sex. Men can be pretty dumb when it comes to pleasuring a woman.

"It's all about the vagina for them, 'cause they don't know any better. They think we're in heaven if they stick their dick inside our pussy. As you know—at least I hope to God you do—that's not bringin' us the magic of orgasm."

"Have you ever climaxed from just penetration?" I smoothed her bedspread with my left hand.

"Oh shit, yeah, but he has to know how to move in there, *and* I need plenty of warm up. Some women come from playing with their nipples," she continued. "I've never been one of them, unfortunately."

"Why *unfortunately?*"

"Because guys love to play with them," she giggled. "They can play all night long with our girls and our little kitten's noses."

"Kitten's noses?"

"Nipples. They love sucking and fingering our nipples, Nick. Promise me you'll insist they move your body so it sings. Pleasure from sex is about the *both* of you. Men don't know any better if you don't speak up. Mom never did."

"What do you mean?" I was shocked she knew anything about sex between our parents.

"I heard Mom talking with Auntie Barbara one day. She didn't think I heard, but I did. She said Dad is a 'two-minute' man."

"What's that?" I asked. "Stick it in and he's done?"

"Yep. No orgasm for Mom—with Dad, anyway." She reached for the bottle of water on her nightstand. "No wonder she's sad."

"Poor mom. Well, screw that noise." My eyebrows knotted. "I'll be in control when I decide."

"Yeah, yeah. You go on thinking that way. I admire your determination, but control over sex? When you're taken away, you just go. That's why you need birth control, so you'll have some protection when your passion roars and you're helpless to do anything except open your body."

"I've already controlled it," I maintained. "A few times. And I'll keep doing it as long as I have to."

"That's sad." She looked down.

"Why?"

"That you feel you have to abstain . . . sex is wonderful."

"I'm conflicted. They need to give me time."

"Yeah, we're talking about Ryan here, not Jerry. He's not going to roll over and let you dictate when and where. Go get your damn pills or shot or whatever," she continued pushing.

"I've already bookmarked a bunch of websites to research. So what do *you* do for birth control?"

"I get a monthly shot at the clinic near Stonestown. If you go, they'll talk to you about all the alternatives so you can decide which is the right option for you."

"Ryan said when he gets back, we can do *other things*—you know, besides intercourse. I told him I didn't want that yet. Well, I didn't exactly say it like that, but . . ."

"For God sakes." Jenise took a swig of water and put the cap back on the bottle. "You drive a person crazy when you go on and on. He's saying until your pussy is ready for his big stiffy, you can have oral sex, sensual massage, masturbation, or anal if you're ready for that."

God, she's calm talking about this.

"You *have* fingered yourself, *haven't* you, sissy?"

I pulled my blouse out of my slacks to get more comfortable.

"The blush in your cheeks tells me you *know* what an orgasm is?" she smirked.

"*Yes*, Jenise. I've had them *many* times. My friends *are* having sex, you know."

"Thank God for *that*. They sure haven't shared much with you from the questions you're asking me. You afraid to bring up the subject because you're the good girl of your group?"

"It's not that. They know I haven't had it. I don't trust they know what they're doing. I trust *you*." Suddenly it was important she believe me and I emphasized the point. "What can an eighteen-year-old know about sex? On prom night, do you know what advice my friends gave me?"

"No idea." She shrugged her shoulders.

"Smoke a joint so I could enjoy my first time. I mean, if sex is so great, why do I need pot?"

"You don't." Her response was harsh. "I hate that so many women *put up with sex* rather than ask for what they want. No wonder men think they just put it in and we're enthralled. I can't say this any other way . . . I have to be blunt. If you understand your body, sex is an experience you'll enjoy forever.

"Knowing your sensual responses comes from touching yourself and daring to let another touch you," she continued. "You have to play with your breasts, examine the way they color when you're excited, examine the fluid and the amount when you have an orgasm, the way your lips swell, if you're more sensitive on the left or right of your clitoris, all of those things. Hold a mirror to your cleft and explore everywhere."

"I'm glad we're talking like this. I don't know who else . . . I got confused the last few years, Jenise. You know you've always been my hero. I never said that to you, but you were . . . are."

"You'll be okay." Her face softened. She put her hand on my arm. "Don't let either of them rush you. Even if they threaten to leave or try and play on your sympathy by saying they're suffering or in pain, let them go."

"Don't worry, I won't put up with that nonsense. Hey, what about condoms?"

"What about them?" She reached into her nightstand and pulled out several different types.

"Oh, my God! You keep them in your bedroom?"

"Why not?" She tried handing one to me. "Here."

"Ew!" I threw it back at her. We tossed it back and forth. "Why are there so many varieties?"

"Some people have allergies to latex so there's polyurethane, animal membrane—but that doesn't help with STD's—different sizes, thickness, taste, some have ridges for better stimulation . . . WebMD has a condom wizard that goes over a lot of this. Check it out."

"Do you continue using them after . . . well . . . how long do you keep using them?" I tossed the foil packet on her lap.

"Until you're sure both of you are STD free. *Make sure* he's tested, Nicky. Do *not* take his word for it. And when you look at the test results pay attention to the date. If it's before you started seeing him, ask him to get tested again. That goes for Jerry, too. If you do go with that one, I'll knock you on your head."

"What do you mean?"

"You're going to take Jerry over Ryan?" She shook her head in disgust. "And by the way, you can get STDs with oral sex, so don't gobble and swallow thinking you're safe just because he didn't stick it in. And don't let their mouth on your pussy without a dental dam or put your mouth on their helmet—even with Jerry. You can get and give herpes that way."

"What's a dental dam?"

"It's a thin piece of latex that protects partners from mouth to skin transmissions." She reached in her nightstand again. Pulled one out and showed me what it looked like. "It's thin enough so each person gets pleasure but strong enough so our tongues and teeth won't pop through. You can use plastic wrap—the kind that's non-microwavable. Sean and I used it for anal rimming, cunnilingus, and fellatio until we got tested together."

"Your nightstand is a treasure trove of goodies! What else you got?" I turned sixty hues of red as I listened to my smart sister calmly explain how she practiced safe sex. "Can I look in there?"

"The rest of what's in there . . . you're not ready for it," she summarized. "Come back when you're deflowered. Are you uncomfortable talking about this?"

"Yes and no. I need to hear it." I gave her permission to continue and took the dental dam from her fingers to examine it.

"I have some books for you." She nodded to the shelves above her desk. "Be my guest if you want to take a look. The photos are pretty graphic . . . as they should be."

"Okay, yeah, I'll borrow a few. Point me to a few you think would be a good start for me." I handed her back the dental dam and we both got off the bed and walked to her desk.

"I know of a couple of positions that are especially good for first times." Jenise pulled two books from her collection and handed them to me. "They guarantee orgasm for a woman even if the guy's a dork in bed, or if he squirts too quickly."

"God, you're descriptive!"

"Fast ejaculation can be a problem when the guy enters you for the first time. He's so excited to have your pussy that he wants to come immediately. There you are, panting and still hot, saying to yourself, *what the hell just happened*?"

I enjoyed watching her expressive eyes and my education.

"Yeah, well, I doubt Ryan's a dork in bed." I thumbed through one of the books absentmindedly.

"He could surprise you," she challenged. "Maybe he doesn't understand what really turns a woman on because so many told him whatever he wanted to hear."

"Why would they do that?"

"To say Ryan Tilton had his cock inside their slit, bragging rights to the competition—a leg up so to speak." She cracked up.

"Yuck."

"Well, you're not with an innocent boy, Sis."

"Don't remind me."

"That's in his past now, right?"

"Right." *I'm not sure.*

"I think it's cool that with all his experience Ryan is going slow with you. It tells me he wants more than a fling."

"Maybe."

"Look, apparently you have a golden opportunity with two great guys—Ryan *and* Jerry—and hopefully your golden pussy will be a happy girl." Once again, she threw a party, enjoying her own joke.

"You're *real* funny, Sis."

"Yes, I am." She agreed and then settled down again. "So, Mom and Dad are pissed because Ryan stayed here the other night?"

"I don't know if it was that or if they don't know what to do with it. Guess I'll go over to his place from now on."

"What do you think you feel for that man? Pretty awesome someone like him is interested in you. You know your eyes light up and your body kind of pushes out when you talk about him."

"What do you mean *pushes out?*" *I wonder how I look doing that?* I leaned over so I could see myself in the mirror.

"You expand and get big." She held my shoulders. "It's like you're so happy you can't keep it inside."

"I more than like him," I admitted. "Actually, I'm really proud to know him. Did you know—" *Don't tell her about what Ryan can do for her. We're not together that way, yet. No sense getting her excited. Those promises haven't worked for us in the past.* "—Um, that he's generous with multiple charities?"

"I've heard about something he started at school," she admitted.

"Honestly? I'd love to be his girlfriend. If you could hear the things he says to me . . . I just let the invisible drool run out of my mouth. I feel like he's seducing me without even touching me."

"That's because you've fallen for him," she said with a giggle. "And it sounds like you've hit pretty hard. Ah, the beginning of lusty love. It's great to be there. I'm still there with my boyfriend."

"How come you didn't bring him to watch me sing? I don't mean I was great or anything, but to the dinner party? Jerry came and Mom invited Ryan, so it wasn't only family."

"Yeah, well um . . . he was busy and couldn't make it, but I'll introduce you pretty soon." She was nervous and I sensed she was covering up an important piece of information. "So what are you looking for? Sex? Dating? A long relationship?"

"I'm pretty sure I'd like to date. Not sure about sex, but then another side of me thinks . . . yeah, a lot of sex, but not a long relationship. I want to be free of everyone here when I go to college. Except for you. Anyway, I guess that's another reason I'm stalling. I'm afraid when I give in to him I'll want to go deep and that'll be it for me."

"I hear ya. I can't wait to graduate and then live on my own— with Sean, of course. But tell you what. Ryan sure is a cutie. If he's the sweet boy you say he is, I'd think carefully about him."

"I am, but . . ."

"You don't have to choose between a career and a relationship, Nick. If he's any kind of man he'll support you. By the way, how come you didn't go right to Stanford? I would've."

"Thirty grand just to take General Ed courses. That's a waste of money. Mom and Dad agreed they'd support me if I wanted to go for my masters."

"I guess. Selfishly, I'm glad you didn't because we can get to know each other again, but for your sake . . ."

"I know. I felt the mistake I made when I spoke with Walter today at Stanford. Seeing all those students gave me a rush."

"Walter?"

"I'll tell you about him later. He was Ryan's high school coach."

"Don't take the same conservative route with boys—or any relationship for that matter. You tend to overanalyze everything so . . . just grab one. Nothing against you, but a sweet, handsome, and smart professional baseball player says you're the one? And the sex! Holy shit, the sex! He'll keep you smiling all day and night from the things he's learned over the years. Fuck, maybe you'll come in your dreams! Wet dreams for Nicky!"

"Ha! Maybe so!" I considered how it might be lying next to him, having orgasms in my sleep.

"I just hope he's not just a stupid jock who tapped as much ass as he could just to brag about it. Still, it'd be worth it for the sex if you dump him later. Somehow I think . . ." she hesitated.

"What?" I grabbed her wrist.

"I have a feeling you might be swept away with him. He introduced himself to your family and you both have twinkles in your eyes," Jenise nodded to the mirror. As if I'd see them, I turned to look. "You don't give in easily and to have these feelings so soon . . . I think he might be the one for you."

"That's what I'm afraid of." I had to change the subject before I completely lost my breath. "Tell me about Sean."

We walked back to her bed and sat on the edge. I enjoyed as I watched *her* body become the one to swell up with happiness, her eyes open wide, and her hands waving in the air.

"I love him!" she exclaimed.

Her face softened and her voice sped up, becoming higher and louder. We talked for hours about their love, their sex and how tough it was for her to be apart from him.

"I have to hit the hay," I announced. "I'm getting up early to go to Yountville. Want to go with me?"

"Sorry, I've got a project to finish for my building design class. Ask me again though?" She winked.

"I will. Thanks for talking with me. I love you."

"I'm glad you finally knocked on my door." She reached for a book and her laptop. "Love you, too."

We kissed each other good night.

I tucked myself into bed knowing she was one of the greatest loves of my life.

Chapter 9

Be Careful When Texting

1:00 a.m.

I took out my journal to write down the conversation I'd just had with my sister.

My phone lit up with a text from Ryan: _Thinking of u. Sweet dreams my baby. I love you._

I responded: _Thinking of u 2. Ok 2 luv the 1 ur with._

Sarcasm—I couldn't believe he'd really commit to me, so I protected myself with it. My habit of pushing people away with a joke was how I kept my distance and prevented the hurt from touching me. It was the way our family handled serious emotions. Each of us polished our armor regularly, keeping our exterior strong. In making sure Ryan was at arm's length, I wouldn't get hurt when he abandoned me.

My phone rang shortly after I answered his text. He didn't wait for me to say hello. The flippant comment I'd sent to him came back to me very loud and very clear—as anger.

"Stop it," he ordered.

"What?"

"I'm not playing games with you."

"I'm not—"

"You've just called me a liar and a cheat without coming right out and saying it."

"No, I—"

"Yes, you most certainly did. Your insecurities don't give you the right to lash out and accuse me of being unfaithful."

"I didn't mean—"

"You didn't mean what?"

Silence.

"You texted exactly what you wanted me to feel—that I'm not taking my promise to you seriously and I couldn't possibly love you the way I've promised. You want to keep pushing me away?"

"No."

"You're waiting for news to come back to you that I'm with another woman?"

Silence.

I didn't know how to respond.

I wanted to be close to a boy. On the other hand, I knew at the exact moment I opened my heart to him, he'd say goodbye.

"I understand you're covering your feelings. When I get back, I'll listen to your doubts and their reasons, but not from a sarcastic text. I'm not *seeing* anyone. I'm not *sleeping* with anyone, and I'm not *partying* with anyone. I'm. Not. With. *Anyone*. I'm asking you to take me at face value. I wouldn't lie to you. Have I misrepresented anything so far?"

"No." *Not yet.*

"Why can't you trust me?" His voice was low and hard. "You told me you did when I kissed you in your bed the other night. You only say sweet things when I make you weak?"

"That's not it." My voice cracked. *I don't believe you really want anything but sex.* "I'm sarcastic—too sarcastic. I'm sorry. I don't believe it when you tell me you're not having sex."

"Why not?"

Isn't it obvious? No one I love keeps their promise.

"I don't understand how you can turn off that part of who you've always been. When I heard you and Kevin talking, you said you've had sex every day since college and now—nothing? It doesn't make sense. I haven't committed to you and we're not having sex so why would you—"

"You think I'm out of control?" he snarled. "Some Neanderthal with a caveman brain? After everything you found out today, that's what you think of me?"

"No." *I don't know, maybe.*

"When I say I'm serious about a relationship with you, I am. I understand you have problems with my past. It's my past. If you want to talk about it when I get back, I'll talk it through as long as you need to. But don't throw jabs at me—especially with a text—when I'm away and can't respond."

"I'm sorry." I pulled my knees up to my chest. "I don't know why I have such a hard time opening up to new people. I don't know how to handle this . . . or you."

"You don't have to *handle* me. I can handle myself. Listen, Nicky. I could have sex as easy as getting a cup of coffee. All I need to do is to walk into the lobby and pick a woman from the dozen or so that hang around. I'll wait for you. I will."

"I know they hang around, that's why—"

"I'm trying to say," he interrupted, "if you think I only want you because I have some kind of sex fantasy, I could've been with a woman your age dozens of times. Women aren't bashful. They walk right up to me and make damn sure I understand what they want."

Oh, yuck, I know. I don't want to hear any more of this.

"Please don't talk about it. I can't stand to hear how many are waiting for you and there's nothing I can do about it."

"Why not?" He knew exactly what he was doing by asking the question. If I didn't want him to be mine, I wouldn't care who he was seeing. "Didn't you just open this door?"

"Because, I'm not ready like they are . . . and you are. I know I can't go with you on a moment's notice. I have my parents and college . . . I'm outmatched in every way. I don't need to be reminded you're sacrificing a part of your life for me."

"I'm not sacrificing anything. I'm yours, Nicky, only yours. I won't cheat on you. Didn't Walter share enough to let you know I'm more than a sexed up jock?"

"He did."

"Didn't you see who I am from all of our visits to Yountville?"

"Yes."

"You're part of an elaborate joke—wasn't that *your* fear? You thought I was making up some scheme and using you, right? And yet, you just treated me the same way. Your text told me I'm only a joke of a man. Your words were very clear. You think so little of my character that you believe I'd string along an innocent woman and promise her love, also playing a game with her family. Don't you see the double standard? Do you really think I'd go out of my way to be so cruel?"

"No, I don't believe that. My response, well, it was a knee-jerk reaction. I didn't think my text through. I'm sorry, Ryan."

"Fine. I'll talk to you tomorrow. Good night."

After he hung up, I was disappointed in myself over what I'd done. He took my sarcasm as an attack on his character and that the good things I'd heard all day from other people meant nothing—and why wouldn't he? He had a right to be angry. I'd just told him I didn't trust him. Worse, he read into my message that I had no faith in us.

I detached through sarcasm.

It was my defense mechanism.

I joked away affection and serious emotions whenever possible.

I could reduce a compliment—or a sweet text from a boy who was only checking in with me—to a meaningless nothing.

When I turned off the light, my stomach was upset and twisting in knots.

An hour passed.

I lay awake.

My cell phone rang.

Ryan.

As I answered, the fear he might have had enough of my insecurities crashed around me.

"Ryan?"

"I'm sorry I was so angry." His voice had an edge.

"I understand." My emotions were writhing and tangled. I was careful not to make the situation worse. "What I texted was flippant. Instead of separating my own past from my present I handled it my usual way—fear of being left alone. And that's the one of the problems you're going to be dealing with. You sure you're up for it?" I laughed nervously.

"I should've waited until we were together so we could talk it through," he admitted. "You hurt me with your comments. I couldn't let it go."

"Please accept my apology." *Please, please, please.*

"I do." The covers rustled as if he'd scooted down in his bed. "Now, I can't sleep until we get this settled."

"I don't always understand how I come across. I'm so used to joking everything away . . . I'll try to be more aware of my responses. Will you help me?"

"As long as you help me, too. I'm partly to blame. I shouldn't have cut you off. I'm sorry I was abrupt. I'm new at this and I want you to trust me. When you didn't, I overreacted."

Come on, Nick. Hold back your tears. Don't let him think you'll be a tearful mess every time he has something difficult to discuss.

"My fears rise up unexpectedly," I confessed. "They rush on me so fast . . . before I know it, I'm not handling them well. You texted so sweetly and look what I did. I don't understand what you see in me. I mean it when I say I'm sorry. I don't know what else to say."

"We'll talk everything through face to face. Until then, let's agree we're both sorry and put this one to bed, all right?"

"All right."

"I'm glad I called back. Sweet dreams, honey."

"You know what, Ryan?"

"What's that?"

"When I put on my PJs I could still smell you from the other night. I hung your jacket in my closet, so your smell would filter through all of my stuff. You have such a masculine scent. I love it. It's like . . ." I giggled. "I'm an animal marketing my area."

"Oh, baby." A long sigh separated the words. "You're a tough woman to have as a girlfriend."

"I know I am," I answered timidly. "I sure miss you. Checking on all those contacts today made me feel like you were home—I mean in town. Now I miss you even more."

"I miss you, too Goodnight, sweetness."

"Good night, my Ryan."

I turned out the light and fell to sleep, smiling, comfortable and relaxed—even if it was only for *that* night.

Chapter 10

Surprises

𝖂henever I volunteered in Yountville, I left the city early to get a head start on the thousands of wine-tasting tourists. By 10:00 a.m. they'd usually overwhelm and jam the one road that went through town.

The staff at Veterans' Hospital was cleaning up from breakfast when I arrived. I quickly poked my head into Paul's office and let him know I'd brought the boxes of jerseys and I needed help to bring them in.

"Ryan's one of a kind, isn't he?" Paul Billings mused as he unloaded the cargo from the back of the car. Paul wore several hats including administration and director of social programming. Ryan introduced us the first time we volunteered together and I'd made a point to say hello whenever I visited. "I hear you're singing for the vets today."

"Oh, yeah? I didn't know *that*."

I'm not prepared at all. What do I sing?

I followed him into his office.

"Seems you've been set up," he said with a wink.

"When is all this supposed to happen?" I tucked my hair behind my ears.

"After lunch in the rec room. You have plenty of time to make your visits before the program starts." He offered a quick smile. "If you're hungry, Grayson can fix a plate for you. I'm sure there are leftovers."

"Thanks, I'm not hungry. Now that I know I'm singing, I'm kind of nauseous. I'm not the only one performing, am I?"

"We have two groups of musicians, several author readings, a couple of motivational speakers, and four singers. Ula's coming."

"She has such a beautiful voice."

"So do you," he remarked. "I'll never forget when you sang with her last year. Are you studying music in college?"

"I hadn't planned on it, although you're not the first to suggest I look into it."

"Hmm . . . maybe you should give it some serious consideration. Don't worry about today. This is all pretty low key." He shuffled some papers on his desk. A knot formed between his brows. "I want to give everyone a little pick-me-up."

"Something wrong?"

"Tough times with funding." He lifted an unopened envelope off the stack of mail. "These men and women wait for benefits way too long before their rehab benefits are approved."

"Ryan told me about their challenges. I'm sorry. They're very lucky to have you as their advocate."

"I do my best." The tone in his voice seemed heavy with doubt. "One person isn't enough, though."

"What am I supposed to sing, Paul?"

"The musicians we hired know most of the popular hits. Just pick a few titles, let them know, and go from there."

"I'm sure you'll get the funding you need." I patted his hand. "Guess I'll see if my favorite patient has a song request."

"Johnny Mantle, right?"

"Right," I nodded. "Paul, he's been in and out of the hospital so many times . . . is he going to be released soon?"

"Barring anything unexpected should be a few weeks." He made a blue checkmark next to one of the listed tasks on his white board, which hung on the wall behind him. "Do you want to take the jersey to him?"

Barring anything unexpected?

"What's his prognosis?" *I have to ask.*

"You know I can't discuss that." When he turned his back to me, I knew Johnny would have challenges the rest of his life.

He doesn't want to tell me it's not good.

"I'd love to take him his jersey." I rubbed my palms together. "Should I just—"

"I'll get it for you. I'm pretty sure I saw his mom's name on the guest log. She'd love to see you again."

"I hope so. Thanks, Paul."

On my way to Johnny's room, I texted Ryan: *You are sneaky.*

He texted back: *? Ms. Young ?*

I texted again: *You know!*

He returned: *Have fun.*

I found Johnny concentrating on a game of Pyramid. The cards were spread on a portable tray that was over his bed. I had tucked the jersey behind me. When he looked up, I quickly held it out for him.

"Look, Johnny! From Ryan!" My voice was loaded with enthusiasm.

"Mine?" He pushed the tray aside.

"Yours!" I placed it in his lap and enjoyed his sweet exploration of the shirt, almost petting it with his hands.

He unfastened each button carefully. When he put it on, a smile fanned his face that was so innocent and appreciative it made me melt into the floor.

"Love it. Thank you Nicky."

"You're welcome. It's from Ryan. I brought it here because he's on the road playing his baseball."

"Is Ryan doing good?"

"Yes!" I blushed and talked to Johnny about all Ryan's saves and how well the team was doing. "First place!"

"He's your boyfriend," Johnny teased.

"No he's not." *Not yet but we'll see.*

"Your cheeks." He patted his face. "Red."

Johnny's got a lot going on in there. I wonder if he'll get the chance to show people what he knows? Hopefully he won't be tucked away like my great aunt, Ethel.

"We'll see." I settled into one of the chairs near his bed.

"I love him," Johnny confessed. "Treats me nice."

Just as I thought I might lose myself, his mother, Samantha, walked into the room.

"Look, Mom!" her son grabbed the tails of the jersey.

Almost as endearing as Johnny's reaction was, the same held true of his mother's voice. She quickly escalated with excitement. I should have visited some of the others, but I couldn't leave the. The three of us talked until noon. As we got up to go to the lunchroom, I told them I was performing in the variety show.

"Is there a song you'd both like to hear?" I slipped my arm through Johnny's while his mother did the same on his other side.

"*Somewhere Over the Rainbow*, Hawaiian style," Johnny offered quickly.

"Oh, my favorite," Samantha cooed.

"It's settled, then." I sat with the two of them at one of the lunch tables.

"Your voice is pretty." Johnny stroked his jersey. "Wait 'til you hear, mama."

His mother looked away. I hoped she didn't start crying because I was sure I'd follow her lead.

"Thank you. I love singing. I'll bet . . . as soulful as you are, you must sing, don't you?"

"Some," he put his head down and smiled.

"It would be so much fun to do a song together sometime."

"Goof around." He shrugged his shoulders.

"I goof around, too." I poured a glass of iced tea from the pitcher on the lunch table. "Let's do one together next time I visit. Do you know any duets?"

"I need practice." His hands drummed a rhythm on the table.

"We can practice together. It's a date, okay?"

Samantha took my hand and squeezed it.

A year had passed since Johnny suffered his traumatic brain injury from serving in the military overseas. He'd been in and out of the hospital since then. Even so, his mother's tender sadness seemed ready to surface with every beat of her heart. Several times I saw her wipe her eyes. I wondered if her worry would ever stop.

"I'll check back with you later," I whispered to her. "I'm really not hungry and I need to see a few others before the entertainment begins."

She nodded her head. I got up to visit some of the newly admitted patients and then checked in with Paul to see where to wait for my turn to sing.

After lunch was finished and the room cleaned, we filtered into the rec room. I took a seat in the back with some of the others scheduled to perform. Ula touched my shoulder.

"Hi!" I stood and embraced her.

"Heard you're singing today." She strummed a chord on her guitar.

"I am. You, too?"

"Yep." Her smile was infectious. "Hey, I wanted to let you know the music program I told you about last year has been approved."

"Congratulations! How did you get the funding? Paul was just telling me . . ."

"The money comes in bits and pieces and my piece is a go! I'd love it if you could help me out sometimes and join in the fun."

"That would be great! Thank you for asking me." *Maybe I should do something with music at Stanford.*

"Would you mind if I taught Johnny a song and you guys can do something together on your next visit?" She nodded to someone who passed by and said hello. "I hear him singing in his room sometimes. He's got a good voice and the outlet might help. He was pretty excited and told me you talked about a duet?"

"I think he'd love that. Of course I would, too." I was already thinking of songs that might work for us.

"Perfect. Can't wait for your song today. You starting Stanford this fall?"

"Spring." My shoulders dropped.

"Expensive, huh?"

"Very. I wish there was some way, but it's ridiculous to spend thirty grand for Gen Ed classes."

"Don't worry about. You're gonna rock the world, Nicky Young."

"If I can be even a little like you? I'm good."

A man who wanted to speak with Ula interrupted us. She patted my back and winked as she turned away, focusing on the veteran who wanted her attention.

As I waited for the program to begin, I texted Ryan: *M singing S/where Over Rainbow 4 Johnny & his mama. I miss U.* ☹

He texted back: *O baby, take U in my arms, thinking of U, miss U, luv U, xxoo.*

I replied: *XXOO*

He texted again: *Talk 2 U L8R, game starting.*

A few hours passed. I was mesmerized listening to the poetry and book readings, speakers who offered inspiration, the music and the singers. When Paul walked on stage, I knew it was my turn.

"Some of you already heard her sing last year. Today she's performing for all of us. Nicky Young, everyone."

The butterflies in my stomach were flying all over the place. After a polite applause, I stood at the microphone.

The band waited for my cue.

I took several deep breaths.

I wondered if magic waited inside the walls of the Yountville Veterans' Hospital the way I thought magic was inside of Ryan.

I wished he were with me.

I turned to the band and nodded. The music began.

You can do this. Remember the national anthem, you were nervous at first, but you were okay as you went along. One more note and it's my cue.

I began.

Plagued with worry I'd forget the words.

It hadn't happened so far. The fear was there, however. One stanza in and my nerves began to settle. As I sung the last word and released a long sigh of relief, I opened my eyes.

"Yaaay, Nicky!" Johnny cheered.

Samantha whistled and clapped, laughing at her son's rapid applause. I wondered if it was one of her lightest moments in many months. Her son's brain injury made him like a young boy in many ways. In others, he seemed to observe and appreciate moments that I often took for granted in my life such as the joy of listening to someone sing.

Before I could walk off their stage, another veteran asked if I'd do her favorite song, then Ula wanted to sing a duet with me. In the end, I sang for over an hour.

As for Ryan's gift, the Goliaths' jerseys, the staff thought it was special enough to save for the end of the program. Many of the vets put them on immediately.

Originally, I'd planned to leave after my performance, but Paul had arranged a special dinner for the vets and performers alike. I knew it would be disrespectful if I didn't stay.

During the day I'd taken quite a few pictures and several were taken with me. As I sat at the table eating and listening to stories, I thought Ryan would enjoy seeing them and I forwarded a few to his phone.

Finally the long day was over and I drove home. I looked forward to a good night's sleep. While driving, my cell phone rang. I hoped it was Ryan. When I pulled over to answer I saw it was Alexandra Flowers. She was a model and the fiancé of Darrell Sweet, one of the Goliaths' pitchers. I'd also met her good friend Tara Summers last year, wife of Matt Summers who also pitched on the Goliaths. The three of us had gotten close.

"Hey, Alex. What's up?"

"Pack your bags, girlfriend." Her voice rang with excitement.

"Why? Where are we going?" *Oh no.*

"LA, baby. Just for two days. We leave in the morning for my photo shoot at Newport Beach."

Damn.

"Oh, I'm . . . I'm exhausted. I should stay home this time. I've been doing so much and . . . I'm sorry, but I really need the rest. Have a great photo shoot and don't forget me the next time."

"Bullshit! It's the *perfect* time for you. Besides, I've got a whopper of a surprise that you'll never forget. Now pack and be ready tomorrow—no excuses. You need to get the hell out of your house and keep me company. Ben wants me to be happy and relaxed and I told him, *that's Nicky's job.*"

"What time are you picking me up?"

I'm sure she did say that to Ben, her photographer. I might as well get ready. She won't take no for an answer.

"Nine," she insisted. "That'll give you the sleep you need."

"See you then."

I should have slept like a baby.

My head hit the pillow at nine-thirty.

I lay awake.

Sat up.

Pulled out my journal and wrote a few pages.

Put the journal away.

Texted Ryan: *Everyone loved your gift. Did you get my photos?*

Left three phone messages, asking that Ryan call or text me.

His baseball game is over. He's been done for hours.

I got no response to any of my messages.

Ryan's voicemail greeted me each time I called.

Face it . . . he's out with a woman or in bed with her and doesn't want to be disturbed. He tells me what I want to hear on the phone, but behind the scenes where I can't see him, it's a different story.

I had no right to expect him to wait for me or be faithful when I hadn't committed to him. Still, after his insistence he wasn't partying, it shocked me he was being so evasive.

My fears were out of control—I knew they were.

The worst scenarios played in my mind.

Vivid scenes of Ryan with another woman in his hotel room, their naked bodies enjoying each other, or him sitting in a bar flirting—perhaps with a woman or two on his lap as he touched her body—all of these came to life in my head.

I knew his reputation.

By the time I was through, I had convinced myself the paranoia residing inside me was really happening. I went more deeply into my dark corner, and began the fear-driven, negative self-talk from my youth.

I tried to stay away from it, but my anxiety constantly kept me within the temptation of engaging.

I knew I'd never be able to adjust to a relationship with Ryan.

He needed to come and go every week—that fact alone stroked my fear of being abandoned.

From the crunch in my gut when walking to Walter's office, listening to the jocks whistle and holler at me, I was certain he would be too much to handle. I could only think of how in ignoring my calls, he'd covered up what he was really doing—having sex and making future connections.

I'd just fallen asleep when Ryan finally called me.

"I got your pictures." His voice was light and exuberant. "Looks like you had fun."

"I tried to reach you so many times." My voice shook as I ignored his comments.

"Yeah, I'm sorry, sweetheart. I wanted to call you, but we had a team meeting in the clubhouse for hours, and then a mandatory dinner meeting . . . it went forever. God, it was torture. I tried to get away, but they wouldn't let any of us go—not even the married guys could call their wives."

Yeah, you call when it's convenient for you because you're accustomed to women dropping everything at your command.

"Not even a quick text hello? Come on, Ryan. You could have sent me a message. You had to go to the bathroom, didn't you? It's been hours."

"They made us turn our phones off."

"Yeah, okay. I'll call you tomorrow." *Whatever. I don't believe you.* "I'm going to LA with Alex, so I don't know when I'll be available. Anyway," I yawned. "I need to go. I feel like I haven't gotten any sleep all week."

"Are you okay?" Worry threaded his voice.

I hear beeps coming through his phone. Did he just turn it on? Maybe he called me first before checking his other messages? No, he saw my pictures, so . . . who are the people behind all those beeps?

"Just tired. I'm sure you've got a lot of messages to return, judging from sounds I hear in the background. Night, Ryan." I hung up, not in any mood to talk or listen to his stories. I didn't want to hear what he was doing, the voices or whispers in the background, or how happy he was in his career of baseball.

We occupied two different worlds—I understood that now.

Neither was compatible with the other.

Just that quickly I was beginning to give up on the idea of us.

You know that's why you couldn't reach him, Nick. Isn't it obvious? It's all lip service until he can get you in bed.

Something was changing and stirring inside me.

My restless spirit, the Evil Twin I'd given birth to a few days earlier, wouldn't let me relax.

Or maybe, it was that I wasn't going to take the consequences of remaining passive any longer.

Chapter 11

LA Style

My cell rang a few minutes after 6:00 a.m.

I had only gotten to sleep a few hours earlier.

I flipped and turned dozens of times, struggling with the disappointment of losing Ryan to a quick night of satisfaction with another woman.

"Alex?" I answered in a slow, groggy voice.

"We're taking an earlier flight. Be at your place in thirty! The taxi won't honk the horn since it's early, so hurry up!"

"Oh damn. Bye!" I threw off the covers, showered quickly, and pulled together a few basic things in a small overnight bag. I woke Jenise to tell her what I was doing and then raced downstairs to write a note for my parents. Just as I finished, the taxi pulled in the driveway.

I grabbed my backpack and carry-on, turned out the lights, and locked the door behind me. The driver opened the trunk and put my bag inside while I scooted next to Alex in the backseat.

"Morning." I wiped my eyes.

As usual, she looked gorgeous. Even when I slept over at her house it seemed she woke up that way.

Her reddish-brown hair hung as if it were a perfect wig— shining and bouncy. Cut in a bob, it was short at the back of her head, tapered so that it curved toward her face and neck and fell on the top of her shoulders.

Alex's big, brown eyes were striking. They seemed to have golden specks in them that were like little lights blinking when she looked at me. She often left both men and women open-mouthed when she passed them with her long and lean five feet, ten inch tall body and legs that went forever. That morning, I was certain her Stella McCartney ripped hem, skinny ankle jeans and white silk blouse, had been designed just for her.

"Hey there, girlfriend." She gave me a hug and a big smooch on the cheek. "Ooh, no sleep, huh?" My eyes showed the obvious. "We'll get coffee at the airport and add a few extra shots. I have some cold packs in my bag that will do wonders for your red eyes. What were you doing last night, you bad girl?"

"It's more like the entire last week." I rubbed my eyes. "Too much going on, Alex." As I said those words, I remembered my mother had asked me to slow down. I brushed her off because I thought she was meddling.

"Oh, babe. Are you spending any time with your friends or has it been all business?"

"Mostly with friends." *Please don't ask me to explain anything further.*

"I worry about you."

"I'm fine," I tried to reassure her.

"You don't get enough down time, Nick."

"Yes I do."

"Boy, you're a wealth of information this morning." She was obviously irritated with me.

Yeah, well, I don't want you to know about Ryan.

"I'm still asleep."

"When we get down there, we're going right to the shoot at Newport Beach. You'll need energy today, sweetheart."

"What's your photo shoot about this time?" Her svelte body and jaw dropping looks shot her right to the top. She was one of the most requested models for her age group and was often called for clothing photo shoots.

"Winter in LA. Now *that's* an oxymoron, right? Pretty lame, but . . ." she laughed.

"What are you modeling? You're going to melt!"

"Evening gowns on the beach. Makeup will definitely have their challenges," she laughed. "When we get to the site, let the staff handle you."

"Oh crap." I put my head back. "I know what that means. I hate that." I really didn't mind the makeup and primping. The real fear was they wouldn't find any clothes for me. I was much larger than the models and never could fit into the size 0-6 clothes in the boutiques my friends frequented.

"Please, girlfriend. I need you to look a certain way. You'll run a few errands and meet a few prominent people. A polished, professional look is essential. No jeans or T-shirts. Some of the people you meet could be contacts you'll want later in your career." Her voice rose higher as she teased and taunted me. It was as if she'd sung the last few words.

"Well, you know you just got my attention." I was already scheming, plotting, and visualizing possibilities.

"Knew I would!" Her eyes shone with a speculative gleam. "I know how to get you."

At the airport, we grabbed a couple of strong, black coffees before boarding our plane. After I downed the much-needed java, Alex placed her eye treatments on my lids. They were similar to tea bags and were cool to the touch. I kept them on until the pilot announced we were beginning our initial descent.

"Let's take those off so I can look at you." Alex carefully removed them from my eyelids. "Perfect! They did the trick!

We'll go to makeup and wardrobe right away. Penny will get you the day's agenda and we'll rendezvous tonight at the Fairmont for dinner. When you check in the hotel, go to the front desk. They'll give you a key to our room. I should be there but don't panic if I'm not. There may be an impromptu meeting or last minute schedule changes. After dinner, we'll get a little downtime."

"I'll hardly see you today?" I made a pouty face with my lips. *Well this isn't any fun at all.*

"Trust me, you'll be too busy to worry about it." She patted my back. "We'll see each other tonight."

After we stepped off the plane and we walked through the secured area, we saw a man holding a sign with "ALEXANDRA FLOWERS" written on it. He introduced himself as her driver and we followed him to a van waiting at curbside. Alex slid in first and immediately checked her messages.

I hesitated a few seconds before I checked my phone, wondering if I should text Ryan at all. I thought it could be the only time I'd get a private moment. I put my phone down. Should I text him? Why bother? He couldn't even take two minutes to send me a quick message yesterday.

Giving in, I sent the message: *In LA, talk to you later.*

He texted back: *Call me ASAP, xxxooo.*

Now *you text me back right away. What happened yesterday?*

My first instinct was to respond with sarcasm. I wanted so badly to write: *Sorry, Alex's modeling agency is making me turn off my cell phone and I won't be able to—even the married women couldn't get a message off to their spouse.*

I fought my internal struggle of learned tendencies and stayed rational, returning the message: *Will be late.*

Ryan texted back: *Want to talk to you! Miss you very much!*

I wrote: *Me too. Talk to you later.*

When we got to the site at Newport Beach, the staff quickly whisked away my girlfriend. A woman named Penny introduced herself and we headed into a tent where people scurried everywhere.

"Sit here." She pulled out one of the many chairs lined in a row and in front of a long mirror.

"What about my suitcase, Penny?"

"Already sent to your room. May I have your backpack?"

"I've got my wallet and journal in there. I'll need my I.D."

"We'll take good care of them." She handed me my wallet. "Empty it, please. Anything else?"

"My makeup."

"We'll put some new things in a purse matching your outfit. You'll be supplied with a new wallet and makeup," Penny comforted. "You can't buy it off the shelves . . . it's exclusively for the models." She leaned closer and whispered, "Covers their imperfections really well."

I laughed at her attempt to mock the beautiful man and women she was surrounded by every day.

"Laura," she straightened and raised her voice to get the attention of a subordinate. "Get this over to Alex and Nicky's room at the Fairmont right away." She handed my backpack to an eager young intern.

"I might want my journal. Sometimes I need to write down—"

"You won't have time," Penny interrupted. "I'll be back in a flash."

When my hair and makeup were completed, I followed an assistant to a changing room. Waiting for me were a caviar and porcelain-colored suit made by St. John, and a red and white iconic flap bag with thinly patterned stripes from Chanel. The sleeveless knit dress had a V-neck and a matching jacket with an open front and ribbon trim accent. A pair of Prada front-zipper, ankle-cut, black high-heeled boots finished the look.

I'll fall and break my neck or embarrass everyone as I stumble along in these but it would be rude not to wear them.

I hid my thoughts about the difficulties I knew I'd have wearing the ensemble. Its length was short for me, the fit snug, and my struggle with heels was legendary—I was a klutz.

When I walked out, I found Penny waiting for me.

"Have fun today. You're going to be a busy lady." She smiled and gave me a leather folio. "There's an agenda sheet attached to a 2" x 10" envelope which explains your day. Your driver is waiting right over there," she pointed.

I thanked her and peeked inside the folio, finding an electronic tablet, a matching pen and pencil set, a yellow writing pad, and an envelope with the sheet detailing my appointments Penny mentioned. My driver introduced himself as Peter Hopkins. We shook hands and he opened the passenger door to a Lexus SUV.

On the way to our first stop, I reviewed the day ahead. I was scheduled to tour several design houses in downtown Los Angeles and bring the items they'd give me back to the beach for the next day's photo shoot.

At each location, I met with designers and their assistants who were thrilled I wore or carried their products—planned on purpose, of course, by Alex's modeling agency, Sonar. The representatives gave me envelopes, bags, and boxes to bring back to Newport Beach along with full-sized samples of perfume, lipsticks, sunglasses, and scarves to take home.

Next, I delivered a sealed 8" x 10" envelope to Veronica, the daughter of the company's founding partners at St. John. While she gave me a tour, she revealed I'd just given her the details of a winter fashion show and charity event sponsored by Sonar and St. John. After complimenting my business suit—one of her designs—she excused herself. Her assistant took over and made sure I had the packages needed for the photo shoot at Newport Beach. She also loaded me with freebies. I chose items that I was sure Jenise liked—a purse, shoes, and some cosmetic jewelry.

Last on my list was a meeting with the Lieutenant Governor at a beachfront café called 3 Thirty 3. According to my itinerary, he was to be the grand master of the winter charity event. The interview with Mr. Xavier Del Sol would be a published piece, promoting the gala. Its focus was to put a spotlight on the thousands of men and women returning from their military tours with Traumatic Brain Injury.

Mr. Del Sol was a handsome Mexican man of average height, in his late forties, with salt and pepper hair. After shaking hands and making small talk, I learned that one of his goals was to bring awareness to the "hidden illness" of brain assault, also known as "TBI." His voice was steady and calm, his demeanor pleasant and polite. I could understand why he had entered politics . . . he had a natural way that made a person feel confident he was in charge.

I typed furiously on the electronic tablet given to me as Mr. Del Sol answered the questions preprinted for me on sheet. He spoke about the unknowns of how those burdened by TBI are in constant recovery. I was fascinated hearing him explain how their brains often struggle from seizures and cognitive challenges, trying to form whole, succinct thoughts—sometimes for the rest of their lives. I couldn't help but note that while informative, the questions as written, weren't enough. I didn't want to make any ripples by posing a few of my own and made sure he answered everything written.

After the last question he seemed ready to excuse himself.

No longer able to resist the temptation, I posed several questions of my own.

"Please comment on the poor outlook and recovery of brain trauma victims. Why isn't there an equal amount of medical attention focused toward rehabilitation after they leave the hospital? Acute and sub acute care doesn't scratch the surface, does it?" I shouldn't have dared to ask I but after volunteering at Yountville, I couldn't resist. "There are plenty of medical measurements for survival but not enough that address the victims' lives after 24/7 care. Why? As Lieutenant Governor, what can you do to help?"

His eyes widened in surprise. He took on the challenge and answered my question with ease. I asked another. Posed a third. I had to. For Johnny's sake and the others at the Veterans' Hospital Yountville, I owed it to them—especially since people who had money would be at the gala.

When we finished, I thanked him for the extra time. He shook my hand, paid for our iced teas and excused himself. He climbed into the back of his limo and was chauffeured away.

Debating whether or not I should send in the complete interview or only the answers he gave to the prepared questions I sat at the table debating with myself.

Drummed my fingers on the table as I reviewed and edited what I'd typed.

In the end, I entered the email address listed on my agenda and uploaded the entire interview to Sonar Modeling Agency. I hoped I hadn't embarrassed Alex or blown the opportunity given to me.

"You've had quite a day." He opened the car door.

"Oh, Peter, I met so many people!" I showed him the stack of business cards I'd collected. "I'm studying business marketing at Stanford and this could be important for an internship and maybe even class credits." I told him all the details of my college program, delighted to explain my future to someone who'd never heard my story.

"Good for you, Ms. Young. They're still wrapping up at the beach," he said. "I'll deliver the larger items to the Sonar reps so you can check into your hotel."

"Um . . ." I didn't want anyone to see me as lazy or handing off a responsibility that was mine. I'd never handed over a task without seeing it through to the end. I wanted absolute control over my own fate from step A through Z.

"It's all right." He seemed to notice the doubt on my face. "Alex said you could go up to the room. You can call her if you need to verify what I'm doing."

"That's all right. Thank you for driving me around today." He tipped his cap. After shaking hands and saying goodbye, I walked through the lobby of the hotel and checked in. I had no trouble getting the key to our room and when I entered, all I wanted was to sleep. My luggage and backpack was on one of the beds. I threw my bags of designer freebies alongside them and kicked off my shoes. I was about to lie down when Alex came out of the bathroom.

"Oh, babe, you look like you're ready to take on the business world right now. I, for one, would hire you on the spot."

"Hopefully you'll have some sway when I graduate," I giggled, but in actuality I knew she had the connections to help me.

"What a great suit. Penny's awesome, isn't she? Did you have fun meeting everyone today?"

"Oh, yeah," I clasped my hands together. "I met fashion designers and their assistants; collected their business cards, and had tea with the lieutenant governor. Can you imagine? And I met the daughter of the founders at St. John. She runs the company now, and here I am wearing one of their suits—*this* suit! And she commented on it! Damn, what a day! Thanks for insisting I go with you."

"Aren't you glad we dressed you up?"

"Pffft," I waved my hand in the air. "How embarrassing if I'd shown up in jeans."

"See what happens when you let go?"

"Which is just about impossible for me, lady." I took off my jacket.

"And yet, you did it. You work so hard, Nick. I loved seeing you reap some rewards for all that effort. You sowed a few possibilities today."

"I hope so."

"I'm telling you that you did." She stepped closer and held my shoulders. "And with more than a few of the people you met, including Mr. Del Sol. He'll be joining us for dinner, by the way. I understand you asked a few questions that weren't on the interview sheet."

"I didn't think he'd notice." I blushed, but knew a man who'd risen in politics the way he did would catch it. I was glad he did. "Wow, news sure gets back to you fast. Wait—I thought it was going to be just us at dinner."

"You'll fit right in. Xavier wasn't the only one who was impressed; my boss was, too."

"Xavier?" I teased.

"Yeah, well . . ." she blushed. "I've made a lot of contacts over the years, you know."

"Oh, I'm sure you have." I bumped her shoulder with mine. "At all of twenty-two no less. How can I go to dinner? I didn't bring dress clothes. They've already seen this suit, and . . . oh, by the way, the driver, Peter Hopkins, said he was taking the boxes I got from the designers back to the photo shoot. He said it was still going on, but you're here . . . did I do the right thing—"

"Slow down, Nick. Yes, it was okay he took the boxes. And all those freebies you got today are yours to take home."

"The tablet, purse, *and* the suit? All of it?"

"Just shut up about it. They're yours."

"Thank you. Please tell your agency thank you, too."

"Tell them yourself at dinner tonight. Come with me, my dear. I have something for you to wear."

I followed her to the closet.

"Please no more heels. My feet are so sore."

"Don't worry." She took down a black, short-sleeved Valentino sheath dress. It was cut just above the knee and matched with a comfortable looking pair of Manolo flat-heeled shoes. "Do I know my Nicky girl, or what?"

"Oh, it's stunning." I ran my hands over the dress. "I hope it fits. My butt, it's . . ."

"Luscious." She tilted her head.

I stood with my mouth open.

"Yes, girlfriend. Completely luscious," she repeated.

"That's not how I think of it." I about choked.

"Maybe not, but just about every man does. Speaking of your splendid ass, did I see you send a text to Ryan Tilton earlier?"

I fiddled with a pair of sunglasses given to me by the Ralph Lauren representative.

"No answer needed." Obviously my nervousness confirmed what she had suspected. "I want to talk with you about him when we get back from dinner. For now, let's get ready. I'm starving."

Chapter 12

Discussions

𝕿he hotel restaurant, bambú, was set in the middle of a four-story atrium amid lush gardens and filled with palms and orchids.

Alex and I were escorted to a private room. It had a large table with seating for twenty-four people. I was grateful she was sensitive to my awkwardness, insisting we arrive together and taking a seat next to me. Hungry and thirsty, I immediately drank several glasses of water. Our appetizers of baked fig with pistachios and goat cheese were served quickly and followed by grilled salmon, a salad of baby greens, and a cheese plate.

The lieutenant governor made a toast congratulating everyone on a well planned winter fashion show and promising charity event.

"So, I had the pleasure of meeting Nicky Young today," he announced after settling in his seat.

The eyes around the table looked at me briefly.

Alex smacked my thigh.

"Ms. Young was supposed to interview me with questions I'd already reviewed with Sonar to promote the winter gala. Imagine my surprise when she asked me several that weren't on the list." He gave me a nod. "Her passion for the TBI issue brought to light several of the most important questions of all. It turns out she volunteers at the Veterans' Hospital in Yountville.

She's especially fond of one of their patients, Johnny Mantle," he continued. "Like so many, the young man is recovering from a TBI and has been in and out of the hospital several times. What you don't know, Ms. Young, because of our interview and talk today, I've gotten in touch with Mrs. Mantle. She and her son will be our guests of honor at the fundraiser."

Immediately I covered my face with my white cloth napkin to hide my tears. The news tugged on every part of my wounded and sentimental heart. The way Johnny's head was slanted because of the portion of skull removed, his mother's pain, the story Ryan had revealed about Sam and Ermina's son . . . they all rushed into my thoughts.

"I think you can see how you touched my girlfriend," Alex put her arms around me.

"Thank you, sir." I tried to dry my tears. "When you meet them," I sniffed, "you'll see for yourself how precious they are."

"We get it." Veronica, the designer I'd met at St. John focused her eyes on me. "I have a daughter who was in a car accident and the result is a severe TBI. We understand what few people do— the ongoing therapy needed once she left the hospital. We're blessed to have the means to give it to her. It's a long struggle."

The conversation about TBI lasted through dessert and as we wrapped up, the lieutenant governor pushed back from the table.

"Ms. Young, I think it's safe to say you'll be an asset to anyone's business," he squared his shoulders and faced me directly. "I'm extending a standing invitation. Please look me up when you graduate from . . . Stanford, I'm told?"

"Yes, but how . . .?"

He gestured to Alex.

"My alma mater." He showed his class ring, which he wore on his right hand. "I could pull a few strings for you."

"Thank you. I'm humbled by your offer." I didn't dismiss his statement lightly and honored it with a simple acknowledgment.

Someone suggested cocktails in the bar, and with that, Alex and I shook hands with everyone, left the restaurant, and went to our room. It was almost eleven.

"How come you didn't go with them?"

"Baby, I like to party, but I'm modeling and can't afford droopy eyes or having to drag my ass around."

"What time do we have to get going in the morning?" I yawned.

"Bright and early at six." She unzipped her dress.

"Oh dear Lord. I don't know how you do it." I stepped close and threw my arms around her. "Thanks for today. I love you."

"Pull a few strings for you—did you hear what Mr. Del Sol said?" She kicked off her shoes.

"*Yes,* I heard!" I kicked off my shoes, too. "I was stunned. I didn't know what to say."

"You're something else, doll." She stepped out of her dress and hung it in the closet. "I told you. You suck us in! Now . . ." She gave me a penetrating look. "What's up with Tilton?"

"He's not the man you and Tara warned me off of," I put my hand up like a stop sign. "I've gotten to know him on a deep level. Actually, he and I are good friends now."

Of course, I won't reveal anything about our kisses or the night we spent together.

"I'll take you at your word." She looked at me suspiciously. "But hear me when I say this: *don't* get serious with him. I don't care that he's older than you—shit, I dated a man who was thirty-six when I was eighteen so I'm no one to talk. It's exciting dating older men. They can show you . . ." She became lost in her thoughts for a moment. I was certain that something juicy passed over her face.

"God, Alex. Is his name Xavier?"

"What I'm saying," she shot me a hard look, "is you have no experience at all and don't know anything about that side of yourself. I'd been having sex from the time I was fifteen. I knew things when I was your age. You need to be with your peers. Those boys won't mind going slow because they don't know anything. You can control them the way you like."

"I'll think about it." My cheeks flushed at her intimate knowledge about me. I hadn't realized I'd been so revealing to her. "Ryan's just a friend, you know."

"Not by the look on your face."

"Oh, damn," I panicked. "Am I *that* transparent?"

"We're always an open book when we're in love, honey. No hiding it, I'm afraid. I'll just say this: whatever kind of man he is, you have Stanford coming. He attended college and it's not right he's asking you to consider an exclusive relationship with him— if he is. I hope he isn't. Well, is he?"

"No." I covered my mouth to stifle a laugh. The way she was stumbling amused me.

Lying to a friend? How healthy is a relationship with Ryan?

"If you're thinking of playing with him, well . . . I can't blame you. He's a handsome devil. Just . . . don't get involved."

"I hear you," I tried to reassure her.

"Let's get some sleep. We have a big day tomorrow."

"Don't tell Tara."

"I won't." She threw down the bed covers. "I'm betting she already knows."

"Oh, shitola."

She laughed and we got ready for bed.

Alex was already gone when I awoke the next morning. It was 10:00 a.m. and panic raced through me—I thought I'd blown it. I pushed up from the bed in a panic and I found a note she'd left on the desk for me. She'd written that I could relax as long as I wanted. She also left the number for Peter Hopkins, the driver, who I could call when I was ready to come to the photo shoot. She'd be working until six that evening.

After checking in with Mom and Jenise, I took a nice long bath. When I felt ready, I put on jeans and a T-shirt, called Peter, and went to the photo shoot.

"There's the girlfriend I know," Alex yelled.

Ben said hello and immediately gave me a list of things to do. I ran back and forth on the set, getting this or that item of clothing or accessory. The second day flew by.

We got back to the hotel at seven. Thankfully, there were no meetings of formal dinners and we had a quiet night in our room. It felt good to relax, snuggling and talking, lounging in our pajamas, and enjoying the thick comforter and crisp cotton sheets on the bed. The next morning we flew back to San Francisco.

Alex had the taxi driver drop me home first. I waved goodbye as she pulled away, already missing her. The pangs of loneliness knocked from within.

As soon as I walked through my door, the push and pull of having Ryan in my life came to the forefront of my mind. Before I left, I couldn't wait to taste the deliciousness of a relationship with him I'd imagined. Now, although I still had those feelings, I was conflicted.

I'd gotten a taste of the business world. Did I want to put my focus on anything or anyone else?

I laid out the two beautiful designer outfits, their accessories, and all the freebies I'd gotten on my trip. Going to LA with my girlfriend, sorting through the business cards given to me, and running my hand over the laminated agenda sheet, now a memento, I heard different whispers.

I didn't want to commit to anyone this soon.

Maybe I'll move to LA with Colleen and go to UCLA.

Part of me felt relief.

And the other part of me was sad about what I'd have to do: I needed to let Ryan go.

While hanging my two new outfits in my closet and unpacking the rest of my things, Alex's words echoed in my head: *Whatever kind of man he is, you have Stanford coming.*

Still, there was something soft and gentle about the man who'd caught my heart. With every day that went by, I was more ashamed and embarrassed I hadn't made a real effort to call him.

He stopped texting me several days after I'd returned from LA. I was sure our brief but wonderful encounter was over. More to the point, I was sure *no one*, let alone a woman whose attention he wanted, had ever left him hanging or waiting for a phone call.

I knew he wouldn't take it well.

Even *I* wasn't taking it well.

I felt like a witch stirring her potion—churning, boiling, and forming something new.

I had no idea of the turmoil that was brewing deep in my heart.

Chapter 13

A Strange Gallery

$\mathcal{J}$erry had come home from his summer league baseball games a day after I returned from Los Angeles.

We hung out a few times during the week. Took in a movie and I went to his baseball games and cheered for him. The night before he was leaving for another week of competitive summer league play he invited me to dinner and a walk through The San Francisco Museum of Modern Art.

The museum is a part of the sprawling area south of Market Street known as SOMA. The surrounding galleries, restaurants, shops, clubs, and hotels were known for having a bohemian undercurrent.

I loved it. We walked among the neighborhood's successful residents, business owners and visits. The evening with Jerry validated my restless feelings—I was a college bound woman on the verge of independence.

Jerry asked me to dress up for our date. Besides much new but much too fancy LA clothes I had only one dress. It was as far away from a designer outfit as it could be. I'd purchased it off the rack of a discount department store. It was black and loose fitting with a tiny white and yellow flower pattern, fell to my ankles, and had a high U-shaped neck.

My long, brunette hair was pulled back with a decorative headband. My curls and waves hung down below my waist. I put on a pair of flat shoes and grabbed a heavy, white sweater just as I heard the doorbell ring.

Mom answered before I could get downstairs and invited Jerry inside. I hung back and eavesdropped on their conversation from the top of the stairs.

On that night, he looked older than eighteen. His black leather jacket emphasized his broad shoulders. The white collared shirt and dark blue jeans showed off a beautiful male body. He was developing into a gorgeous man.

The expression on Mom's face was relaxed and confident. The question of whether I'd be *safe* didn't seem to cross her mind like it had with Ryan.

"Hey you." I walked up behind Jerry, slipped my arm in his, and kissed his cheek.

"Your daughter is such a flirt."

"I know she is," Mom agreed.

"No I'm not."

"Yeah, you are." He kissed my cheek. Turned to Mom. "We'll be out late, Mrs. Young. Don't worry."

"I won't. Have a good time." She waved goodnight and closed the door.

"What was *that*?" I asked as we walked to his car.

"About you being a flirt? You *are*."

I've never thought about it that way. Am I?

"So, where are we eating, Jerry Stowe?"

"MoMo's. I'm in the mood for some appetizers and they always rock 'em." He licked his lips. "Then we can go to the museum. Sound good?"

"Fine with me. Let's try and peek in Club 111 Minna on our walk. I've always wanted to see what it looks like." My eyes widened. "Alex and Darrell go there sometimes. I know it's racy. I'm so curious."

"Me, too. I've seen some mighty hot women go in and out of there," he joked. "I'm happy to give it a try."

"Oh?" I narrowed my eyes. "You don't think the same can be said for the hot men? God, I love their scruffy look."

"Yeah, yeah. You don't always have to even the score. You look nice, by the way. I like you in a dress. You look, uh, soft."

I guess soft *is a compliment? It's the second time he's said that. How do I take it? Does he mean less aggressive, more feminine, less threatening?*

"What do you mean by *soft*?"

"I'll show you later." His voice dipped in a slow, sexy tone.

After waiting thirty minutes at MoMo's, we were seated. Music blasted. Voices were loud in the always-crowded restaurant. It was fun being with him, garnering extra attention from the servers since they assumed we were a couple.

Next, we toured the museum. It stayed open late on Friday and Saturday nights, catering to the patronage from society types, tourists, and clubbers—in other words, people with money.

Jerry had an affinity for art—modern art in particular. He was unique that way. Normally I liked predictability. I laid out plans and gathered friends I felt I could control. In his case, the differences I'd come to know, especially from those of his jock friends, drew my curiosity.

We did our best to persuade the bouncer at Club 111 Minna to let us peek inside. After teasing us mercilessly he refused. He suggested we look up the club online instead. After our failed attempt there, we walked through the bookstores, coffee shops, and nearby galleries. Lovely, shining objects were illuminated in the bay windows.

One gallery in particular seemed to sparkle brighter than the others. The name of it was Bellissima.

Bellissima . . . Bellissima . . . This gallery is beautiful.

Several bronze sculptures of naked men and women were on display. The strategically placed lighting made their patina finish glisten as if rainbows were all over them. Beckoning from inside, but partially hidden from passersby, were paintings of nudes. They were carefully positioned to leave the rest to our imaginations.

I felt enchanted as we walked in.

The artist who was on display was a master at transferring intimate facial expressions to canvas. The delicate curves of both men and women's bodies were breathtaking.

Jerry followed behind me until he noticed nudes of women on the other side of the gallery. I stayed focused on the males.

One painting in particular drew me in.

A delicious man faced away and to the side, his broad shoulders and muscular back in full view. A shaving towel hugged his thick neck. His big, luscious arms were expertly painted. Even the details of the veins in his athletic forearms were visible. I thought the artist perfectly captured the man's amused and seductive look. Perhaps the scene was of surprise as the subject realized his lover was near. His head, turned slightly, revealed the hint of a smile. One eye looked out from under his eyelashes in what seemed to be unspoken desire.

"Never too early to start developing your taste in art, young lady." A woman came up from behind me.

I'd been so engrossed in the painting that I jumped a little.

It was as if she had swept across the room and her feet never touched the ground.

I wondered if she'd come from some invisible place.

Where did she come from? She came on me like a ghost!

"Cassandra." She extended her hand.

"Nicky," I shook her hand. Jerry walked over and stood at my side. "And, this is my friend."

"Charmed." She held her hand out for him to kiss.

"Jerry," he introduced and gave her hand the kiss she desired.

She had long, blond hair that was pulled back, braided, and wound around her head in circles, ending in a point. Her skin was fair. Her frame was very thin and petite. Even so, her six-inch heels caused her tower over me. Her professionally styled hair, designer clothes, and ultra-polished appearance spoke of money—and a lot of it.

"This is one of my favorites," she said, gesturing to the painting that had me hypnotized. "I'm so curious. What draws you to this piece?"

"His look."

"Explain." She rested a thin index finger on her lush, red lips.

"The anticipation in his expression. His eyes. His smile." I paused. "It makes me want to put my hand under his chin and make him turn to me. He's a kiss waiting to happen."

"Brilliant," she laughed seductively.

"Are you the artist?"

"I am."

"It's incredible. Do you mind me asking, I don't mean by name, but in general, who was your inspiration?"

"Someone I used to know," she sighed dramatically.

"His expression is really . . ." I paused to gather the right words. "It looks as if he just noticed that you were behind him and he can't hide his desire. It's obvious he's dying to make love to you."

"God, Nicky." Jerry turned to Cassandra. Was he intentionally trying to gain the favor of the attractive woman standing before us? "She's so dramatic." He flashed her a flirtatious smile.

How rude! Wait until we get out of here, Mr. Stowe.

"She's actually right about that, young man." As she chastised him, she seemed to exalt herself. "You're very perceptive, Nicky. Do you do anything creative?"

"I've been told I have a gift for writing. I see the deeper layers of people," I confessed. "I write down all my observations. One day I hope to turn my journals into books."

"Very ambitious." She touched my arm lightly. "Do you live here? In the city, I mean?"

"Yes, all my life." I looked up at the painting again.

He's so handsome. God, I'd love to caress that cheek. What a lucky woman she is. Those arms . . . look at those veins in his neck . . . ooh.

"Let me give you my card, Nicky. After all, today's youth are tomorrow's wealth. Be right back. What's your last name?"

"Young. Nicky Young."

Her head jerked as if she'd been hit with a line drive. Her eyes seemed to lose their focus. "I . . . I'll . . ." She stumbled over her words. "Be back."

Jerry and I looked at each other.

In an awkward silence, we watched her walk away.

A dangerous and icy-cold tension seemed to make the air around us too heavy to breathe.

"What was *that*?" Jerry whispered.

"I don't know. Now I'm uncomfortable," I put my hand to my mouth to shield my words from her. "I think we should go."

As we remained, undecided on what to do, a tall, muscular Latino man came in the gallery. Cassandra noticed him immediately. They quickly kissed once on each cheek, as if they were high society. For all we knew, maybe they were. The way she laughed so dramatically, I was certain the kiss was more than a casual hello. This wasn't just a friendly meeting.

"Let's make our escape." Jerry tugged on my elbow and then reached for my hand. "Thank you!" Jerry yelled to her.

We were almost through the door when I turned back to wave.

Cassandra's cold stare seemed overtaken by a desolate darkness.

I looked away and quickly walked out the gallery's door.

"Weird," Jerry shook his head. "Something off about her."

I tried to put the strange experience behind us.

A shiver crept through me.

The chill shook my body.

Stayed with me for days.

Chapter 14

Jerry Gets an Education

$\mathcal{A}$ drive to the Marin Headlands topped off our evening.

Jerry parked at one of the viewpoints overlooking one of the many dramatic vistas of our City by the Bay. He grabbed his jacket and a blanket and I put on my sweater. We fanned the blanket on the ground and sat down to enjoy the 180-degree view spread out before us.

It was a clear night.

The Golden Gate Bridge was awash in orange light.

The San Francisco skyline twinkled against the bay.

The homes dotting the distant hills blinked. One by one their glow dimmed and then darkened.

"It's so beautiful and quiet out here." I folded my arms. "I love the ocean."

"I do, too." He put his arm around my shoulders.

We sat completely still, trying our best not to disturb the nature around us. Bushes rustled. Some little animal scurried along a gravel path in the distance. The buoy's bell rang as another ocean swell pushed through.

The cold breeze made the dry blades of grass sound like motors as they rapped against the bottom of our shoes. It was as if we were lying in a wheat field. The green hills had turned golden months ago and the straw radiated a magical glow as it cradled us.

I enjoyed being held within Jerry's masculine body. His arms had found their way around me. When he kissed my cheek my mind wandered into daydreams.

Who is Cassandra?

Where have I seen her?

Why did her eyes seem to so cold when I said my last name?

Was it weird or did I imagine it?

Does she know me?

I wonder what Ryan is doing.

When Jerry stroked my arm, I felt the electric connection of his body. I became restless. Couldn't sit still. Finally got up to move behind him.

"What are you doing?" His shoulders shook when my hands massaged him as if chills had rushed over his skin.

"Giving you a nice massage." I flattened my hands to knead the muscles under his skin. "I've wanted to do this as soon as I saw you talking to my mother. God you look good tonight."

He turned to face me.

"Damn, woman! What's gotten into you?"

"Turn around," I commanded. My hands dug into his shoulder muscles and his back.

"Oh, that feels so good. I get sore from playing so much baseball; especially in my upper body."

Yeah, feels good for me, too!

"Mm-hmm." I cooed in my most seductive voice.

He breathed deeper. His upper back rose in obvious and dramatic ascents. I continued pressing my thumbs and palms into his body, my elbows working in circles.

"Can we lie down together?" He grabbed hold of my hands to stop my massage. Led me to the front of his body. "Can we . . ."

We embraced. While holding me in his arms, he lowered me onto the blanket. His body squirmed, slowly edging to a position of making love. He seemed to lengthen. His feet parted my legs.

Urgent kisses and shallow, raspy breaths sang in the night. Before I could put a hand up or express hesitation, he was fully on top of me. A hand slipped underneath my head, the other nestled against my cheek.

"I want you tonight." The look in his eyes seemed to be one of pure lust. His hips pressed into me. I felt his erection.

"I don't want to get serious, Jerry." I marked my invisible boundaries and stood my ground.

"Please don't . . ." he swallowed. "Don't put up stops signs. Not with me. You're with a boy you've known all your life."

"Sorry." *Why do I do that?* "I'll try. I was doing . . . I'll try."

Okay, here we go, you can do this. Get comfortable, take a breath and loosen up.

He kissed my neck and opened my lips with his tongue. I opened my mouth to receive his seduction. My body arched. Easy kisses turned hard as he pressed into my jaw. He seemed to cover me in every way.

I enjoyed the feeling of his stomach and hips the way they tensed and moved side to side. He'd positioned us for intimacy.

Starting to lose the sense of where I ended and he began, even the ground underneath me seemed to soften.

Had the cold breezes stopped?

I was not only warm, I bordered on being too hot.

Shielding Jerry's hands from touching my skin, my dress was a fragile barrier as he squeezed and seemed to measure my breasts, perhaps gauging them for the fit into his mouth. His fingertips shook. His exploration was in full motion.

The hem of my dress, now in the grasp of his hands, slipped above my panties. When I heard his zipper open, every one of his intentions was plain and clear. He braced his body on one elbow. His hands moved toward my waistband.

I only wanted his deep kisses.

Needed to stop him.

I went into reverse immediately.

"Jerry, don't. I'm not ready for you inside of me—don't."

He raised his head. His eyes were hooded. By the distant look in them, I wasn't sure if he'd heard me.

"Please don't," I begged softly.

"You're ready," he continued to lift my dress. "I can feel the way your body moves under me. Let go."

"Jerry . . . I'm not . . ."

"Baby . . ." One finger stroked my panties where they covered my vulva, and then moved again to the elastic waistband. With one pull, my feminine body would reveal the soft opening unique to a woman. "You're wet."

"Stop." I grabbed frantically for his hands, trying to pull them away from my legs. "I'm asking—"

"Come on."

"No," I insisted.

His hands fell away. I felt his body soften.

"I thought . . . isn't the perfect place?" He took deep breaths as if trying to calm himself. "It's just us and . . . are you sure?"

"For a minute I thought I was. I'm . . . sorry. Shit. I didn't mean to lead you on, I thought . . ." I sighed. Completely disgusted with myself. "I don't know what's wrong with me."

"What are you worried about?" He hovered over me, as if he hoped I might still give in to him.

"We need to get tested and neither of us knows what we're doing. A million things are spinning in my mind."

My hips were in his hands. His quivering fingertips danced slowly on my legs. It was as if he was pretending I'd given my okay. He wouldn't let go.

"But you . . . you know me," he insisted. "I'm clean. You're clean. Come on." He leaned in to kiss me again and his hands tried to pull my legs open.

"No." I pushed against his chest. "I need to see your test results."

He stared down at me.

Minutes seemed to pass.

"Jerry, snap out of it." I tried to bring him out of his dreamlike state. I grabbed for my dress to pull it down. "Get up."

He closed his eyes.

His mouth was open.

His hips were still moving as if he were inside me.

"I said get up." I wriggled to get out from under his heavy body. "I'm sorry. This isn't going to happen."

"Wait," he swallowed hard. Almost gulped the words. His hands let go of my clothes. He rolled to the side. "Give me a second."

I sat up quickly. Straightened my clothes. Buttoned my sweater—all the way up to my neck.

This is my fault. I've crushed another person. What am I doing? I have no business dating. It's obvious if there's no sex I can't see anyone. They're all ready for it and I'm not.

I waited quietly, hoping he was done and we could go home.

Once more, he took several deep breaths.

"Okay, I'm ready. I have to pack for my next round of baseball games anyway." He stood up. Was the excuse he offered to help soothe my feelings . . . or was it for his ego?

"How long you away this time?"

"They start again tomorrow and go through the week. Can I ask . . . if we were tested, would we still be lying on the blanket?"

"Do you have protection?" I challenged.

"Yes."

Do you automatically bring it with you these days?

"I'm not sure," I confessed.

"Why? What can I do to change your mind?"

He turned away from me to zip his pants.

"I want it to be good for us." I shook the blanket a few times, trying to get out the remaining burrs that stuck from the dry grass.

"Why wouldn't it be?" He walked to his car bowlegged.

My body tried to relax. I wasn't sure if I wanted intimacy this way with Jerry—or with any man this soon. The way he was ready, so forceful, so aggressive, I knew nothing would have mattered except his relief. His only concern was pulling it out of his pants. That wasn't foreplay. On the other hand, he *had* stopped. He listened. He asked me questions after-the-fact, which . . . I supposed was better than not talking at all.

The more I watched him walk, the more I held back an urge to laugh. It wasn't funny. It was how I reacted when I was nervous. I wondered if "it" was in the way of zipping up his pants.

"It would be great for you, no doubt, but what would you do to pleasure me?" I was as bold as I could be. "In fact, you seemed more than ready to complete the act without stimulating me at all. What was your plan back there?"

"To move inside your vagina and slide through your wet—"

"Jerry," I caught his attention before he went too deeply into another vision. "It's not about the vagina for women." I confidently repeated part of my sister's education about sex and pleasure. "Not like you just described."

We drove home in silence.

I could feel him thinking about my answer.

When we got to my house, he turned off his car.

"Tell me how it is for you, then." He came back with his own brave response.

"It's about being slow, stimulating my clitoris, kissing me, slowly stroking me—"

"You've done it before," he said disgustedly.

"No," I put my hand on his forearm. "I'm telling you what my sister told me. It's also the way I bring myself there. I have to create the mood in my head. I do it by reading a sexy story or I watch something . . . I'm um, also in the middle of everything." I was totally embarrassed to admit I wasn't safe for sex without protection. "You know what I mean?"

"You're fertile." His eyes darkened, and the response from my feminine body sent a quivering pulse between my legs. *Well that definitely helped to get me ready.*

"Jerry, I want to know, I mean, when it comes to sex, you seemed to know um, something, like . . . you had condoms, so have you, well, do you—"

"Do I—what do you mean? Have I done it before? Do I know how to *get there*?"

"Of course you do—I know every boy can stick it in and come. I'm asking do you know how to please me? My sister says I need to be sure we're protected, get tested, have the right birth control, and that I'm supposed to guide you on my body."

"Guide me as in . . . take me in your hands?" He raised his brows.

"As in take your hands in mine and make sure I have an orgasm." I pursed my lips and let a breath out slowly so I didn't hyperventilate. "I don't want to be left wanting more, while I see a smile on *your* face and then two minutes later you fall asleep or zip up your pants. Have you done it before or talked with an adult about sex?"

"No to both."

"Are you sure?" I watched his face carefully as he answered.

"You doubt me?"

"Terrie told me you've been flirting with her and that you've made moves on Sabrina, too. I know Terrie wants to go out with you. I don't blame her . . . or you for that matter. I want you to be honest, though. I have no right asking you to wait for me and I don't think you should. I'm confused about sex. Still, I want to know if you're—"

"I'll wait for you," he interrupted.

You didn't exactly answer my question.

"Okay, well, don't you think we should . . . I don't know, ask someone who's done it, so both of us have a good experience the first time?" I flattened my hands on the dashboard of his car. "I'd at least like to have some idea of what we're doing. We've talked about it, but neither of us has really researched what good sex is—at least, it doesn't seem like it."

"No, I haven't," he admitted. "You're right, it's a good idea."

"I bookmarked some good stuff online. I'll text you the links. I want to know how to please you, too. Does that sound stupid?"

"No, not stupid," He ran his hands through his hair. "Damn, Nick. Sometimes you overwhelm me the way you talk. None of my buddies have girlfriends who talk with them like this. You make me feel like I'm a kid."

"Sorry, I'm only—"

"You're intimidating. You're great, but . . . intimidating."

"I'm not trying to make you feel awkward talking with me. It seems like everyone's too embarrassed to discuss it. Sex is something . . . well, I think it should be talked about in every way possible, don't you think?"

He nodded.

"I don't know about your friends. My girlfriends seem to plunge in and learn as they go. I don't want to open my legs and we're done. I want to be completely honest so each of us gets what we want."

"I can understand that."

"I know it's hard to talk about. Believe me, I have to force myself to say every word out loud to you. I'm lucky to have a sister who took the time to care about sharing a little with me."

"I've talked with my friends and—"

"Oh God, no," I interrupted. "Please don't rely on a bunch of eighteen-year-old guys—and jocks at that. Chances are if they're having sex it's only good for them."

"What do your girlfriends say?" He seemed lost.

"The kissing's good, some masturbating is good, but the act itself? Not so much. They say their boyfriend never takes the time to make sure they're ready and it's a race instead of an intimate journey. They say the oral sex is awful, too. All the focus is on the vagina instead of . . . you know."

"Your little button?" Desire colored his voice.

"Yeah." I looked away.

"Are *any* of your girlfriends happy with sex?"

"Colleen. She's dating a twenty-one-year-old and pretty damn happy," I giggled. "My other friends say their boyfriend just wants to—"

"Spill the cream?" he grinned.

"Oh, that's . . ." I covered my eyes for a second. "God, Jerry. Anyway, are you comfortable talking with your dad?"

"Hell no," he said emphatically. "That asshole will probably punch me just for bringing up the subject. I'll ask my coach or pastor."

"I'd like to give your father a piece of my mind," I admitted.

"Don't. I'll be the one who gets the short end of the stick if you do that."

"Yeah. You could go to the clinic." I wanted to change the subject and talk about getting away from his father, but continued talking about sex. "Please, whoever you talk with, make it with someone older than us—much older—please."

"Okay, I will. You know, I've waited a long time to have this talk. Well, not exactly like this. I wish we were still at the ocean."

"We both need to show our test results to each other. And condoms; we need those. I guess you already have them, but I need to look into them, too. Oh, and a dental dam."

"Wow, you, um . . . What the hell is a dam? You sound pretty educated for a virgin. Are you really?"

"Yes. Geez, Jerry. You already asked me that. I saw my first one the other day. My sister showed me. She told me quite a bit, actually. A dental dam protects us from getting herpes when we have oral sex. Don't you want oral sex?"

"Hell, yeah."

"I do, too. Why would you assume I wouldn't want your mouth on me like you want mine on you?"

"I don't. I didn't." A knot formed between his brows. "I don't know."

"I want to talk it all through so there aren't any big surprises for either of us." I reached for his hand and held it. "I know we'll have some surprises. If we can at least try to prepare by talking to people and reading about it . . . send me a text if you find something interesting while you're away playing baseball."

"Where the hell do you get a dental dam?" he asked.

"I didn't ask," I confessed. "I guess the clinic?"

"No, I know," Jerry kidded. "You go to your dentist and say, 'Hey doc, I'm planning on having oral sex Friday. Can you spare a dental dam or two?" He threw his head back in hysterics.

"I guess we'll research that, too." I laughed with him and then reached for the door handle.

"My parents are going with me this trip," he informed. "Otherwise, I'd invite you to come with me. Seeing you in the stands cheering for me would be awesome. Could you imagine us in a motel room? I don't know if I'd get to any games."

He had a happy twinkle in his eyes.

"We can't have that," I waived my index finger in a warning. "Not good for your baseball career."

"Won't it be great going to college together?" He played with a strand of my hair.

I nodded. In reality, I didn't intend to commit to any boy when we went to college. I had made a silent covenant to break out from all my restraints. Meeting new people was high on my list of priorities. The box in which I'd kept myself was beginning to choke me. Fully intending to shed all my reservations about sex, come hell or high water, I was going to experiment.

I thought so, anyway.

Well wasn't I?

"Jerry, do you think I'm fat?"

"What? God, no! What kind of question is that? You're built like the freaking Hoover Dam."

"Sabrina and Terry are so much thinner." I shook my head. "Any boy would go for them and their little skirts and short tops."

"You're crazy." His hands cradled the back of my neck. "You have nothing to worry about."

"I know I'm crazy. But I've always been embarrassed about my belly. It's round and sticks out. I can't change it. Most of the other girls, their bellies are flat and go in, but I have this bump. Plus, my hips and ass are big. When I was in LA with Alex, I about died when she told me she was having her staff dress me. I didn't think they'd have anything that fit. Those models are so thin, you know?"

"Guess they made a trip to the big girls' shop," he joked.

"Shut up! They probably did!"

"You got nothin' to worry about girl. I like your belly and butt. I especially love your tits."

"Shut up!" I punched his arm. "Don't call them that."

"Boobs, then. You're a triple threat—the killer Bs."

"Okay, good. I guess. Is that a backhanded compliment?" I frowned and then smiled quickly so he knew I was teasing him. "I'll see you in a few days. Good luck with your baseball games."

We kissed good night and I got out of the car.

I spun around quickly so I wouldn't have to watch as he drove away. Instead, I focused on his return.

Small steps. Baby steps.

As I went upstairs to my room, I thought about the words that Alex had said: *Boys who are your peers will allow you to go slow and you'll be able to control things just as you like.*

I wanted to go slow, but if I was going to take the dive in the deep end of the pool, I wanted to get the strokes I needed to manage the warm waters.

A director in my own play—that's what I intended to be.

I vowed not to be the kind of woman who was like a dying fish when it came to sex, afraid to speak up—like my mother and her two-minute man.

No one was going to push me.

Only when I was ready for sex and intimacy would I give in— but when would that day come for me?

Was it possible for me to fully embrace the love of a man—or even a friend—and allow myself to be so vulnerable that I could let old fears fall away?

Could I fall boldly into the depths of love and intimacy, finally transitioning into the brilliance of joy?

Chapter 15

Dressing Up

𝔗he Goliaths came back into town on a Monday, the last week of June. I was ready to go for a workout when my cell phone rang.

Ryan.

His name blared at me as if it was in neon.

Panic interrupted my initial exuberance.

Oh no, what do I say? Should I ignore his call? I should tell him our timing isn't right. It's best to go our separate ways. I don't want to, but yes it's what I should do. I should. I . . .

Ten days had passed since my wonderful day at Yountville and the night Ryan had stayed over. We'd slept in my bed together, only hugging, kissing, and caressing each other.

The day he left? I felt anything was possible with him.

After LA and after Jerry?

I needed time.

I needed college.

I needed focus.

Why didn't I call him? Do I really want to say goodbye?

Ashamed, I knew I had taken a child's way out, once again hiding under the dining room table as if I were still that eight-year-old girl, cowering from my fears.

Damn it, Nicky. Crawl out of there!

Had I also taken advantage of his trust? Had he of mine?

We promised to be a good boy and girl for each other. Did I break that promise? Did he on the night I couldn't reach him? Was it right to expect either of us to keep that promise? What about kissing Jerry at the coast? I never committed to Ryan, but I asked him not to party. What was I doing?

Paralyzed, I stared at my phone, certain his reason for calling was to pick up his jacket and say goodbye forever.

He's too sophisticated for me. You've already decided you wanted to be free. So what if he says goodbye?

I battled the two sides of having Ryan in my life.

My cell phone faded to the last ring.

A second before it went to voice mail, I picked up.

"Hi, Ryan."

"Nicky."

"How are you?" *So far, we're very polite. When are you going to drop the hammer?* "You guys had a good road trip." I said the words quickly, trying to dodge his oncoming goodbye.

"You weren't too busy to watch?" His words were purposeful and they stung.

Sarcasm. I deserved that.

"I managed to sneak in a couple of games," I responded nervously.

"Are you free tonight?"

Silence.

"I'd like to get together." His tone was even and steady.

"Sure." My stomach dropped. *What happened to telling him you aren't right for each other?* "That would be great." *He's obviously the kind of guy who is gracious enough to break up in person. I need to allow him that at least.*

"Good, I'd like to take you to dinner," he said smoothly. "I can't wait to see your pretty smile again."

Well, at least you're being gentle.

"What should I wear?" *I might have to pad my bedroom walls. Dare I let myself feel this excited?*

"Something nice—not formal, but not jeans." I heard a phone ringing in the background. "I've got to get this. I'll be at your house around six-thirty."

"Where are we going?"

"It's a surprise." His voice jumped up a note, as if excitement pushed through him. "See you in a few hours."

Oh . . . he didn't say good-bye. He's breaking it off. I knew it. What did I expect? Of course, he is. He said me missed my smile. He wouldn't . . . no. It's better not to hope.

After Ryan had spent an innocent night in my bedroom, the feelings I had for him had grown sweet and sticky. Like making saltwater taffy, we pulled and stretched each other, trying to form the new relationship and learn how to be intimate without scaring the hell out of each other.

My fear of letting people get too close had probably blown any chance for the two of us. I mourned the thought of never again having a deep conversation with him or the feel of his kiss.

I feel as if I'm in high school giving the jock back his jacket.

My heart banged with the constant beat of panic when I thought of not having Ryan as a friend.

What have I done?

I felt sick as I envisioned him at the ballpark flirting and seeking out another woman to share his dreams with. Just picturing him taking her hand and kissing it made me teary.

Something casual, but nice—what does that mean?

I'd worn the only casual dress I had for my date with Jerry. Somehow, it didn't seem right to wear it for whatever the evening was going to be with Ryan. The Valentino dress I'd worn in Los Angeles was probably too much.

"Jenise!" I knocked on her door.

"For shit's sake, come in!" she yelled.

"I need you." I stood in her doorway. "I have a last minute date with Ryan tonight and I don't have anything good to wear. Please help?"

"What do you mean, *last minute*?" Her eyes shone with mischief. I was sure I saw a twinkle in them.

"He called me out of the blue and asked me out."

"And you want me to help you *how*?" Jenise had enrolled in summer school and was trying to handle three courses normally taken over a full semester. Add to that her deepening relationship with her boyfriend, Sean, plus my busy schedule, and we hadn't seen each other much.

I bounced on the bed, sat next to her, and filled her in on everything that had happened during the week. I started with my singing at Yountville and covered my latest date with Jerry.

"You made a big mistake not returning Ryan's call. Why the fuck did you do that? Lame-O! And why the fuck do you care so much about how you look?"

"I don't know. I think he's breaking up with me tonight. I want him to remember me looking nice, I guess."

"He's going to set you straight—*that's* what he's going to do," Jenise corrected.

"That sounds gross and way too domineering for me." I scrunched my face. "What do you mean *set me straight*?"

"He'll expect you to see *only* him. You know the night he spent with you in your room?"

"Yeah?"

"I didn't say anything when we talked before . . . that was a serious move." She held my hand. "The way you told me he teased you, kissed you, and didn't press you for sex? He's serious and he'll explain it all tonight."

"How do you know that?" I piled my hair on my head.

"He can get sex and casual relationships whenever he wants them. Coming to the house after you sang the anthem and staying the night even though you told him you're not ready for sex means he's not letting you go easily. It's like he's being old-fashioned just for you. For a guy who has women vying for his attention—damn, Sis. I'd say he's not only starry-eyed but quite a sweetheart. Do you really know what you've got?"

"No." I was telling the truth. I *didn't* understand. "I was sure I only wanted freedom. But hearing his voice . . ."

"I think you have someone special—really special. Maybe like Sean," Jenise grinned. "So before I pick something for you to wear, tell me what you feel for Ryan."

"I like him. I *really* like him. But when I was with Jerry that felt good, too. God, Jenise! We came close do doing it!"

"You listened to your smart sister and told him to back off?"

"Yes." I tossed a pillow at her. "Like you said, we need to get tested. Mostly, I'm confused about sex. My feelings for Ryan were strong and then he left for his road trip. Alex took me to her photo shoot in LA and I got a taste of that business world. I liked that, too. I came back and got closer to Jerry. Then, Ryan calls . . . wait. Before that, I got angry he didn't answer my calls when I was in Yountville, and I acted ridiculous."

"Why?"

"I'd convinced myself he was out carousing—"

"*Carousing*," she cracked up. "You're such an old lady sometimes."

"I know. Shut up."

"Go on Ethel."

"Remember her?"

"I only saw her briefly when we visited grandma."

"Remind me to tell you about her sometime." I folded my hands. "Anyway, I was certain breaking up with him was the

143

right thing to do. Then I hear his voice and I melt. I hope he doesn't tell me goodbye. I think I blew it."

"When a person lusts—and sissy, you're lusting—it's messy. You get twisted up. So, you're feeling hot and sexy for Ryan?" She waited for my response with obvious anticipation.

"Yes, but it's too soon to dress hot. I just want something pretty—not sexy. Shit. What the hell happened to me, Sis? I didn't want any of this, and now, boom."

"Funny how everything we think we have under our control suddenly isn't." She pushed herself off the bed.

"I don't like being vulnerable. Damn it." I clenched my fists.

"Why not? Being vulnerable doesn't make you weak." Her eyes were alive and peaked with interest. "It means you're open. That's how you learn to embrace intimacy."

"Too scary for me right now." I shuddered.

"News flash—Ryan isn't going to date you without sex. He sure as hell won't wait while you go to college and find yourself."

"I know. Dad made sure to tell me the same thing." I traced the pattern on her bedspread with my finger. "God, I hate it when Mom and Dad talk about that stuff. How did you handle it when you had those discussions with them?"

"Well . . ." Her bottom lip quivered. "They didn't have those talks with me because they figured I was damaged goods."

Her reveal stunned me.

When I matured, I never considered my sister as anything but a strong, wonderful woman, regardless of her being raped. I never could understand why our parents weren't in her room constantly, offering support, discussing sex and how strong and intelligent she was. Sex was so much more than having it for the first time. It was also about mental readiness, social stigmas, physiological responses and health issues. A storm of anger thundered inside me that they hadn't taken the time to show the deepest of concern for their oldest daughter. How dare they make her feel damaged.

"I don't think that was it." I tried to shove down my rage. Our parents were ashamed because they couldn't handle their daughter being violated? They couldn't accept how she had transitioned into an independent woman and someone who made her own choices about sex regardless of how she was judged?

How were the two synonymous? I didn't understand why one had to do with the other in the minds of our parents.

"Yes, that's exactly what happened, Nick. I'm past it now. At the time . . . pretty brutal, huh? It took months before they could even look at me. Remember when Grandma came to stay with us? They wouldn't even let you sleep in my room."

"That *was* weird," I concurred. "I never did understand why I had to sleep in their bedroom. Still, I don't believe they saw you as anything except their wounded daughter. You know how they are; they can't even handle themselves."

Deep down, I realized she might be right.

"Thanks, Sis, but—"

"That's the end of it," I interrupted. "You're an incredible woman, sister, daughter and girlfriend. That's that. Let's look for something to wear. I hope you have something that fits."

"You're sure different now. Only a few weeks ago you'd hardly talk to anyone at home—especially me. What happened to you? Ryan has something to do with it, right?"

"I think it's all the wonderful women in my life." I nudged my shoulder into hers.

"That *must* be it." She socked my arm gently, returning the affection. "So what are your intentions with Ryan?"

"I want some kind of relationship with him. Not a permanent one, though. Or maybe I do. I don't know. I'm afraid of taking a chance." I picked at my fingernail. "I think about having intercourse with him and then—"

"God, Sis," she scolded. "Say the words! You're thinking about sex! Fucking! Getting a beef injection, the cucumber rumba, the slap and tickle, diving in the deep end, making love."

"Okay, well—"

"What you're saying," now she was all business. "Tonight you want to reestablish your friendship and let him know that you're okay with more but it has to move slowly."

"Yes."

"Finally! All I wanted is a straight answer. You're murder."

"Sorry. I know I talk in too many circles. I don't mean to. Anyway, my connection with Ryan has always been incredible. Ever since Yountville . . ." I stopped when I noticed my sister smiling.

"Take a peek in the mirror," Jenise suggested. "You'll understand when you see yourself."

I glanced at the mirror . . . but refused to actually look.

"Alex said the same thing when we were in LA. I was so embarrassed she'd noticed whatever I did to give myself away."

"Even if you don't admit it, the way you *really* want to dress is not for friendship, Sissy." She poked at my chest. "I get it—you want to go slow."

"What does that tell you about how I should dress?" *How does she know so much?*

"A hot dress is out of the question or you'll give him the impression you're open for sex tonight. We'll dress you like the innocent, pretty sister you are. You'll look soft and lovely with a pinch of virgin. *That* part shouldn't be too hard for you to play."

"You're not funny." I swatted her on the arm.

There's that word "soft" again—first Jerry and now Jenise.

"Yes, I am," she grinned confidently, sorting through the clothes hanging in her closet.

"I concede."

"Smart sister." A look of pure satisfaction warmed her face. "Tonight, you need to wear something pretty, flowing, and covers everything on your curvy body. Do you have anything like that?"

"I have an extra-large t-shirt that fits like that." I tried to hide my smile.

"Sis, get some clothes, would you?" The hangers were flying to the side. She was on a mission for something specific.

"Tell you a secret?" I tugged on her T-shirt.

"What's that?" Her nose crinkled as she focused on finding the right outfit from her clothes.

"I was in your closet last year and took one of your dresses to wear for the Goliaths end-of-the-year party," I laughed.

"What a shit you are! You could have asked, you know. I would have given you—oh, this is perfect! Here you go." She pulled something white from her large collection. "If I leave it up to you, Ryan will see you come bounding down the stairs in jeans wearing your big, innocent smile, shouting, *I'm ready*!" She laughed again, thoroughly enjoying herself. "You know, if you're going to keep seeing him, you'll have to do some shopping."

"He knows who I am," I said confidently.

"Do you know who *he* is? You'll be exposed to his friends and business associates. Alex showed you the same thing in LA not too many days ago, didn't she?"

"Yeah." I looked up at the ceiling, thinking about the important lesson I'd almost let slip by. "I'm not sure he'll want to see me again after tonight."

"You said that earlier. I don't agree." She took a scarf from her dresser that matched the outfit. "Why do you feel that way?"

"I ignored him, Jenise. I was certain he wasn't someone I should have in my life right now and I ignored his calls."

"Like I said, I don't think he's breaking up with you." She handed me a pair of white silk pants and matching top. "All of this goes together." She draped the scarf over the clothes and shoved them in my arms.

I held the ensemble in front of me.

The softness and the layers of cotton and silk were like foamy waves. One folded over the other. Alternated in creamy white, opaque and sheer fabrics. The neck was cut in a U-shape and was wide from one shoulder to the other, dipping in the back.

"It's beautiful." I gave her a kiss on the cheek. "Thank you."

"The pants have an elastic waist for your big ass. Please try not to stretch the top with your boobs."

"I have a sports bra I can use to squish 'em." I was glad I had something of my own to contribute. "It's what I wear when I cheer and exercise so they don't bounce."

"The top dips too low in the back for a bra like you're describing. You either go braless—which, um," she looked at my breasts, "I wouldn't recommend or you might give Ryan a heart attack."

"Funny," I lamented.

"You need a special bra that's made for an outfit like this. I'm betting you don't have one. Do you?"

Silence.

"Never mind." She looked disgusted. Dug through her lingerie drawer. Tossed one of her bras to me so I could try it on. It was tight. I stretched the hooks.

"Oops." *Damn. I've ruined her bra already.* "I'm sorry, Sis. This won't work."

"Here, let me help you." She stepped behind me and adjusted it. Even though the bra was tight, we made it work.

"I'll pay you back if I ruin it."

"I don't think I have to worry about *you*; it's that big boyfriend of yours and the way he takes it off of you." She smiled a tantalizing grin.

You and Ryan and your grins—what do you do, practice them in front of a mirror?

"What time is Ryan, um, coming to *get* you?"

"Around six thirty." I ignored her comment.

"Oh good, you've got plenty of time to play with your hair and makeup. You can wear any of my jewelry," she offered. "Don't ask, just go ahead and get what you want. Maybe I'll set out a few pieces since you have no sense of style."

"Thanks." I put my arms around her. "I appreciate all your help. I know I'm interrupting your studies."

"No, you're not." She put the empty hanger back in her closet. "I hope you'll interrupt me again."

It was a moment I had to write about before the vividness of all the little details—the tones of our conversation, her facial expressions, the conversation, the colors, noises, and things in her room—faded from memory. As soon as I went back into my bedroom, I put her outfit over my chair and grabbed my journal.

I was restless and unsettled.

I couldn't write too long before I turned on music and then the TV. I wrote more. When I couldn't sit still any longer, I decided to work on my hair.

I wonder if I should bring his jacket and sweat pants. Will he ask for them or just expect me to bring them?

As I was primping, my cell phone rang.

Ryan.

I'd put on a brave front and try not to cry when he said, "*I've changed my mind. Good luck to you, Ms. Young. I'll be by to pick up my stuff later this week.*"

"Hey, Ryan."

"I'm early. Are you close to being ready?"

It's only three. He wants to get it over with. I knew it. Why didn't I just wear jeans?

"Not yet. Are you canceling?"

"No." I thought I heard him laugh a little. "Can you be ready in a half hour?"

"I think so." I glanced at my clock.

"Good, because I'm coming to get you. I can't wait any longer."

Is this what having a heart attack feels like?

His voice made my heart slam. Why didn't he just tell me on the phone he wanted to end everything? Why go out?

Maybe he's going to tell me what he'd planned and saw for us and then kiss my hand, coming full circle.

I could hear him say, "*This isn't working, but since you cheer at the ballpark, I hope we can still be friends.*"

"Help!" I knocked on Jenise's door.

"What is it?" She broke into a laugh when I peeked in.

"He's coming early. Can you help me make sure everything looks okay? Please don't make fun of me, I guess—"

"Oh man, girl, you *are* gone, aren't you?" Jenise took my hand and we walked into her bathroom.

"I guess so. Do you think it's too late?" I grabbed her arm. "I think it's too late. I'm sure it is. I hope it's not too late. What do you think?"

"I don't think it's too late." She flashed another grin. By the time Jenise was through, half of my hair was up while the other half fell down my back. "One big pin to hold your hair."

"I think I need more than one! Look at this mop. Maybe I should just pull it back. What if the wind blows? I'll be a mess."

"One pin, so that when he embraces you, takes you to his bed and covers your lips with his . . ." I watched my sister lose herself. " . . . You both lie down; he caresses your back as he lays you on top of him. Big, masculine hands slide up your body. They glance across your breasts and move through your hair. The hairpin drops. Your hair falls all around him . . . Bingo!"

I began to envision that scene.

I was sure my face revealed how lovely I felt.

"What are you smiling about?" Jenise provoked.

"Nothing." I answered flatly doing my best to deny it.

"Oh yeah?" She gave me a pair of her silver chandelier earrings. Each had several shining filigreed chains dangling from the fulcrum. They sparkled as they fell to my shoulders.

"What about your shoes?" Jenise looked me over.

"I have sandals."

"Oh, damn." She went into her closet and grabbed a pair of open-toed, silver shoes with a low heel. "Here, take these. Your feet are longer than mine, but they should fit okay."

Feeling like a woman who looked damn good that afternoon, I finished with lip-gloss, like my friends had so often.

I should have worn a hot dress. Maybe if I showed my boobs he'd give me another chance.

"What do you think, Jenise?" I walked into her bedroom.

"Oh, Sissy. I've never seen you look so pretty. The way your eyes shine . . . he'll know you're opening to him. Even *I'm* not ready for the way you look—you *never* look this good."

"Thanks a lot."

"You know what I mean. I feel a little . . . sad. My little sister is growing up . . ." She tossed her hair as if shaking away the unpleasantness. "I just realized something . . . I'm not ready for you to date!"

"I'm not sure I am, either."

We laughed nervously.

"I owe you one." I hugged her and then the doorbell rang.

Chapter 16

Cranberry and Orange Juice

"*M*oment of reckoning!" Jenise teased.

Feeling frantic, I checked myself in the mirror once again. Started to leave my room. Realized I'd forgotten my wallet. Back to the mirror for another check. *Shit, where are the earrings?*

I put them on and walked out of the bedroom.

Down the hallway.

Partially down the stairs.

I looked at my feet. No shoes.

Ran up to my bedroom, grabbed them. Peeked in the mirror.

Threw the wallet on the bed.

Sat down. Put on the shoes, grabbed the wallet and stumbled into the hall.

Damn heels.

My mother answered the door and invited Ryan inside. My father was in the living room. Immediately, Ryan started a conversation with both of my parents.

I relaxed when I heard their laughter.

After several slow and deep breaths, I walked downstairs. My feet felt as if there were weights on them. The shoes Jenise gave me to wear clacked on our wooden steps.

When I came into the room, the three of them looked at me. I felt like running away.

Ryan wore a dark gray linen vest and matching slacks with an open-collared, pale blue shirt. The rolled-up cuffs and his thick, silver chain-link bracelet made me want to lick the entire length of his forearm. Peeking out from his chest, the "BLESSED" tattoo on his upper pectorals beckoned. I was sure I heard them whisper *you know what I'm covering. Come get us.*

Ooh! Your magnificent chest! Hello to you, too!

"Let me take a picture." Mom reached for her cell phone on the coffee table. "You both look nice. Don't they, Bob?"

Dad nodded.

We posed with Ryan's arm around my shoulder. After Mom snapped two photos, I was more than ready to go. The chance of being embarrassed increased every second, especially as Dad sipped more of the wine from his glass that rested by his chair.

"I'm ready if you are," I hoped he'd take my cue.

"Mr. and Mrs. Young, I want you to know I have such a hard time looking away from your daughter. She's taken my breath away from the moment I saw her." He took my hand in his. Although he spoke to my parents, he looked only into my eyes.

Ooh, I'll miss this.

"Thank you." *His words always shake me.*

"You look . . . so pretty." His eyes sparkled.

"You look nice, too. Then again, you always look good even when you wear your T-shirts. So, anyway . . ." *I'm nervous, nervous, nervous. I want to bite my cuticles.* When Ryan chuckled at my T-shirt comment, I looked away from him before he put me into a trance.

I noticed my dad focusing. My parents wore the biggest smiles I'd seen from them in a long while. Neither had any idea of how powerful their gestures of approval were.

To Jenise and me, they meant we could relax.

They meant love.

They meant everything could be all right.

"We'll be in late, so don't wait up, Mr. and Mrs. Young." Ryan shook their hands. "I'll make sure she's safe."

"Byeeeeee, you two," Jenise said in a long, exaggerated voice from the top of the stairs. I could see invisible horns sprouting from her head.

"Bye Nicky's lovely sister." Ryan's stunning grin was on display. I knew I'd never see anything like it again. He took my right hand in his and brought it around his waist.

I was an absolute wreck and could hardly stand to touch him. As we started out the door, his left arm went around my shoulder.

I'll never make it down the driveway.

It was the second time we had walked out of my front door holding onto each other that way. I turned to see my parents waving goodbye. I waved back. Suddenly sentimental, I realized a time would soon come when they wouldn't be there to see me off. For that moment however, unaware of the full effects of those future moments, their attentiveness embarrassed me.

Ryan drove an SUV that afternoon. He opened the car door for me. I hesitated. *How do I get around his body when he won't step aside?* My stomach knotted. When he moved closer, I thought I'd drop to the ground.

"God, you look beautiful." He kissed my cheek.

"My sister helped me. I've never taken so long to get ready for a date. I almost forgot to put my shoes on before I came downstairs." I cracked up. I was nervous and it was what I did when I was spinning. "Then I couldn't find my wallet, and I hate these heels you know? I can't walk in them. You might have to catch me as I fall in front of everyone, so be ready. Whelp, anyway, thanks for the compliment."

He waited for me to get settled. A delicious smile reflected his amusement. While he walked to the driver's side, I examined him thoroughly. I appreciated the way he'd dressed for our date. He had to have spent a lot of time getting ready to look like he did—or not. Maybe he was just that damn handsome.

"You look nice in your vest and slacks. Where are we going?"

"My brother and sister-in-law are in town. They're staying at the Embarcadero Hotel and I'd like you to meet them. We'll talk for a while and then leave for dinner. Is that all right with you?"

"Sure."

"Nicky, the way you look, I didn't expect you to . . ." He let the words hang.

"You didn't think I'd dress up for you?"

"I didn't know what you'd do." He ran his fingers through his hair. "I can't figure out what you're thinking."

"I almost put on a pair of sweatpants." I saw his shoulders drop in relief, as if a little icicle had broken away. "I'm just kidding." I put my hand on his arm and stroked it a few times. *So luscious.* "You were probably worried, huh? Thank God, I dressed this way. Look at *you.* You call that *casual?*"

"I, um . . ." He blushed as he gathered his thoughts. "I couldn't decide what to wear."

You were fretting over me? Sweet.

"Maybe we can get a room while we're at the hotel so our primping doesn't go to waste." He looked at me from the corner of his eye.

"I didn't do all this just to get tossed around." *Maybe this isn't goodbye after all.* "I'm sorry my parents feel as if they have to greet you." I suddenly shifted the conversation, uncomfortable with the attention. "It's a little embarrassing. I guess in their eyes I'm still their little girl."

"I wish I had parents to see me off on my dates." Tones of sadness weaved in and out of his voice.

"Ryan?" *I have to get this out.*

"Yes?"

"I'm sorry I didn't call you back. I should have."

"I accept your apology."

"Are you upset?" *I'm waiting for the boom to drop.* "I don't know how to talk about this." I tugged on my earrings.

"If I'm being honest, I don't get it. You wanted more time with me; you even initiated when we went to Sammy's. We had a sweet night together in your room and you spent an entire day checking on my contacts. Then the surprise in Yountville—I still don't understand. I know you enjoyed the day, yet all I got from you that night was the brush off because you were tired. When you landed in LA . . . couldn't you have called and talked to me a few minutes? What the hell happened?"

"I don't know. It was—"

"I don't understand why you didn't phone me at *all*," he interrupted. "Not even when you came home."

"I did, though. I called the day I went to Yountville. During the day and when I got back around nine. I couldn't reach you. I tried several times. I knew your game had been over with a while. You weren't around for me."

"Like when I called and you were at the beach?" he said knowingly.

"Yes, but—"

"You couldn't have taken a few minutes to say hello? Not for my entire road trip?" He was rolling like a snowball, gaining momentum with each word, the same as I'd done with him. "I tried you at least a dozen times. No, more than that actually. I finally gave up."

"Why didn't you keep trying?" I turned my palms up as if my hands had asked the question.

"I tried every day after you got back from LA. For five days I tried." His tone was stern and filled with disappointment. "How many times did you expect me to call, trying to get you to pick up or get back to me?"

I looked out the window.

I didn't know how to answer him.

"Your silence told me you weren't interested." He bravely continued. "Did you lose interest? Should I keep trying? Or will this be our final evening together?"

"I'm interested." I may have not known exactly how to explain myself, but I knew what he was saying to me.

"Were you still upset with how abrupt I was on the phone to you when you accused me of being with someone else?"

"No. I accepted your apology and I meant it. I was . . . well, I, um, I really don't know how to describe what I felt."

"Try."

"Okay." I took a deep breath. "After being in LA with Alex, I didn't want to be serious. With anyone. Calling you would have brought me back into your world, or . . . being with men too soon, I guess."

"I see."

Silence.

"See what?" I pushed.

"The adjustment I need to make," he said confidently. "I know what I need to do to get your attention. I want you to see me like you've never seen anyone before. Now you will."

"Get my attention?" I smiled nervously.

"Yes." He made no apologies. His hands flexed on the wheel.

I'm going to faint. I'd better hold onto something. Should I give him a warning? Is my face pale? Did I bring some blush? My face must need some color.

"What is this adjustment?" I tilted my head, trying to stay involved in the conversation.

"You'll see it all unfold, Nicky. In fact, you'll *feel* it all unfold." He looked straight ahead.

Just let me rest my head on some pillow. I'll open my mouth, listen to him talk, and let the lust flow out of it.

"I love this hotel." We pulled into valet parking. "See how the glass elevators go up the side of the building? And the structure—it's geometrical, see how it cuts in an angle? Jenise said the design approval took three years."

He looked at me with his wry grin showing off for me.

"You know?" *Don't start with your sexy looks.*

"You're sure cute when you talk about your sister. It's obvious you're proud of her. Your face lights up."

"I *am* proud of her. The way she picked herself up . . . I hope she can design a project as big as this one someday." I felt my body expand with pride for my sister. "Have you ever seen it decorated during the holidays?"

Slow down, Nicky.

"I'm usually back East with my family or taking a vacation that time of year since it's the off season. I've got to fit in my personal time from November through January. Mid-February—"

"The pitchers and catchers report. Yeah, that's right. You must see it, though. They have a thousand strands of lights hanging up and down the atrium from a dozen stories above the floor, several train displays, a huge Christmas tree with big, gaudy decorations and . . . ooh! Then the Embarcadero lights up with a fireworks show. We grab a soft pretzel and a dog . . . it's great." I was starting to ramble.

"What do you mean *we* grab a soft pretzel?" He turned to look at me, his lips forming a tempting grin.

"I mean, we, my friends and I, well," I cleared my throat. "I meant you and me. That's what I meant." *I give in.*

"Maybe we can go there together this December."

"Mm-hmm." *You'll be tired of me by then. I've already caused each of us to take a time out from being together.*

We left the car with the valet and walked into the lobby of the hotel. Within minutes, a number of people recognized Ryan and rushed over to him. Looking at me apologetically, his hand, previously resting on the small of my back, lifted slowly. He turned to greet his fans.

Having lunch with him in St. Helena last year popped into my mind. He'd made a comment and at the time I'd brushed it off: *It's especially difficult when I'm trying to pay attention to the woman I'm with and people won't leave me alone.* I didn't understand what he'd meant by it until now—he had been talking about *me* that day.

I was overwhelmed.

I wanted to run to him and tell him I understood what he was saying. Give him a big hug. Let him know I'd just put the pieces together. Restraining myself for the sake of his privacy, I forced myself to hold back and kept my moment of discovery to myself.

When he finished talking with the last fan, he took my hand. We walked over to the lounge area. Without warning, my body seemed taken into his masculine essence.

He wrapped me tightly in his arms. The lips I'd missed took my mouth, making it moist, making it tingle and making me want more.

Whispers covered me in delicate, lacy threads.

It was as if some promise had been newly sealed in our soft moment.

Our bodies pressed together. He rubbed my upper back. His chest expanded. His moans grew louder. A little sound of pleasure rolled off my tongue. I was taken away. Much too soon, his body said good-bye. As he let go, I was reminded of how good it felt to be with him.

"Can you give me a second?" I was so weak for him. Whenever he kissed me like that it was as if he started the primal beat of my heart's rhythm. I lost the strength in my legs.

"Only a second," he teased deliciously. He leaned close and said in his low voice, "You're such a fragile baby."

"Shh, don't make it worse for me."

"Should I carry you?" His eyes looked as if they were ready for a scandal.

"God, no! I just need . . . oh look, Ryan. Look at that beautiful flower display." I pointed to the arrangement in the atrium to distract him.

"Good try. I'm not taking my eyes off of you." His focus was possessive. He pinned me with his gaze. "My only desire is to take in your sweet face so I can watch you react to my kiss."

Oh holy mother. Please look somewhere else.

"I'm all right now," I informed softly.

His wicked grin led us into the lounge.

"I admire the way you're so open with your emotions." I was nervous and off to the races. "I watch other couples, like Matt and Tara, Alex and Darrell—even my school friends. They're all reserved when they're out in public. Sometimes it's hard to tell they're together; they don't even hold hands. With you, it's obvious and it feels good. Your girlfriends must have been in heaven being with you."

"I'm glad you approve." He paused a few seconds. "Just to be clear, I've never had girlfriends or kissed a woman in public."

What?

"You're trying to make me feel special," I offered in disbelief. "Thanks for that. Your sweet to be sensitive to my phobias."

"No, Nicky. I didn't tell you that because it's what I think you want to hear. I've never had a reason to show my affection in public until now. I've always been guarded about my emotions."

I couldn't look away.

"What are you thinking?" he asked impatiently.

"I'm trying to process this."

"Two?" the lounge host asked.

"Yes." His arm slid around my waist. "Somewhere quiet, please. My girlfriend has a lot on her mind."

I shot him a smile; almost giggling at the way he so naturally lightened a conversation—and then a mere second later, buried me with passion and depth.

"Follow me." The host smiled and led us to a quiet corner. Ryan slipped him a few bills as we took our seats.

"Let's have a drink and talk before we go upstairs."

"I thought you didn't drink." I raised my eyebrows, curious at this new twist.

"I don't." He went to the bar and came back to the table with two cranberry and orange juice drinks.

"I don't drink, but I *have* tasted alcohol," I informed him when he sat down. "Plus, my friends drink so don't feel as if you have to protect me. If you want a beer or a cocktail, just have one."

I need to get over my anxiety when someone is only drinking in a social way.

"You're not twenty-one. You don't need to drink or have a boyfriend who does. I wasn't hiding anything when I told you I didn't drink alcohol last year in St. Helena."

"I believe you."

"We need to talk before we see my brother." Ryan looked directly in my eyes. His gaze was deep.

I had a hard time returning it.

I knew his questions were beginning.

"I'm so hurt, Nicky. Why didn't you call me?"

I started to answer.

"Why?" He leaned forward, his elbows on the table. "I'm not an insensitive asshole. You made me feel like one. I need to understand—you, of all people."

I stirred the ice in my cranberry drink.

"Paul told me how you stayed on stage for an hour singing at the Veterans' Hospital because you had so many song requests. I enjoyed getting your texts, yet after that, nothing except *you were busy*? I was really down." He waited for an answer.

I didn't have one.

I could only look down at the table.

"I thought we were becoming close," he started again. "I felt like we were sweethearts." His eyes welled with tears.

Instantly I felt ashamed.

As I sat across from him, I realized I'd stabbed him by taking advantage of his kindness.

"I don't know why I did that." I rolled my glass between my palms.

"I felt used. It was as if you were no different than any of the other women who try to hook up with me because I'm a professional athlete."

I reached across the table and held his hand.

"I'd never do anything like that intentionally. To make you feel like an object . . . I don't give a damn that you play professional baseball other than I'm a fan of the team and I love to cheer you on. When I think of you, kindness and generosity are the first things that come to mind, not the spotlight of baseball."

"I believe you, still . . . you left a kind man waiting for your hello." He stared at our entwined hands.

"I'm ashamed." I drew in a deep breath. "And embarrassed."

"Tell me why you felt you couldn't call me." He squeezed my hand slightly. "I heard what you said about LA and the way it took you into another world. I understand those new feelings. It wasn't too long ago I was drafted from college and could barely contain my excitement. I've already told you I support that part of your life. What's the real reason?"

"Being in LA made me realize . . ." I gulped. "Our timing isn't right." The pressure pounded in my temples. "I'll hold you back."

"How?"

"My insecurities. They rise up constantly, Ryan. I've already caused you too much trouble because of my fears. I can't compete with the other women out there. They can give you what you want. I can't. Shall I go on? I've got a long list."

There, I said it. Now you understand, you're better off with someone your age.

"What do you mean, *our timing*? Timing of what?" His thumb rubbed mine. "Tell me why you feel that way. I need to know. I need to hear what you have to say so I can understand you."

I don't even understand myself. How do I explain that the only example of a relationship I've seen is my parents and that example is twisted?

I can't take the chance that you'll trade me for a vice like the bottle my father coveted.

I can't take the chance time with the guys is more important than time with me. They'll take you away the same as my father let his friends take him away from Mom.

I can't take the chance another woman catches your eye.

I can't bear to hear, "I'm sorry, I know I said I'd support your career, but I need someone who can be with me on the road."

I can't take the chance you'll drop me once you get tired of dealing with my dark places.

I don't want to get the call I know will come from another woman who tells me she's captured your attention. I know you'll feel too badly to tell me it's over and instead I'll hear the whispers all around me, "she doesn't know."

I don't want to live in an alternate world of fantasy and detachment like my mother did because I'm facing too much pain from someone I once thought was amazing.

Jerry's safe. Don't you get it? He's safe.

I need to be safe.

I need to be around people that make me feel safe.

My education is safe.

I'm used to working hard and keeping everyone at a distance while I strive for my complete independence.

You're too confident.

CRANBERRY AND ORANGE JUICE

You promise everything I see for myself but haven't achieved.
Too many people desire you.
I don't want to get lost.
I don't want to feel lost.
With you, I'm lost.

Chapter 17

Can I be that Woman for You?

"All week long, I've been up early and out late." I began to summarize my reasons for giving up on our relationship even though I'd initially feared it was what he was going to do.

My fear of being abandoned was choking me. Wouldn't allow me to explore. At the first sign of trouble I ran.

Ryan and I sipped our cranberry and orange juice drinks. Throughout the majority of his questioning I'd remained silent, trying to gather my thoughts.

Now it was time he heard me.

Maybe after I was through explaining myself, he'd understand I wasn't right for him.

"I was on the run before you left or your road trip. The pace continued through Yountville. When you finally called me I was beat. The edge I found myself teetering on . . . I mean, you didn't respond to any of my texts or the pictures I sent you during the day. Where were you?"

"I already said—"

"I tried to reach you for hours. Then I'd just gotten to sleep when you finally called me back. I was overly tired, and . . . I guess . . . well, I was pissed off."

"Pissed off at me?"

"Yes."

"Why?"

"I don't know, exactly. I hadn't heard from you. To top it all off, I had to get up again the next day to go to LA with Alex. She said she was picking me up at nine. Instead she called me at six, announcing she'd be at my door in thirty minutes. I had to rush around after only a few hours of sleep. I hadn't even packed."

"Why couldn't you get to sleep?" His voice was laced with concern and innocence. "You just said you didn't talk with me because you were so tired. In fact, you pretty much hung up on me after you said good night."

"Because." I answered defiantly. *Don't try to put me in the corner. I'll cut you right out of my life.*

"Because?" He kept pushing.

"Because I couldn't reach you. I couldn't *reach* you," I emphasized. "You said you were in meetings. Okay. Before they started you couldn't have sent me a quick text? You just accused me of doing the same things to you when I was in LA, right? Well, I was busy, too, Ryan. Then—"

"Wait a minute," Ryan interrupted. "Let's back up. I told you what I was doing. I was in meetings."

"Yeah."

"You don't believe me." He put his head down.

"No. I'm sorry, Ryan. I don't."

"We need to discuss that later." His finger ticked as if he'd made a checkmark on an invisible piece of paper. "Go on."

"I was literally on the run all the next day. I met so many business contacts; I felt as if I was in a different world. I *wanted* that world—not this one. I knew I could start my career and my adult life with the contacts I'd made during those two days in

Newport Beach. In fact, I know if I asked her, Alex would help me right now."

"Who did you meet?" He scratched his cheek.

"Lieutenant Governor Xavier Del Sol, executives from Alex's Agency and the head designers of Chanel, Gucci, and St. John. What struck me the most was how so many of their employees were around my age. They were already off and running in their careers." The scenes in LA rushed through my mind like a slideshow. "It made me reconsider everything about having a relationship with any man." I put my hand on his. "It wasn't right that I didn't call you. I admit that. The more time that went by, the more embarrassed I was. I know I sound confused. I *am* confused."

Two couples came into the lounge laughing and I was momentarily distracted.

We were silent.

Our eyes locked on each other.

"I don't know what to do about us." My voice cracked as I looked at the worried expression on Ryan's face. "We really should stop seeing each other before it gets too hurtful." *Keep going, Nicky. You have to talk about this. Stop hiding your feelings for the sake of others. You need to heal, too.* "For your sake, I think we should move on. I felt so close to you when you left. Then, the longer we were apart . . ." It was difficult to continue. I could see the hurt in his eyes and my heart felt as if it was breaking in two pieces.

"Get it out," his voice cracked.

"The longer we were apart, the more I was sure it would be better to stay away rather than take a chance on a relationship with you." I let out a long sigh. The pressure in my face was bordering an explosion.

"So you *have* given up." His body seemed to collapse on itself.

"No."

He looked up.

"I think about you a lot. If you want to know the truth, I told Jenise it's you I want, Ryan. But your desires and dreams are about a life I haven't experienced. We haven't even begun anything and already we seem . . . like we're doomed."

"Don't say that." He closed his eyes.

"I'm sorry. I hate talking about any of this." Two beats of silence. "Do you want me to stop?"

"We need to get over the obstacle in our way," he encouraged. "I don't want you to stop . . . no matter what."

"I haven't dated more than one boy my *own* age let alone someone like you." I played with the hair on his forearm. "You should be dating someone who isn't confused about her life and knows what she wants. Someone . . . ." I looked at the ceiling. The hotel had little lights on it that were like stars. "Someone who wouldn't second-guess being with a lovely man like you.

"We need to face it—you need a woman with cool confidence, who can handle all the limelight that comes with you and your female interruptions. The perfect woman for you is a woman who doesn't get weak when you kiss her. Wouldn't it be better to have someone who knows what to do with you romantically—you know, sex, I mean? I feel like falling to the ground every time you take me in your arms."

Ryan placed his hand on my cheek.

Ooh, your beautiful eyes.

"First of all, you were invited to a dinner party with people who carry international fame—if that doesn't give you a clue about how you present yourself . . . How could you think I wouldn't be proud to have you with me wherever we go? Second, I told you I've never taken any woman in my arms in public or kissed her like I did with you. I've managed my public persona carefully and kept my emotions in check at all times. I don't care about that with you. I welcome the attention. The more that people know we're together, the better off we are. In fact, I intend to take you in my arms and kiss you whenever I can—in private or in public."

Really? That would be . . . nice; so nice.

"That is, if it's okay with you." His wry grin appeared.

I looked down at the table unable to hide my smile.

"Yeah, it would be okay with me." *Just when I start to get my sea legs, he says this stuff.*

"I know you haven't had the chance to explore other relationships. I'm an adjustment in your life. I'm asking you to let go with a baby step." He pinched his fingers together, dramatizing his words. "You might find being with me isn't as daunting as the picture you've drawn in your head. You could be terrified when I say this . . . I know you're the woman for me and I'm the man for you."

There wasn't the slightest waver in his voice.

"It's . . ." My thighs closed, tightening against my hands, which were folded together as if in prayer. "Way more than that."

"Tell me what it is." He put up two fingers. The waiter nodded, understanding Ryan's signal for two more drinks.

I knew it was time to reveal everything.

Each of us fidgeted.

We looked around the lounge, focusing on everything but each other, waiting for our drinks to arrive.

My cell phone beeped.

I hesitated.

Decided not to get it.

Several women walked by us giving Ryan the eye.

He didn't flinch.

I did.

They reinforced everything I was going to say.

Our drinks arrived.

I stirred mine, watching the cherry sink to the bottom.

"Let's start from the top," I said nervously. "You're—"

"Excuse me," a soft, feminine voice interrupted us.

Our bodies jerked, as if they were drawn out of our solitary bubble, scraping against its sharp, jagged edges. I looked up to see a bombshell of a woman—gorgeous, blonde, her makeup in place, dressed in chic couture, and long, long legs decorated with a diamond anklet and in expensive heels—standing at our table.

"Ryan?"

He blinked a few times. His face flushed.

Is that anger or embarrassment?

"How are you, Tabitha?" He looked at me and seemed to gulp as he answered.

I shook my head.

Closed and then opened my eyes.

Looked at the table.

He stumbled for a few seconds.

"It's good to see you." She put her hand on Ryan's forearm and traced his wrist with her finger.

Oh, God.

"I'm busy, Tabitha. Something I can do for you?" He withdrew his arm. Put it under the table. Sat back as if trying to break contact with her.

"Oh, I see." She leaned over and flattened her palms on the table. Doing so, let the top of her dress dip to reveal a view of her breasts. "I didn't know you were . . . are you exclusive?"

"Yes."

"I'll make this brief, then. I was wondering," she licked her bottom lip. "Are we getting together like last year? The summer is dwindling away, and . . . Kevin, Lance, Sheila, Hunter . . . God, I don't remember everyone there were so many of us. They've all stopped by and I haven't seen you. None of the girls have. Those nights were endless, weren't they? Sorry to interrupt." She extended her hand to me. "Tabitha Sable."

What kind of a name is that?

"Nicky Young." I shook her hand.

"And she was just leaving," Ryan pushed up from the table and stood next to her.

"I can take a hint. Don't worry, Ryan. I'm not here to ruin your evening. We have a couple of new dance routines. I'd love for you to stop by the club. Everyone would love to see you. Most of the regulars have said hello a few times. Now I understand why we haven't seen you." She turned to me. "You must come with him, Nicky. Well, cheers. So sorry to interrupt."

She moved close to Ryan as if she wanted to give him a kiss on the cheek . . . or more. He backed away and she turned with an elegant grace, looked seductively over her shoulder, and with hooded eyes, blew Ryan a kiss.

I watched her as if that kiss floated through the air and onto Ryan's cheek. I felt defeated. The confidence I'd begun to build with him had been shot down.

I was ready to give up.

"Sorry about—"

"What are you sorry for?" I was shaken. "That you're attractive? Desired? An athlete that continues to draw any number of people to him wherever he goes? What exactly are you sorry about?"

"Sorry she interrupted us," he said calmly.

"Yeah." My voice was laced with resignation. "What just happened? That's everything I was trying to say to you in a nutshell. She shouldn't bother me. She does, though. And she knows what she's got and how to give it you. That she can come right up to you even though you're sitting here with me? They'll never stop. And you let her continue right in the middle of a serious conversation. Tabitha Sable? Let me guess. She's an exotic dancer?"

Silence.

"Why didn't you stop her?"

Silence.

"The way she rubbed your arm, blew you a kiss . . ." I shook my head again, not certain if I wanted to continue. "I know you've been intimate with her."

"What she did was completely out of line," Ryan's hand swiped the air.

"Out of line or not, you let her interrupt."

"I know her."

"Obviously."

"I was only being polite so she'd leave."

"Ha! So polite that she leaned over to give you a view of her breasts in case you forgot what they look like. Let's face it. She's got something I don't and she wants you to remember what it is. I'll never have that kind of swagger."

"I'm not looking for swagger," he replied bluntly. "I didn't want to make a scene, that's all. I was about to ask her to leave when she wrapped it up and I let her to leave on her own."

"Oh yeah?" I challenged. *I don't believe you.* "You're not looking for women who exude sensuality and confidence and yet that's all you've been with. You don't want swagger? Really?"

"No."

"Fine. You expect me to have the strength of women like *that?"* I nodded in Tabitha's direction. "I won't, Ryan. Hear me and understand what I just said is a fact. Women like her will haunt me forever. Anyway, I'll continue where I left off." I sighed, watching Tabitha confidently weave her way through the lounge. "Even though you let her interrupt me." Tears welled in my eyes. "What I just witnessed? I'm second. It was like you didn't care."

Just like my mother was second.

Just like my father chose the bottle over his family.

I'm used to being second.

He rose from his seat and lifted me into an embrace.

As I lay against his chest, I saw Tabitha looking from the corner of her eye.

"I'm sorry." He kissed my temple. "I hardly said a word to her. I just wanted her to leave. I didn't want a scene. Everyone has a camera ready in his or her phone and an overreaction causes publicity. I can't risk it. Please believe me."

"I'm trying."

"Hey." His hand cupped my cheek. "Please focus on me."

I hesitated.

Cleared my throat.

"Okay. Let's continue." I pulled myself together and sat down.

Ryan pulled his chair close to mine.

"You're almost twenty-six. Been to college. Successful in every way. You're confident like Tabitha and others around the ballpark. You know what you want. I'm the opposite of everything you are and the people you know." I nodded in Ms. Bombshell's direction. "I don't know what the hell I want except my career. One thing's for damn sure—I am not going to battle women like that."

"You don't have to battle anyone," he said softly. One of his hands rubbed my back.

"Right."

"Please believe me when I reveal my heart to you." He reached for my hand and held it. "I'm not a liar. I wouldn't say things to lead you on."

"I believe you have good intentions . . ." I hesitated.

"That's as far as I go? There's nothing real in here?" He put my hand on his heart.

"I know you're real and you think you're in love with me. I'm still confused and trying to figure it out. And when you say things like *I'm the woman for you* and *you're the man for me*, it sounds like you want us to be together for a long time. How can you really commit like that? You don't know me. *I don't know me.*" My stare was serious and unwavering. "Is it even fair to talk about commitment when I haven't done anything yet?"

"Making promises that mean forever is easy, Nicky. I know exactly what I want. I'm sure about us. I'm ready for us to be a couple."

"When I go to college?" My gaze was firm. "I want to stay out late without worrying the man I'm committed to will be upset because I'm with friends. I want to experience boyfriends, and swagger through a club like Tabitha did and . . ."

I stopped there, not wanting to say the words aloud.

"And what?" He asked the question appearing so naïve I felt guilty when I answered him.

"When I'm more comfortable, you know, that time may never come as backward as I am about boys, but if it does . . . it seems like I'll never get there, but if I do, I mean, well, I might want to have sex with a few boys at college." I hesitated and then added, "You know, like you did with the college girls. And of course now, with women like Tabitha."

"Oh."

I looked in his eyes.

"Remember, I heard you talk about all the sex you had in college when you and Kevin were in the outfield last year."

Silence.

"I've just graduated high school. It's not fair to expect me to be exclusive before I get to explore the world. I've played it safe all my life, Ryan. I don't want to look back and regret that I compromised—again—instead of being brave with my life. I'm afraid I'll be sorry that when I'm older, I gave up the kind of opportunities that come to us only when we're young. You didn't want to be committed to one girl at eighteen, so why should it be any different for me?"

He never looked away.

He didn't have an answer.

I should have waited for him to say something. Nervous as usual, I couldn't wait and started again.

"I want to date you. But to swear to be true and not look at another boy?" My finger rimmed my glass. "I don't know. How will we handle it when our lives are in two different places? What do we do when we cross paths for only an hour or two each day and then not for a week at a time?"

"We—"

"Be honest," I interrupted. "Don't you expect me to drop everything for you?" More silence. "I want parties, boyfriends, staying out late, study groups, having pizza together with new friends—that's what I'm going to do in college. You won't like it, but it's a part of the experiences I should have, right?"

Chapter 18

Please Commit to Me

"❤he life you envision . . . I want you to have it." Ryan jumped in, perhaps unable to remain silent any longer. "I'll wait for you when it comes to having your career and graduating college. I promise I will. I have to be honest, though. I couldn't stand to wait while you see other boys. I do want you to see me exclusively. I know that's asking a lot. I really . . . I know we're meant to be."

"How?"

"Your magnificence has called to me from the day you walked into the bleachers. I felt it—felt *you*. You speak to me." His hands tightened around his glass. "When I told your parents I couldn't take my eyes off you from the first moment you walked into the stadium, I wasn't telling them some fluff story to make them feel good."

Oh, damn! He's murder.

"I feel the same way. When you introduced yourself—"

"No, Nicky, you're not hearing me." He leaned forward. "It wasn't at our introduction that I noticed you. When you sat in the bleachers, even before your first performance, the kindness and love you carry radiates from your soul. To me, the entire area of the stadium lit up. My heart was on fire from the moment I spotted you. You. Are. Light."

"I don't know what to say." *I'm exhausted.*

"I didn't mean to make you stumble." His chest expanded in a deep breath. "I just want you to know how I see you."

I reached for his hand.

"You're a warm man." I stroked his fingers. "You deserve to have what you want in every way. You need *that* woman." I nodded in Tabitha's direction.

"I need *you*." His voice rose in volume.

"Do you know what the biggest obstacle is for me?" I looked down and then raised my eyes to his.

"Tell me. Please don't hold back."

"I'll bring you down while I try and find myself."

"No you won't. How—"

"You'll constantly have to reassure me. It's not only women like Tabitha. She was only the boldest. Several have walked by giving you those *come on* eyes. They're waiting for me to get up so they can sit down and take my place. You can try and reassure me all you want, but I know I'll face them every day we're together."

"You don't have to worry—"

"That's just one fear. I have about a thousand others. I can't— scratch that, I *won't*—handle the kind of intensity that follows you." I reaffirmed my position. "You're a part of a special life, Ryan. You've achieved what few men do and this is your chance to have an incredibly sexy, gorgeous woman at your side. I don't want to know someone is waiting for you the moment I make a mistake or have to look polished every second so your eye doesn't wander. I'm tired of walking on eggshells and being afraid. I've done that enough with my family."

"You're afraid of me?" He looked as if he were a little boy.

"No," I shook my head. "No, I'm not afraid of you at all. What I'm afraid of is not being able to be myself with you, saying the wrong thing, pissing you off because I don't have the maturity you do and exhausting you with all my fears. One day, you'll leave on your road trip and drift away in frustration or anger. Trust me, when you really get to know my family and our dark secrets, you'll leave." I crossed my ankles under the table. "There's a lot of crap that comes with me. For the man who wants to be my partner? I don't know how to make room for an intimate relationship."

I wanted to stop but couldn't.

My Evil Twin wasn't a silent being and she was pulling on me, perhaps giving me the courage to say what I had to . . . *needed to*.

"Being with you won't help me get over any of the feelings I just revealed. Plus, the big killer for me is you leaving every week or so. That fact alone is deadly to someone like me." I could see he was struggling. "I'm sorry. I'm just trying to be honest. A man like you . . . you're too much for my first relationship. You have an aura that's pure sex appeal. I've seen it. Plenty of others see it. I mean, let's face it, *I'm* attracted to it."

"That's a bad thing?" he pushed.

"For most people, no. Maybe if *I* had some experience with sex, I might understand. I can't relate to why you've been with so many women," I continued. "There's tons of stuff about you online—more than just baseball. I haven't even looked that deeply and I've found dozens of posts with you and Miss Somebody or Other and all of them in little panties or low cut dresses or bikinis."

A variety of emotions washed over his face.

Mere seconds passed between a look of what seemed like sadness, anger, frustration, and . . . hope?

"I'm tired of fighting," I managed to say in a voice so raw it didn't sound like my own. "What I want is for someone to fight for *me* for a change."

Another attractive female came to our table, obviously dressed for an evening out.

Her face lit up.

Her eyes were bright.

Her body was already opening to Ryan.

She started to speak.

Before she could, Ryan stood up.

"I'll be right back, sweetheart." His stare never wavered from me and our hands stayed connected longer than usual. It was as if he'd sent a silent message to me.

"How rude," the woman standing at our table scoffed. Even so, she didn't leave. "You his girlfriend?"

I was afraid to even speak. I had concerns about social media and what she might post about Ryan or me. I smiled like an idiot, not knowing what to do and pulled out my phone pretending to text someone. *Go away. Maybe I'll get up and give her my seat. This is all too much and I know it.*

A minute later the host came over to our table.

"Here she is." Ryan stood behind him. "Please don't let it happen again. I tipped you well so we'd be left alone."

"Follow me, Miss," the host said to Ryan's visitor. "They've asked not to be disturbed. I'm sorry, Sir. Mam."

Ryan nodded, accepting the apology.

She snorted and followed the host.

"I was saying—"

"You're tired of fighting. You won't have to do that for me." Ryan settled in his seat and continued without hesitation from the exact point of where our conversation was interrupted. "What do you think I'm doing?"

His blue eyes were penetrating. One of his big hands cupped my cheek while the other hand exposed my palm. He circled it with a long, thick finger.

"I don't understand your question," I exhaled roughly.

"I'm battling for your heart, Nicky. I'm fighting so that you'll see only me. I'm fighting to take away your hurt. I'm fighting to gain your confidence and love. I'm fighting for us."

Why does he make me feel so defenseless? After everything I've said, how can he be so certain? And am I still interested?

He leaned so close that I had no room on the table's surface. His hands framed my cheeks.

My body naturally responded and moved toward him.

He kissed me.

I kissed him.

Even as I tried to push him away, we came together.

It seemed as if our spirits had lifted from the table, the lounge, the hotel, and soared somewhere above all of it. Had a part of life that was meant for the two of us already begun?

His lips were gentle as they sealed my mouth.

Love was around and on me.

"I've had enough meaningless sex," he whispered. "I don't want someone who's used to public situations or knows what to do with my kisses. I could have had that woman already." He paused as if mulling over his thoughts. "You'll think this is nonsense, but . . ." He looked down at the table. His finger drew circles on it. The little boy was with me again. "I've already imagined what it will be like when you go to Stanford."

"You have?" My mouth dropped open.

"You come out of my bedroom in the morning. I prepare your coffee. You're sweet and sleepy-eyed, like that night after you sang the national anthem. I remember that look on your face as if it was moments ago. I'll never forget it."

I tried to look away. He held my cheeks.

I had to look into his eyes.

I *had* to.

"You came down from your bedroom in your robe determined and fiery. You were ready to let me have it, weren't you?" His silent demand forced an answer from me.

I smiled at the memory.

How can I stay focused with this boy? I can't fight him.

"We sit at the kitchen counter. Talk about your day. I fix you breakfast. Kiss you goodbye. Go for a workout. Play my baseball game. When we come home, we kiss. Have dinner or a cup of hot chocolate. Talk about everything. I'll help you with quizzes and tests. Be there for your graduation. Watch as you rise in the business world. I dream coming home from a road trip and you're there to pick me up at the airport. I'll cover your face in kisses in front of anyone. Everyone. Most of all"—his eyes hooded—"I look forward to the nights when I'm on and in your body."

Embarrassed as I was, I had to let him know I could stay focused with him. Even as I felt taken over, my body possessed by his stare, I kept eye contact.

"You're putting limits on us because of a picture that's in *your* head, not the picture *I* have. You see us only in these moments, fixed and unchanging. That's not real. We'll adapt." He played with a strand of my hair. "We're limitless. I know we can make room for the dreams each of us has. At least, I'm pretty sure I've read that in you."

We didn't move.

We were quiet.

It was as if the hotel lounge had closed and our energy filled the entire space.

I heard no other sounds.

I saw no one but Ryan.

"I want to be good for you." I put my hand on his heart. "I want to be such an outstanding woman that I'll blow your mind. I have so many doubts . . . so many."

"I'm a good man." He kissed me again.

"I believe you. Only, I don't know if I can be a good woman in the relationship you're looking to have with me. I'll think about everything you said." I looked all over his face. "I promise I will."

An ocean swell had arrived.

I was overcome.

Muscular, tattooed arms wrapped me inside them. I felt as if he were a thick, succulent, leafy plant. Wet. Growing. Covering my heart. Attaching to everything about me.

"Nicky," he called to me with seductive notes of comfort and reassurance. He made me want to believe in what we could be together. While looking into my eyes, he took my hands in his.

"Please stop seeing Jerry. Try our relationship first," he pleaded. "We won't be able to get anywhere if you have him as a safety net. I need you to leap with me. Take a chance. Let me soothe your fears. Let's figure out if we work together. If we don't, then okay. You'll be free to explore and experiment with him or other boys."

There it was, Ryan had asked me to commit to him, just like Jenise told me he would.

My head told me to run.

This boy was coming on much too fast.

But my heart . . . it sang and filled with the gloriousness of new joy like never before. The tenderness he'd shown made me want to embrace him, lie down next to him and let him take me inside his life in every way.

My defenses softened.

Moment by moment Ryan weakened my resistance.

I wanted to let go.

He made me want to jump into magnificence.

That night, it was as if a thin veil of cloth lifted. Layer after layer of resistance peeled away, leaving me more transparent and vulnerable. I could see my struggle form a mist and swirl in a circle around me.

"I promise I'll think seriously about everything we discussed. Jerry and I are good friends. We grew up together and I can't just cut him out of my life because you're uncomfortable." *You can't? You've been good at cutting people away so far.* "I want and need to have my friends like you had at my age. We're going to the same college, so we'll see each other there anyway."

He kissed my hand and put it on his heart.

"Tell him you're with me. Won't you please tell Jerry you're mine and I'm yours?"

He unlocked our hands, turned them over and kissed my palms, my wrists, and continued to travel in slow motion up my arms—all the way up my arms.

"Yes, I will. Soon, Ryan." Weaker by the second, I finally pushed the words out of my mouth.

My cheek felt the soft caress of his hand.

I closed my eyes.

His fingertips, rough from where he'd built up his calluses from pitching, ran across my face. When his wrist turned, I could sense the small movements and twitches in it. I indulged in the possibility that he was warming me up for something more.

God, he's taking me apart little by little, telling me everything any normal woman would want to hear. I wonder if he can see my face throbbing.

"Let's go see my brother." He stood and offered his hand. I took it and walked to the elevator with him. We stepped in.

It felt as if I'd stepped into another story—another life.

We held each other until we arrived at the eighth floor.

Chapter 19

Chris Tilton, Jr.

"**H**ere's my brother's room." Ryan stopped at a door several removed from the elevator. It was at the beginning of a long hallway.

"How old is he?" I leaned against the wall.

"Thirty." His cheek twitched.

"Four years older." I looked at him from the corner of my eye. He seemed hesitant to knock. "Sort of like my sister and me."

"Hmm. Like you and your sister, indeed." He flashed a smile.

He let go of my hand.

I felt cold without it.

I was vacant.

Needed to have the warmth I'd felt only a second earlier, when a part of his body was connected with my own. I reached for him. Brought his hand to my lips. Kissed it and stood at Ryan's side.

I felt him gather me up against his big body.

Oh no . . . my legs.

"Nicky." His voice was soft.

His body pressed on my innocence as he framed me against the wall. Bulging forearms were on each side of my head, caging me. I felt his body push out to mine. This little preview of what it would feel like to be his woman, made my not-so-innocent inner sexual priestess announce her presence. His chin nudged upward against my cheek. Soft lips opened my mouth. Letting his breath come into me was like a hot desert wind before the monsoon. Oh, how I wanted that warm rain on my body.

The sounds in his throat made pulses stir from deep inside my belly. Our mouths teased playfully. Gently. I gave myself over to the story his kisses were telling me. His arms hesitated and rested on my shoulders. His ear delicately brushed mine.

I could feel his heart beating as he pressed against my breasts. They ached for my surrender. My flame was becoming fire. My hands rose slowly to his thick neck. I was ready to welcome more of his rhythms just as his body lifted.

Oh no . . . more please.

"Are you starting to understand?" Ryan's moist lips touched my ear as he said the words.

"Mmm."

"You may not see everything we're capable of," he tilted my chin back with a gentle nudge. "But you will."

That's good, because right now I could be capable of way more than you know.

He turned to knock on his brother's door.

"Wait!" I reached for his arm. "Let me catch my breath!"

Oh, damn that shitty smile he has. He knows I'm weak. If his brother answers the door after what he just did I'll be like a fish flopping on the ground.

Ryan's arms flexed. Luscious biceps began to orchestrate their symphony, ready to play my body and ripple through my soul. If he embraced me in that slow, sensual way he had perfected, I knew I might not recover before his brother opened the door.

"Please don't hug me again." I put my hand out. It landed on his chest. My palm burned with heat. "I'll never be ready to meet your brother if you do that."

He laughed his sexy laugh and knocked on the door.

Easy for you to laugh; I can't breathe.

"How are you, Ryan?" A man who was obviously Ryan's brother answered. The two shared a brief handshake.

"Great. You?" Ryan's body stiffened.

"Just hangin' loose, feelin' the love," he kidded. "Come on in." Chris stepped aside. "You must be Nicky. Pleasure to finally meet you. Chris Tilton." He extended his hand and I took it.

Their smiles seem forced.

The two men seemed to purposefully move their bodies so they wouldn't touch or make direct eye contact.

The air thickened.

You guys didn't hug . . . what's going on here?

Chris had a certain mature look that his little brother didn't have. I loved how I could sometimes see Ryan's baby face when he smiled, while laugh lines paved a few roads near Chris's eyes. The roundness of getting older filled his face. His hair fell to his shoulders and was darker and longer than Ryan's. His body was slender and not quite as tall.

The hotel room was modern with floor-to-ceiling windows that looked out on the Embarcadero's Ferry Building and its famous clock. There was a small lanai, which offered views of the bay. It was furnished with two chairs and a bistro table. Luxuriously appointed in dark woods and marble tabletops, the small living room included a working area with a wooden desk, a large curved-screen television, a small sofa, and four chairs that surrounded a matching coffee table. On it were four wine glasses and a bottle of something chilling in an ice bucket. A king-size bed rested against the window with the puffiest comforter I'd ever seen on top of it. A crisp white coverlet and throw blanket made me want to bounce on the bed.

"You guys look great," Chris commented. "Going somewhere special?"

"Dinner and dancing." Ryan looked at me with a smile that had bloomed with warmth. His proud chest seemed swollen with the anticipation of our evening.

"Sounds nice. Let's sit down," Chris gestured to the four chairs surrounding the table. "Frances is freshening up; she'll be out in a minute. I ordered some sparkling cider for us." He opened the bottle and poured it in the four glasses.

That's sweet. He doesn't drink either? Or is he sensitive to his brother's resolve?

"How long are you in town?" Ryan questioned.

You don't know? That's a little weird.

"Friday night when we leave for Seattle. After your game." He playfully socked Ryan's arm. "That is, if you can get us tickets."

Finally, an act of affection!

Ryan's smile seemed a surprise as if his brother would have no interest in his career. It was timid and bashful. I wondered if it stemmed from a time when the boys were little.

"Mom sends her love. She's looking forward to seeing you in a few weeks." Chris plugged the bottle and put it back on ice. "I didn't know she was coming out so soon after her last visit. Isn't that a little unusual for you two to see each other so quickly?"

"I'm sure it surprised you." Ryan's sarcasm was obvious.

"Let's not go there," Chris snapped back.

"You went there first, *older brother*."

Ten seconds.

"Are you going home after Seattle, Chris?" I tried to break the heavy air.

"This is only the beginning of our tour." As he shared his schedule with us, I found out he was a musician and in a band. They were about to tour the western United States for most of the next two months. As he told us about some of the stops they were scheduled to make, Frances came out of the bathroom.

190

She was a striking woman with well-defined cheekbones, a thin, straight figure, black hair, and magnificent violet eyes.

"Nice to see you, Ryan." She gave him a hug.

"You too, Frances." He returned the embrace and kissed her cheek.

"Nicky, it's lovely to meet you." Instead of shaking my hand, she hugged me. She seemed to be an exuberant woman.

"Nice to meet you, too, Frances. My God, you have beautiful eyes," I said aloud. "I've never seen purple eyes."

"Thank you," she said graciously. "They're violet, actually."

"Violet," I repeated. "Beautiful."

"To family." Chris offered a glass of cider to each of us and then raised his. "May we be together often."

"To family," we all repeated in unison and took a drink.

Our early evening began pleasantly enough. Still, I knew something was off. Everyone seemed to be going a kind of robotic motion. The typical notes of excitement and the drama of family were missing from their voices.

No arms or hands waved in the air to express joy.

The lack of passion was uncomfortable.

As we talked, I felt the rift between the two brothers.

I was no stranger to buried family secrets. I could have run entire seminars on how to hide them.

It was half past five when the two brothers stood up.

"Excuse us for a minute," Chris announced. He held open the hotel room door for his brother and then followed him into the hallway. The door closed automatically behind them. Frances continued talking even as their voices escalated outside.

"Brothers." She shook her head. "Always arguing. Do you have any siblings?"

"One sister."

"Do you battle like this?"

"No. Although . . . we've had our rough spots. How about you? Any brothers or sisters?"

"I'm an only child." She took a sip of the cider and then put the wine glass on the table. "I like your earrings."

"Thanks, they're my sister's—the fashionista in our house. She's got a closet full of clothes and all this jewelry. I'm not much for any of that, really. In fact, my grandmother gave me—"

The brothers came back into the room.

I was distracted, trying to understand Ryan's expression. He wasn't smiling. His eyes were unfocused.

"Sorry about that," Chris interrupted. "What did we miss?" He bent over and kissed Frances on the side of her head.

"Nicky was saying . . ." She waited for me to complete my sentence. When I didn't, she coached, "Your grandmother . . ."

"I've forgotten." I struggled to remember but the moment was lost. My only concern was how Ryan was feeling.

"Where is Romeo taking you for dinner?" Chris chided.

"I don't know." Annoyed at the nickname he used for his brother, I bit my lip and held back the things I wanted to say about his lack of etiquette. "Where *are* we going, honey?"

"Robin's." Ryan's answer was short. The way his mouth curved in a smile made it obvious he enjoyed the pet name I'd used for him in front of his brother.

"Ooh! Robin's is delicious," Frances added. "Remember, Chris? We all went there last time we visited."

Something was—or wasn't—happening between the two men. I didn't understand how everyone could keep talking around *it*.

I felt the dangerous air, charged with something uneasy.

I was sorry I was in the room.

Their bodies wouldn't let them hide the awkwardness.

As Frances began talking to me once again, the two men moved to the lanai and closed the sliding glass door behind them. They tried keeping their conversation private. Their frustrations carried into the room with the obvious sounds of anger. When Ryan put his head down, I could see he was still just a boy and he was hurting. I wanted to hear what they were saying and reassure him it would all be okay.

"Where did you and Ryan meet?" Frances asked.

"What?" My head jerked hard. I was back in the moment.

"You and Ryan—where did you meet?" she repeated.

"The ballpark."

"How?"

What do I say? I cheer for the Goliaths? That sounds ridiculous.

"I presented a business marketing plan. He introduced himself." I proceeded cautiously.

"What kind of business marketing?"

"An entertainment idea I had."

"Like what?" she shrugged both shoulders and raised both hands, turning her palms up so they faced the ceiling.

I explained my business plan the same way I'd done with Ryan in Yountville, leaving out the part about me being on a cheer team.

"How did you catch Ryan's eye? We've never seen him so enamored with a woman. His feelings are so obvious for you."

"You'll have to ask Ryan, I guess."

"Well then, what caught *your* eye?" I felt as if she had grabbed a fireplace poker and used it with every question.

"His eyes, the way he uses his voice . . . his voice is like a melody to me."

"Tell me more," she giggled.

"Well his eyes tell everything about him; I feel as if I can see into his soul when he talks to me." I was into it, proud to brag about the man I knew. "He hides nothing when he talks. He's so expressive and he easily reveals the gentle the man inside him. And his voice, you know, he's got the gift of—"

Ryan seemed to burst through the sliding glass doors as he returned to the room. "Nicky, you ready?"

I nodded.

Yes! Take me out of here!

"I hope we're able to do something together before we leave town." She stood, smoothing her dress.

"Me, too." I followed her lead.

Not sure if I want that, but maybe if she stops questioning how I met her brother-in-law . . . On the other hand, I've just met part of Ryan's family and that's pretty great. I'd love to get to know that side of him.

We all stood in a circle.

The last few words of unimportant chitchat filled the room. As they talked about events from their past of which I hadn't been a part, I thought about the people I'd met since cheering for the Goliaths. High on my priority list was getting over my resistance when it came to making new relationships and meeting people. I considered how I'd already met more than I'd ever dreamed of so soon in my life. These people were successful. They didn't sleep on the beach next to a bonfire. They had money, could afford to stay at five-star hotels and some were in government and international business.

"Nicky met the lieutenant governor last week," Ryan boasted.

"*Really*," Frances said with wide eyes. "How wonderful."

"It was!" I shared my enthusiasm. "He gave me his card and told me I could look him up when I graduate college."

"What college?" she asked.

"Stanford."

"How wonderful!" Chris exclaimed. "You're major?"

"Business marketing," I said. *Please don't ask me what year I'm in. I'll die if I say I'm a freshman.*

"Tell us about the lieutenant governor," Frances interjected.

"Well, I was in LA with my friend, Alex. She's a model and she travels all over. She planned a day for me and he was part of it. I was helping her agency with some errands. But before that, what was so ironic is that I volunteered with Ryan at Veterans' Hospital. I've learned a lot about brain trauma there, and that's why I could talk with him so intelligently when I interviewed him. I really owe how well things went at my meetings to your brother." I slipped my arm around Ryan's waist, partially to claim him in front of Chris and partially to take a breath. "It was everything I learned from being with Ryan that gave me the opportunity in LA."

"Thank you," Ryan said, kissing me on my cheek.

"Oh, you two are so cute!" Frances clasped her hands together while Chris snorted.

I hoped I'd given Ryan enough credit to quash any more sarcasm from his brother. Maybe it hadn't been enough. He'd been condescending with a few of his comments toward his younger brother, and while I understood fault generally fell on both sides, I was defensive of the man I knew . . . I knew . . . *I loved.*

"Seems like you'll have your hands full trying to keep up with this one, brother," Chris said flippantly.

This one? Maybe my lengthy speech made me his target. Does he mean I was one of dozens Ryan introduced to them?

"Nicky, so nice to meet you." Chris shook my hand. "I hope we'll see each other again soon. Continued success with college. See you tomorrow, brother."

We hugged briefly and wished each other good night.

As we waited for the elevator, Ryan's eyes seemed caught in a rising storm.

He held onto my hand, keeping my arm tight around his waist and stared straight ahead.

The color in his face had drained away.

When the doors opened, I stepped forward, but he squeezed my hand and didn't move.

The doors closed.

"Can you let my hand go?" I whispered. When he released me, I stood on my tiptoes to kiss his cheek. I took his hands in mine.

"Are you sure you still want to go out? I don't care if you'd rather drop me at home. You don't seem—"

I couldn't finish before his arms wrapped around me. His embrace tightened as if he tried to squeeze us into one being. When he pressed my body to the stucco-covered walls at the elevator, my breasts felt the weight of his chest. I realized he was sobbing. My cheek was wet with his tears. Returning his embrace as hard as I could, I did the things I'd always done when comforting a friend: patted his back, offered words of comfort, and did my best to reassure him it would be all right.

He's my man.

Sliding my hands through his golden brown hair, all I wanted was to find a way to make him feel better. I cradled his gentle spirit as softly as I could.

Take away what happened in the hotel room with his brother—that's what I longed to do. How could I protect Ryan from his hurtful memories? Stroke by stroke, I visualized how I might caress his entire body and wash away the hurt.

He's exposed deep emotions . . . maybe if I did the same, taking a risk like he had just done with me, I could make him understand how even in turmoil he was helping to tumble down my walls of protection.

If both our bare bodies could soothe each other as we lay together in an innocent embrace, perhaps he could see, without me having to claim it out loud, I loved him.

Through our deep conversations, most recently in the lounge of the Embarcadero Hotel, I felt a kind of strength gather around me. It was as if held a golden lasso and rode the power of the four seasons with the goddesses of fire, water, wind and air.

That late afternoon, I was ready to roar like a lioness for the man in my arms and my growl had begun.

Chapter 20

Half Moon Bay

The feelings Ryan had revealed in the hotel lounge caught me off guard. His passion, desire, vulnerability and sweetness had a physical hold on me the same as if he'd gripped my body. Now, as I held him in my arms, I'd discovered his grip on my heart was just as strong.

"I need to be loved." His voice cracked and was uneven. "I need to be loved by *you*."

I wondered if the words had been bottled up ever since his father had died when he was fourteen. Before me, was Walter the only person who'd witnessed the pleas Ryan made for love?

"I'm here." I caressed his hair.

He made desperate sounds while kissing me, sometimes moaning and covering my mouth with his own, pushing his hands through my hair, keeping me in place, pressing hard, as if exchanging his spiritual energy with mine.

In the middle of a kiss, he unexpectedly gasped with grief. For a few seconds, I couldn't breathe. His sadness was devastating.

As if we were frozen in his past and also in the present moments of letting go, it seemed like an eternity before the rush that had initially overcome him, faded. He rested his head on my shoulder. I caressed his back with every breath, moving up his spine as he inhaled and down his sides as he let go in deep sighs.

He began to settle.

His shoulders relaxed.

The rigid tightness of his muscles eased.

Who knew how long we'd be together—or if we'd last?

Maybe we wouldn't like each other once we were intimate.

Could he even be faithful to me?

Could I be faithful to *him*?

What I did know was that night Ryan had called me to be with him and I wanted to comfort the frightened boy in my arms.

I knew it was time to dive more deeply into a life I hadn't dared to dream I could be a part of. That night, I took a baby step toward a promise of brilliance.

"Okay, Ryan." I squeezed his biceps. "It's okay. You're okay."

"I understand your dreams—believe me, I do."

"I believe you." I pulled back so he could see the conviction in my eyes. "I believe you."

We continued to hug each other, still buried in our past, trying to embrace our present, fearful of our future.

"I'm sorry." He straightened. "This isn't your problem. I had no right." He wiped his eyes and pressed the button for the elevator.

"Don't apologize because you showed your emotions." I gripped his wrist as if putting my hands around his demon—maybe it was my demon, too—this thing that kept us bound and chained in our past—and kept us embracing our fears. "There's nothing wrong with what you just did. I still have trouble sorting through my childhood. What happened to you back there? I'm honored you shared it with me. You certainly don't need to apologize. Do you believe me?"

"Yes." He smiled.

I knew it was forced. I had to change something about our evening or we might never have had another date.

"You know what?"

"Hmm?"

"I have an idea. How about we skip dinner and go out to Half Moon Bay?" I took a chance that I'd read the moment correctly.

A sudden change washed over his face. It replaced the knotted expression he'd worn a few minutes earlier, to one that indulged in the promise of comfort and calm I'd just suggested.

"We can stop at Sammy's and order those oysters you like." I licked my lips. "I'll get some chowder and bread. We can sit on the beach and just talk. Or we don't have to talk. You'd probably like me to be quiet for a while, huh?"

"Keep talking," he said quietly. "I need you to keep talking."

"When I want to empty out, I love to spend time at the ocean." I briefly drifted back to all the times Jerry and I went there to escape our family's rage. "I stare out at the water and try to let my mind unravel as much as I can. I have a hard time letting go so believe me I go there a lot. I think that's why I talk so much. I'm trying to get everything out to the person I'm talking with, like I'm doing with you now, even though sometimes I'm not sure what it is I'm getting out. Anyway . . ."

I was already lost in the way he looked at me. When the elevator doors opened, we stepped in, ready to make our escape. My poetic side always came to life when I talked about the ocean. Dreams and images circled through my mind and burst into visions I could only hope to capture with words.

"Don't you just love listening to the waves roll onshore? They sound like a big wall of wind coming toward you. It's so powerful."

"Mm-hmm." Ryan's natural smile returned.

"When the water crests and then folds over on itself? Ooh, it's so . . . the force of the wave unravels and when it breaks—the way it pops and sizzles—it's like a string of firecrackers." I raised my hands and opened all of my fingers at once, demonstrating the explosion. "When the full force of it tumbles on itself—the way it splashes, pounds, and pulls on everything beneath and then rushes back out to sea—it's so symbolic. Have you ever watched it? I mean *really* took the time to watch?"

He shook his head. As thoughtful as he was, I suspected he'd watched the ocean more than once, but in this moment, wanted to stay quiet a little longer and listen to my voice.

"I love when the water rolls over the sand and leaves ripples in it. All the little bits of shells and pebbles, little crabs and creatures . . . it feels life affirming. It's biological—like the rhythms and pull of life. Come on, Ryan; let's go there. Do you want to?" I grabbed his hand. "It's only an hour from here. I have such sweet memories being on the beach with you from when we first talked, don't you? What do you think?"

He kissed my temple and sighed heavily.

"I shouldn't have brought you to meet Chris. I've been talking to him about you and . . . I'm sorry if you were uncomfortable. I wasn't thinking clearly. I should've gone by myself."

"Don't worry. I know how hard family stuff is. It shouldn't be so hard, but it is."

He nodded.

"I hope we're always here for each other." I declared boldly. "If we're careful with our friendship and keep it honest, I have faith that we'll be okay."

"You have faith in me?" His knotted eyebrows seemed lost in the possibility.

"Yes." I was embarrassed and nervous that I'd been so forthcoming with my feelings.

Careful, Nicky.

After I made the suggestion of going to the ocean, I focused only on what he needed. I wanted to get all the insight I could about this big, gentle man. If I had a clearer picture of his dreams, perhaps I'd understand more about the pain he carried with him.

We stepped out from the elevator, walked through the lobby, and exited the hotel. Ryan gave his ticket to the valet. While we waited for his car, we stood in a tender embrace. For a few precious minutes, even those who recognized him didn't interrupt. Somehow, the universe understood. Gave him a break.

His head was deep into my shoulder. An inch at a time, his arms took me inside them. My lower back was alive with his touch. As soon as he knew he was released from having to be *on for the public*, I sensed his whimpers. He let go of his sadness.

I let myself experience his release.

The late afternoon began to cover us.

Soon, the valet brought his car to the curb. After tipping him, we slid into our seats. Ryan let out a long sigh and gripped the wheel.

He must get tired of always having to accommodate his fans, the press, maintain his swagger at social events and in public, or have the right comment to a fan to avoid a negative write-up.

We drove to Half Moon Bay.

It was a place that stood at the edge of one world as another began. Away from the traffic, noise, and congestion of the city.

The road hugged the cliffs, defined and sharp, then dipped near the water and rushed down into possibilities. Traveling there brought a certain yearning for something more. Anticipation teased and ran with the ocean's power, then pulled back against the rounded sand dunes. Finally, the road soared to the edge, not quite ready to reveal the full wonder of what awaited us.

Dozens of grassy fields supported cattle and horses. Their heads peeked over old, gray, wooden fence posts as they watched us drive by. Bent and twisted pine trees on the side of the road showed the effects of the constant coastal winds. In some areas, the ice cactus was in full display. Beautiful and succulent flowers bloomed in pink, purple, and white.

Even though Ryan appeared strong, playing the powerful role of an alpha male and competing at the top level of his sport, I wondered if on this day *he* needed someone to fight for *him*.

Did he ever get to relax and enjoy his precious moments? Was there anyone who stood by him and really loved him for the strength of his convictions *as well as* his fears and insecurities?

Had he talked to anyone else about the things that made his body shiver?

Had he faced what he was afraid of, only by himself?

Like me, was he keeping dark secrets?

How would I be that person to comfort him?

How could I fight for him when I'd previously only fought battles for myself?

How could I stay, when every instinct said, *run?*

Chapter 21

Learning to Fight for Another

"*I*'ll go in and order while you close your eyes." I turned on the car radio. "Here we go. *This* is the station I listen to when I'm by myself and need the smallest amount of something. It's soft jazz. Have you ever listened to it?"

"Once or twice. Now that I know you like it . . ." He pushed a button and set the station as one of his regulars.

"You know what?" I turned the volume down.

"What?" He leaned back in his seat.

"I know I told you I'm sick of battling for everything. I do get sick of it. Well, except when it comes to my education, I never get tired of that, but your brother? He um . . ."

Should I open up so honestly? Is it too soon to talk like this? What if I offend him? It's his brother, after all. Oh well, here I go.

"Go on." He turned and sat with his arm resting on top of the driver's seat.

"Well . . . I'm sorry to say this; I admit that I don't know Chris and I really don't have a right to talk about him. He was kind of flippant back there. He me want to fight for you."

"You put your arm around my waist." His finger traced circles up and down my arm.

"Yes."

"That was a strong move, Nicky. Thank you."

"You're welcome. Tonight I'm going to take charge of you." His wry grin appeared and before he could tease me, I corrected my mistake. "Take charge *for* you is what I meant." I swallowed. "So, just let me do everything and you can relax. Is that okay?"

When he put his arm around me, I felt his body deflate. Perhaps he turned off his protection—if only for one night.

"Thank you." He handed me the money. "Here you go."

I kissed his cheek and climbed out of the car. I wanted to rush back to him and say *I give up. I'm yours.* I visualized taking his entire body in my arms, cupping his cheeks and taking his lips with mine in a passionate kiss. Maybe I could finally run *to* someone instead of running away.

Hardly able to wait to get back to Ryan, I forced myself to keep the appearance of control. My pace was steady and even.

When I opened the door to Sammy's the smells of garlic and malt vinegar filled the air. My mouth watered. I looked for Ermina and Sam, the restaurant's owners whom I'd met just two weeks earlier. The woman at the counter informed me it was their day off. The locals crowded the cashier, picking up their own dinner orders, while some waited patiently for a table or booth to open up.

I was glad Ryan had decided to take a moment for himself. The way he so readily agreed to let me handle the order told me he needed a time out from the usual autograph and photo requests.

When it came down to it, I needed a time out, too, but for me it was from his young and pretty female fans.

On my way back to the car, I couldn't help but take a piece of bread and dip it in the chowder. The creamy broth was rich and delicious with the sourdough.

"Cheater!" Ryan's laugh was robust and warmed me to my toes. "I saw you take a bite."

"I did!" *Your smile is back!* "It smelled so good I just couldn't wait. Here." I dipped another piece and then held it out for him.

"Feed me." He opened his mouth. I put the chowder-soaked bread on his tongue. He licked my finger and closed his eyes. "Mmm, I like that."

Ooh . . . so do I.

"It's delicious," I agreed.

"The chowder's good, too." His sexy laugh made the warm bubbles pop inside my belly.

That tongue of his. The things he says . . . he's got . . . like . . .

"God, Ryan. I see you're feeling better."

"Mm-hmm." He smacked his lips and then lifted my finger to his mouth. "You have a little bit of chowder left here." He slowly sucked on my finger with his eyes open and flirting, his magic tongue circling with its tip.

It feels like he has a separate muscle on the end of his tongue. The way it . . . I wonder how it would feel on my . . . maybe I'll dip my finger in the soup again.

As we drove to the beach, I was well aware of the big waves of joy cresting inside of me.

Whenever he started his comments, it was as if I was a runner on first base and he was the pitcher. He'd look back at me, daring me to advance. He seemed ready to throw his ball in my direction at only a moment's notice. I wondered, would I ever cross home plate or would I be left standing on base, too afraid to move.

Ryan pulled off the road to a deserted beach and carried the food when we got out of the car.

"There's a good spot to sit." I pointed to a smooth, sandy area.

"Your clothes—you'll get dirty. You're dressed so pretty."

"It's all right. My sister will kill me, but so what? Besides, I was the one who suggested we come here. And you dressed nice, too, so if you're game, I am. If there's one thing you'll get to know about me, it's that I don't care where we go or how we're dressed when we go out. Except—don't take me to the snow because I can't ski."

I saw his shoulders go up and down and heard him laughing softly. I felt good that I had lightened his mood.

"I probably shouldn't say this because you might think I'm a cheap date, but I'm more of a sitting-on-the-sand kind of woman when it comes to being with people. Come on, let's eat."

"Here, hold the bag." He handed me the food. "I'll be right back." When he returned, he had a Gladiator's blanket and two sweatshirts. Locals generally carried them for an impromptu drive to the coast and I was impressed he had them. We each put on a sweatshirt and after fanning the blanket, sat down.

"Anyway, do you remember what I was saying, Ryan?"

"Yes." He laughed again.

"Don't worry. Jenise and I were talking today. She said I've got to shop for clothes when we go out together, and—ooh! I have to tell you more about LA. You should see the outfits I got from Alex! I can't believe she was able to find stuff for me. I have a beautiful business suit and a dinner dress now. I was afraid it wouldn't, you know how skinny those models are so . . ."

"So?" he pressed.

"Sew buttons on your shirt, that's what."

"What?" He cracked up. "Buttons on my shirt? I thought you were the one who needed shirts—and now buttons apparently."

"Yeah, well at some point you might think, *My God, she's wearing those jeans and that T-shirt again.* That's what I own, though. I guess my sister will have to loan me her clothes until I can get to the store."

"I see." He seemed to enjoy my story.

"I'm just kidding."

"Uh-huh," he teased.

"Really, I am. You don't care that I'm a casual girl, do you? You don't want to see me in tight tops that sparkle and dip low, I hope, I hope."

"I love your jeans and sweatshirts." His eyes twinkled. "You know what, Nicky?"

"Mm-hmm?" I dipped one of the last pieces of sour dough bread in the clam chowder.

"I don't care what you're wearing. In fact, it'd be great if you wore your sweet little birthday suit."

"Uh-huh." Embarrassed, I looked away.

He's back.

He put his arm around my shoulder while we sat on the blanket. Then, he opened up about a part of his childhood. "Sorry about what happened at the hotel."

"It's all right. I understand."

"Chris and I . . . I have a tough time forgiving him."

"How come?" I didn't want to pry too deeply. I knew how it was to have feelings locked away and how easy it was to close down when probed. "What did he do?"

"When our dad was killed, Chris was entering his first year of college. It was still summer. He had just started to move into the dorms and school didn't start for another few weeks. That didn't stop him from leaving us. He only came back for the funeral and then never looked back. Mom and I were alone. We didn't know how to deal with the emptiness of Dad's death."

"And he left *you*." I tried not to interrupt his thoughts but I needed him to know I understood and could relate to his trauma. He regretted losing his brother. I wasn't sure he understood how much those feelings resonated even now.

"I called him every day, begging him to come home. I told him Mom was asking for his help and support. His response? *You're there. You help her.* What the hell was *I* supposed to do at only fourteen?" Ryan closed his eyes. "Have you ever had a family member die?"

"My grandma on my dad's side. She lived at our house for a while. She took over my room and I resented her for it. At first . . . all I wanted . . . anyway. Sorry. This is your story. Yes, my grandma to answer your question."

"I don't know how you handled it, but what happened to Mom and me . . . we became numb. It was like we clicked into automatic and were zombies. We took care of the necessary details of his funeral, insurance and veterans' benefits . . . all of that kept us occupied. As soon as everything was done and there was nothing left to distract us? We fell apart and it went dark.

"When they lowered Dad's body into the ground and the flowers and handfuls of dirt were tossed onto his casket, the finality of it literally crashed into me. We . . . I needed help. I needed to have people around us. I needed my brother," he continued. "Only problem was the calls and offers to help faded away when we needed them most. It seemed like everyone deserted us. We were alone—I was alone."

He took a deep breath.

I rubbed his thigh.

"I'd steal a moment to secretly hold his dog tags, medals, and fishing gear . . . the sadness really shrouded me." He brushed a tear from his cheek. "Dad was gone, Chris had left, and Mom just cried and cried . . . there was no one left. Friends of the family and relatives got back to their own lives. God, it was tough watching her struggle. I needed someone to talk with but my friends didn't know what to say. Plus, no boy wants to mope around his friends. That's not cool, you know. No way I could show weakness around them. It felt like I was abandoned."

"I'm sorry." I put my hand in his.

"One day, Mom finally packed some of Dad's stuff. She didn't know I was watching her. She brought each piece of clothing to her face and cried. It was so sad."

"You were too young to be her savior." I put my arm through his, thinking back to all the nights my father came to my bedside drunk to share his misery with me. I thought by listening to him I could help. It took me years to understand—he didn't remember anything we'd discussed from the night before. He was too drunk. I was like a fly batting itself against the window, repeating the same, sick pattern and hoping to change the outcome.

"I knew that—at least somewhere deep down I did, but there was no one around except me. My asshole brother couldn't even help us call our relatives and friends to tell them about Dad's death. Then Chris left again—it was like another funeral. Mom needed the love of both her sons. She was left with a son who didn't know anything." Ryan put his head down.

"You knew enough." I praised him. "The both of you got through a terrible time together stumbling through the dark. I'll bet if you ever had the chance to ask your mom, she'd admit you helped her survive." I slipped my arm through his.

"I really missed Dad," he said quietly. "I still miss him, but back then I was so sad, angry . . . a stupid adolescent who needed to talk to him about teenage stuff. After he died, whenever I had a question for him—even months later—I couldn't wait to see him. Then, that empty feeling would hit—the one that reminded me he was dead. Those times were the hardest.

"I finally understood." He paused as if still trying to comprehend the finality of it. "He was dead. Forever dead. He'd never walk through the door again. I'd never see him sitting in the stands at my game. He wouldn't be there to teach me to drive or see me go to my prom . . . or get married."

Just then a sneaker wave rushed in. The water pushed up the beach and we scrambled to save the blanket. We ran as fast as we could, our arms full, both of us laughing and me screaming like a child to avoid getting my feet wet. When the water receded we set the blanket down, this time higher up on the sand.

"That was close!" I shouted in excitement. "I almost got it!"

"Well . . . I have to admit, it would've been kind of . . . amazing to see you get wet."

Is he being sexual?

"Yeah? Well you would have been something in a suit all drenched. What about that, mister?"

"True." He slurped down an oyster. "Anymore of that soup and bread?"

"A little."

"Be sure and dip it for me and then put it in my mouth." He smirked knowing I couldn't look at him when he looked that way.

"Here's the container," I handed it to him without looking. "I'm not feeding you. I'm afraid I'll lose my finger."

After a few pieces of chowder-soaked bread, I opened the conversation once again so he'd continue his reveal.

"What kind of questions did you want to ask your dad?" I hoped saying them out loud might help ease the pain he felt.

"Why girls were so confusing, for one."

"We're not that confusing," I punched his arm playfully.

"Uh . . . yeah, you are. And you top the cake." He kissed my hand.

"I challenge you on that, but continue."

"I wanted to get his opinion on how to date a girl and get her to like me, millions of questions about sex; peer pressure at school, the clumsy way my body felt, wet dreams, when would pimples go away, masturbating . . . you know how odd everything is at fourteen."

"I get it. I ask my sister about all that stuff. There's nothing like talking about those things with your own gender, I guess. And friends just don't cut it. They're as stupid as we are."

"You're naive, but not stupid. Isn't that what you told me?" He looked at me from under his eyelashes.

"Don't tease me." I pushed my shoulder into his.

"I'm not. I'll never forget when you said that to me," he confessed. "I thought, *naive*? She's innocent, but no way is she naive. They're not the same."

"Good point." I felt special he had remembered what I told him when he first volunteered in Yountville. "Go on, Ryan."

"I was broken. Mom was broken. Chris didn't give a shit about us. My mother would hug me and cry while I was in her arms." He shivered. "I couldn't . . ."

"You didn't have the answers. She was looking for them through you because you were there, but you couldn't give them to her. I can't wait to get out of my house, but that doesn't mean I don't love my parents—or in your case, you with your mom."

"I wanted to get away so badly. There was a point where I didn't think I could endure one more hug or long talk." Ryan put his head down. "All I wanted was to get away like Chris."

"You were a confused boy," I counseled. "That's understandable."

"I was so tired of talking about death. Dad was gone and nothing was going to bring him back. I wanted to move on, but it seemed like Mom wanted to live in his memories. His death was all she talked about from the time she got up until she went to bed. I needed to be with friends so I could try and fill up again."

"What do you mean fill up?"

"Replace the sadness with doing. Getting on with life. Being happy again. Doing *something* to move forward. Chris did, after all. What was wrong with me wanting the same thing?"

"Nothing. You had every right to want that." I rubbed his forearm, tracing the powerful looking veins that stood out all the way to his wrist. "I like these."

"My veins?" He was obviously amused.

"Yeah," I admitted. The way they stand out on your forearms."

"Good to know. Anything I should do to get your attention elsewhere on my body?"

"You've got my attention everywhere," I confessed. "Continue, Mr. Tilton."

"Okay." His expression was showed a mixture of amusement, titillation, and a hint of desire. The heaviness of his mood was lifting. "On Chris, I understand my brother wanted to start his new life, but that wasn't the reason he chose to stay away. It was because he'd have to face Mom and he didn't want to grieve with her. The bastard didn't even come home for Thanksgiving. It took her four years to recover and stand on her feet again. Just when I was off to college, Chris came home."

What an ass.

"He acts like the big man in front of you, throwing jabs at me? He's a phony and an ass for trying to make me feel guilty. I've been through enough and I don't need his sarcasm when it comes to mom visiting me."

"No, you don't." I sat up to face him. "You were a strong young man, Ryan; much stronger than you should have needed to be. Your mom was lucky to have you at home." *I think you were lucky, too, in ways you haven't seen yet. Maybe I am, too.*

"Back there in the hotel room? You caught it when he called me Romeo?"

"That wasn't nice." The anger kicked in my belly. I wanted to knock Chris on his ass for what he'd said. I wondered if he was trying to drive a wedge between mother and son so he'd have her all to himself and deny Ryan the love he needed.

"That was all for show. He wants you to see me as a weak man who isn't settled and can't be faithful to you. He tried to make me look ridiculous and play on your innocence so I won't have the chance to show you who I am."

"Well, he failed if that was his intention," I reassured him. "That's so far from the man I see. Strong and weak—what are those anyway? All I see in you is good. I've always bragged about how compassionate you are, Ryan. You have a gift of noticing what people need. It's unique, the same as you are. Your work at the Veterans' Hospital and SF State . . . Weak? No. You're incredibly strong. I think that's the gift your father left you. Because of what you went through, you're able to have empathy for others in a way that's really unusual."

Why is it so easy for me to see other people's struggles and so difficult to peel back my own defenses?

"Mom and I should have gone to counseling. We needed it but didn't know see it at the time."

I know that feeling.

I wanted to take him in my arms and make it all okay, while reassuring him he could be whole again.

Before you can do that for someone else, you *have to be whole yourself, Nicky.*

"Maybe your father's death was so painful for your brother he couldn't process it so he ran." I wanted to go on, but was afraid he'd stop sharing. I quieted once again and sat with my back to his chest, tucked into the envelope of his body.

"If he just called once in a while . . ." He caressed my hair.

You were abandoned. I know how that feels.

I rubbed his arm up and down only caring about the man it was a part of and not the physical excitement I'd felt minutes earlier when I'd traced the veins.

"Don't get me wrong, I know I've had it better than most people. Being able to play professional baseball is a privilege."

"Thank God Walter came into your life."

I felt his muscles bulge as he squeezed me tight.

"If he hadn't come to my high school . . ."

"I really enjoyed meeting him at Stanford. Did I tell you he was late for our appointment because he was helping a *female* athlete with a problem?"

"You didn't mention that."

"I couldn't believe it. The head of men's baseball—the athletic director of the whole college—taking care of a woman instead of some stud male athlete . . . you two are a good match."

"Thank you for saying that." He kissed my temple and let out a long sigh. Perhaps he was searching for answers even as we sat together, looking up and down the shoreline. When his cheek rested against my neck I felt him sigh.

"What was your dad like?"

"How much time do you have?" His response was warm and friendly.

"All the time you need." I held each of his arms and brought them around me. Leaned back and kissed his cheek. Watched as he squeezed his eyes shut, took a breath, and began to tell me his story of Christopher Tilton Senior.

Chapter 22

Memories in Softness

"*D*ad was everything a man should be." Ryan's voice resonated with sadness and also admiration. "He was typical military—strict but always fair. Whenever he handed out discipline, my brother and I didn't challenge him; he was usually right. Even if we disagreed, he was not a man to bullshit and we didn't get away with much." His eyes softened as if his heart had smiled at the memory.

"That's how it was with my mom." I kissed the back of his hand. One of his fingers twitched. "She worked at juvenile hall with troubled teenage girls. She always said she'd seen it all. Trust me when I say there wasn't a story we could make up she hadn't already heard. Not that I ever did anything much to rouse her anger, but when I did—wow."

"Yeah." Ryan seemed transported back to his childhood. Perhaps his dad was right there with us. Maybe some ripple in the universe brought us all together and now his father was at his side, soothing his son's feelings his tender moment.

"Dad pushed us in every way: homework, school projects, sports, our chores at home . . . he sat with us every week and went over our personal goals. We didn't have much downtime together. When we did? It was magical."

"Do either of you look like your father?" I could see Ryan was still dreaming.

"I do." His chest seemed to swell.

"Your dad was a handsome man, then."

"Yes, he was." His tightened his embrace. "Thank you for saying so."

He's like a boa constrictor!

My heart beat hard. My throat closed as the revelation of our future came over me—I'd be leaving for college soon. Would I leave him the same way his brother had? As I thought about getting close and then having to say goodbye, I tried to keep the tears from spilling but my body shook and gave me away.

"Is my story too sad for you?" Ryan kissed my cheek.

"It's not that." I turned to face him. I was on my knees. "I mean, it *is* sad. The thing is, you make me feel different. Here I made such a big deal about committing to you when we were in the hotel lounge . . . I'm really confused." I sat between his legs once again, my back against his chest. Perhaps my intimate reveal was something I couldn't do while looking into his eyes. "You get to me. It's like you're reaching inside me. As if my heart can feel your hands, emotions and all your hidden messages."

The way his arms insisted on surrounding my body was sensual. Powerful. I was in a maze of love and had no interest in finding the way out. I squeezed his biceps as they held me.

"Nicky?"

"Yeah?" I'd been looking out toward the water. I looked back at him. He lifted me onto his lap and closed his legs underneath me. Tilting his head, he sealed his sculpted lips over mine. I'd snuggled into a nest of power. He'd transformed into some sea creature, swallowing me in a passion that sucked everywhere on my body.

When we finished kissing, we looked toward the oncoming darkness in front of us. The water crested in a steep wave as if it would crash on shore but then broke gently. The foam bubbled and coaxed open holes in the sand. It was as if the water gave nourishment to the life underneath. Little creatures waited open-mouthed, ready for the chance to fill up.

I was sure my heart worked overtime, squeezing pools of blood into all of my extremities and moist places. Pulses began to form rhythms in my fingertips, neck, and face. When his muscles tightened, I knew I was in for a nice embrace or a wet kiss.

As if answering him, my belly began a sensual ache. Liquid electricity surged from my chest, through my pelvis and down my legs. I was full of hope, like the night Ryan laid next to me in my bed.

"Feed me again," he requested.

"There's no food left." My voice shook.

"Let me taste *you*."

I closed my eyes and waited for Ryan's kiss. Anticipated the gentle press of his lips and the little beads of moisture on them that would make my mouth wet. I lifted my chin with my lips spread open.

He took them.

Made them his.

I was his.

Too soon, he lifted from me.

Wanting to hold on a moment longer, I opened my eyes and lightly traced his mouth with my finger. He held it to his lips, making a popping sound when he kissed it, as if the last bubble broke in the foam of a receding wave.

We were two frightened people sitting in the hope that our hearts might soon be free—perhaps even fly together.

The breeze lifted my hair. I imagined a new promise covered me. Ryan and I sat until the fading blues above turned to the golden orange of an early evening. The cold wind swirled through the pine trees. Their limbs strained and creaked behind us. A farewell gust swooped across the sand. Lifted what had once been part of an erupting and furious Earth, now spread before us in fine grains, soft under our bodies.

I felt as if the wind was the rise and fall of our dreams— blowing, swirling, twisting, straining to touch . . . and then becoming still and silent.

My heart seemed one with the evening and elements of nature, floating on the water and flying in the wind—pulsing, fluttering, crashing, beating, the blood pushing through my body.

Like the mouths of all the little creatures underneath the sand, I was opening. And the nourishment I needed—was Ryan.

I wanted to tell him how I felt.

I was afraid.

I held back.

Decided to protect my heart from the inevitable pain to come. Kept the words *I love you*, to myself.

"This is a night neither of us expected, was it?" I asked, rather than share how I was falling in love with him.

"No." His mouth rested against the side of my head. "I'd only hoped," he whispered.

"I feel as if I'm slowly going mad with you. Beware, Ryan." I giggled, too nervous to sit still or be serious for long.

"How come?"

"Because you make me feel open—too open. I don't know what to do about it. My rooms are dark." I grabbed a handful of sand and let it drain through my open fingers. "Sometimes even the most brilliant beam of light can't penetrate them. Everything I've held deep inside rushes to the surface when I'm with you. I'm sorry—it's not fair."

"Not fair?" Ryan repeated.

"I'm afraid of new relationships. You shouldn't have to put up with someone who's still discovering herself. You deserve a woman who's gone through the things you have. I know we talked about this back in the hotel lounge, but you should really be with a lady who already knows herself and wants the things you want right now. Not in four years from now. I just can't help but feel that you're making a mistake."

He lay back on the blanket and pulled me down with him.

Oh, it's nice in his arms.

I was on top of his body looking down at him. His eyes bounced from left to right, deciding where to settle on my face.

"I don't want someone who's poised. I'm not looking for or interested in a woman who knows how to maneuver in relationships and is used to the spotlight. My job in baseball is temporary. So is the attention. What I want is a life with someone grounded and doesn't care about fame or society. Someone real. It's you."

"You've had all of that and more and *you're* not jaded. The women you've been with, the press, society, famous people—"

"I'm not jaded because I knew who I was looking for," he shared. "I've always known. With you, I'm beginning again. That's why I want to kiss you in public and take you in my arms wherever we are. All I want is to be near your fiery heart. I love the way you explain your thoughts and how you stand up for what you believe. I welcome all of your dark rooms and look forward to opening your doors one by one. By the way, you're stronger than anyone I've ever known, man or woman."

His arms slid under my lower back.

He turned so he was on top of me.

I felt as if my insides would push out of my body, trying to touch him. When he kissed me, my legs naturally rose against the thickness of his thighs.

"I don't want to go home." He looked at me for several heartbeats. "There's a bed-and-breakfast just across the harbor where we can lie together all night. If you want, we can even lay on top of the bed. I promise I'll be a good boy. I just want to be with you."

"Sounds perfect," I agreed.

The little boy in him reached out to me. My intuition told me he needed to be protected that night.

I wanted to be that someone.

Reshaped into a tender possibility, our evening had become deeply intimate in every way. We trusted each other enough to share a part of ourselves that we'd never dared before that evening.

We started to open a door—*our* door.

Now, we needed the courage to step through.

Chapter 23

An Interlude

𝔗he Harbor Inn Bed and Breakfast was a two-story, sea green Cape Cod style home. It had a white picket fence and was adorned with cream-colored shutters on its windows. Typical coastal accents—shells, statues of gulls, and netted glass balls— were strewn about a country garden. Flowering shrubs and grasses lined the walkway to the front door.

We both agreed it looked inviting. Ryan rang the bell. The hostess answered, introducing herself as Paula. She informed us she was one of the owners and said she had availability. We were invited inside for a tour.

Thank God she didn't greet him by name. I'd hate to think of this being his regular sex pad.

As we followed her, she talked about the history of the home. She and her husband had remodeled it from attic to basement, converting the rooms into six guest suites.

"Let's take a look at this one." She opened the door. "We also have one upstairs with a broader view of the coastline."

We could see the ocean through the large sliding glass doors immediately walking into the room. Two Adirondack chairs were strategically placed on the deck outside near a small table, offering moments of relaxation and the chance for guests to enjoy both nature and the spectacular views. Inside and to the right of the sliding door was a love seat and coffee table. In front of them a large picture window offered another spectacular view.

As we stepped further into the room, I noticed the bathroom on the right. A claw-foot tub, stall shower, and an old-fashioned pedestal sink were perfect accents. To the left was a king size bed. White sheets were folded over the top of a beautiful quilt in turquoise-green. Two creamy white knitted blankets draped across the foot of the bed. A nightstand and reading lamp were on each side.

"The kitchen's open twenty-four hours a day," Paula informed. "Help yourself to bottled water, a glass of wine, iced tea, coffee or soda. I have some home-baked cookies and a fruit and cheese plate in the dining room right now."

Ryan looked at me with raised eyebrows.

I nodded.

"We'll take it." He followed her out to take care of the necessary details.

After walking around the room exploring, running my hands over the rich textures of the bed quilt and over the smooth surface of the coffee table, I stood looking out toward the ocean.

Suddenly, the situation hit me.

I'm spending the night with an experienced man. Am I doing the right thing? Is this too soon?

I didn't hear Ryan come up behind me. When his hands rested on my shoulders, I jumped.

"Sorry," his voice was soft and low. "Nice view, isn't it?"

"Beautiful. I'll be right back. All those cranberry drinks . . ."

"I'll wait outside." He smiled knowingly at my excuse to go to the bathroom and set two bottles of water on the coffee table.

I closed the door. Turned on the faucet to let the cold water run, soaking one of the thick, white washcloths. I wrung out the excess and then laid it on my face. It was cool and refreshing.

When I came out, I saw Ryan standing on the deck. He rested his elbows on the wooden railing as he looked out to the ocean. The orange light of evening was on his skin. He looked majestic. The sadness from earlier in the evening had slipped away. Calm seemed to cover his face. It was obvious to me he'd closed and locked the doors to his hurt.

The light within the soft colors of the setting sun lit up the gold highlights in his hair. A palette of reds, oranges, pinks, and violets were thrown across the sky and splashed on his body. He looked like he was part of an exquisite painting.

I walked out to meet him. Lay my head against his back. With a sigh of pleasure, I wound my arms around his waist. My hands flattened and rested on his stomach.

"Ooh, Ryan." I squeezed him. He put his hands over mine, covering them on his belly. "You should see how your skin is all lit up."

His fingers laced through mine and he lifted my hands to his lips, kissed and pressed them against his mountainous chest.

"You feel so good," I admitted. "*Everything* about you feels good. When you first called today I thought you were breaking it off because of what I'd done."

He turned around to face me.

I was captured in his burning eyes.

The backs of his fingers on my cheek made me feel like a wisp of love had touched me. When he gathered me into his arms, I was sure a slender, silken bond wove our sacred spirits together.

Some connection—something bigger than the moment—lingered near us.

"Breaking what off, Nicky?"

"Well, um, your, uh, our, you know, our friendship."

"Mm-hmm." His massive chest pressed against my breasts as he leaned closer. His muscles began their concert, flexing and gathering their adrenaline to move on my body. "You're so close, Nicky. So close to seeing me in every way. You don't even realize it."

"Close," I repeated in a tone barely audible.

"Baby." His breath went past my ear in a sigh.

"Hmm." I looked up at him. I knew he loved that.

"You're wonderful."

My emotions rose so joyously, I thought the sun might reverse its direction and bring a new day as it skipped over night's shadow.

Finally, my heart was exposed. My inner core had revealed itself. I felt as if I was shining.

"Ryan, this is crazy."

"What's crazy?" he challenged. "Being here?"

"Not that." I stared at the bed. "What I'm about to suggest is insane of me." I shoved my hands in my hair. "Can we lie next to each other tonight? You know, just be together?"

"Of course, I will," he anxiously agreed. "I already said—"

"What I mean, God, I can hardly believe I'm asking, but— *naked.* I want to feel our skin touching. Is that too forward of me?" I nervously waited for his answer, but started talking again before he offered one. "Can I feel everything about you without sex getting in the way? I want to rest alongside you as if we've been friends for a lifetime. Did you know I've felt close to you from when we first volunteered together?" I placed my hands on his cheeks. "I want to hold you and just . . . can I bring my head to your chest? I'll . . . I'll . . ."

"You'll do what, sweetheart?" His hand rested on my lower back. "What will you do?"

"I'll rub your arms and back so carefully. I want to bring chills down your spine and legs." I put one hand over my heart and the other on his chest. My woman's body ached as his masculine essence reached into every heartbeat. "We can be quiet and listen to them beat for each other. Let's enjoy the simple beauty of touch. The softness of a kiss. The delicious flavor of a memory. Would you do that? Do you want to? I know it's corny, but—"

"Only you. You have an uncanny ability to see what people need." He sighed. Rested against my body. "I love you."

Inside I burst with love. Still, I couldn't repeat the words. I listened, I heard, I pressed against his chest and circled my arms around him. I still couldn't say those three words.

We watched the fiery orange ball of light slip under the ocean. The turquoise color of the water faded to gray. As we walked inside, Ryan started to close the sliding door to the balcony. I put my hand on top of his.

"Do you mind leaving it open and just slide the screen closed? I love the fresh air. There's something about . . . I don't know."

"What, sweetheart? Tell me."

"It's like I can breathe when I open everything; the curtains, blinds, windows, doors . . . I need it all left open. Silly, huh?"

"No." His arm rested on my shoulder. We walked over to the sound system and tuned in the same jazz station as we had on in Ryan's car. I put my arm around his waist. It was as if we were saying *let's go on this journey together*.

He rubbed his stubbly cheek against mine. Touched the back of my head. Pulled me close. I was nestled under his chin. When I sensed his shift, I knew he was moving into position and my mouth would soon tingle from his kisses. Covering my lips with his, I heard the sounds of my lover—low, masculine moans—from deep in his throat.

For a brief moment I considered reminding him of the friendly agreement we'd made for that evening. Instead, I let him explore where he wanted, trusting he'd respect my boundaries.

He suddenly broke our embrace.

"Do you want me to get you anything to eat or drink from the kitchen besides the water I grabbed for us?"

"No, I'm good."

"Are you ready?" He took my hands in his. "I know it's early. I'm so tired. Can we lie down for the night and hold each other?"

I nodded in agreement.

"Will you let me undress you?"

"Yes." I didn't hesitate with my answer. I quickly took off the sweatshirt he gave me to wear at the beach.

"Turn around." His request was firm but respectful.

I witnessed his slow, seductive gaze move downward. When he was done looking at my body, each of his hands fell gently on my arms. He coaxed me to turn away from him. I felt him search through my hair to take out the pin that held it in place. My waves and curls bounced against my lower back.

How wonderfully romantic! Thank you for insisting on having only one pin in my hair, Jenise.

When I no longer felt him on me, I turned around and faced him. His eyes were closed.

"Ryan?"

"Hmm?" his hands were at his sides.

"Why are your eyes closed?" I asked naively.

"I'm making a memory. I'm burning the outline of your body into my mind. You're above me, like when we were on the beach. Your sweet face looks down at me. Your hair is all around me. Your naked breasts brush my lips. I take your nipple in my mouth. Your head tilts back in pleasure. I'm quietly listening to your body's silent language. She's shouting for me to love her."

Yes, shouting . . .

One of his hands held my arm. The other pulled down the bed covers and reached to turn out the light. Our bodies glowed in the kiss of the evening. The newly risen moon threw its soft light over our silhouettes.

Ryan unwound the sheer scarf from my neck. After folding it, he placed it on the end of the bed. His hand traveled to the dip of my shoulder. When his fingertips touched my skin, I thought they might burn through to my bones.

"Let me just . . ." His head tilted slightly. I felt his mouth on my neck. His breath was hot. "I want to suck your little heartbeat here," he whispered.

I opened my mouth from the pleasure of the way his tongue moistened my skin. My breath escaped into the air, no longer able to be silenced or restrained. The loveliness of his fingers as they touched my earlobe and held the clasp of my earring was delicate—as were his lips when he removed each earring with them.

"Do you trust me?" he asked again.

"Yes."

"Raise your arms." He held them above my head but in reality, I raised them without hesitation.

He lifted my top. Folded it. Placed it with my scarf. His fingers seemed alive with their own thoughts. My body shivered with their touch. Soft breezes crept in from the ocean and danced lightly on my skin. Chills traveled from my lower back to my neck and then down my arms as his big hands touched my sides. When Ryan unhooked my bra and laughed his sexy laugh, I thought my knees might give way.

"What?"

"Is this your bra?" His voice was low. Its tone stirred my aching belly.

"Why?"

"The hooks are bent. Buying them a little too small?"

God, he notices everything.

"Or maybe . . ." he hesitated.

Just say it!

"Maybe you're still a little girl who's going through quite an amazing growth spurt."

His laugh sizzled.

The air was hot around me.

"No, it's, well, this top, it dips. I don't have a bra to go with it, so I borrowed my sister's. This whole outfit is hers. I don't have anything this nice. Well, now I do, with my suit and dress from LA, but they weren't right for tonight. Well, I really didn't know what we were doing tonight, but I just figured."

"I see." He was obviously amused.

"God, Ryan, you don't have to point out everything you notice."

"I know." I could sense his smile.

He took off his vest and then his shirt. When I felt his swollen, naked chest touch my bare breasts, it was all I could do to keep my body from saying hello to the floor.

"Oh baby, the breezes make your nipples . . ." He stopped talking as we embraced.

Our arms tangled. Weaved together. Everything about us seemed to yearn to love each other. Our lips met passionately.

We stood with our bodies pressed together.

He trembled.

I looked up at him.

It was as if we shimmered in the gray light of the room.

"Ryan?"

"Mm-hmm?"

"Are you cold?" I asked naively. "Should I close the door? You're shivering."

"Because, I . . . Nicky, I'm . . ." His arms tightened around my body. He never finished his statement. I finally understood. He was physically and mentally excited and trying with all his strength to keep himself under control.

I could feel his erection.

I wondered if this was the night to go all the way.

I was all too conscious of where his flesh touched me and questions about staying a virgin were rapid fire through my mind.

Why *should* I hold out?

What was the purpose?

Everyone I knew was having sex, why hesitate any longer?

Was it because once Ryan was inside me, I believed his sweet words would quickly fade away? Maybe his gratification would be so instant, that once satisfied, he'd turn over and fall asleep— or worse—get up, dress and drive me home for one final and chilling goodbye.

Where would that leave me?

After we had sex, would I be classified as a *bad girl*? I scrunched my nose as I considered, why wasn't there a widely accepted definition of a *good boy*.

Why was a *bad boy* cool?

Why, at least with the jocks, were they encouraged to accumulate as many sexual experiences as they could? Their conquests were "stripes," and yet, they weren't considered *"bad,"* or called *"sluts"* and *"whores"* like women. Why not?

If two people were consenting adults, what did it matter how much sex they had? Did "too many hands" somehow make a person "used up"?

Would I be punished on a spiritual level because of the lovely act of sharing my body with someone who wasn't random? If I gave myself freely, willingly, and respectfully in love, would that be wrong?

And what if I *did* have random sex? Was physical pleasure immoral when it was between two adults who had consented to be intimate with each other? Wasn't it just another way to play together and have fun?

Before *going-all-the-way* sex, my friends had all masturbated and had oral stimulation. So why, other than having protection and consent, was it such a big deal when a man's penis enters a woman's vagina?

I'd gone to confession every Sunday, from when I was nine until I was sixteen-years-old. When I began to masturbate as a young girl—and I did it a lot—I told a priest, "I touched a bad place." He led me to believe what I did *was* bad, and that *I* was bad for doing it. Or maybe it was only that *I* believed I was bad and my guilt had interpreted the priest's words to be woven in sin. It had only been a few years earlier that I stopped confessing when I realized it was normal.

But this—this with Ryan would be full on sex without being married. How would I confess this?

Would I be used for pleasure, and afterwards hear the zipper of his pants rise, facing the same fear I had with Jerry a few nights earlier? Would he fasten his belt and leave me with nothing but a kiss that meant, *so long*?

The old doubts of being a part of an elaborate joke for Ryan, a twisted bet that he could make me fall for him, brushed by me.

Before I became *aware* of Ryan and Jerry, I was certain I'd wait for sex until marriage. Now . . . there was that *other* side of me—the evil twin who seemed to be a sexual priestess in hiding. She had awakened and at every moment encouraged me to play.

I didn't know what path to choose.

"Sit down on the bed." Ryan's gentle command brought me back into our moment. I sat down. Held my breath as his body moved closer. His hands rested on my shoulders.

Ooh, your big hands. I love them.

"You're tense." His masculine voice filled the room. "I won't abuse your trust." His hands cradled my back as he lowered my body to the bed.

Is this what asthma feels like? My chest is so heavy. My throat feels like it's closing. I wonder if I can even speak? Maybe I need a drink of water . . .

His hands moved along the waistband of my pants, as if trying to understand how to take them from my body. All his touches against my stomach were strange sensations. I was reminded of the honeybees—fingertips doing the work for their queen, buzzing on my waist, fuzzy and soft, careful and light, touching each nerve underneath my skin. My body seemed ready to ooze honey wherever he touched.

When he slipped the waistband below my navel. His arms tensed and the muscles inside them bulged, giving him the strength to support his body as he leaned over me. I moaned when I felt his lips kiss the area around my belly. I breathed hard. Rapidly. I could no longer hide the sounds of my excitement. I lost count of the number of pulses sending liquid heat to my legs.

His mouth connected with me in a slow and easy motion, circling my stomach. His tongue licked my skin. Moved higher. Found the crease of my breasts. Just as I thought he might take one of my nipples in his mouth, his soft lips kissed along my sides and made love to my hips.

A storm gathered over my body—waiting, watching, hovering, ready to trigger lightning everywhere inside of me.

"Ryan?" I was losing my breath.

"Hmm?"

"I'm getting lost," I confessed.

"I know you are." He looked down at me as I lay underneath him. "I won't let you go and I won't take advantage of you."

Something sensual was pushing through me.

To be rubbed all over my body—that's what I wanted.

With only one more kiss, I felt as if I'd burst open; the intimate throbbing in my pelvis carried an obvious message—my entire body and millions of nerves inside my brain wanted sex.

Chapter 24

Undressed

Visions of having Ryan inside me became more vivid with each kiss from his lips.

They rippled through me.

In one way, I felt as if I'd slowed down.

Another breath.

I sped up; each gasp for air more desperate than the last.

His hands and mouth created an intense heat and a fire that lie just under my skin. The flame of my desire had been lit.

I put my hands on his head. Petted him gently as if he were my little lion cub. Grabbed bunches of his hair in my hands. Enjoyed the man who wanted me to open with him.

Subdued notes called out to me.

Little sounds came from his throat that let me know he enjoyed my touch. He didn't have to say a word.

Every inch of my belly was lifted inside his mouth. His lips seemed hungry for their next destination. They pressed and marked me with long pathways of moistness, preparing his roadmap for more.

I was swollen—a victim of Luna's power—wet, rushing in and out with the tides. One by one his fingertips caressed my hips; they grasped and took hold of my pants.

"I want everything." His masculine voice echoed through the room and covered my thighs as he kissed them. My legs opened naturally, without any thought of resistance. His hands flattened on my hips, guiding my swell.

Even though he held only part of me, my whole body was his.

"Are you okay with what I'm doing?" The look on his face told me he understood: he had complete control and could do whatever he wanted.

"I haven't ever felt . . ." I swallowed.

"It's you and me," he reminded. "You and me."

Lifting my left foot, he held it so the silky pants slid down and partially covered my right leg. My thighs were covered in chills as Ryan's seduction moved through me in a way I'd never felt. When he placed my ankle on his shoulder, my knee naturally bent toward my chest to make it easy for him to touch me. His tongue said hello, slowly licking the crease behind my knee.

I tilted my head back without thinking and without question.

I was his.

My body arched.

I wanted to give in to him.

He put my leg down. Continued to take off my pants. The material fell as if exhausted. He tossed them somewhere in the darkness.

We could've been outside, the wind blowing, and the water pounding against my breast. I'd still have felt his heat.

"Nicky," he called me back from my sensual paralysis. "I'm going to take off your panties. I won't push you for sex; I'm just letting you know. Are you okay?"

"Mm-hmm." I was incoherent.

My lips were stuck.

My body was weak.

My mind spun.

My sensual ache was on the edge of hurt it was so powerful.

Lower. Lower. The aching . . . my legs . . . lower . . . please.

His fingers traced my hips. Grasped the waistband of my panties. My skin felt every fiber of the material as it slid over my thighs, knees and ankles. He tossed them aside. I imagined them keeping my pants company. Each article of clothing chatted about how they'd almost burned up.

He growled.

"What . . . why, why are you . . ." I sounded like I'd just come in from a long run—I could hardly breathe. I swallowed rapidly and hard, trying to moisten my mouth.

"Your panties are uh . . . wet." His seductive, deep voice filled with appreciation because of the way the woman he'd held inside his hands had responded to his seduction.

My body involuntarily gave itself over. There was no question about why or how nor any need for conversation. I was sure my Evil Twin had taken charge and numbed my brain to make sure it stayed out of the way.

No, Nicky. You did that all on your own.

With each touch, I came to life differently. Rather than analyze and resist, I moved naturally and willingly. His physical power took me away. Wherever he wanted to go, I was with him.

Ryan's lips gently sucked on the tender softness of my inner thigh. Those lips made me feel as if I were lying in the ocean, riding its swells and power.

My moans were dramatic. They danced inside and outside of my body. I was so vocal that Ryan stopped.

"Are you still okay?"

"Uuuuuhh . . ." I could only groan. My *Y* called to me. She was alive and demanding. "It's like, I've never . . . mmm . . . feels so good."

I let go of what seemed like hundreds of short breaths and groans. I was fighting hard to keep control. Like all my battles with Ryan so far, I was losing this one, too.

"Let me take you where I want you to go," his deep voice purred.

"I'm already there." My fists grabbed for the pillow.

He was on his hands and knees. His big, muscular body hunched over me, looking at all that lay underneath him. I knew if his legs settled in between mine, I'd let him inside me.

Instead, he seemed frozen in the silvery gray of our night, the same way as when he was in my bedroom more than a week ago. His desire was suspended in the dividing space of seduction and promise, deciding whether to take a naive woman into a new journey, or touch only the innocence of our beginning.

I didn't dare look when he pushed up from the bed to take off the rest of his clothes. When his briefs dropped to the carpet, he slid next to me. Immediately, his body gave me its warmth.

The feeling of his big frame—his naked male body—brought a new awareness of how it carried his magnificent strength, and the barely contained desire he kept inside.

Being touched by a man I'd fallen in love with helped me realize the same desire beat within my body. It screamed for release.

"Turn over and face me." He pulled the covers on top of us. Unashamed, I face him, ready to lift off into a dream. He pulled our hips closer. "Are you glad we're here together?" Ryan caressed my head.

"Yes."

"Are you relaxed?" He ran a hand through my hair and kissed me on the forehead.

"Yes. Like mush." I giggled weakly. "You've made me question everything about sex and this woman having it."

"I'm glad I've risen those questions in you." He kissed me.

"Yeah," I giggled. "I know you are." My hands held the nape of his neck. "So am I. What about you? I was supposed to help *you* relax, not the other way around."

"Whenever you're with me, I relax." His foot rubbed mine.

"Thank you for being so tender." My toes stroked his calf from his knee to his ankle. "I think you've been in my dreams since I was a little girl." My fingers brushed his cheek. When I spoke, I felt as if a wave had rolled through the murky intoxication of our darkness. "In many ways, I already trust you." I outlined the tattoo that ran under his collarbone. "What you've shared about your family . . . you wouldn't have told me those things if you didn't care for me. And the way you've already made calls for my dad, sister, and Jerry . . . someday I hope I can do for you what you just did for me."

"I'll be waiting." He kissed me and drew all of my body to his.

Our chests, stomachs, and thighs touched throughout the night.

My cheek rested against his beautiful chest. His hands caressed the curve of my head and his embrace held me, preparing us to fly away in our dreams.

Our very souls seemed to relax after we'd shared some of the pain from our childhood. For the first time since becoming close to my sister again, I'd felt a deep and intimate connection with another person.

It was glorious.

Ryan fell asleep before I did. His muscles relaxed. His arms went limp around my body. His chest rose and fell in a regular rhythm. His breathing went from shallow to long and deep.

My body sang him a silent lullaby.

Together, our spinning minds slowed. They finally stopped to say good night. After the rush and sleepless nights of the past week, I closed my eyes and joined him not too much later.

My body was secure, loved, and content.

I knew we were heading into the unknown.

Chapter 25

The Morning After

When I opened my eyes the sun shone through the windows. Rays of filtered light sprayed on our bodies.

I felt the breezes through the screen door.

I imagined the pine trees bending on the hills.

The gulls and sea lions had begun their songs of life and the stars of night had fallen away.

The beautiful man with whom I'd lain during the night moved on top of my body. He was erect. When he kissed my lips, the soft notes of his love began to play like a melody.

"Morning, sweet Nicky."

"Morning." I stretched toward him.

"God, you feel good." He opened my legs and put them around his hips. "I love the feel of your body surrounding me."

His hard penis lay between my legs touching the entrance and warmth to my soft inner core. I didn't ask him to reassure me he wouldn't push further. I didn't hesitate or resist—I opened. My heels rested on his back and my legs hugged his sides. With one movement, he could've gotten pleasure inside me.

Fingers danced up and down my sides. Outlined my hips and the curve of my breasts. Long, slow kisses from his lips were delicious treats. I'd never been brought into a new day so beautifully. Even in my vulnerable position, I felt comfortable and safe.

I kissed and wiggled underneath him, trying to feel his beautiful, hard chest and his loins against my belly. I didn't understand what I was doing to him.

"Don't." His tone was firm.

"What?"

"The way you're moving, you're . . . inviting me to . . . we both agreed I wouldn't push you. Don't you feel me? I could . . . it would be so easy to . . . your sweetness covers my entire world. I've never experienced anything like it. When you squirm under me all I can think about is the tender depths of your vagina. The thought of your feminine softness around me is almost unbearable."

"I don't mean to tease you, it's only that I want to feel you like this. You're everything I knew you'd be." I shared my joy more boldly than ever before. "I want to get closer."

"There's a way we can do that." He lifted his head. Looked at me in surprise. Another look—a look I was coming to know well—replaced it. I saw his body unravel its layers of protection. He'd very slowly sliced them away each time we were together, showing me that he was ready for me in every way.

"I know." I ran my hands up and down his back. Placed them on the curve of his head pulling him down for a kiss.

We were in and out of sleep and desire the rest of the morning.

When only a few precious minutes remained before we had to leave our little nest, Ryan rolled off of me with a sigh and got up.

I enjoyed the view of his strong back, his defined and round behind and his muscular thighs. He seemed to shine with the colors of wheat and honey, blessed by the late-morning sun. His body was beautiful and I looked forward to enjoying more.

"You better not sneak a peek." He turned to see if I was looking.

"Sorry, I already did." I covered my eyes.

"Nasty, Nicky," he chuckled and made some coffee for us. He brought me a cup. Sat down on the side of the bed.

Wouldn't this be lovely if it were a regular routine in my life, this wonderful man loving me, bringing me coffee, and whatever came next . . . what a nice daydream.

"You owe *me* a peek." He set the cups down on the nightstand and reached to pull the sheet down from my chin.

"Nope." I gripped it tightly, holding on with both hands, giving myself a fragile sense of security. "You'll have to take a rain check on that one."

"Uh-huh. I'll take that rain check—soon."

I'm a liquid mess under this sheet.

When he went into the bathroom, I threw off the covers and grabbed for my clothes. I tried to dress before he came out. I couldn't find my underwear.

Where are they? Where did he throw them? Tear the covers apart! Strip the sheets off the bed! I'll never get that bra on so it fits right before he comes out of the bathroom.

I finally saw my pants. I remembered he'd tossed my panties in the same area. I started to look by the sofa and then heard that low, masculine laugh.

"God, Ryan, turn around!" I pulled one of the creamy white throw blankets around me.

Of course, he ignored my request and instead came close wearing his naughty smile. When he put his arms around me, my heart began its serenade, speeding up, calling him closer.

"I promised I'd be a good boy. I'm true to my word. The thought of you under there . . . damn, woman. You know you're hard to resist."

He took a few steps back and retrieved my clothes from across the room. The smile on his face grew as he held up my big-girl panties.

"I know what you're thinking." I waved my hand. "I don't like the skimpy stuff. So if you're expecting me to wear little panties, thongs, and lacy bras, you won't see them. That's not me."

When he closed the distance between our bodies I was certain the air between us had been displaced. I was sure he'd moved in slow motion when his big hands reached for my hips. When they held them it was all I could do to stand.

Oh, damn!

"I love that about you." His fingertips squeezed my skin. "You don't need to explain what you like. I accept everything about you. Let me know when you're ready." Ryan opened the sliding door and walked onto the deck.

I headed into the bathroom. I was so tense that it took several deep breaths to stop the pounding in my face. Just as I feared, I couldn't get the bra to fit right. I tucked it into my pocket and fixed the scarf so it covered my chest. After using the little bottle of mouthwash the Inn provided to freshen my breath, I turned out the light. I'd barely finished with my scarf when Ryan stepped back into the room.

"That was quick." His gaze was hot on my face.

That look—the sound of his voice—he's going to give me heart failure. I'm here with a man—a big juicy man.

"Quickest I've ever dressed." I fastened my earrings.

He sat down on the love seat that faced the large picture window and brought his coffee with him. I eagerly followed.

"I guess I should have showered." I scooted closer.

"Did you think I might follow you in?"

"Think? *Knew* is the operative word." I didn't hide what I was certain he had considered.

His seductive laugh seemed to vibrate through my body, the sofa, and the entire room. I wondered if it was the reason a big wave suddenly rose up and crashed on shore. Even the sea lions rushed away from it, their belly muscles working to move them higher on the rocks to avoid being pulled into the ocean's fury.

It's too late for me to move on the rocks. I've already been pulled in.

He put his arm around me and let out a long sigh. He drew circles on my shoulders.

"Couldn't get that bra on, huh?" he teased. "Need some help?"

"Nope."

We sat together until the housekeeper knocked on the door.

"Hard to let go of this." His arm tightened around me.

"Yesterday, I was so sure you were telling me good-bye and now? I'm in a place I never thought possible. I'm sorry I didn't call you back, Ryan."

"Thank you." He kissed the side of my head. "For everything."

It made me feel good that I had been able to comfort him.

I knew how hard it was to calm childhood fears.

I had plenty of them.

"Let's go." He stood up and held his hand open, ready to take mine.

When I took it, I felt renewed, strong, and excited that our relationship had just jumped far above any level I'd ever envisioned with any boy— or any friend.

"Tomorrow I'll take you out for dinner. Promise." He kissed the back of my hand. "We'll dress up and wine and dine ourselves."

"It doesn't matter where we go, except . . ."

"Skiing?"

"Right. No skiing."

We both laughed and it made me feel good that he'd repeated my little joke from when we were on the beach. It was endearing and told me he was paying attention.

We said goodbye to Paula, the owner of the B & B, and walked down the little pathway from the entrance, back to our worlds of question, excitement, and the possibility of being together.

When we pulled up to my house, I didn't move. I didn't want to speak and break our bubble. As the silence lay between us, it was clear he waited for me to say something. Perhaps he was in the same dreamlike state that had covered me.

"I can hardly say good-bye to you. Did you know, even when you dropped me off from our visits to Yountville last year, I didn't want you to go? Could you feel *me*, Ryan?"

"God, you're . . ." He kissed each of my cheeks. "When you bare your soul, there's an honest beauty that reveals itself in your eyes. It's like an aura around your body. Even when you're afraid, you speak to me. I didn't expect you to so open this soon."

"Guess you bring it out of me. I feel like I can spill anything on you. I hope you feel the same way." I patted his hand. "Of course, the same applies to your kisses. I'm addicted to them!"

His big arm slid to the back of my head, bringing me to his lips, pressing me close, almost ending our embrace and pulling me back for another kiss. His unrelenting smile appeared. We'd come together and start all over again.

"I'll call you later." His face beamed. "Did you get your fill or do I need to kiss you again?"

"I could stay here all day if you're going to kiss me. I'd never let you pull away. You'd run out of gas as your car idled for hours."

"Can you move?" he taunted.

"Barely." My smile went from cheek to cheek. " I'll struggle to make it." I got out of the car.

"Nicky!" I turned and walked to the driver's side. He rolled down the window. "You can call me whenever you want. It doesn't matter how late. Don't worry about excuses. Even if I'm on the road and it's two in the morning, call me. If I can take your call, I will. If I can't, I have an honest reason and I'll call you back ASAP. Do you believe me?"

"I do. See you tomorrow." I gently kissed his cheek. "I'm not going to watch you leave, so go ahead and take off."

"Why not?"

"I don't like goodbyes." I looked at the sky until he spoke.

"All right, sweetheart." His face softened. "I'll call you later."

"Bye, Ryan." I patted his hands and then ran up the walkway.

When I went into my house, I leapt up the stairs to my bedroom. Immediately, I opened my journal to capture everything as accurately as I could. Then I changed my mind and decided to take a bath. I wanted to soak in the water, keeping the memories from Half Moon Bay circling around me, the same way I felt Ryan circling into my life.

Chapter 26

Checking In

When my cell phone rang, I was deep into my daydreams.

I was sure the golden vision of Ryan standing on the deck outside of our room at the Inn had burned into my brain forever. Seeing his picture on my phone brought the joy from my heart into my voice.

"Hi, Ryan!"

"You sound like you're a happy girl."

"I'm a *very* happy girl. I'm taking a bath, imagining you're the water circling around my body."

"Oh, baby . . . I've just . . ." He took a deep breath and remained silent for so long I thought we'd been disconnected.

"Are you still there?"

"I can't get the image out of my head."

"Image?" I grabbed the side of the tub. His words made me squirm. I wished he were there with me in the wet liquid.

"The one I have of you right now: naked, wet, and ready to be rubbed. I wish I was there to wash you . . ." The sound of his voice dipping and fluctuating made my breasts tender. "I called to hear your voice again. I also needed to explain why I couldn't invite you to be with me today."

"I don't expect you to feel obligated to be with me every free second you have." *Yes please, keep doing it.*

"No, I know you don't," he reassured. "Still, I want to make sure I don't elevate any fears you have about me."

That's thoughtful. "Thanks for being sensitive."

"I promised to spend the day with my brother."

"Aw, Ryan," I wanted to kiss his check. He was still reaching for the love of his older brother. I wondered if he even knew it. "That's very tender of you."

"Well, family is important regardless of our arguments," he paused. "I'd rather be with *you,* of course."

"I believe you." I held one of my breasts, gently squeezing and enjoying its softness. *Please keep reassuring me.*

"Believe me enough to commit to me?"

"I'm getting there." I admitted as much as I dared.

"You feel the pull, don't you?" He made me shiver in the memory of our pleasure. "The fears you have about me? I think they'll dissolve and wash away just like the bathwater around your beautiful body."

"How is it you always know the right thing to say?" I filled a sponge with water. Squeezed it over my belly. "Do you have some book of responses you've memorized? Can I borrow it?"

"I don't need a book, sweetness. I'm in love with you. Everything I say comes from my heart."

I'm a goner.

"Yeah, well, from your heart or not, I've never heard anyone talk like you do," I cautiously admitted.

"Except for you," he countered.

"Oh, you just . . . do you know you constantly chip away at me? You'd better be careful or pretty soon there won't be anything left of my body except a beating heart lying somewhere on the floor." I joked to stop spinning from the things he said.

All the layers and walls I'd built up since I was a little girl were cracking and crumbling; they still hadn't thinned enough for me to say aloud and without fear, *I love you.*

"I've already seen your heart." The sound of his voice slid through the water like a snake, circling and waiting for the right moment to bite me with sensual venom. "I don't know how I'll go a whole day without you. Maybe I'll throw a pebble at your window tonight. If you hear tapping, it's me, so let me in."

"Deal," I giggled. *I'll be listening!*

"See you tomorrow."

"Ryan? I heard um . . . you know, the words. I understand I'm not a joke to you anymore and I don't take what you said lightly. I have strong feelings for you. Well, more than that, I just need some time to sort through everything."

"I respect that. But sometimes . . ." He hesitated. I could hear him breathing. "Time isn't all that helpful."

"Ryan?"

"Sweetness?"

"You can throw a pebble at my window no matter how late it is. I already miss your chest; you have a lot of merit badges on that thing and I want to look at all of them."

"I can't wait for you to explore me." His husky laugh followed. "I'm an Eagle Scout so you'll need to spend a lot of time on my body. See you tomorrow, baby."

After I hung up, my emotions poured out.

They were shocking, unexpected, dramatic, sudden, and not the mountain-high joy I'd just felt with him.

These were the exact opposite.

Big sobs racked my body.

Typical of the way my feelings came to the surface when I let go, they exploded.

Pain.

Gut wrenching.

I'd held so much of myself—the person I longed to open and become—inside. For years, I'd carefully guarded the fears I was most afraid of, making sure no one got close to my locked rooms. I realized I'd lost possible relationships of all kinds because of my fears. The fences I'd built to guard and protect me had previously helped to keep stability in my life.

The curtain that parted for me made me realize I'd missed the high peaks of joy and low valleys of anger and sadness. Unable to face those dramatic upsets growing up resulted in being naïve and emotionally insecure. I had to confront he wonder and the peaks and despair of life—that was living.

Now, a good man loved me.

He'd reached out.

Exposed his heart.

Shown his vulnerability.

Was he ready to take every part of me—weak, strong, good, bad, flawed and brilliant? It seemed so. He needed to as I needed to accept him.

Just that realization in itself was emotional.

Incredible relief, confusion and fear—each of them tangled inside my mind.

I knew I was on the edge of something.

Even as I saw the possibilities of another life, I felt my feet dig in and resist. Why? What were those feelings telling me?

Was it that I looked forward to moving on and yet mourned the loss of sweet innocence as well as the finality of childhood?

For perhaps the first time in my life, I felt a little flame of desire light in my heart. I wanted to feel it burst into fire. The dream of love taking me into the embrace of a new life and all of its beauty, ugliness, joy, disappointment and vulnerability seemed a reality. Could I finally stop living to survive and instead welcome the chance to be elevated like never before as I experienced the promise of an intimate relationship?

I gave myself the time to experience the deep emotions that had just surfaced. When I was ready, I drained the bath water. Still wrapped in a towel, I knocked on Jenise's bedroom door.

"Come in!"

"Sorry to bother you. I need to go shopping today and was wondering if you'd go with me. Please, please, please?"

"Nice evening with Ryan?" Jenise smirked.

"Oh, yeah." I clasped my hands as if trying to hold his light inside them. "*Really* nice! He's wonderful."

"Sis—you're floating."

"I can't wait to be with him." I plopped on her bed. We bounced up and down. "I miss him so much. Twenty-four hours is too long to wait. I feel empty." I told her about my date. When I finished my story she had starry eyes of her own.

"Man, he sounds like he's really into you." Her smile was gorgeous and genuine.

"Do you think he could be . . . well, just infatuated?" I offered. "Men get confused that way, don't they?"

"Are you telling me that a twenty-five-year-old man," she replied sarcastically, "who's had all the pussy he wanted, probably fulfilled every sexual fantasy he's ever thought about—someone like him doesn't know the difference?"

"Oh, that's . . . yuck. When you put it like that—gross." My eyebrows furled. I shook my head.

"I'm not saying he's had all that. Well, pretty damn sure he has. You told me before Ryan is constantly surrounded by women. That probably means he's been with a fair number."

"They all want him. When we were at the hotel lounge before we went to see his brother last night, an exotic dancer he knows came to our table."

"Wow! How do you know she was a dancer?"

"She invited him to see her new routine. And guess what her name is?"

Jenise shrugged her shoulders.

"*Tabitha Sable.* Can you believe it?"

"Ballsy lady."

"I'll say. Shook my hand and everything, making sure she didn't seem like she was after him. Baloney. She wanted to send a message she was around. Then another female fan tried to talk with him—all kinds of women were staring."

"He's striking! Why wouldn't they?" She knelt on the bed with her arms crossed. "It's not a big deal."

"To you, maybe," I scoffed.

"He knows the difference between infatuation and love. "And *you*?"

"What do you mean, *and me*? Of course I looked at him."

"No." She laughed. "I mean do *you* know the difference between love and infatuation?"

"Yes."

"How?" she challenged.

"I'm infatuated with Jerry. The way I feel about Ryan is way different."

"And?"

"I love him. I'm afraid to say the words out loud. God, I *do* love him. I hope everything doesn't change if I say it. Our date was magnificent, Jenise. I mean really special. It's just . . . I'm not ready for any earthquakes. I don't want any more of those."

"Why?" She raised her arms with such force she jiggled the bed. "Shout the words! An earthquake could be what saves you!"

"Saves me from what?" I was on edge and wanted her to get to the point. "I want peace and quiet until I get out of here. Don't you want that?"

"Fuck no. Peace and quiet is for chicken shits. Rebel! Be different! Dare to challenge yourself! All your rigid and high-minded morality . . . Sis, no black angel is going to come down and take you to hell if you have sex. Give into your feelings."

"If I do, I mean, do you think someone like him would really support my dreams? He'll expect me to change and give up the things I want as soon as I do it, won't he?"

"I can't see that." Jenise tucked one leg under her. "I'll bet he could've had dozens of women who'd be willing to drop everything for him. As you get to know each other you'll know if he doesn't encourage you to reach for your goals. Then? You simply move on."

"That sounds easy enough. What if I'm in too deep? And the other thing is, we've only been seeing each other a few weeks. Can I really believe what I'm feeling? How can I really know? Don't you think it's too soon?"

"The hell with that." My sister was fierce and determined. "*No*, it's not too soon. What do you *feel*?" She poked her finger on my chest. "What's inside there?"

"Last night, I came close. I wanted to admit I loved him. All I could say was I have strong feelings for him." I held her upper arm. "I've never dated like this and I don't have any other experiences. I mean, it's the first real relationship I've had and I'm already in love? Maybe it's only a crush."

"Oh, shit, Nicky, you go on and on, circling the same question. Honestly, tell me," Jenise repeated. "*What* do you *feel*?"

My voice broke.

Tears poured.

"I really love him."

She held me in her arms. It felt so good to be wrapped inside them after so many years of my self-imposed distance from people—and not too long ago—from her.

"I know you do. Get out of your head." She patted my back. Repeated, "I know you do. I know."

"I feel like I'm sinking." I gradually let go of our sweet embrace. "Sometimes I feel like it's all bright and rosy and then suddenly I can't see the bottom of some forbidden, endless and dark hole that surrounds me."

"Nicky, look at me and listen carefully." She took my hands in hers. "*I* am a rape survivor."

"I know."

"*I* am a rape survivor," she repeated.

"Yes."

"How do you think I made it?" Jenise's hands were turned up. Her palms seemed to symbolize her spirit opening to me.

"I don't know."

"Yes, you do." Her eyes were penetrating. "How do *you* survive? How have we survived our home life?"

"We focus on other things."

"Right," she agreed. "And how did I do that, knowing those boys might still be waiting for me to come home from school one day and could've attacked me again?"

"I don't know how you did it." I put my head down. I could hardly stand to hear my sister relive the trauma of being raped at fourteen.

"By keeping my head up." She lifted her chin a little. "Letting people help me. Do *not* put your head down, Nicky. You can't stay closed off. Remaining frozen and afraid doesn't solve anything. Take one little step. Reach for what *you* want, not what you think Mom and Dad wants. Otherwise? You'll never really come to life."

I fixed my eyes on her.

Watched her.

Noticed the strong women she'd become in a new way.

"Don't *ever* hide. You're unique," Jenise admonished. "You're my beautiful and brilliant sister. Ryan would be lucky to have you. Not the other way around."

"I won't hide," I affirmed. A light bulb went on.

"When you decide about Ryan, forget about what anyone thinks except for the two of you. He's obviously putting his heart out there for you to grab. If you want him, screw everyone else. Our parents had their chance. They fucked it up. It's up to them to live their life and make their marriage work. Don't let them make you afraid and fuck you up, too, Nicky. You said you felt something even *last* year, when he first approached you, right?"

"When he kissed my hand."

"You've mentioned that moment several times." Her smile lit up her face. "So, the feelings you have are from much earlier than only the few recent weeks together. He knows what a good person you are. All the things he's done to get your attention—volunteering with you, the Goliaths' party, roses on prom night—I'd say he's been looking at you for a while."

"True."

"So . . . he's *seen* the inside of you." She drummed her fingers on her cheek. Has he *felt* the inside of you?"

"God, Jenise."

My cell phone beeped.

"Hold on!" I ran into my room, anxious to see if Ryan sent me a quick hello. I brought my phone into Jenise's room.

He'd texted: *Still soaking in the bathtub?*

"What's with the smile?" Jenise coaxed.

"He's hard to resist," I reported. "Hang on. I have to respond." I texted back: *Have a towel wrapped around me and nothing else.* "Ha! That'll teach him. Look what I wrote." I showed Jenise.

Another beep: *If only you'd showered with me.*

I returned: *If we'd done that I'd still have bathed.*

Ryan texted: *Nasty, Nicky.*

I laughed out loud.

"Sexting?" Her eyebrows rose, reminding me of how Ryan's face brightened when he was up to no good. I felt so hopeful at the thought of the two of them being friends.

"Look at you bursting with happiness."

"That's not only because of Ryan," I shared. "My big sister has something to do with it."

"Quit putting limitations on your relationship before you've even begun to explore what you have." She took my hands in hers. "What I can picture for you is happiness. I've often wondered if you've included it in your plans. You've visualized everything so you can get out of the house and go to college with your predefined picture of how your life is supposed to be. That's fine. When it comes to love? You think something magical happens when you suddenly decide you're ready for a relationship? Mr. Charming isn't going to show up right on schedule, sis."

"I don't think that."

"No?"

"No!"

"You sure act like everything will play out like a romance novel. Come on. You think you have that much say so over love and relationships?"

"But I'm not looking for—"

"Well?" she probed. "Do magical dreams fill that smart head of yours? Snap your fingers, twitch your nose, wave a magic wand, and when you're ready, a sexy man comes along for you?"

I sat in silence, waiting for her to continue.

What she'd just pointed out . . . was exactly how I saw my life.

"I'm afraid you'll look back and regret how you pushed aside someone who could've been the love of your life or at least, a special memory. The feelings you have don't come around all that often. Sorry to say this, but you tend to throw happiness away with both hands. It's as if you don't think you're worthy."

"I guess I can't believe someone loves me. I'm so afraid he'll leave me after I open up to him." I answered in a whisper as if someone else was in the room eavesdropping. "Once he sees my insecurities, I'm scared he'll run for the hills."

"This is *your* life, Nick. If he leaves you, then he does. You gamble. Take a risk. Move on. It will hurt like hell. That's life.

That's risk. That's taking a chance on love—on everything. You learn from your mistakes. Maybe you chose to risk yourself a little differently next time. Don't close down. And what if he takes off? You said yourself you really don't want to be serious."

"I know I said that. Now I don't want him to go."

"I could be wrong, but . . . crap, this is hard to say." She looked out her window. Then looked back at me. "You can stop taking care of Dad."

"What? I'm not—" I started to defend myself.

"Let me finish. You don't need to be Dad's good girl or any kind of example to your friends. Ryan doesn't need to be taken care of like that. For once, let someone take *your* hand. You're not a nun, for fuck's sake."

I was sure that if I held onto my emotions, there was a chance to end the screaming. Hitting. The abuse. I thought if I could keep my father close, I could take his danger away from my mother and sister. It was the only way I knew how to help them.

He didn't hit me like he did them.

He wasn't violent with me like he was with them.

Except for his verbal insults and rage, which I'd learn to accept and deal with, I wasn't attacked.

Except for holding his belt in the air, threatening to strike me, I wasn't in danger.

I remained passive with my father. I learned that challenging him would pull his trigger.

And that passivity caused him to drive me home from the bar after he'd gotten drunk.

And listening to his drunken stories for hours while the only thing I wanted to do was sleep.

Staying passive and putting him to bed with conversation or literally pulling the covers over him, got him out of our lives— for the night.

My passivity allowed me to slip in and out of our family's dysfunction. I didn't speak up.

I was hardly noticed and I wanted it that way.

The only place I stood out on purpose was at school and where I volunteered.

Those times needed to be over.

I could no longer trade temporary peace for staying quiet.

It was time to make a stand.

"We were expected to be tough girls," Jenise continued. "How many times were we left on our own—even when Mom and Dad were home? They'd forget about us, assuming we were okay until dinner, which was hell, wasn't it?"

"Yeah." I covered my face, remembering the evening our father choked my sister. My mother had to pull him off of her before he killed her.

"I took the physical bullshit of Dad's drunkenness," she pulled my hands down. "You had to watch his lifeless face as he sat on your bed, sought your company, and gave you those gross, stinking hugs.

"Do you think I've forgotten the nights when Mom was late and you tucked him into bed? She stayed away on purpose. She knew you'd take care of him. That wasn't right. We took it because we had no choice. Now we do."

Yes, now we do.

"Ryan isn't Dad, she continued. "He isn't one of your friends who depend on you to tell them it's okay. They know you'll do whatever they want and take them where they need to go because you're always there for them. That's how you've retained their friendships—by making it easy for *them*."

I guess I did do that. I wasn't even aware.

"This life needs to be about *you*, Nick. And the man that loves you? He wants you as you are. Stop trying to be the perfect friend, daughter, and now girlfriend. It's time to relax and show your individuality. If he doesn't take you as is? He's not worth it."

"God, I'm so sappy lately." I looked at the bedcovers and tears spilled down my cheeks.

I had to joke away my struggle.

It was our way and what I knew.

"Let go and enjoy your exploration," she encouraged. "Check him out and let him check you out. See if you get along before you start worrying about commitment and other women. Both of you might decide it's not right after all and you'll be friends. On the other hand, it could all fall into place."

"Yeah. It's more than that, Jenise."

"What is it?"

"Dad's in danger of losing his job. He's on strict probation at work. I'm afraid he's going to be fired."

"*What*?" she shouted.

"I spoke with his supervisor and it's bad. Remind me to tell you about that meeting. His name is Sid Freeman. Ryan knows him. That's how I got the appointment. I'm afraid I'm going to lose Stanford, but I don't know how to bring it up. Do you think Mom knows?"

"We need to talk to Mom *and* Dad," she was obviously concerned. "It's not only you; it affects me, too."

"Please keep quiet for now."

"Why should I?"

"Ryan's trying to help," I shared.

"How?"

"He asked a guy he knows in the union to start filing disability papers," I told her. "If it goes through, Dad can go out on paid leave and won't be in danger of being terminated. Most importantly, his retirement will be safe."

"*Your* Ryan is doing this?"

"Yeah."

"And you're having doubts about someone like *that*?"

"I don't doubt his generosity. Honestly? I'm afraid if I give in, we'll be so right there may be no turning back. I have a feeling I'll be in so deep I'll drown."

"I'd love to witness you drowning in love. Then *you* can be the one to do exotic dances for him in private!" she giggled. "Your name can be Nicolette Faire."

We both cracked up.

"So, when do you want to go shopping?"

Chapter 27

Do You Think We're Weird?

Once again, the tears filled my eyes.

"God, I'm a blubbering mess. I start to cry at the mere thought of something sentimental."

"You're in love." Jenise put her hand on mine. "The emotions have only just begun."

"*Great* news." I shot back sarcastically. Appreciating how my sister took the time to share her wisdom with me, I gathered myself to compliment my wise sister. "Damn, you're smart. When did that happen?"

"You haven't been around a lot to notice. You're different yourself these days. I think . . ." She trailed off, but taunted me with a knowing look. "I think it's because of Ryan."

My foot rapidly tapped the floor and my leg jiggled the bed.

"You're a strong woman." Jenise grabbed my wrist, subtly acknowledging my nervousness. "I cherish that part of you. He's had an effect. A softer side seems to be coming through."

I started to argue. I never wanted to be seen as weak.

"Now before you get huffy, I don't mean you need to be soft to be a woman," she elbowed me in the ribs. "It's just that in the past you weren't easy to reason with. Once you made up your mind there was no changing it."

"Okay . . ." I still wasn't happy with her explanation.

"You're approachable now and it's pretty fucking great."

That made sense. I had to admit I did feel something inside me turning over. It was as if my inner core had been covered in layers and as they dropped, someone new was gradually exposed. Having my sister in my corner to recognize and validate my feelings felt damn good.

"Why I came in here in the first place is Ryan is taking me out to a fancy dinner tomorrow. I need a knockout dress and your help with a couple of other pieces. I don't know where to begin and—Ooh! Let me show you what I got when I was in LA! I have gifts! Plus, I've got your clothes to give back to you, too."

"Are they clean? You know . . . no sex residue?" she cackled.

"No. Geez." I went to my closet and took out the suit, dress, purse, and shoes I got in LA as well as the extra goodies given to me by the designers and their assistants. When she saw the labels, her eyes widened in curiosity.

"Wow! They're beautiful, you lucky girl!" She applied the lipstick, sprayed the perfume and tried on the makeup. "Can Alex hook me up? *Chanel*! Can I borrow this purse?"

"It's yours."

"Which?"

"All of it except for my suit, dress, sunglasses, and leather folio. You can have the ankle boots, too." I picked the boots off the floor and put them on her lap. "And take one of the scarves. There. Now we're even."

"How? This is so much stuff!"

"Because . . . well, your bra. I ruined it." I took it from the pocket of her silk pants. "Look. The hooks are toast."

"I knew your boobs were too big for it. Or was it *Ryan*?"

"One hundred per cent me." I felt my face flush. Once again I was embarrassed about my body. "You like the make up?"

"This is designer stuff. Who wouldn't? Thanks, this is so cool of you—wait. You want a sexy dress for dinner with Ryan? Didn't you dress last night so you *wouldn't* be sexy?"

"I still don't want a dress that shows boobs or ass, but I do want him to do a double take—maybe a triple take," I joked. "I guess some skin needs to show. As little as possible, okay?"

"So, how *was* sex with your sweetie?" She folded her arms, ready to hear a juicy story.

"We didn't have any."

She looked at me as if I were crazy.

"You've spent another night in bed with him, and—you're kidding me. You had sex with him, *didn't* you?"

"No."

"No, as in you didn't spend a night in bed with him?"

"No as in no sex." I turned away from her. "Why is it so unbelievable?"

"It's just, you seem to be two very passionate people. Like, how did you resist his body? Shit, how did he resist those tits and that ass of *yours*?"

"He managed," I scoffed. "Let me get this straight. Because we haven't had sex we're not serious?"

"It doesn't mean that at all. You've slept in the same bed twice—you're telling me both times you only made out? I can't imagine someone like him—"

"We kissed," I interjected. "He kissed—"

"Tell! Now we're getting to the juice!"

"He kissed my inner thighs. I thought I might get his face wet." My thumb rubbed across my cellphone where Ryan's picture had been moments ago. "When he took off my panties he made a point to tell me they were wet. I about died."

"I bet he loved that! Did he put his mouth on Miss Puss?" She seemed barely able to contain herself.

263

"No, but his forehead brushed my hair down there. We had the lights out. He didn't see me."

"You don't wax?"

"Why should I?"

"Um, you'll find out soon enough. On the other hand, maybe he likes it bushy. By the way, if you do? Ask for a landing strip," she laughed.

"What's—"

"I'll show you later. Anyway, damn, Nick. For that man to restrain himself and let you lie next to him naked . . . I'm not sure you understand how serious he is. Wasn't his waving schlong trying to enter your wet lady? He didn't try to put it in?"

I completely turned around so she couldn't see my utter and total embarrassment.

"Ah! I'm on to something! Tell!" she pressed.

"This morning I had my legs open around his hips and his penis was right there. One push and hello Mr. Magic." We cracked up. My eyes were wide open. "And for your information, *I'm* the one who wanted to lie naked with him."

"He's pretty intense, isn't he?" She grabbed her hair and pulled each side up into ponytails. "Why didn't you let him bring you to orgasm with his tongue?"

"Too early for that."

"Oh, fuck no. It's never too early for a tongue bath. Come on. Let that man on and in your body." Jenise was like a cheerleader with invisible pompoms.

"I didn't have that um, that dental dam and—"

"Oh, yeah?" She cracked up. "If you had one, you'd have said, *here's my dental dam, Ryan. Now get to work?*"

"No. God, you're intense just like he is."

"You must've felt him. He was standing at attention, wasn't he?" Her face was alive with delight.

"We were standing on the deck together, watching the sunset."

"No, I mean wasn't his dick hard?" She held an erect finger near her stomach.

"Shut up!"

"Well?"

"Of course," I rolled my eyes at her. "It seems like he gets hard if the wind blows the right way."

She cracked up. "Because you haven't had sex with him. What do you expect? So you were naked, you felt it now, right?"

I smiled and played with the bedspread.

"Is he as big as you suspected?"

"I don't know." *I don't want to talk about it.*

"Yes you do. Don't be so tightly wound. You're so afraid of intimacy," she accused. "You can't even stand to talk about it."

I've been trying to tell you that. How can I be intimate when it means giving in? Isn't that what Mom did?

"No! I can't. Happy? Just drop it," I argued. "Besides, Ryan and I have already been more intimate than a lot of couples at this stage, so don't judge us."

"Ooh, so defensive, little sissy. You. Are. Most. Definitely. In love." The smile soon faded and she became serious. "I'm not kidding when I say this. Listen to me. Trust me, okay?"

Trust? How do you do that?

"You haven't fully admitted how you feel. I get it. If you take him for granted, you may never get anyone like him again. I'm telling you, please grab him like he's trying to grab you. Otherwise? It may be a few weeks or months for you to realize what you had, but you'll regret it. He'll move on with another woman if you don't open up. He loves you now and he won't wait long. No one can tell another person they love them without hearing the words repeated back to them for long."

A crash!

We both jerked hard.

A loud bang on her bedroom door shocked us.

Something smacked into it from the hallway.

Loud.

The wood sounded like it had cracked.

We looked at each other.

Dad.

We heard him stumbling down the hallway . . . drunk.

"God." I shook my head.

"He started early today," Jenise whispered.

"I'm afraid it's getting close at his job," I confided.

"Let's ask Mom."

"Please give Ryan a little more time," I begged. "This is delicate and needs to be done carefully. If we confront him, Dad could reverse in denial and everything might fall apart."

"Well," she shrugged her shoulders. "I guess there's nothing we can do. We'll have to trust that Ryan knows what he's doing."

"When I spoke with Sid Freeman it seemed as if things were in motion, so . . ."

"Back to Ryan."

"Who knows? Maybe if I told him I won't be able to commit right up front I'd save myself from being hurt. He has a bad reputation, after all."

"Bullshit. I hate that fucking reputation stuff. Sex is just sex. It's not wrong. He's single. For a while *I* had a reputation, too. What about that?" Her jaw stiffened in defiance.

"I didn't mean—"

"Get over the purity shit, would you?"

"I'm trying," I frowned at her.

"Picture him kissing someone else while you're cheering. Or you watch him walk up to another woman. He flirts with her and gives her a wink. What if he takes her hand and kisses it?"

"Stop!" I snapped. "I hate what you're saying!"

"Then shout your feelings! Grab him! He's waiting for you to do it! Maybe I'll call him tell him before you blow it."

Would you, please?

"I'm messed up. Alex believes we're all damaged because of our family trauma. Maybe I'll never be ready."

"Maybe we are damaged." She seemed in full agreement. "I've got a good head on my shoulders. So do you. *Use* it. Understand?"

"Yes mam," I poked. "I feel funky now about all this. Can you go with me today or what?"

"Sure I'll go. I didn't mean to make you feel bad. I'd never do that on purpose."

"I guess." I pouted.

"Come on." She nudged my shoulder. "Don't you?"

"Just kidding. Yes, I do."

"I've been through some things and can see how special Ryan is to you. I don't want you to send him away because you're afraid to take a chance. We all have fears. At some point you've got to stake your claim. Loving someone isn't a sin, Nick. Neither is consensual sex. By the way? Everyone's damaged in one way or another. That's life. We straighten ourselves out the best we can. I work on myself all the time. I don't think we're ever done, you know?"

"Doesn't seem like it. Would it be okay if we left in an hour?"

"I'll start getting ready. I have a new designer purse to bring with me!" She held it to her chest. "Be careful going out the door. Let me know if he cracked it. He fell pretty hard."

I opened her door and examined it. Didn't see any obvious damage. After I went back to my room, I couldn't help but obsess about the conversation with my sister. I felt odd. Was my relationship with Ryan valid without sex? I had to call him.

"Hi, sweetness, what's up?" He answered immediately.

Oh, you make me feel so, so lovely.

"Are you out with Chris and Frances yet?"

"I'm on my way to meet them now. How can I help you, Ms. Young?"

"Do we have a relationship if we're not having sex?" I blurted. "I told my sister about our evening and she thought it was weird that we didn't, you know, have it."

"*Have* it?" Sensuality wove through his voice.

"You know what I mean." *I can just visualize the smile on your face.*

"Of course we have a relationship." A cable car bell rang in the background.

"You shouldn't be driving and talking on your phone," I reprimanded.

"Will you punish me for being bad?"

Silence.

"Kidding! Just kidding, Nicky," he laughed nervously. "Don't hang up!"

I let out a deep sigh of relief. *I wonder if he's into all that kinky sex. Makes sense he is with the variety he's had.*

"I have hands free, babe. My cell is synced to the phone in my vehicle. You don't have to worry about your man."

"That wasn't nice."

"But it was wicked fun."

"Anyway . . ." *What a bad, bad, boy you are, Mr. Tilton.* "I didn't think about us being weird until I talked with her. You and I were naked, but sex wasn't the reason I wanted to take our clothes off. I didn't give you mixed signals, did I?" When he didn't answer, I quickly continued. "Am I strange to be with?"

"Oh, sweetheart, your innocence—"

"I'm sorry; I know I'm a pain."

"You're maddening. Wonderful. Frustrating. Lovely. Baby, you're anything but weird—at least in a bad way. The only pain you cause me?"

"Am I damaging your reputation?" I changed the subject before he started talking sexy. I wasn't going to see him that day and didn't want to spiral into lust so soon.

"My reputation?"

"Your wild boy rep," I exhaled.

"That's all bullshit. You know my feelings; it's you and me. Anyone else forms an opinion? None of their business."

"How can you be so patient when it comes to having sex with me. You never have been, have you?"

"I'm not out of control."

"Hormonal urges are pretty powerful and you've been with lots of women. They're all after you. Tabitha, for one."

"Honey, I'm almost twenty-six. My hormones aren't raging. Yours, on the other hand . . . I'd *love* to soothe them."

"Yeah, well I—"

"We'll find out soon enough what makes each of us at ease," he interrupted at just the right time. "When two people are serious about each other, they push to the next level gradually. I'm enjoying you revealing yourself to me."

"I worry I'm not revealing things fast enough." I flipped positions on my sofa and held my toy bunny, Mr. Blackberry.

"I do want sex with you—God, Nicky, I want it. I believe the right moment will arrive for us. When that happens, I hope we'll both recognize it."

"Why is it taking me so long to get comfortable with having sex?" I was frustrated with myself. "My sister thinks I'm in danger of letting you slip away. What if I'm so backward I can't give in the way you want?"

"You do scare me."

"Why?" *What?* "I can't believe you said that." I switched my phone to the other ear.

"Just being honest. I'm afraid you won't enjoy my body the way I hope you will and your walls stay up. My fear is you'll shut me out before you really get to know me. Or the opposite might happen—you use me to get your confidence with sex and leave. You keep warning that you're gone in January. It doesn't feel good to hear that."

"Oh, I'm . . . I'm sorry. Until you just repeated it back to me, I never realized how bad it sounded. I didn't mean to be threatening. That's my fear talking."

"I tell myself that. You're still intimidating." There was sudden commotion in the background. "Hang on." A minute later he was back on phone.

"What happened?"

"Police car siren. I muted you so it wouldn't blare in your ear. I'm trying hard to make your fortress weaken. It's another kind of strength to be patient and talk things through. Believe me?"

"Yes."

"Nicky?" Ryan had a little hint of mischief in his voice.

"Yeah?" I closed my eyes. *Something sexy is coming I just know it. I'm going to squirm all day long from what he says.*

"When we explore the physical part of our relationship more deeply, you've got a lot of love coming."

Oh, my throat—it's closing up again. I'm sure I have asthma. I'd better make an appointment with the doctor.

"Nicky?"

"Yeah?"

"Are you still afraid of being with *me*?" Ryan asked.

"Sometimes I am. The conversations we have, the kissing, it's all so good. I'm afraid it's only a bubble waiting to pop." *Just like every other bubble in my life.* "I worry your magic will sweep me away."

"That's a bad thing?" he asked sincerely.

"I don't want all that I've worked toward to be for nothing. Regardless of what happens though, I don't want either of us to be afraid."

"We'll get there. I promise I won't leave you just because you're not ready for intercourse. My past isn't important because I've been with a certain number of women. It's that it brought me to you."

"How come you're attracted to me, Ryan? I mean, really. Be honest and tell me."

"Your kindness. The hope you have about people and what could be. Your views on life . . . I feel like anything is possible when loving you. You've touched me in ways I've never been." He took a deep breath. "I watched you for weeks when you sat in the bleachers before the game. Your gentle way . . . I haven't seen it before. You have a light and it's all around you. To me, everything I once hoped for when I was just a boy is possible with you. It's like I still have my childhood in front of me when we're together."

"Speaking of your childhood, Mr. Blackberry is sitting with me and says hello. *And* I just told him I'm going to buy a hot dress for our date tomorrow." I changed the subject before he pushed me to say, *I love you.* "He's very excited about it."

He opened his heart and was vulnerable. You ignored him.

"A hot dress—*you*?"

"Jenise is helping me pick it out. You're taking me somewhere I can wear a nice dress, I hope. Remember last year when I talked about going to that hamburger joint in St. Helena? We're not going for burgers, are we? I mean, it's okay, but I don't want to wear the dress I'm thinking of buying just for hamburgers."

"Your sister." His voice was soft, as if beginning a nice thought and then he went into a laughing fit. "Hamburger joint— yeah, I remember that sweet girl who suggested we go there. I already told you we'd go somewhere nice, silly. Anyway," he laughed again, "what I started to say is that your sister is next on my list. I'd like to invite her and her boyfriend to go out with us."

"Maybe they can come with us tomorrow night?" I checked.

"Tomorrow, I'm going to dazzle only you, my baby."

"You already do. God bless America, do you ever."

"Uh-huh, I know."

"And you're so humble," I kidded. "I know you've got to go. Thanks for talking. I'm trying to understand moral and spiritual beliefs that have been a part of me for a long time. I know it's difficult for you to be patient. I still haven't decided about having sex before marriage.

"My friends are having it," I tried to give him as much insight as I could. "So is my sister. It's not that I think any less of anyone having sex or that it's wrong or dirty, but I'm still confused about that part of our relationship. I'm weird, I know."

"I wish more people were weird like you. Call me whenever you want," he offered. "Can't wait to see you tomorrow."

"Ryan!" I called out to him again, wanting to stay connected for another moment.

"Yes, sweetheart?"

"I really like you . . . a lot."

"I really like you, too. *Ciao, Bella.*" As he hung up, I heard him chuckling.

Chapter 28

Shopping for a Hot Dress

*J*enise made a unilateral decision to go to Union Square for the clothes I needed. It was the oldest and in my opinion, the most charming shopping area in all of San Francisco. In addition to stores like Neiman Marcus, Saks Fifth Avenue, and Nordstrom, there were also many expensive designer boutiques.

"Let me pick out some dresses and I'll tell you what looks good. You don't know any better," my sister joked.

"Hey, not nice," I protested.

"Trust me, I know what'll look good on your curvy body."

"Don't pick anything that shows my boobs or ass," I warned.

"Why worry when you can't hide those," she giggled.

"I'm serious, Jenise."

"So am I," she countered.

We talked more about Sid Freeman and Walter Dixon as she looked through the racks of evening and cocktail dresses. I revealed more of the details of Ryan's acquaintance, Mr. Tremmel and the time needed for Dad's disability to come through. Then, I told her about my meeting with Walter Dixon, the Athletic Director at Stanford and how I believed he was Ryan's angel on Earth. I strategically hid from her my conversations with Misters Woodson and Blockley, In case my budding romance didn't work out. I didn't want to set her up for disappointment.

"Here, take these three dresses into the changing room." She shoved them into my open arms. "Be sure to come out and model each one for me. They're having a clearance sale, so you'll have money left over for the other pieces you need. Do I know how to shop or what?"

"We'll see," I teased. I tried on the first dress and modeled for her. I got a thumbs-down. Tried on the second dress and walked out to show her.

"That's it!" She threw her arms up.

It was a royal blue Adrianna Papell sheath dress, with intricate lace overlays, softly pleated cap sleeves, a U-shaped neck and an alluring back cutout. It fell at my knee.

"Oh, that's so your color! Your green eyes, your wavy flowing hair on your bare shoulders . . . his tongue will hang out so far it'll be on the ground. Plus, there's the right amount of hug against your ass to spin him into a wild fantasy."

I felt my edges begin to round. My feminine side gently stroked me from within as it yearned to expose my soft underbelly. It seemed as if a shiny brass ring hung in front of me.

If I could reach it, what would I do?

"You're unbelievable at this, sissy girl. Now that we're done, can I take you to dinner or do you have a date with Sean?" I batted my eyelashes mocking her affections.

"No Sean tonight." She made a pouty face. "He's going to some function with his folks. I'm up for an evening with you."

"Pick where you want to go," I suggested.

"I can't turn down an offer like that! How about Daily Grill?"

"Great." I adjusted the bags with my new clothes for a tighter grip. "I love their burgers and I haven't been in ages."

"Don't fill up too much—you don't have a lot of room in that dress. Of course, wouldn't he'd love to see you rip a seam!"

"Well great. You've given me something else to worry about." We walked by Maiden Lane. It was an area of boutiques, jewelry stores, expensive stationery and office chic, salons, and sidewalk cafes. I glanced at the brightly lit store windows filled with Prada, Xanadu, Mont Blanc and Chanel, among other items from top designers and artists. I knew they were too expensive for me, but I hoped someday I'd be able to afford them.

"I love Maiden Lane, too." Jenise obviously noticed the dreamy look in my eyes.

Perhaps I'll sit in my own chair in some corporate office overlooking the San Francisco skyline. I'll run in on my lunch hour, buy a lovely scarf and wrap it around me, and then skip back to work.

Over dinner, my sister talked about her goals. Until that evening, I hadn't realized how she'd quietly planned her career without anyone noticing—except Sean.

"I need this." She dipped her beer battered cod filet into some malt vinegar. "I *have* to make it to prove to myself I've achieved everything in spite of what happened."

"Do you mean—"

"Yes." She assumed I meant her attack. She was right. "I need to shout to those fuckers who raped me, *you assholes didn't kill my spirit*. After all, living well is the best revenge, right?"

My sister had long ago emerged from a cocoon. I thought her to be beautiful in every way. It wasn't only her long, thick, dark hair falling against her fair complexion and striking hazel eyes that drew me in. The determined spirit coming from her heart— the same heart I'd shunned as being weak seven years earlier— had become strong. The brilliance shining from within her was like the northern star.

"In my opinion? You've proven everything already." I offered all my encouragement, still thinking about my parents overlooking the need to have a heart-to-heart talk with her. "You're the bravest person I know."

"Thanks." Her smile went cheek to cheek.

"I never understood your courage until recently." Overwhelmed with so much love, I could barely contain myself. I reached for her hand and held it. "I'm so sorry I turned away from you. I promise I'll never do that again."

"You didn't know—"

"I *did* know. I knew exactly what I was doing," I confessed. "Maybe I didn't understand your trauma completely. I still don't, really. I was disgusted you didn't take those boys and their families to court and sue them for everything they had."

"Did you know they moved away and did jail time?"

"No. I was always afraid to ask you anything about it." I held my burger firmly between my hands and took a big bite.

"Yeah, their families moved to another state," she said defiantly. "So who kept their head held high?"

"You."

"Damn right."

We high-fived.

"Thanks for letting me back in. I promise I'll never let go of you, big sister."

"You'd better not."

"Even though you have every right to get revenge on me for the way I acted."

"I've never held anything against you, sis. You were only eleven. And plus, you were going through your own shit."

"Will you ever tell me what happened?" I tread carefully.

"Oh, I don't . . ."

"I'm sorry, I didn't mean to make you uncomfortable." I silently kicked myself for stepping over the line.

"No, that's not it. I don't have a problem talking about what happened. The boys who raped me were disturbed and violent. Why should *I* be ashamed? The only reason I hesitate . . . I don't want to make you more hung up on sex. Ask me again after you've started a physical relationship, okay?"

"Okay." I was sorry she felt I was so uptight that she couldn't confide in me. "Tell me about the school project you're submitting for the City Architecture award."

"I'm developing a green community, and . . . wait. Did I tell you about that already? I don't remember."

Oops.

"Well, I heard about it somewhere, so you must have said something." *I almost blew it!*

"I guess I did." She shrugged her shoulders and her eyes came alive in delight as she described her idea of an apartment complex that was one hundred percent green. "The materials are all recycled or reclaimed and a system of rewards and incentives will be in place for the tenants who live there, possibly leading to ownership." Her enthusiasm was only diminished by the next brilliant detail of what she hoped to create in her working life. "I'm working so hard on it. Sean is helping me, too." She got teary. "He's giving up his own chance for the internship for *me*. His parents are pretty well off, but the prestige that comes with it is long lasting for anyone's career."

Sean loves my sister!

"You met Sean at college?" I poked carefully.

"Yeah!" She finished another bite of her fish filet. "God these are good. How's your sandwich?"

"Delicious," I mumbled in the middle of another juicy bite.

"Sean and I sat next to each other at an art history class of all things. We began to see each other in more classes and we took off from there." She looked at the ceiling and sighed. "The rest is . . . hopefully our history together."

"How romantic," I said dreamily. "College sweethearts."

"It is, isn't it? He's even helping me draft the CC & Rs. And he found a nonprofit legal group who's making sure I have the language correct and the project is feasible."

"What are CC & Rs? Yes, I'll have another iced tea," I said to the waitress. "Jenise?"

"Please." She looked up and smiled and then returned to our conversation. "It's a document that outlines the conditions, covenants, and restrictions of the common areas." She sounded like an attorney. "If I get chosen, I'll be a shoe-in at City Architecture!"

I kept quiet and acted as if I didn't know anything. In some ways, I didn't—at least not about the details of her project. After she was through talking about her design, she finally opened up about her boyfriend, Sean Taylor.

"Why haven't you brought Sean home to meet Mom and Dad?" I dipped a French fry in ketchup.

"He's African American," she said guardedly.

"Wow, that's so"—I struggled to find the words—"progressive of you." *Is this her "fuck you" to Dad?*

"Yeah, I'm afraid of how they'll react because of the gun incident with Dad. What do you think?"

Our parents had endured their share of bad experiences in the workplace. Whether or not it was real or exaggerated by our parents, the majority of them involved people of color and that jaded their thoughts. Of course, the biggest event was the African American man who had held a gun to Dad's head while at work and we were often reminded of it when our father went on a bender.

We both knew Sean wouldn't be an easy introduction.

"I can't wait for you to meet him. He's old school. A gentleman. Smart and handsome, too." she giggled. "He's got these long eyelashes and big brown eyes . . . I don't want to jinx it, but I think he's going to propose. Keep your fingers crossed."

"Oh, no!" A rock dropped in my stomach. "I'm losing my sister just as I'm getting to know her again?"

"Even if he proposes, we won't get married until after we graduate. Besides, you'll be living with Ryan by then."

"Oh, right. I think not!" I mocked, using an English accent. "I can't imagine living with *anyone*—at least not before I graduate. Besides, I'm too moody. I would drive *me* crazy let alone the other person."

"Moody or not, he'll ask you. *Drive yourself crazy*. What a nut you are, Nick."

"Why would he ask? He's away half the time. He couldn't stand reassuring me all the time and I couldn't stand his coming and goings from being on the road."

"Whatever. You're so in denial about the pull he has on you."

"You were saying, about Sean . . .?" I slipped into a daydream, visualizing Ryan bringing me coffee, snuggling under the covers, and warming our bodies on a chilly morning.

"We've been seeing each other about five months and it gets better every day. I've met his parents—they actually like me! Thank God! And best of all, I like *them*! Can you believe it?"

"Why wouldn't they?" I exclaimed. "You're a sweetheart!" My sister blushed. I wanted to pinch her pink cheeks. "I'm so happy for you. I—oh yeah, I almost forgot. Ryan wants us all to double date. So hopefully I'll meet Sean soon?"

"Sure! I'll give him a heads up. How great is that? We're going on a double date!"

"Isn't it funny how things twist and turn?" I reflected on the rush of events that seemed to be pushing through my life. I dipped another French fry in ketchup and just as I held it to my mouth, a customer bumped into me.

"Slob!" She cracked up and wiped the corner of my mouth with a napkin. "Ketchup all over you!"

I dipped my finger in the tartar sauce on her plate and put some on the tip of her nose.

"You're dead meat when we get home." She took out her pocket mirror and made sure to wipe it off completely. "Watch your back, sistah."

"I'll do that." I reached for the check.

Soon after we got home, my sister went back to her studies, and I went up to my room. I had energy to burn and began a silly task of dividing my closet into *Ryan* and *Other*. I put the new items I'd purchased with the two outfits from LA on the *Ryan* side. Then I cleared a spot in one of my drawers for my cool new leather folio, sunglasses, electronic tablet and beautiful silk scarf.

I was the last person to recognize the subtle changes happening inside me.

Sitting with my feet on the beige sofa in front of my bed, I opened my journal. I quickly wrote two poems and then outlined the events of the last few days. For a third time, I reviewed the classes I needed to take at City College. When I finished my checklist, I turned on the TV.

The Goliaths were in the late innings of their baseball game. Ryan had just come in to pitch. He shut down the three batters he faced and the Goliaths won 3–2. I watched him high-five his teammates and hoped I'd get a shot of his butt. No such luck. I turned off the TV, opened the window, and got ready for bed.

The fog had rolled into our West Portal neighborhood. I was instantly reminded of Half Moon Bay and pretended it was the same ocean air surrounding me, making everything moist. When my phone rang I just about floated out of bed, loving that I'd get another chance to hear Ryan's voice before the night ended.

"I saw you come in the game to pitch," I purred. "Congratulations on your save."

"How'd I do?" He had an easy and light tone in his voice.

"Who cares?"

"Meaning?" He sounded confused.

"Meaning, as a fan of the team, I'm glad you guys won and you got the save. As your girlfriend, you're pretty damn cute out there. I wanted to jump through the TV and give you a big smooch."

"*Are* you my girlfriend?" His voice wriggled into my belly as if it were his finger stroking sexual places.

"I think . . . um, I think I am." *I just committed to him!*

"You know what I want to do after hearing that?"

"What?" *I'm afraid to ask.*

"The lights are out in your house and I quietly walk upstairs after letting myself in with the key you've given me. I get under the covers to snuggle with you. Your body easily fits into mine and you tell me about your day. I stroke you with tender caresses. I rub your back. The evening ends with a long kiss before we go off to dreamland. Do you think about us that way?"

Oh, Ryan—more please.

"All the time," I answered eagerly and honestly. "I can't wait to see you tomorrow. I'll sleep like a baby because you called. Did you get game tickets for Chris and Frances?"

"Yep."

"I'm glad. Everyone get along?"

"No bullshit sibling rivalry today." He had notes of sadness in his voice. "I wish it could've been that way last night."

"Think of what we would have missed in Half Moon Bay, though," I reminded. "Everything worked out exactly how it was meant to be." I heard his long sigh. I thought it might sing me to sleep. "Oh! You know what I did today?"

"What's that?"

"I bought . . ." I hesitated. I wondered if it might have been too forward. In the end, I took the chance. "Jenise not only helped me buy a dress for our date tomorrow, but some other stuff, too. Now I won't embarrass you if we're at an important event together."

"*Embarrass* me? You'd never embarrass me. Your tenderness alone makes you stunning. May I point out, Ms. Young, you talk a lot about the vision you have of your future, but the way you think of others? Baby, being with you is an unbelievable privilege."

"Thank you." I felt appreciated in a way I never have before. *I wonder if Jerry feels this way about me.*

"Chris and Frances are in the parking lot. I'd better go, love."

"What did you guys do today?" *Don't go yet.*

"Shopping in Marin and a nice lunch at the Inverness Inn. Frances wanted some new clothes. I needed some things, too."

"Sounds fun. Guess we were both shopping. So everything is okay with you and Chris?"

"As much as we can be okay."

"Like it or not, we're stuck with family, huh?"

"You hit the nail on the head. Baby, I miss you so much."

"That's why I want to talk another few seconds. I'm having trouble hanging up. It's like I want to sing you a lullaby, Ryan. What's happening to me?"

His sexy laugh went straight to my inner thighs.

"Let's pretend we're still at the bed and breakfast," his words dripped with sensual flavors.

"How? I can't even touch you." His request was enchanting. I tried hard to immerse myself in his vision.

"Close your eyes."

Seconds passed.

"Are they closed?" he asked fervently.

"Yes."

"We've just turned out the lights. You shake your head and your hair bounces at the top of your gorgeous behind." He took a deep breath. "In the moonlight I can see your beautiful smile. The way you've let your guard down—it's like warm desert rain. Can you feel me, Nicky?" Another deep breath. "Can you understand how much I want to touch you?"

"Mm-hmm."

"The way you speed up and talk one hundred miles per hour, explain all your observations about life, your day, me . . . I miss that. I hope tomorrow's game goes by like the speed of light. Maybe it will seem like we've only been apart a few minutes. Goodnight—until tomorrow, goodnight."

"Now that I have no breath, goodnight, Ryan." I said the words as sweetly as I could and went to bed with dreams of him lying next to me.

Chapter 29

I've Got Plans

My cell phone rang around ten the next morning. I was sure it was Ryan. Without looking at the screen, I answered, "Hey, baby."

"Nicky?"

Oh damn. Jerry!

"Jerry! Hey! What's up?" *I'm awake now, that's for sure.*

"*Baby,* huh? I like that, gorgeous. What should I call *you?*"

"Oh," I forced a laugh. "I don't know. I was in the middle of a dream and still half asleep when I answered the phone." I tripped over every word.

"Sure, you were," his response almost dared me to defy him. "It's okay to call me baby. I like that."

Silence.

"Whatcha doin' today, gorgeous?" He knew I hated it when he used that word. I let it slide, wanting only to get through the conversation.

"I thought you still had a few games out of town. You're back early, aren't you? What happened?"

Please don't pop over today. I want to take my time primping for my date with Ryan.

"I'm not back yet; I'm just calling to say hi . . . *baby*."

"Funny, Jerry."

"We almost got canceled." His voice held a smile. "We were scheduled to play Friday and Saturday and the other team started a fight. They had to forfeited, but then won their appeal."

"You fight anyone?"

"Well . . . ya know how it is." He paused awkwardly. "Gotta join the fellas."

"Yeah, yeah. Still knocking the cover off the ball?"

"Smokin' it!" His voice rose with excitement.

"Very cool." I shifted on my side and leaned on my elbow.

"So . . . whatcha up to this week Nicky, Nick, Nick?"

If only I could tell you.

"Um, today I'm going to meet my college advisor and then I'm supposed to help my mom around the house."

"There's a chance I'll be back a day early. I'll come over as soon as I get home."

It may have been anything but a warning, however that's how I took his statement. Could it have been that my guilt caused me to interpret him that way? "This week isn't so good." *Don't press me.* "I have a lot of volunteer work to do with Tara."

Lying to my friend . . . ouch.

"Think of something great to do when I get back."

"Okay, I'll give it some serious consideration, Jer."

"Don't strain your brain," he laughed. "We don't want Stanford to be in danger."

"Can't have that," I flirted.

"I'll drum up a few alternatives and bring three to the table. Between the two of us we'll have a fabulous night, okay, Nick?"

"Of course."

"You're busy, huh? Slow down, girl!"

"You should talk with all your baseball games," I reminded.

"Maybe you could drive down and see me play?"

"Maybe." *It sounds like fun but I'd like to see where things go with Ryan and it's probably not a good idea.*

"Bye-bye, *baby*," he teased. "See you Sunday—in more ways than one."

"Bye, Jerry." *God, he's already planning to get right into sex when he gets back. How am I going to tell him I don't want that kind of relationship with him any longer?*

I showered and then got ready to meet with my college advisor. Everything I needed to do could be completed online. Still, I was so looking forward to college I had to walk the campus that afternoon. I needed to look at the buildings and browse the bookstore and student facilities. I wanted to take in the smells of the classrooms and run my fingers over the whiteboards. The tactile sensations at junior college made attending Stanford seem much closer. I needed that.

For incoming freshmen, it wasn't uncommon to be locked out of a course; we had last choice. I met with my advisor and asked her to *please* put in a personal recommendation with the instructors I wanted. Even after I'd enlisted her help, I dropped off my own note at the offices of my potential instructors, trusting no one when it came to my education. I knew how to maneuver when it came to my future.

At five p.m., I tore myself away from the junior college campus to get ready for my date with Ryan. While waiting for the streetcar home, I got a text from him. Despite the magic of the past few days, I was afraid the good things we'd shared had spiraled down into a bad ending.

I couldn't escape the fear of knowing one day I'd hear him say, "Nicky, I've reconsidered things and I wish you the best. You were right. I need someone my own age."

Instead, his text read: *See you at six. Can't wait.*

When I got home, I jumped in the shower, quickly dried off, and pulled my new dress off the hanger. I slipped it on in front of the mirror and watched as it fell around my body. I ran my hands over the lacy folds, straightened the sleeves, and touched up my makeup. I'd barely finished my hair when the doorbell rang.

Jenise answered and invited Ryan inside.

I could tell she was excited. Her voice always raised a few octaves when she was stirred up. I could hear her high-pitched giggle from my bedroom.

The magic of my evening began to cover me.

Just for that night, I imagined our household normal and ordinary. My sister had already reintroduced my boyfriend to Mom and Dad. They were talking freely, casually . . . almost lovingly as they waited for me. I imagined our parents engaged and not detached, mom present rather than fearful of Dad saying the wrong thing and dad with no glass of wine in his hand or the threat of a bottle near him.

I put on a coat to cover my new dress and went downstairs. I didn't want to explain anything to my parents and especially didn't want to look at Jenise. I knew she'd embarrass me once we made eye contact and I couldn't stop laughing at her suggestive expressions and comments.

A few weeks earlier, I'd been angry when she chided me for purposefully playing with two boys and insisted that everything came easy for me. Now, our relationship had morphed into something completely different. I felt emotionally healthy with her. She made me believe in the possibility of our family.

Relationships are worth fighting for.

What a difference it was for me living in our household since I'd met Ryan. Possibilities were opening in ways none of us had anticipated. Taking a deep breath, I walked down the hallway and into the kitchen.

Ryan carried the conversation with my family.

Even from where I stood, I could see his blue eyes shining. His full smile seemed made of promises; completely attentive to the people I loved.

He wore pressed chocolate-brown slacks and a black linen shirt, which he'd tucked inside his pants. The three-quarter sleeves highlighted his magnificent forearms. His shirt was unbuttoned just enough to reveal a copper cross dangling from the gold chain around his thick neck.

I walked up to Ryan, took his hand and kissed him on the cheek.

Jenise smiled at my kiss.

My parents, unsure about their daughter's change in behavior, were surprised by it.

"Show us your new dress." My sister turned to Ryan. "Of course I had to help her shop for one since she doesn't know the first thing about style."

He smiled with genuine appreciation and squeezed my hand.

"I'm good." *No way in hell I'm taking off this coat.*

"Come on." One of her invisible horns peeked through her hair. "I went to a lot of trouble to pick out that dress for you. Don't cover it up. Show us!"

"That's okay."

"I'm sure mom wants to take a picture, don't you Mom?" She winked at Ryan.

Mom nodded her head.

"Another time. We have to go, don't we, Ryan?" I shot my sister a dirty look. "See you guys later."

"Wait!" Mom grabbed her cell phone and snapped a photo. "Okay. I wanted to get that."

"Looks like we're off." Ryan returned a wink at Jenise. "I have a long evening planned. I promise to bring her home safe and sound, Mr. & Mrs. Young."

My parents nodded and gave us a short wave goodbye.

When no one was looking I stuck my tongue out at Jenise.

She promptly returned the gesture.

Ryan closed the front door behind me, a pleasantry I was still getting used to.

"What a troublemaker my sister is. I can't believe she kept going on about my dress."

"She's wonderful." He took my hand in his. "I'm looking forward to going out together."

"Me, too." Instantly my agitation settled. "Where's your car?"

"Around the corner. Someone's apparently throwing a party on your block. I couldn't find anything close. So, your kiss in front of your family was a nice surprise. Was that your way of telling me you're ready to show your affection in front of them?"

"Yes."

"That means a lot coming from you, Ms. Young." The warmth on his face made me feel good. "So, your hot dress . . ."

"Yeah?" *He's going there already?*

"I've been waiting to see how it slips over your gorgeous ass ever since you told me about it." We approached his Land Rover SUV. "Here we go." He started to unlock the door. Stopped and turned to face me. His eyes narrowed as they took in my body.

"Don't tease me, Ryan."

He straightened.

A sexy grin kissed his face.

He stepped close.

"I'm not teasing." His hands fell to my hips. They pulled me against his body. His mouth moistened my ear. Muscular arms held me inside them. In only seconds, we passed a few luscious secrets over, on, and between our lips.

The softness of his kiss made me feel elegant.

"It's been too long since I've felt you." He kissed my left ear. Lingered purposefully and slowly. "Even an hour is too long to be apart. Do you feel that way?"

"Yes."

Scoop me up. I'm melting into puddles.

When he finished nibbling my ears, he held my bottom lip in his mouth. I stood perfectly still until it slipped from his gentle suck. Slow. Hesitant. Blatantly sexual. His move expressed every hidden and bold intention.

Ooh those lips. God, he just knows.

"I was really hoping I'd hear that pebble you warned me about on my window last night." I chanced a sensual reveal. "I fell to sleep thinking of you and your wonderful kisses."

"Is that what my phone call did for you?"

"It definitely helped to stir me up when I imagined your hands and mouth on me. I couldn't sleep after that and I . . ." I swallowed. I stopped short of telling him too much.

"What, Nicky?" his mouth whispered dangerously close to my ear. "What did you do?"

"I, um, well, I just wished we were kissing each other." *I indulged in a finger fantasy but he doesn't need to hear that.*

He pressed me against the car.

"Did your fingers do the walking instead of letting mine do it for you?" Ryan's nasty smile flashed, almost blinding me.

I shoved my hands in my coat pocket and looked away.

"You shouldn't say things like that, sweet baby." His hand cupped my chin. My eyes met his. Desire filled them. He couldn't hide the primal male animal within. I felt helpless, as if caught in his sensual trap, waiting to be eaten alive.

"What do you mean?" My heart raced. "I didn't say anything."

"Without saying a word you told me everything and you know it. I'll take care of what you need tonight."

Oh God, here we go. His fingers, walking, stroking . . .

His stomach pushed into mine.

My cheek felt the touch of his lips.

"If I'd come in through your window do you know what I would have done?"

"I can't imagine." My laugh was a naive response to a situation I didn't know how to handle.

"I'd study your body with a long, slow look from your head to your toes. One finger would slowly lift the sheet from your body. I'd push your hair back from your face. Take off my clothes. Carefully slide next to you. Press my chest against your back." His eyes were steady, searing, and lustful. I could see the next wave of intensity gather inside them. "You wouldn't even know I was there until I tucked your luscious ass against my belly and thighs. As you became aware of my hips moving and my lips sucking on your neck you'd try to understand what was happening to you. The bruise would remain for weeks."

For weeks and weeks.

"Before you even opened your eyes, my hand would slip into your pajama bottoms." His voice was invisibly undressing me. "I'll rock you in a slow, sensual rhythm. You've just become aware that I have you in every way, when you feel my finger sliding back and forth over your soft lady spot. I'll coax her from her little hood, making you moan and squirm until you can't stand it. Against every resistance in your body, your legs will strain, wanting to open for me even as you try to keep them closed.

"You turn your head. I see your beautiful smile. You kiss me. But that's not enough. I put my tongue in your mouth. My finger moves your sweet flower. Circling her until I feel your body bump up and down against mine. As you break apart into your orgasms, I'll coat my finger with your intimate fluids and slide it into your vagina so I can feel the way your body pulses and ripples again and again and . . ."

He turned my cheek as I tried to look away. I closed my eyes. Opened them again when I heard his voice.

"Mmm, my woman." He took a deep breath. When his chest pushed out to my breasts I thought he might crush me in his power. "Your body's waves of pleasure, jerking with the hard crush of your blood filling that tender spot so protected . . . your sighs escaping your body, your mouth open, and your head tilted back . . . I'll be there to see all of it. So you'd better lock me out unless you want me, um . . . inside."

"I . . ." I gasped, trying to recover from what he'd just said.

Thank God he had to park away from the house so my family can't see me!

He kissed me all over my lips, face, ears, and neck. Then, just as he'd suggested in the sensual vision he'd just painted I felt his moist lips on my neck. I put my hands up to stop him. Even though he could've easily continued, his lips lifted from my skin.

"I can't let you do that. As much as I'd love you to keep going, I'll look ridiculous if I have a big hickey. My dress reveals too much of my neck."

"I'll hold back—for now." He opened the car door for me. "I can't tell you what it would do for me to see my mark on your neck." His laugh slithered through me. "My possession tonight."

"God, Ryan, what a thing you said."

"Did I stop in time? Or did your knees get weak?"

"You know they're weak." I locked my seatbelt in place.

"Serves you right for your suggestive comment. That wasn't nice telling me you fingered yourself."

"But I didn't say—"

"Don't act innocent. You were anything but that with your comment." With a nasty smile he closed the car door, walked to the driver's side, and got in.

"Where are we going?" *Change the subject—fast.*

"You'll see," an edgy melody danced in his voice.

I felt shaken and breathless. I knew I'd have to fight hard to keep from falling even more deeply under his spell.

Chapter 30

Dancing

We pulled up to an elegant gallery on Maiden Lane.

Ooh! What's he picking up here? A gift for Frances? His Mom? That's right, must be for her visit in a few weeks.

My thoughts ran wild. A mere twenty-four hours ago I'd fantasized about buying something in this exclusive area. Here I was with someone who could afford some the items offered in the dazzling window displays.

Lucky guy. Oh well, someday . . .

"Aren't the arrangements beautiful?" I pressed my nose to the car window. I unlocked my seatbelt and scooted up in the seat. "What are we doing here?"

"You'll see." Ryan's body seemed to bounce like a little boy as he got out and then walked around my side to open the car door. "Will you take off your coat for me so I can see if what I got for you works with your outfit?"

You got me something? Here? Oh, I'd love another pin. Maybe it's earrings. I wore a pair of Jenise's earrings that were shiny enough for him to notice in Half Moon Bay. He probably thinks I like those. What will I say? I'd better get ready to fake my reaction and be ecstatic. Maybe a bracelet? Wouldn't that be sweet? Oh, a charm bracelet to match the charm he gave me on my birthday! I can start collecting them now. Oh, look at the sculptures; I love running my hands over their blue patina finish. Maybe it's an artist he loves. He's picking up something for his place. I—

"Nicky?"

Back into the present. I took off my coat and placed it on the car seat. When I turned around, his face said it all.

What's the matter, Mr. Tilton?

His lips parted.

His mouth remained open.

Blue eyes changed from sparkling to dark and lustful. They raced up and down my body. Several times, he shook his head back and forth.

"I'm, uh . . ." Ryan cleared his throat. "There's, I um . . . I have a surprise." He fumbled and it made me laugh.

"What was that?" I teased. "I couldn't understand you."

Now you know how I feel.

"If I touch your skin, I might completely lose myself. You look so pretty."

"Thank you! Obviously my sister knew what she was doing since it's you stumbling and not me for a change," I giggled. "Just let go, Ryan. Isn't that what you're always telling me?"

"Letting go is exactly what I have in mind." He held my hand as we walked into the gallery. He carefully put his arm around my shoulder.

Tingles of pleasure moved in my belly.

"Good evening, Mr. Tilton." The saleswoman standing behind the counter seemed pleased to see him.

"Good evening, Ms. Stonefield. Is my purchase ready?"

"Right here, Mr. Tilton." She reached under the counter and pulled out an 8" x 8" green velvet box.

Ryan opened it and revealed a gold omega chain with a diamond-shaped emerald hanging from it. A gold border held the shining green stone securely. Each of his hands held an open end of the necklace.

"Let me put it on," he commanded.

I turned and lifted my hair, so he could fasten the clasp. When he leaned down, his lips touched my neck in a soft kiss. Chills raced through me. His hands rested on my upper arms as if holding me inside a fantasy.

"Here you go, miss." Ms. Stonefield handed me a mirror.

"This is so thoughtful." I ran my fingers over the smooth gold and held the emerald. "It's beautiful. Too much, but beautiful."

"No. It's not enough to show you how much I value your friendship. I've wanted to get you something since last year, but I thought you'd take it the wrong way. You like it, then?"

He asked the question bashfully as if needing my confirmation that what he'd done was okay—I didn't realize until much later, the confirmation he searched for was about far more than the necklace.

"I love it." My eyes teared. I turned to face him. "Thank you."

"I knew the green in the emerald would bring out your eyes. What a perfect match. I'm so lucky to have found you."

"It does look beautiful on her, Mr. Tilton." Ms. Stonefield gave her approval. "If you don't mind me saying so, I think her eyes actually bring out the green in the emerald."

You're one hell of a saleswoman, Ms. Stonefield.

"Now I have two special pieces of jewelry," I immediately thought about my grandmother's pin. "I'll cherish this forever." I put my arms around Ryan's neck and looked up at him the way he liked.

"Do you know why I got the emerald?"

"It's my birthstone. Is there anything you miss?"

"What a month it was that brought you into this world." He lowered his voice. "And to me."

"Who knew you were waiting for me when I was a baby all those years ago?" I mused quietly.

He put his arm around my shoulder and thanked Ms. Stonefield. I let him escort me out of the shop.

"You have me spinning hard," he confessed. "I can't focus."

"That was the idea." I was more than satisfied with my effort. "This dress—I'll burst out of it when I take my first bite of food. If I grab my coast and run out of wherever we're going you'll know it ripped to shreds. Do you think my belly sticks out too much?" I asked as he opened the car door. "See this round spot? You say you like it, but it sticks out no matter how much I exercise. I've never—"

When his lips pressed to mine, it felt as if a thousand wings from little hummingbirds stirred the air. His mouth tasted like the sweet nectar from a velvet tulip. Its sweetness coated my lips.

"I love that spot." His hand rested on my belly. "It's just right."

Love that spot . . . your hand on my tummy . . . love that spot.

With weak knees and a heart that was beating ninety miles per hour, I slid into the passenger seat of his car. As Ryan sat behind the wheel and started the engine I tried to breath, quietly releasing the pressure in my face and body.

We pulled up to Gary Danko's, a sophisticated restaurant in North Beach. Known for its five star menu, lounge and soft music, it was frequented by couples wanting an elegant evening.

"Do you think they'll let me in?" I asked shyly.

Ryan looked at me with his devastating and mischievous smirk. He might as well have spelled out sex in the air right in front of us.

Of course they'll let me in. They won't even question me because I'm with you and you know it.

Two valets opened the car doors. I waited for Ryan to sort it out with the young man on his side of the vehicle.

As usual, I fell into a daydream, seduced by my boyfriend, the atmosphere, my new necklace, and the romantic evening that lie ahead of us. Just as the valet took the car away, I remembered I'd left my coat in the back seat.

"Wait!" I absentmindedly started to run after it.

"Where are you going?" Ryan caught my arm. My handsome beau tried to hide his grin and I suspect hold back a laugh.

"I forgot my coat," I said breathlessly. "How can I get it?"

"Uh-uh." He held my hands.

"What do you mean, *Uh-uh*? I might get cold. What if the dress rips, or . . . don't you want your date to be comfortable?" My chin lifted just a little. "I seem to remember a few weeks ago, a certain boy in the parking lot gave me his jacket so I'd be warm, and now—no?"

"I want to see your moves." He didn't know the moist trail that formed on my body with only the dip in his voice.

"My *moves*?" I was nervous. "I don't have any moves."

"Your bounces and wiggles—they're a feast for me. That dress—before we take one bite of food, or dance one dance, I'm done. I'll be so saturated with visions and fantasies of your body, I might have to carry you right off the dance floor and make you sit on my lap through dinner."

I'm in deep trouble.

"Please, don't do that." I literally pleaded, believing he would do exactly what he'd said.

"In fact, if you become too much for me to handle, I'll have to carry you out of here and take you to my place." His fingers flexed against my back.

"How quickly could you get my coat if I needed it?" I asked the head valet.

"With your ticket, only five minutes." The man was stoic in his response but I could see a twinkle in his eyes.

"Where's the ticket I need?" I persisted.

He nodded to Ryan.

When I looked at my big boyfriend, he waved the ticket back and forth, blatantly slow, his mischievous look telling me he had thoughts in his head that would make my mouth drop open.

"God, Ryan," I walked as fast as I could to stay ahead of him.

His wonderful, masculine laugh rang through the air. He easily caught me at the entrance of the restaurant, took my hand, and stepped up to the hostess.

A tall, blonde woman who looked to be in her early twenties greeted us promptly. She wore a long, white gown that hugged her svelte body and had no trouble giving my date a look of hunger that traveled up and down his masculine frame. It was obvious she wanted to be of service to Ryan after hours.

I know what you're thinking, lady. Everyone feels the same way about him.

"Tilton, reservation for two," he announced and turned to kiss my cheek. "You're going to love this place."

We'll see. Hopefully she won't be one of too many distractions, like the ones at The Embarcadero Hotel lounge.

She checked us off her list, very sweetly wished *us* a good evening and asked that we follow another woman to our table.

"Did you see that dress she wore?" *I can't measure up to that.*

"What dress?" He tightened his grip on my hand.

"Never mind."

Soft lighting formed a path beginning at the entry of the restaurant and continued through its interior. Candles and a variety of colored lights highlighted the deep, rich, oranges, yellows and chocolate browns on the walls, floor, and ceiling. The booths and tables were arranged in an intimate setting near the bar and small dance area.

We were seated in the open. In a way, I felt like we were on display like those diamonds and rubies in the windows on Maiden Lane. We were in full view of the other diners.

"Aren't you afraid you won't be left alone? I can already hear people talking and we haven't even been here five minutes. And that hostess back there wants you for dessert."

"I'm not concerned about any woman but you. This place is known for its discretion. We won't be bothered." Ryan pulled out the wooden chair with a black leather padded seat. Once I was comfortable, he sat down and then moved his chair next to mine. He took my hands in his. "Tonight, I want everyone to know I'm with my woman. Can't you see it's over for me? I'm bursting with love for you."

I fiddled with one of the forks on the table doing my best to hide my emotions. Thankfully, the waiter arrived with menus and asked what he could get us to drink. Ryan ordered sparkling water with lemon for both of us.

"Dance with me?" He pushed up from his seat and held his hand out for me. Just watching him reach for me made my chest get tight. The intensity of his eyes was as if an azure fire was held within glassy volcanic rocks from an ancient time.

We walked onto the dance floor. His arms slipped around my waist. Our hips moved together effortlessly, naturally.

Ryan whispered the words of a song the band played. I looked away, trying to steady myself. One of his hands lifted from my waist. Softly caressed my cheek. Turned my cheek so my eyes stayed fixed on his. The desire, written plainly on his face, was too penetrating for me to handle.

I closed my eyes.

"Nicky." He leaned in. Whispered my name. "Look at me."

"You know you can't . . . I'm already a mess."

The kiss from his lips was simple, sweet, and sent my stomach into a wild swirl. I opened my eyes to his beautiful but deadly grin. Those blue flames that burned in them were plain in their meaning: he was ready to be as savage as I wanted.

We swayed on air.

It seemed an evening had already passed when the music ended.

"Thank you for the dance, Sweetheart."

I turned to go to my seat, trying to keep from losing myself completely.

Ryan's hands stayed me. Held me close.

This is it. My heart is pounding way too hard—call an ambulance!

"Dance close with me." He teased me with the slightest touch of his cheek against mine. "Connect with me. Brush against me. Make me hunger for you. Coax every ounce of desire and make me ache with the rush that pours from my body and into yours. I've waited to have this evening for so long."

"You know what happens to me," I admitted shyly. I can't stay out here."

"Relax against my chest. Let me lead you into our evening while you tell me what happens when I make you weak."

We moved rhythmically. Let our bodies flood with passion. Our hands locked together. Energies rose slowly and met with bursts of heat. It was as if he channeled a magical spell from an enchantress. His low voice came to life. Little grunts and growls of pleasure put me on notice—they were wild, ready to be unleashed.

"Why are you hiding from me," Ryan sang the words to a beautiful ballad. His fingertips lifted my chin. I could see the restraint held within his eyes. "I'm ready. I want you in every way. Believe me?" His masculine voice vibrated against me.

Several heartbeats later and I found my man nodding to the lead musician. Another slow song began to play. The line between control and chaos blurred within my body.

"This song is just for you, Nicky." One thick finger traced the base of my neck, my spine, and lower back. "From me to you."

The ballad that played was the kind that brought lovers to the dance floor. They almost rose from their seats as if a siren had trapped them in her cry. As the singer spun the song's lyrics into a sexy heartbeat, patrons seemed hypnotized. Words spoke of warm, wet, kisses, being with a man I could be proud of, and lying in each other's arms. The bells in the melody were softly ringing, and the steel strings of a guitar resonated low. The polished piano keys quivered underneath light fingers that danced on them. Notes that were released from the hairs of a violin's bow were soothing as they were into the night.

Ryan turned my body so I faced away from him. His pelvis rubbed against my bottom. His muscular, hard, and beautiful chest was a massive wave of emotion crashing down; the weight of its rush tumbled me as if I were a seashell within its curl. I was helplessly tucked inside his body; held firmly by his hands as they rested on my belly.

"I'm burning for you." His head rested on my shoulder.

I couldn't respond.

He pressed himself against me in a way that made me feel as if we'd been carved by a master sculptor; we fit together perfectly. When finished, the artist had planned to make us one, each man and woman inside one skin, hearts beating together, our breath hot as we melted and formed a new being.

The nuances of the body that contained the virile man who was pressed against me were about to make themselves known. His muscles moved on my arms, his chest rose and fell on my back, and his freshly shaven cheeks were gentle against my face. His hot breath moaned into my mouth as my head fell back. His lips whispered silent expectations, filling my lungs with new life.

Feelings I'd never experienced before Ryan bloomed inside me. It was a force that seemed fueled by an intimate and ancient passion that got bigger with every touch. One erotic burst after the other sent scarlet pulses down and between my legs.

I need to say something. Everything has come to a stop and all I feel is his body, his low voice, and his fingers revving the little motor inside me . . .

"Let's order some dinner." I patted his hands as they rested on my belly. I needed to lift them. I had to lift them . . . didn't I?

Obviously satisfied for the moment, he turned my body to face him. My back felt the treat of his arm as it slid around me. I was held firmly against his frame. I took several deep breaths as his low, masculine moan ripped through me.

"Don't make fun of me," I ordered gently.

"Me?" His cheek brushed up against mine.

"And don't tease me," I added weakly.

"I won't, but . . . I do enjoy how you submit to me. It's so touching. The way you let me in . . . you don't realize it but you're all woman, you know." We walked back to our table to continue our journey. "Will you order for us?" Ryan tucked my chair underneath me.

I took a sip of water and gathered myself.

"Is there anything you don't like?"

"Not tonight." His lip twitched in a luscious tease. "I love everything I see."

"Whew, it's hot in here, isn't it?" I fanned my face. "I wonder where our sparkling waters are? I wish they'd turn on the air conditioning. Are you hot?"

Ryan's expression was neutral.

"Well, let's look at what they have here." I looked at my menu. As I did, the waiter served our drinks.

"Ready to order?" He looked at me and then to Ryan.

"My girlfriend is handling everything for us," Ryan's eyes steadied on mine.

"We'll begin with the heirloom tomato salad, drizzled with balsamic vinaigrette." I pointed to its spot on the menu. "Is that big enough for two?"

Our waiter waived his hand back and forth, signaling we may want to consider ordering two portions.

"We'll need two of those, don't you think?" I looked up from my menu seeking Ryan's approval.

"Whatever you say." His stare was unwavering.

"I'll make sure to ask the staff to make enough for two," he smiled. "The tomatoes were purchased today from the farmers' market, by the way. Good choice."

"Oh great! Hear that, babe? I made a good choice!"

My boyfriend's approval made my pulse quicken.

"We'll follow the salad with your crab cake appetizer. Oh, I just love crab cakes. Make sure there are three, please—one for me, and two for Ryan. In fact, if they're very small, can we have four? He's got big appetite and honestly? I can eat them, too. I sure don't want him to go home with an empty belly and although I have to be careful, well, I love them just so you know. Maybe we can get four, but make the fourth small."

Ryan's face went from seductive to relaxed and amused.

"For the entrée . . . let's see. We should still have our appetites, right? The salad and crab cakes won't be nearly enough, will they?"

"We can adjust your entrée to smaller portions if you need them that way." Our waiter made notes in his tablet.

"Great! So then we'll share the blackened mahi-mahi and vegetables. But, again, if the filet is small," I pinched my fingers together, "please bring two. I won't eat more than one of those, but you know, what I said earlier. Oh and please give us plenty of vegetables; my boyfriend needs them. They're steamed, right?"

"Yes. Smart selections, miss." He seemed entertained. "Did you decide on something to drink besides sparkling water?"

"I want a virgin strawberry daiquiri," I handed him my menu. "Do you make those? They're delicious. I've had them at Chevy's, so anyway if you do, I'll take one of those."

"Sure. And you, sir?"

"The same." Missing no opportunity to tease me when the waiter left, he said, "Virgin—"

"Please don't say it," I interrupted.

"Say what?" His smirk was delicious.

"Was my order okay?" I tried to deflect.

"Even watching you order turns on all the switches inside of me." He scooted his chair closer until our hips touched.

"Ryan, don't." I put my hand out as his body leaned in. He kept advancing, taking my hand in his, kissing my palm, and holding it to his cheek.

"What will it take to get you to say you're completely mine?" he asked softly. "When will you say the words?" He held the back of my head as he pressed my lips to his—deliberate, moving and tilting, finding his perfect fit.

"Close," I muttered like I was waking up from an operation, still dazed and groggy. "I'm closely . . ." Once again, I mixed up the words. "I'm getting closer, I mean."

"Now that we've ordered, we have time for another dance." Ryan stood and then held his hand out once more.

Oh hell.

I took his hand, and stood with him.

Chapter 31

Turn up the Air Conditioning

"*I* can't dance anymore. My knees, they're—"

"Sweet woman, it's the first time I've been able to take you out. I've planned a night like this since last year. Please don't deny me. The man in front of you is only trying to be with the woman he's dreamed of asking to be his. I need to give you a sweet memory and soothe my aching heart. Won't you let me?"

"Are you *kidding,* Ryan—a *memory*? I won't *live* through this," I teased. "*A memory* he says. Sure. By the way, my parents don't have instructions on what to do with my body, so I need to write a note. Make sure you give it to them, okay?"

"I know what to do with your body . . . and I don't need a note." He growled and ran his hand along my shoulders.

"God, you're—"

"Just one more dance. We'll stay right here at our table." His arms slipped under mine and held my waist. As we stood together, I was sure if he didn't hold me my legs would give way.

"Have you ever considered how perfectly we fit together?" His voice was calm. His eyes seemed at peace. I thought he had steered away from sex and was talking about something different.

"We do have a lot in common. I've felt that from last year."

"I mean the way our bodies naturally slide into each other's curves and valleys." His hand crawled up my back and rested on the nape of my neck. "You naturally reach for my waist without me asking or guiding you to touch me." I found myself leaning against him, straining to hear his seductive comments. "Have you ever thought about why?" His hand cupped my chin. I lifted my gaze and watched the light shift in his eyes. "Nicky?"

"Yeah."

"You're so . . ." He looked all over my face. "Your lovely body is the perfect height for me. Don't you notice how easily my arms slip around your shoulders?"

He kissed my cheek.

"Don't you?"

"Uh-huh." *Don't ask me any more questions.*

"Your cheek fills my hand perfectly; feel the way you respond to my caress and welcome my kiss. It's as if we've been made for each other. Our souls waited so long to come together. We're here. We're ready. The way you look up at me . . ." He sighed. "The expression in your eyes is so innocent and yet they tell me, without any doubt, you've opened your heart just for me.

"When you take my hand and give me a little kiss? I can hardly contain myself," he continued. "If any part of your skin touches my nakedness, even my forearm, hand, or finger, I come undone. My body hardens and the muscles fill with blood in the anticipation of getting ready for you. You don't even have to speak. All I need to do is watch the way you help others, or brush against me and flash your brilliant smile. I want to be all over you. I've been thinking about it for more than a year.

"You bought that dress for me so you'd have something special and even shopped for extra pieces so we could be together more often. You must know how you're inviting me into your life. You want me like I—"

"Yes!" *Enough! I can't take it!* I was morphing into a sloppy mess. "Yes, Ryan. I did. I do. Please stop talking."

"Sweetheart?"

"I know."

"What do you know?" he pressed on.

"Just . . ."

"Are you weak?" he smiled.

"You know I am." I looked away. "I'm sure you've been told hundreds of times, you're not fair. Not fair at all."

"*You're* the one who isn't fair. Don't you understand how weak you make me? You have since I first saw you sitting in the bleachers. I couldn't believe it. There you were. The woman of my dreams." His arm covered my shoulder. His hand slowly turned my head. He sucked and bit lightly on my bottom lip and then covered my mouth as his desire strengthened.

I took several breaths as we sat down, but never broke eye contact with his handsome face.

I have to show him I can match him this way.

"So, are you doing something with Chris and Frances before your game tomorrow?"

"We're going out afterwards. I kept the first part of the day open in case you, well, first tell me what's on your mind."

Our heirloom tomato salads arrived. I put an entire slice of tomato in my mouth and savored the simple salt and pepper seasoning with drizzled balsamic vinegar.

"I was thinking maybe we could go to Yountville. I know the vets want to thank you for the jerseys you gave them; they'd love to see you." I dipped a piece of bread into the dressing. "Johnny and his mom were so excited—you should've seen their smiles.

He put on his jersey right away. Oh yeah! I've wanted to tell you, they're going to be the guests of honor at the Brain Injury Awareness fundraiser this winter in LA!"

"We'll have to go to that," he said confidently and then took a big bite of the salad.

"That would be so great. I hope we get invited." I crossed my fingers. "I wonder if Alex can get us invitations? Her agency is a cosponsor for the event. I'd really love to go. I need to make sure Mr. Del Sol doesn't forget me."

"I don't think an invitation will be a problem." He laughed his sexy laugh. "Yountville it is."

"Where were you going to suggest we go?" I took a long drink of my virgin daiquiri. "Mmm that's good. Before, when you hesitated and said you kept the day open, where did you want to go?"

"The same as you suggested," he confirmed. "I had a suspicion you might want to go there. I owe you a few visits per our original deal, after all."

"Yeah, I forgot about that."

"You're not keeping score?"

"Not anymore," I confessed.

Our crab cakes came and we went through them in no time. The chef had thoughtfully given me one that was oversized. When dinner arrived, our conversation began to flow like running water.

"Saturday, we have a day game as I'm sure you know," he moistened his lips.

"Well, yeah, we're cheering."

"I talked to your sister about double dating Saturday. Is that okay with you?"

"When did you talk to her?"

"Tonight, when I picked you up."

"What did she say?"

"Yes." He winked and the twinkle in his eyes said hello.

Of course she said yes. Does anyone tell you no?

"Jenise met someone at school and she's afraid to bring him home." I swirled the cream in my daiquiri.

"Why?"

"Because he's African American. She's worried our parents won't approve or they'll say something to embarrass her."

"Hopefully when your folks meet him, they'll look beyond that and see him as an individual."

"It'll be a tall order. A black man put a gun to Dad's head and he's held it against the entire race ever since. Unfortunately, it seems his worst experiences were with people of color—at least that's how he remembers them."

"For your sister's sake I hope he's able to put that aside." He shook his head.

"I hope so, too." I finished the last bite of my rice. "Ryan?"

"Yes, honey?" He held my hand.

"Please put in a good word for my sister with your contacts." My eyes began tearing. "She's worked so hard to overcome her trauma. I didn't realize how important her career is to her. When we went to dinner last night, she really opened up. We're getting so close again and it would mean everything to her. Of course I'd be grateful and I'd give you a few extra kisses."

I giggled and ate the cherry at the bottom of my drink.

Ryan's expression became serious.

He could throw a mean fastball, but that night, I threw him a big curve. I shifted the question of trust back into his lap. He had asked me to have faith and try a relationship with *him*, but my silent question was, *are you able to let go and trust me enough to know I'm not using you for the things you said you could do?*

"What is it, sweetheart?" His brows were knotted in concern.

"I feel bad that I didn't see her struggling. She's come through her trauma a strong woman despite her family's doubts. You know she was my hero for years when I was little. The things she did for me . . ." *Stop before you go too far. You don't know that you can trust him with your dark secrets.* "She protected me so many times. My dad bea—he, she um . . . she just needs someone on her side. Someone like you."

I could see his mind racing. He seemed to drift away while considering the possibilities of my request.

"I'm so confused."

"How so?" His body jerked a little as if jolted back to the moment.

"All I've ever wanted was to leave my house as soon as possible. For years, it's all I've focused on. Now, I don't want to leave my sister and I don't want to leave you. My life's vision seems blurry and I'm not sure that's a good thing. That's what I mean about you having someone with experience. What if I can't be a good girlfriend to you?"

"I won't let go of you." His smoothed my hair. I gave myself freely to the passion in his lips. He looked taken over as if only wanting to comfort me. "It's natural to be afraid of things unfamiliar to us. We'll work through them together. I want you to have the life you envision; I only want to be a part of it."

We were quiet as we finished the rest of our meal.

"Would you like any dessert tonight?" Our waiter had the table cleared and had two dessert menus in his hand. "We have a molten lava cake that takes twenty minutes. Fudge spills out as soon as you cut into it and it's served with our homemade vanilla bean ice cream."

I shook my head.

"It sounds delicious, but just the check please." Ryan answered.

"Take you time," he left the check with us.

"I have another spot I'd like to take you. Is that all right?"

"Sure. Hey, Ryan?"

"Hmm?"

"Thank God, we're not going to dance anymore," I felt my shoulders begin to relax. "We're not, are we?"

"No. No more dancing tonight." He laughed his beautiful, low laugh. Paid the bill and left a large tip in cash. As we got up, I felt as if the room stopped to watch.

"You're a generous man. I'm so proud of that part of you."

He gave me a nice squeeze.

When the hostess who'd fussed over him earlier gave him a sweet goodnight, he never looked up. Instead, he dipped me in front of her, held my body easily with one arm and his other hand caressed my cheek. His mouth curved against mine and I melted at the touch of his lips. Several patrons clapped in approval and when he lifted me to his body.

I flattened my hand on his chest. "Thank you." I knew what he'd done without making it an issue.

We walked hand in hand to the valet. In only a few minutes the car was at the curb; both of our doors opened.

"I guess you didn't need that ticket after all," the man said as I started to get in the car.

"What ticket?"

"Your coat," he reminded me. "It looks like the temperature inside is fine. You didn't get cold."

"Oh, that's right!" I leaned over to his ear. "It really wasn't because I was cold."

He nodded with a knowing smile.

"To be honest, though, it's really warm in there. You might want to turn on the air conditioning for a while. Have a good night."

Ryan cracked up.

"What?"

"Nothing, sweetheart. *Warm in there*."

We drove to the Irish Cultural Center located in the Sunset, one of San Francisco's many pocket neighborhoods. I was Irish, but I'd never been to the venue.

"The Irish Cultural Center?" I questioned him when we parked. "What's going on here?"

"You'll see."

We walked in, and as I surveyed the lobby I saw his sister-in-law standing off to the side as if waiting for us.

"Chris and Frances are here?"

He started to tell me more, but once some of the audience members recognized him, a small group gathered for autographs and photos. I never lost interest in watching how he conducted himself in public. I stepped away from the circle for a better view. Dozens of fans wanted to say hello. The time he took to make them feel good was endearing. I not only got enjoyment from watching the look on his face, but also the faces of his fans.

Frances walked over and gave me a hug. "Was this a surprise?"

"Yes! I had no idea we were coming here. The whole evening was a surprise. I can't keep up with your brother-in-law."

"That's the idea, Nicky."

Chapter 32

Chris Tilton Plays His Guitar

"**D**on't you get tired of having to stop for his fans?" Frances nodded toward Ryan and then led the way to a less crowded corner of the room.

"We haven't been on that many dates. No, not so far." I glanced back at Ryan and found him looking at me while he signed someone's cap. A shot of hot liquid surged through my legs. "His fans are important to him. Truthfully, I enjoy how thrilled they are just to shake his hand."

"You're a better woman than I am." Her hands went to her hips. "I couldn't put up with it. When that happens to Chris and the band, I step in immediately." She ushered me through the lobby and into the small theater. She had three seats reserved for family in the front row.

"A little tip?" She put her hand on my shoulder. "Don't let them get too close. Plenty of women wait for just the right moment. If you allow them to interact too often, you're daring temptation to make its move. Women aren't bashful, Nicky."

Is Frances subtly revealing that Chris cheated on her?

"I'll definitely keep that in mind." I pretended to take her advice in a healthy way when in reality it was a fear I battled each time we'd gone out.

"Wow, that necklace looks fabulous on you! May I?" She held the emerald in her fingers. "We were with Ryan when he bought it. Gorgeous, just gorgeous."

"You *were*? When?"

"Yesterday." She took off her gold lame jacket and draped it across her lap. "Ryan was such a love. He rambled on and on asking our opinion of it."

"What did he need to know?" I bumped into a chair. "Ow."

"If we thought the necklace was enough or too much, was it a gift that was too soon to give it to you—he was so worried you wouldn't like it. I tried it on for him. I started to tear up when he said, *I can't tell because you don't have her green eyes.*"

"Oh." I folded my hands in my lap, holding the moment as if I'd cupped a butterfly inside them. "That's so sweet."

"It was," she agreed. "I wish he and Chris would let that soft side show to each other."

"Me too. That Ryan's here is a good sign," I offered.

"It means a lot to Chris." She crossed her ankles. "Anyway, I've been dying to tell you, we've seen Ryan with so many women . . . oh, shit, I'm . . . I didn't mean—"

"I know plenty about his reputation." My toes curled in my shoes. "You're not revealing anything I haven't already heard."

Or seen.

"Don't pay attention to me." She playfully slapped her cheek. "Sometimes I need to keep my thoughts to myself."

"That's okay," I encouraged hesitantly. "Go on."

"What I meant is we've seen plenty of random photos showing him with a woman at some social event or nightclub but we've never been introduced to anyone. You're the only one he's talked about *and* you're the first lady he's ever brought to see Chris perform. Did you know he's talked about you since last year?"

"I'm overwhelmed by him." My hand flew to my chest.

"Guess that means you're a special lady. What took you two so long to get together?"

Well, I was seventeen and in high school. God, that sounds ridiculous. What do I say?

"Don't know. Frances," I quickly changed the subject, "we both understand I'm not the sophisticated woman who should be on his arm." I discounted myself once again; believing almost any other woman would be a better match for him.

My feelings hadn't been acknowledged during my childhood and when I got older and presented my opinions they were discounted as unimportant. Until recently, I'd followed the pattern my parents had set for me—I believed my emotional struggles were unimportant.

"My intuition tells me Ryan knows what kind of woman he wants." She fanned herself. "After all, if it was only social standing and beauty, hasn't he been with her already? It's chemicals and primitive stuff wrapped around things we don't understand."

"My brain tells me what you're saying should be true. On the other hand, Ryan has only been with those women. So no, I don't believe it. The doubts I have—I really don't understand what it is about me that attracted him. It's like trading a Ferrari for a Jeep."

"Even so . . ." She started laughing. "A *Jeep*. Not quite, Nicky. Chris told me until you, he's never seen his brother so watchful or concerned about any woman. Neither have I. We've both encouraged him to bring dates to dinner and when he visits us in the off-season. He never has—until now. The way he touches and looks at you . . . anyone who's paying the slightest bit of attention can see the longing in his eyes. The look he gives you is about having it all."

"How did you know Chris was the one?" I was embarrassed and changed the subject to make her relationship the focus.

"His lingering touches, a certain look in his eyes, the fire of passion and warmth in my heart from just the sound of his voice. He'd call me with a little love wish or make up an excuse to see me. I guess it was his little bits of sweetness. Well," she giggled, "some of the big bits, too."

Nasty stuff! I'm included in conversations about sex now!

"I do see and feel all those things. I'm still afraid."

"You love him, don't you?" She sat up straight.

"Yes."

"It shows. Have you told him?"

"Not yet."

"I understand." She adjusted her pearl necklace. "It's a big deal." She turned to face the stage. "Chris is playing after this set."

"Oh, fantastic! I can't wait to hear him."

"Thanks! I think you'll enjoy their music. At any rate," she turned her head and smiled. "I wouldn't wait too long if I were you." Her voice held a warning. "Know what I mean?"

"Yes."

The lights blinked and then dimmed, leaving only a faint glow by the entry doors of the theater. A strip of lights illuminated along the aisle.

A man introduced the opening band.

Applause and cheers rang out.

Bright strobe lights flashed. They began to play a mix of the hard edge of rock with a lyric and beat of an Irish folk song. It was a style of music I hadn't followed but found interesting. They had no shirts on and wore black leather pants and spiked cuffs. Each had dyed their hair and their boots were decorated with chains and metal studs.

"I don't even know your story," Frances yelled in my ear, trying to be heard over the loud music. "There's obviously some reason for the sweet look in Ryan's eyes. I sound like I'm crazy, talking like this, but I'm known for speaking my mind."

"No, not crazy," I yelled back, clapping in time with the audience. "I appreciate your honesty. He's very considerate, but his life is big and I'm afraid I won't handle it well."

"When you realize your love is in front of you, it *is* scary. Your gut screams *he's the one* and you think maybe it's too good to be true. You know what, Nicky?"

"What?"

"It's *fucking* scary." She roared with laughter, perhaps trying to ease my worry, but the result was that my heart thumped hard.

Another song began.

I turned around to see if I could find Ryan, but I couldn't locate him in the standing crowd.

Why is he taking so long? I would have thought he'd be here by now. Maybe a woman caught his attention.

A show of bright colors circled and swept over the stage, keeping time with the music.

"I didn't know there was such a thing as Irish folk rock," I shouted.

"They're pretty unique." Frances positioned her cell phone and snapped a few pictures. "They've opened for Chris' band a few times and always get the crowd into it."

There must have been close to a thousand people in the small theater, maybe more. Heavy green draperies decorated the interior and dark woods paneled the walls and stage.

Three, four, five songs passed. No Ryan.

I was anxious.

Had someone gotten too close, as Frances had suggested? If I went into the lobby, would I see a woman or two flirting and pressing to be with him?

I pushed down those worries and tried to immerse myself in the music. Frances held my hand and we raised them in the air.

I began having fun.

I danced.

High-fived the people sitting by me.

Yelled.

Tried to sing along to the verses that repeated.

Let go until intermission came.

"Let's stretch our legs," Frances said. "Want a water or something?"

"Water sounds good." *Maybe I'll find Ryan.*

We walked into the lobby. He wasn't there.

"Two," Frances said to the vendor behind the counter, pointing to the bottles of water. "Here you go." She handed me one of the bottles.

"Thanks." I craned my head.

"He's backstage with Chris," Frances smirked.

"Oh, I—"

"Don't worry," she patted my back. "It's too soon to stray. He's deeply in love."

Do I feel better about that or . . . wait for it all to be over?

I recognized a teacher from high school who was with her husband and introduced them to Frances. Then I regretted it, afraid she'd reveal I had just graduated and embarrass me.

"I seem to remember you're a baseball fan, aren't you?" Ms. Pringle asked.

"Yes, a devoted Goliaths' fan." *I'm especially fond of one of their team members.*

"We saw Ryan Tilton here earlier and got an autograph for my grandson." She showed me her signed program. "I thought of you. Maybe he's still here."

I hope he's still here.

"I'll have to look for him." I winked at Frances. From the smile on her face I knew she had difficulty stopping a giggle.

The four of us stood together and talked until the lights flickered, which announced the beginning of the second half of the show. When we walked back to our seats, I saw Ryan and his brothers near the back of the stage. Chris was strumming a few chords, absentmindedly, it seemed, as he talked to Ryan.

Phew, there he is.

The band warmed up, tuning their guitars, the drummer rapping a few beats on the drums, and the horn players tooting a few seemingly random notes.

"Do you and Chris tour often?" Frances and I took our seats.

"All the time," she laughed in the way I thought a lady of society might. "That's our life. He performs most every week or weekend during the year."

"What's your favorite place?"

"San Francisco, of course." She answered without hesitation. "It's so diverse; he always plays to a good crowd, open and ready to have a good time, and yet in many ways the city is old school."

I jumped when Ryan sat down next to me. I had been so engaged in my conversation with Frances I hadn't noticed him leave the stage. She smiled as he kissed my cheek and when his hand slid around my shoulder, she turned her eyes to the stage.

The lights went out except for one.

It was on Chris.

"Is this okay?" Ryan said softly in my ear.

"When I'm with you?" I put my hands on his cheeks. Kissed his lips. "I'm beginning to think that anything is okay."

He took me inside his embrace, his muscles beginning to bulge, his head tilting and his lips parting, ready for my surrender. I let his mouth seal mine.

"You have . . ." He swallowed.

"What?" I whispered as the crowd quieted.

"Me. Completely." His long fingers traced my cheek.

One of his arms dropped to my waste.

Chris began a soft ballad.

His voice was beautiful, haunting, penetrating . . . he was one with the music. It got into the depths of me and I knew those sitting around us felt the same by their devoted attention. He immediately pulled the audience inside the lyrics and melody. He made us feel like we were his friends.

Now I understood the fear Frances had briefly shared with me.

He seemed easy. Trusted with everything. And then? Only a moment later, he was a dangerous lover. The words he sung dared any woman to conquer him and yet the aura he seemed to exude told her he'd never be tamed.

The song was haunting.

He was haunting.

His blonde hair glistened.

As I looked at Frances I saw she was mesmerized.

After the opening number, the band changed it up and went into hard rock. It was the contrast we needed, shaking us, the buzz of a rock band humming through us. Immediately we stood, danced together and yelled loudly.

"He's good!" I shouted to Ryan.

"Yeah!" he yelled in response. "Incredible."

Another look took him over; much different than the one I saw him wear at the Embarcadero Hotel. It was a look of pride. He was happy for his brother. There was no jealousy, no envy, and no hurt in Ryan's expression.

He loves Chris. Oh, thank God. Maybe they can fix the broken things that lie between them.

Ryan stood behind me. His arms wrapped around my waist. My hands rested on his, moving back and forth to the rhythms of the band.

Chris played for over two hours, with an intermission between sets. After an encore, the crowd went wild and applauded for many minutes even as he left the stage.

"Come on!" Frances yelled. "Follow me." She led us back stage, flirting with security along the way.

A few people recognized Ryan. This time he didn't stop. He only smiled as he continued with us to the band's dressing room.

"Isn't he fabulous?" Frances threw herself into Chris' arms.

"You guys were great." I shook hands with several band members.

"Awesome bro." Ryan gave his brother a few solid fist pumps. "Love that new set you added."

We chatted ten or fifteen minutes. Ryan mentioned we were going to Yountville in the morning and needed to leave. The hugs that he shared with Chris and Frances seemed sincere and made me feel good.

Instead of shaking my hand, perhaps still on his high from performing, Chris grabbed me and pulled me in for an embrace.

"See you tomorrow." Chris nodded to Ryan.

"Adios." Ryan nodded back.

"Bye Frances!" I shouted.

"She waved and once again crushed her body into Chris, giving him a taste of what it was to have her French flavor.

"Wow, what a great evening," I said as we walked to the car. "I saw one of my high school teachers and she said she got your autograph for her grandson. I was so afraid she was going to reveal I just graduated and Frances would think I'm a dolt."

323

"Even if she had, my sister-in-law wouldn't have thought anything like that."

"Still, I'm glad she didn't say anything." I slid my arm inside his. "You're a fun boyfriend."

"I'm glad you enjoyed yourself. Speaking of extending the evening . . . how do you feel about staying overnight with me? We can go to Veterans' Hospital first thing in the morning."

We'd already spent the night together twice, once in my bedroom and the other when I'd made him promise abstinence in Half Moon Bay. This would be in his apartment where I would be at his mercy. My next question was ridiculous, but fear-based.

"You have a guest bedroom at your place?"

"I was thinking more along the lines of staying in Yountville tonight," he said with a heated stare. "It's a weeknight. I'm sure a room won't be a problem."

"I can't visit the vets in this dress."

"Have to admit, I'd like to see their reaction if you walked in like that. I have something you'll like. It's in the backseat."

I unzipped the little suitcase and found a pink sports outfit with a pair of white sneakers and socks.

"Well . . ." I felt myself revving up. "How did you know my size? Like, um, who gave it to you? Are you an expert on women's clothes? I mean, well, I don't mean that as an insult. Sorry. God, I'm so sarcastic sometimes I can't turn it off and that's not what I meant, you know. I'm trying to understand, uh, what made you bring it? When did you—"

"Your sister. I had a suspicion you might want to go to Yountville in the morning. And I owe you a few visits, so . . ."

"Okay, but I don't have any pajamas. I think there's a Cost Less on the way. Do you think they're open?"

"I don't think we'll need any clothes after Half Moon Bay." He wore his wry grin. "Do you?" His gaze was void of any bashfulness. Everything about him felt bold.

Chapter 33

Night Falls in Yountville

We drove the hour to Yountville in relative silence.

Anticipation enveloped our bodies.

The little bits of conversation that we attempted focused on Chris and Frances, rather than what remained of our evening.

What will he expect? Sex? Complete, full on sex? Or maybe he'll want a blowjob? Will this be the night I get a tongue bath?

He pulled into a ranch-style motel called The Vine Leaf Inn. It was a single-level accommodation and shaped in an L. The signage was bright enough that it illuminated a color scheme of greens and purples. Thick with bunches of grapes growing on them, vines wove in and out of the lattice that formed arbors over each doorway to the guest rooms.

"Is this okay?" His hand was on the car door handle as if ready to jump out and get a key to our room.

"Sure." *What am I going to say? No, this isn't good at all?* "Should I come in with you?"

He flashed a nasty smile. "We can pretend we're on our honeymoon and we're checking in."

I'm cooking inside. It won't be too long before I'm done.

Ryan opened the front door for me. Once through, we walked hand in hand to check in. When the woman at the front desk smiled and asked if we needed a room with one or two beds, he held up a single finger and took out his credit card. After he registered, she gave him a key to room ten and informed us there was coffee all night in the lobby.

"There's a continental breakfast in the morning from 6:30 until 10:00," she informed. "If you're hungry, there's an all night diner we locals enjoy around the corner and an I-Hop a little ways up the highway."

Ryan thanked her and we wished her a good evening. After getting back in the car, we pulled in front of our room. Two vending machines stood a few doors down. One held water, soda, and juice. The other held snacks such as crackers and candy bars.

"Want a water or a little something to nibble on?" His bottom lip quivered.

"A water would be good." I hesitated, knowing the mistakes and bad habits I continually battled when it came to substituting food for love or soothing a stressful situation. "Do you want to split a candy bar?"

"We could get something from the store if you'd rather." he held my wrist. I felt a knowing squeeze of concern.

"No, this is okay." *Yes! I'd love to go to the store and get a bag of goodies for us to chow down!* "Grayson cooks in the morning for the vets and I'm sure Paul will let us grab a bite."

"Or if we get up early enough, we can get some pancakes."

"True." I felt foolish suggesting we eat at the hospital when we were in a town filled with cafes.

Ryan slid his credit card into the vending machine's scanner, pushed the buttons for two waters and from the other machine a candy bar. He opened the wrapper and handed me a half.

"If you're as hungry as I am, I'm sure you want this now," he quickly gobbled the chocolate and caramel coated cookie. I ate mine as rapidly as he did.

"That hit the spot," I said after a long swig of water. "Do you have anything to take in?" I wondered if he'd planned the evening so carefully that he might have brought his toothbrush.

"Just my baby." He kissed the back of my hand.

"Well then."

He unlocked the door and stepped aside, letting me walk in first. It was quite different from Chris and Frances's room at the Embarcadero Hotel or the Half Moon Bay Bed and Breakfast Inn. I felt a world away.

An inviting four-poster queen-size bed with a rich purple comforter and grape-leaf design sat squarely in the middle of the room. Two chairs and a pine table sat near the window. Against the wall was a cadenza. A TV sat on top of it.

I hung my coat on one of the hangers in a make shift closet near the bathroom.

Behind me, I heard the door close and lock. Ryan threw his keys on the table.

I can't get over this—I'm here with a man. A man who wants to be with me—with me!

"I wish we had a deck of cards," I announced. "I'd beat you in a game of hearts."

"I know how to play that!" he said excitedly.

"Really? Cool. My grandma taught me a lot of card games. Plus, when relatives came over, they'd let Jenise and me play before they started their poker." I ran my hand over the bedspread. "Pretty."

"Just what I was thinking . . . not about the bed."

"You can turn off the charm now," I teased. "I'm here."

"That would be so boring," he laughed. "I'm going to take a quick shower. Can you see if there's any late news on TV?"

"I'll surf the channels." I picked up the remote. "I'll bet the tourists that stay here are too soused to care after their day of wine tasting; probably not much of a selection."

"See what you can find," he repeated.

At first I amused myself with my analysis. Then I considered how riddled I was with the fret and worry of being around alcohol. I had a hard time understanding how cocktails could be enjoyable and considered wine tasting an excuse for an alcoholic's bliss. I shook my head as if trying to stop the dysfunctional thought.

"Want to join me?" Ryan asked, one arm on the bathroom doorframe. He was texting something on his phone.

"You know the answer," I replied. "Who are you texting?"

"Turner wants to teach me a new pitch tomorrow at practice," he frowned. "I thought I was through with new stuff."

"Maybe he's thinking of your longevity."

"I'm thinking about my longevity right now." With a devilish laugh he tossed his phone on the bed and closed the bathroom door. I heard the water flow and the shower doors close.

God, he's always on play. How can I keep up with him? Ooh, I could look through his phone and see his blacklist. It's pure temptation sitting right in front of me.

I fought the urge and continued surfing TV channels. I finally found MSNBC and left it on for him. The little table had two binders on it, one explained the benefits of staying at the motel and the other highlighted things to do that were nearby. I was in the middle of leafing through them when Ryan came out of the shower. He had only a towel wrapped around his waist.

I could take that thing off; run my hands on his body . . . what then? We'd have to go all the way at that point, wouldn't we?

A sudden knock on the door.

I looked at Ryan in panic.

"Who—"

"My text earlier wasn't only to answer Turner. Hopefully the office is here with a little surprise. I'll duck into the bathroom."

When I opened the door, the woman from the front desk stood with a small bag in her hand.

"Here you go, miss. Have a good night."

"Oh, do I, do you need—" I didn't have money on me and wanted to me sure was tipped.

"It's taken care of. Enjoy." She smiled and walked away.

I closed and locked the door. When I emptied the contents of the bag on the table, a deck of cards fell out along with two bananas, two yogurts, and two spoons.

Ryan slipped behind me.

"Surprised?" He kissed my ear.

"Always." I turned and put my arms around his neck. "You're really a love, you know."

"Am I?" He looked down pretending to be bashful.

"And too confident," I added.

"Why don't you um . . . slip into something more comfortable and we'll play a game or two of hearts?"

"Dare I let you see me without makeup?" I began walking toward the bathroom.

"Oh yes, please," he begged. "I've seen that pretty face blink in innocence before. You're beautiful without any makeup. I'd love to see you that way again."

Damn, the things he says.

"God, Ryan." I grabbed the robe hanging in the closet and closed the bathroom door. *I have a man waiting for me outside this door. He's waiting to play cards, but then what? Do we go to sleep? Cuddle? Kiss? Make out? What do I say? How do I stop him? How far is too far?*

I washed my face and used the complimentary makeup remover pads for my eyes. I slipped off my dress and put on the robe. When I was finished freshening up, I hung my dress by my coat. "Don't let me forget these when we leave tomorrow." I rattled the hangers.

"Oh, Nicky." The story of what he wanted was written all over his face. "Come here and let me give you a little kiss."

"Promise?"

"Just a kiss," he repeated.

I walked to the table and he took me into the nest of his arms. They were luscious, bulging life, and they felt so right it was as if I was made to be in them forever. When he squeezed me, I felt his heart beating fast.

I was helpless on his lap.

I wanted to submit to him.

He kissed me on the lips.

"I'm going to stick you with the queen of spades, babe. I'm the resident Hearts expert in the clubhouse and I intend to beat you handily." He kissed my forehead.

"Get ready," I warned. I sat in the chair at the little table and rubbed my hands together, ready for the challenge.

We played the best three of five, ate our bananas and yogurts, and although the last game was close, he beat me with a lucky run of taking all the hearts in the last game.

"Lucky," I chided. "Damn it. You were lucky."

"I know." His voice seemed to lower a full octave. "If only you'd trumped that diamond trick you would've stopped me. Whelp," he stretched. "We'd better go to bed." He pushed up from the table and turned off the TV.

"Yeah, we have an early morning," I agreed. "Yikes! It's already after 2:00 a.m."

I put the cards back into the deck and got up to throw away the empty yogurt containers and banana peels.

"Leave those for now." He reached for my hand and walked us to the bed. His body fell on top of mine. His eyes narrowed. I knew he wanted to begin another kind of game—one I'd never played.

My robe was loose.

When his big pitcher's hands flattened on my belly, his hips moved as if he'd already begun the rhythm of making love. As he continued caressing my body, I fantasized how I might become his instrument. I imagined him moving his bow all over me, resulting in a bedtime lullaby for new lovers. Although he'd showered, I could still smell all the scents of the Irish Cultural Center in his hair. Frances's perfume seemed to linger from their hug goodbye as well as the mixed air of being in a crowd.

"Ryan." I struggled to stay in the moment.

"You know I love it when you look up at me. Your beautiful green eyes are hypnotic as they try to figure out what's happening to the woman they're guarding." He drew in a long breath. "Don't you sense that I'm breaking through your walls?" The lush carnality of his voice was an invitation my body responded to in every way. "Soon you'll be wide open—everywhere."

He rolled to the side. Stood and then lifted me so we pressed together. We moved in little sways. I drifted back to our night on the beach, watching the breezes blow the pine trees side to side. That night in Yountville, my body was like one of those, bending and swaying from his force. When he placed my palm on his volcanic chest, it was enough to bring me to my knees.

His hands opened my robe. I was dressed only a bra and panties. A slow smile spread greedily across his face. Fingers lifted and reconnected as if they were matches striking against my skin, igniting and exploding in fire. There were a million nerve endings lighting up inside me as he squeezed, released, and

331

squeezed again. Our primitive souls circled. Called out. Came together as if we were in a tribal dance.

His big hands were already on my shoulders, silently waiting for my permission. His eyes were heavy-lidded.

I knew I'd show a lack of trust in our relationship if I didn't do as he asked. I nodded my okay, granting his request.

Each of his big hands grasped the collar. He bared my shoulders. Leaned over. Kissed each of them. His soft lips brought chills that ran down my back. His hair brushed my cheek. I felt as if I was suspended in an electric moment, hovering in the thick air, waiting for the next touch of his fingers. After untying my belt the entire robe fell open and dropped at my feet. I stood before him wanting to cover myself. I resisted and instead enjoyed his smile, lust-filled and wicked.

"You are . . ." His gaze darkened almost dangerously.

My stomach tightened.

Betraying me with each second that passed, my body seemed to lose the ability to stand on its own. My Evil Twin was rising. As she showed herself, I felt her encouragement of letting go. My strict and unmoving boundaries were in question for the first time in my life. Only moments from surrendering to his urges—as well as my own—pulses rolled and ached in my belly.

Invisibly, my white flag shot into the air as his mouth went across my collarbone. Licked its hard ridge; summiting and conquering my crest. He covered my bare shoulders and arms with his kisses. I bowed my head. Weak and no longer able to withstand the engulfing waves of desire that consumed me, even my mouth gave in and opened to his passion.

His body became bigger.

Gathered the power it needed—power he'd depended on and had come to know with other women. The blood circled in his pelvis, readying him for his sensual release. I felt small, but also safe in his lion's lair. When he rubbed his cheek against mine, a warm sensation moved through me.

Every part of my body was on alert.

Aware of a new pulsing need, I felt his long, moist tongue, thick and swollen on my face. The way he used it lulled me into complete and utter wonder—and brought tormenting pleasure.

"Mmm, Ryan, that feels nice."

"Turn around." He released me from his embrace. His hands lightly traced my back, touching me at the base of my spine.

I was certain I had left my body and hovered above, watching invisible arms grab for Ryan with wild abandon, impatiently reaching for the essence of a man I knew I wanted . . . I wanted for . . . ever.

Chapter 34

A Draw

$\mathcal{R}$yan's hands framed my shoulders.

Slipped down my arms in a caress.

His fingertips traced my navel and in a slow and exaggerated motion, slid around my sides to my bra. "Your breasts . . . I've waited so long to see them again." He unfastened the hooks, freeing them to be fondled and held.

My nipples hardened in the anticipation of his fingers—or tongue—circling and sucking them.

"Your big, beautiful behind." One hand flattened on it. "I want to take your panties down and play with your ass all night long."

My backside felt the press of his thighs and stomach. Once again, his arms circled around me. Firm and persuasive, I became liquid in his embrace—heated, spilling, and running over.

I covered my breasts.

His head rested on my shoulder.

Man-sized hands found mine. They rested on mine, on top of my breasts. I wasn't a small girl and yet I felt that way against his body. Was this his silent acknowledgement of my feeble attempt to shield my nakedness? Urgent whispers breathed in an almost rhythmic desire. I found my soul moving with our music: gentle, soft, wanting to be caressed.

"I want you . . . all of you. Will you lie with me tonight and give me your love?"

What do I do, what do I do?

His body pushed so hard into mine that I had trouble breathing. I could feel his erection straight up against my lower back. He was ready to be tucked inside my feminine folds, moments away from new relief, bringing me into a very different life . . . together.

This new language of desire seemed to rise from the depths of his being—and mine. I felt cravings everywhere—inside me, from his body, my stomach and thighs . . . all circling around us. I was covered in a misty dream; aware that my passion had reached a level I hadn't known existed.

Ryan walked us closer to the bed.

I knew we were about to make love.

His hands held the back of my thighs.

He lifted me.

I knew he wanted to lie on top of my body. I wasn't ready for that. Instead, I wanted to immerse myself in our possibility and began an exploration of my own.

Kneeling in front of him, I put my hands on his rugged jaw. I held it in my palm. Squeezed gently. The back of my hand ran over his cheek and the stubble that covered it. My fingertips walked delicately on his neck, tracing its throbbing veins, imagining I could take a bite of the life force inside. I outlined his shoulders. Unable to resist, I leaned close enough to kiss the hollow of his neck and ran my tongue along one of the heartbeats hidden inside. Heavy breaths from his mouth were like wispy words covering my face. Flattening my hands on his chest, I hesitated as if holding his heart under them. It was thumping. Strong. Fast. Racing. Next, I splayed my fingers and rested them on his stomach. I was at the mercy of this tribal man even though he was allowing me to take my time on his body.

He lifted me onto his lap. "Open your legs and offer me your body as you cradle my thighs. I need the feel of your breasts touching my chest when you lie on top of me."

"Mmm." I was floating in some other woman's dream—a woman who was unafraid and ready for sex.

It feels so . . . Oh, God, this ache . . . it's so powerful. If I could just rub my . . . against his . . . should I remove his towel? No. That would mean . . . I want him. No. I can't. Can I?"

My legs opened to embrace him just as he wanted.

His devil-may-care-smile was revealing.

I could hardly look at him.

"You're soaking." His tone was low and delicious. "You know that, don't you?"

"No." I knew he meant my underwear was wet. I didn't know what to say. Instead of admitting it, I denied my awareness.

"Uh-huh." He looked over my face as if he were taking my picture and looking for the best angle. "Yes, you do."

Oh damn, I'm going to faint. My head—there's too much blood rushing and pounding everywhere.

"Take your hands away. It's time to stop hiding from me."

"Wait. Wait, I—" *What should I do? How is this, why, I need to slow down. Wait.*

"I want to look at you."

"Okay, and uh . . ." I swallowed. "Tell me what—"

"Should I take you through what I want to do to you?" He hesitated. Gauged my response. My hesitation was his cue to continue. "All the parts of your woman's body will become familiar to me. I need your breasts," his soft sigh brushed my lips. "I'll caress them gently, take a small taste so that I know everything about them. I've yearned to feel your little nipple in my mouth from last year. I dream about sucking its hardened peak. I have to understand your sensitivity from the opening where your milk will flow one day. My hands want the warmth you hold in the crease of your breasts. I need to make them mine. I want to know all the things that make you excited, what turns you on and causes a fever to burn in the split of your body and makes you wet for me."

"Maybe," I gasped. "I . . . um, think maybe . . . I, we should stop and . . ." I trailed off.

"Do you trust me?"

"Yes."

"I won't go further than you want me to. Believe me?"

"Ryan, I won't—"

"Put your arms around me," he interrupted. He helped my arms partially circle around his back, while he pulled me closer.

My belly touched his.

My breasts ached as they touched the volcanic chest I adored.

"Open your legs wider." His breathing was labored. "Wrap them around my hips and hold me inside them; hold me tight. Let me feel your embrace around my body." The way he slipped his tongue inside my mouth was as if it were his penis making love to my vagina. It was creamy, wet and luscious. The little muscle that seemed to rest on its tip moved expertly, lubricating both pairs of my lips. "I want you. I'm ready. Can you commit to me tonight?" His hand caressed my cheek. "You feel how much I love you, don't you?"

"Yes," I inhaled sharply. "I feel you."

"Unwrap the towel from around my waist. Slowly. Will you stay on my lap and do it?"

"Mm-hmm." *Oh yes!* I began to unwrap the thick terrycloth from his body.

What do I do when "it" pops out? I'll close my eyes, I guess. How can I, though? It'll be right there. I want to see it. Can I look at it? I wonder what it will look like this close? I've only felt it in the darkness before.

"I'm desperate to be held by you. Desire me. Take me as if I'm what you need to be alive. Let me feel your hands on me. Run wild on me. Let me feel your passion come to life." He ran his hands through my hair and grabbed bunches of it. "Even now, I'm imagining the moist beads of your inner thighs on my belly as you move and squirm on my body while we make love. You've opened your mind to our relationship. Now open your body. Tonight."

His hips rose up and down as he spoke. His eyes were fixed on my breasts.

"Ryan, I can't . . . get this . . . you're sitting on the towel. I can't . . ."

He leaned back.

Lifted his hips.

Enticed me to come closer.

Flattened his hands on my stomach.

The heat radiated through me.

My nipples stretched.

"Don't let go," he warned.

I wrapped my legs around him. He stood up. I trembled. Tried to grip his waist as tightly as I could. I was sure the strength in my body had dwindled away. I was weak and my legs shook.

He finished taking off his towel.

Quite unexpectedly, I found that he'd worn his briefs. Once again, he sat down on the edge of the bed.

His chest rubbed against mine.

Our two spirits danced, absorbing each other.

"I love lifting you. Have I ever told you that?" His hands rubbed my shoulders and then slipped down the length of my spine. "I love feeling your body move. When you reach for me and hold me? I want to fall into you." He looked at his stomach and then in my eyes. "I think you got me wet."

His voice was searing and brought the ache in my pelvis to an unbearable level.

"I . . ." I breathed a long sigh and closed my eyes. "I need—"

"What do you need, baby?" he asked softly. "What is it, sweet woman?"

"I can't breathe and I need to . . ."

His hips pressed up to my open legs; his obvious erection begged for my attention. I was nervous, scared, and excited all at the same time. It had been a beautiful night. I knew I should be ready for him.

The old voices of doubt whispered in my head.

I hesitated.

Give in and he'll leave you.

Anything this good is bound to end badly.

Abandonment is inevitable.

"Ryan, I can't stand anymore. I'm . . ."

We fell back on the bed.

He put his arms around me and rolled over.

I was caged. A prisoner. Seduced by the loveliness of his hips, belly, and chest. My soaked underwear and his briefs weren't hiding anything.

Our lips met. Dreams pressed the promise of us together. A glorious evening had been crowned.

During my ecstasy, I tightened and then loosened my legs as they surrounded him. The ways my muscles clenched and squeezed were signals he'd felt. They told him my body was ready. I didn't understand these were his guides—and he was paying close attention to them.

I didn't know that when my body was excited, he could feel it the same way I felt it.

I didn't know how in tune we were in those first weeks of trying to come together as lovers.

My quivering limbs clung to his athletic body as he changed positions. Now I found myself on top of him, stretched open around his hips, ready to receive a man inside me for the first time.

His chest was in full view. I felt him move, positioning his sensual stem to make my flower bloom with brilliant colors.

A monsoon of desire began flooding, completely taking me over. Everything about him was ready to love me. My body had been prepared to love him.

"Are you ready?" His hands reached for me, ready to touch my breasts, stroke my belly, and hold my ample behind. "Say it, Nicky. Please say it. Tell me you want all of me like I want you. Commit to me tonight—say you're mine."

I did want him.

Out loud and without hesitation I practiced, "Yes, you're mine, I'm yours, and I want all of you."

But I couldn't say it aloud.

I couldn't let him in.

Once I opened my body I knew I'd lose control of my life.

After he asked me to give up everything—school, career, friends, and family—he'd leave me.

This is too much too fast. Nothing can last when it comes this soon. Get out now while you can.

Even though college was only an hour away, it would be another world—a world I was convinced would demand I enter exclusively.

If I told Ryan yes, I could never gain the independence I needed to leave my house once and for all, escaping the abuse, the suffering, the dysfunction, and sadness of my youth.

I knew I had to stay tough.

I couldn't let myself be vulnerable . . . or take a risk that happiness might be waiting for me.

I couldn't depend on anyone else.

Had to get out.

Couldn't stay there. Live there. Remain there.

I was afraid of ending up like my mother.

Afraid of choosing a life that in the end I didn't want, I refused to end up the way my father had.

I was afraid of getting pregnant.

Afraid of getting lost.

Afraid to trust Ryan.

Afraid to trust myself.

All these years later, the little girl remained frozen under the dining room table, still hiding from the monster in her house.

This time, *I* was the monster.

This time, my fight would be with my own demons.

YOU MADE IT!

CAN YOU PLEASE TAKE A MOMENT AND LEAVE A REVIEW FOR ME? I'D REALLY, REALLY APPRECIATE IT IF YOU WOULD:

AMAZON: bit.ly/FireHeart
GOODREADS: bit.ly/GoodreadsFireHeart

Resources

Books

Dirty Words, Ellen Sussman

How to Please a Woman In & Out of Bed, Daylee Deanna Schwartz

It Will Never Happen to Me, Claudia Black, PhD

Oxford American Writer's Thesaurus

The Bald-Headed Hermit & The Artichoke, A.D. Peterkin

The Complete Idiot's Guide to Amazing Sex, Sari Lockner, Ph.D.

The Romance Writer's Phrase Book, Jean Kent, Candace Shelton

Thinking Like A Romance Writer, Dahlia Evans

The SEXaurus, Stefanie Olsen

The Emotion Thesaurus, Angela Ackerman & Becca Puglisi

Organizations/Web sites

sexualityresources.com

crimescene.com

pandys.org

joyfulheartfoundation.org

Acknowledgments

$\mathcal{A}$s with any project, there are many people who influenced my journey. Some friends exist only in my memories, and others have crossed my path in sweet or dramatic ways. I hold all of you to my heart, even if you're not mentioned below.

For my beautiful sister, whose life ended much too early—I understand you more now than I ever did.

For my father, at times your disease took you over. I miss you. I wish I had the maturity back then to have understood. I couldn't have stopped you, but I would've spoken differently. You gave me so many twisted gifts, and I thank you in spite of everything.

Claude and Aaron, I love you guys so much that sometimes I think I'm sick because the joy is so mountainous and hurt so deep.

Louise—I couldn't have done this without you.

My sweet girlfriends from childhood—Colleen, Patty, Lorraine, Kathie, Marilyn

TS Babes: (Santo, Spanky, Uno, GG, Wiseone, BL, Nine, Catnip xxoo) thanks for allowing me so much.

Mom, you have problems saying I love you, but I get it now.

About the Author

PAMELA TAEUFFER, BIOGRAPHY

My passion is writing books about a family saga, which tell a love story and of leaving old fears behind as the characters embrace intimacy and transition to joy. My first series, Broken Bottles, details those fears of growing up in a family battling alcoholism. Along with the struggle and pain of a parent's rage, there is intelligence, strength, and survival. The challenge is to love intimately in all relationships. For children of trauma, it can take years to let another person come close. When they do? It's like rainbows cover their heart.

Slowly, you'll read how my characters become vulnerable, reach for deep, sensual intimacy, and try desperately to let go of their fears. They struggle and risk everything to trust others—and themselves. My stories are about daring to take the baby steps that let them really come alive and in every way, experience and give love.

MAKING MONEY TO CREATE: The small, vacation rental/ property management company I run with my husband and son in Sonoma County, California allows me to have the money for my creative life. I love that I was born and raised in San Francisco. My father introduced me to baseball when I was six. I've rung a cable car bell, and went to concerts in Golden Gate Park with my sister where Jimmy Hendrix and Santana once played.

WHAT I'VE DONE/AM DOING – IT'S A JOURNEY OF DREAMS: Broken Bottles is a five part series. Part I is finished: *Shadow Heart, Fire Heart, Jagged Heart* and *Amazing Heart*. I'm honored to have 3 poems in an anthology called *The Beats Go On,* and a story in *Sisters Born, Sisters Found.* I have released the first book in a series for introverts called, *The Introverts Guide to the Galaxy: Attending Conferences.*

My Dream? To create beautifully decorated and custom journals with gorgeous paper that accompany with each book series: The Introvert's Journal, Growing up in Family Dysfunction Journal, My Body's Journal, and the Trauma Journals: You Can't Stop Me. Journaling was a lifesaver for me. I was in shock. You may be in shock. Don't let that keep your heart frozen!

Website: www.PamelaTaeuffer.com
E-mail: PamelaTaeuffer@gmail.com
Facebook: www.facebook.com/pamela.taeuffer.9
Twitter: @PTaeufferAuthor
Pinterest: www.pinterest.com/ptaeuffer/broken-bottles

For live chats, freebies, advance chapters,
and pre-publication dates of future books
(and sometimes free giveaways!)
visit www.PamelaTaeuffer.com

Also available by Pamela Taeuffer

Shadow Heart

What if you were afraid to even turn the doorknob to your front door because of the What if family dysfunction that waited inside: rage, mental and physical abuse, the fear of sharing love, a kind word or the embrace of your mother. What would it take to bring you out of the shadows, breaking out of the numbness you've used to protect your heart? Could you take a risk that might change everything? A sexy, professional baseball player wants my mind, body and heart. All my life I've controlled whom I let get close to me. The light of risk means terror. This is the slow, intimate reveal of how I finally learned to open my heart to another person, and just as important, how I learned to trust myself.

Jagged Heart

I walked quietly so I didn't disturb the fragile web that stretched throughout our home: Nothing good would last; I would ultimately be abandoned; my feelings didn't matter; as long as I looked okay, I was okay. My name is Nicky Young. I stay away from hurt by not risking too much. Ryan Tilton, a professional baseball player, has swept me off my feet and I can't let go. I refuse to be intimate, but then I'm desperate to fall into his arms. Adding to my fears, I've learned about Jesse, a beautiful and successful artist and socialite from his past, may have moved to San Francisco to follow him. My boundaries are softening, melting, being redefined, becoming "Jagged."

Amazing Heart

It's amazing, but I am filled with the desire to open my heart and love another, a new person, out of the comfort zone of my childhood, not a relative, not family and breaking through every chain of dysfunction I'd bound myself with.

Amazing is how I feel, that I seem to have the love of someone who will accept me for who I am, a bundle of insecurities and fears, wrapped inside my body of round curves that I tend to cover in jeans and sweatshirts. Having someone who seems to want me in spite of all my demons—it feels as if I'm set free! I walk with a light around me: bright, open, shutting out the darkness of my youth—the alcoholism of my father, his rage, his violence, my mom's codependence and support of his addiction—I know I can risk everything now. The freedom to ask for what I want; dare I dream of feeling safe enough, trusting myself enough to share my thoughts, wishes, fears . . . dare I actually hope in another person? Won't his promises fall apart? Am I really free? Can I dare to really, really, be alive and through being vulnerable, open to deep, sensual, intimacy?

OPEN
HEART
PRESS

Open Heart Press
Broken Bottle Series
www.openheartpress.net

www.ingramcontent.com/pod-product-compliance
Lightning Source LLC
Chambersburg PA
CBHW050914250626
47155CB00001B/224